Phenome
for the novels

Silent Snow

"Thayer uses his mastery of historical detail to build his own spellbinding version of the original kidnapping. He also balances the icy clarity of his investigative thinking with the welcome warmth of his characterizations. And in the end, he leaves us with the chilling thought that the snow might never melt on some buried secrets."

—*New York Times Book Review*

"A fine story . . . Thayer provides a blend of history and fiction that is quite satisfying. . . . Restores one's faith in the craft of storytelling: logical yet surprising, cleanly written yet intricately argued, compelling of locale and enterprising of plot—just what we need to end this long hot summer."

—*Boston Globe*

"An author who is not afraid to take chances. . . . His story moves, the characters are made real enough, the tension never diminishes, the weather gives no one a break, and the tightrope resolution pulls it all together . . . all the visceral emotion a reader can take. . . . The climactic scenes are fire and ice. . . . If Thayer wants to take a chance, I'm in."

—*Cleveland Plain Dealer*

Continued . . .

"A better, more exciting book, and it will be bigger than *The Weatherman*. . . . You'll want to read this book." —*Minneapolis-St. Paul Pioneer Press*

"Enticing . . . quirky and complex. . . . The kidnapper's identity and the links between past and present are real surprises." —*Publishers Weekly*

"Adept and fascinating . . . an intricate story line . . . interesting forays into character." —*Booklist*

The Weatherman

A *New York Times* Bestseller

"Masterful . . . even the savviest readers will change their minds about who the killer is several times before the heart-stopping conclusion. "

—*Chicago Tribune*

"I read *The Weatherman* with mounting excitement and a sense of involvement which few novels can elicit in me these days. It has one of the highest take-off points of any novel in recent memory . . . and from there it just keeps on shooting the thrills and suspense. . . . I recommend it to everybody." —Stephen King

"A dandy, dark, serial killer thriller. "

—*Cleveland Plain Dealer*

"A Minnesota thriller with an unpredictable, highly satisfying ending." —*Washington Post Book World*

"High-level tension . . . a fascinating, frightening, and shocking novel." —*West Coast Review of Books*

"Explosive . . . one of the more provocative and fascinating serial killer thrillers." —*Orlando Sentinel*

"With its reams of meteorological lore and an ironic twist ending, this should appeal to weather buffs as well as to thriller fans looking for something a bit off the beaten serial killer path. " —*Publishers Weekly*

"Thayer is a natural storyteller . . . a vital talent."
—*Mystery News*

"Succeeds in making the implausible stunningly believable." —*Minneapolis Star Tribune*

"A highly readable thriller." —*Dallas Morning News*

Saint Mudd

"At once raw-boned and unflinching . . . *Saint Mudd* succeeds." —*Milwaukee Journal*

"All the roughness and toughness of the best gangster fiction—with a bittersweet ending in the finest tradition."

—Robert Lacey, author of
Little Man:
Meyer Lansky and the Gangster Life

ALSO BY STEVE THAYER

Saint Mudd
A Novel of Gangsters and Saints

The Weatherman

SILENT SNOW

STEVE THAYER

SIGNET
Published by New American Library, a division of
Penguin Putnam Inc., 375 Hudson Street,
New York, New York 10014, U.S.A.
Penguin Books Ltd, 27 Wrights Lane,
London W8 5TZ, England
Penguin Books Australia Ltd,
Ringwood, Victoria, Australia
Penguin Books Canada Ltd, 10 Alcorn Avenue,
Toronto, Ontario, Canada M4V 3B2
Penguin Books (N.Z.) Ltd, 182–190 Wairau Road,
Auckland 10, New Zealand

Penguin Books Ltd, Registered Offices:
Harmondsworth, Middlesex, England

Published by Signet, an imprint of New American Library,
a division of Penguin Putnam Inc. Originally published in a Viking edition.

First Signet Printing, September 2000
10 9 8 7 6 5 4 3 2 1

Grateful acknowledgment is made for permission to reprint excerpts from *Hour of Gold, Hour of Lead: Diaries and Letters of Anne Morrow Lindbergh 1929–1932*. Copyright © 1973 by Anne Morrow Lindbergh. Reprinted by permission of Harcourt Brace & Company.

REGISTERED TRADEMARK—MARCA REGISTRADA

Printed in the United States of America

PUBLISHER'S NOTE
This is a work of fiction. Names, characters, places and incidents are either the product of the author's imagination or are used fictitiously, and any resemblance to actual persons, living or dead, business establishments, events, or locales is entirely coincidental.

For
Dennis Putney
1950–1995

More like a brother than a brother-in-law

Prologue

It always rains when a child dies. The baby the world was praying for was found murdered on a cold, damp day in the season when hope springs eternal. The May sun in the overcast sky was trying in vain to push the afternoon temperature another degree toward summer. Cherry and apple blossoms were in bloom along the Mount Rose road, which was nothing but a rolling ribbon of narrow mud the color of blood. Farm fields were sprinkled with violets. Dandelions awaited the sunshine. Dogwoods gushing pink and white decorated the hilltops like a giant birthday cake. The birds were back, but they had nothing to sing about. The dark cedars and old oaks were still missing their foliage, and the brisk winds down from the Sourland Mountains were chilly and dank. It was here that a truck driver looking for a place to relieve himself found the body beneath a copse of cedars about seventy-five feet into the woods. What little remained of the baby boy was lying facedown in the wet earth, faintly covered by rotting leaves. A shallow grave. Buried in a hurry.

"At first I thought it was like one of them little green Martians . . . I mean, it was hideous . . . didn't even look human."

The remains were in an advanced state of decomposition. Dust to dust. Most of the limbs and vital organs had been eaten by animals, the leftovers devoured by insects. Within the rib cage only the heart and the liver remained. The right leg was missing. So was the right arm and the left hand. But the most striking feature was the smashed skull, bulbous and covered with patches of light hair. A massive fracture from the top of the head to just below the left ear.

Still not sure the gruesome creature was of this world the truck driver picked up a stick and rolled it over. Much of the black, leathery head was veiled in vermin, but most of the face was intact. Preserved in earth. Saved by mud. The facial skin was ash white, wet and shiny from the rain. Locks of golden hair curled up to the forehead. The lips were swollen and pulled back over the teeth—eight baby teeth on top, eight on the bottom. It was the cherub from the wanted posters tacked to trees and poles across the countryside. It was the face that stared out from the front pages of newspapers around the world. Now it was staring at him, giving him the shakes.

He looked around. Lying nearby in the weeds was a burlap bag. Then a sliver of silver caught his eye. The truck driver picked up the shiny piece of metal and examined it closely. It was a Baby Alice Thumbguard. Rich white folks tied them to their babies' wrists while they slept so they couldn't suck on their thumbs. Without thinking the man slipped it into his pants pocket.

The truck driver wasn't running moonshine; he was running a load of timber. And he wasn't looking for trouble; he was just looking for a place to piss. Now he had discovered the gravesite of the missing child. The Little Eagle. No sooner had the man from the lumber truck realized what kind of hellish trouble he had come upon when the cold wind and the deadening drizzle began to turn the ash white face of the murdered baby to brown and black. Rotting before his eyes. The flies arrived. As much as he hated the thought of it, the man knew he'd have to find a cop. White man's problems. He turned and stumbled back through the thick underbrush, forgetting what he went in there for, back to his truck on the blood-red road that snaked over the countryside.

It was a dead body along a dirt road. That's all. The baby's mother would understand. She was a saint.

"If you can say 'Then he was living, then he was dead,' it is final and finalities can be accepted."

Her golden child had ascended into heaven months before, and like a star in the sky he was now in God's hands. And so was the fate of those who had murdered him.

BOOK ONE

THE ABDUCTION

Long ride down—very blue. The eternal quality of certain moments in one's life. The baby being lifted out of his crib forever and ever, like Dante's hell.

—Anne Morrow Lindbergh
May 11, 1932
Hour of Gold, Hour of Lead

Rick

March comes in like a lion. Roaring. Savage. Unforgiving in its ferocity. A childish game the winter weather plays. Come the end of February the snow melts, the air warms and spring appears on the way. Then the temperature plummets with little warning, the winds pick up, and snowflakes begin to fly sideways. Hell hath no fury like a Minnesota blizzard. It was only 4 P.M. but already the sun was barely visible through the cloud base.

The man without a face came in from the cold. He blew warm air into his bare hands, bounded up six flights of stairs and into the newsroom. He was mad. Snow. Sure as hell it was going to snow. The wind had numbed his fingers, whipped through the holes in his mask and stung his eyes. Rick Beanblossom had no business living in this frostbitten state. He read there were parts of Arizona that averaged three hundred days of sunshine a year. The average high was 82 degrees. *The thought of it.* And after a long, hard winter he thought about it a lot. But it was only a fantasy. His sweat glands had been destroyed in the fire. The heat would kill him.

The newsroom was clearing out, the day shift going home, the night shift coming on. Today Rick was night shift. Andrea was home with a cold. The baby was napping. A perfect time to slip downtown and get some writing done. He mumbled a few hellos and crossed into his office, which was nothing but a big cubicle with a glass partition. No door. Still, he was one of the few people below the editors with his own office. At the *North Star Press* Rick Beanblossorn was a star. Features only, just two or three stories a month. Always front page, usually above the fold. For this he was paid handsomely and nobody in the newsroom begrudged him his salary or his perks. They knew the masked newsman could very well be writing for the evil paper across the river. That was the great thing about working in the Twin Cities. If they didn't appreciate your talents in St. Paul, you could always shop them in Minneapolis.

Rick Beanblossorn took off his navy flight jacket and tossed it in a chair. He stole a peek out the sixth-floor window. It even looked cold. The first snowflakes sailed up Cedar Street. The advance team. Getting home was going to be a real bitch. He probably should have driven, but one of the advantages of living on Summit Avenue was being able to walk to work. Twenty minutes. Fifteen if he hustled. Besides the exercise and the fresh air the walk afforded him, people on the street got used to seeing a man with a sky-blue mask pulled completely over his head. It was the kind of mask worn by a comic book hero, only this mask had a black leather triangle for a nose. A nose that lived and breathed the news. The mask was as much to protect him from infection as it was to hide a face made hideous by fire. He was a burn victim. This was how he would go through life. No graying temples. No crow's-feet. No receding hairline. He'd just slip out every year and buy a new mask.

Rick Beanblossom no longer kept track of his age. He was forty-something. He knew only that he had now lived longer without a face than he had with one. A great athlete in high school, an All-American boy, he was still in pretty good shape considering that after high school he'd been given three torturous tours of Dante's inferno. He slid behind his desk and gathered his mail, most of it junk.

Hung prominently on the wall behind his desk was a gold-framed propaganda poster from World War I. Painted in 1917 by artist Charles Dana Gibson, the poster depicted a khaki-clad doughboy in skin-tight puttees and a broad-rimmed helmet standing in a field of wheat with his bayoneted rifle poised to smash the Hindenburg Line. In bold letters the caption read, JOIN THE MARINE CORPS. Rick Beanblossom had paid five hundred dollars for the rare poster at an art gallery in the warehouse district. Something about the corny patriotism struck a chord deep inside of him. *Esprit de corps.*

Compared to other reporters Rick's desk was tidy. Almost Spartan. Tucked under a sheet of tempered glass was a handwritten note from Mrs. Howard welcoming him to the *North Star Press*. Atop the glass was a picture of his beautiful wife. A picture of their baby boy. A crystal vase stemmed with fresh flowers. A remote control.

The television set was atop a file cabinet in the corner. Despite numerous awards for journalism, Rick Beanblossom was probably best known as the most famous husband in Minnesota. He was married to Channel 7 anchorwoman Andrea Labore. Sky High News. Number one in the ratings at six and ten. She had the most recognized face in the land of ten thousand lakes. Beauty incarnate. Local columnists went from calling her Princess Andrea to calling her Queen Andrea. Every night thousands and thousands of men in the seven-county metropolitan area went to bed at 10:30 and jacked off with Rick's wife in mind. When she got pregnant the show's ratings went through the Sky High News roof. When the baby was born congratulatory mail poured in from as far away as Iowa, South Dakota, Wisconsin, and Michigan's Upper Peninsula where they picked up her broadcasts on satellite. Then the TV cameras showed up at the hospital for the requisite photo op of Andrea in bed holding the baby, which later that night was dutifully broadcast across the Midwest, and to all ships at sea.

Forget that her husband had been awarded the Navy Cross for the lives he saved in Vietnam, not to mention the face he lost. Forget that as a young newspaper reporter in Minneapolis he won a Pulitzer Prize for investigative reporting. Or that as a television news producer at his wife's own station he earned a Columbia/Dupont Award for his story on a missing child. Oh yeah, he also had a novel published. Good reviews. Modest sales. He was at work on another. But forget it all. He was the husband of Andrea Labore. The father of her golden child.

"Isn't she married to that burn victim guy?"

This was hero worship in the 1990s. If Rick didn't love Andrea so much he'd resent the hell out of her. Still, if the general public showed him little respect, his wife and his peers showed him plenty.

Rick was still sorting through his mail when a gust of March wind rattled his office window. Startled him. He shot a glance that way. It was getting dark. More snowflakes. Dancing now. Then his eyes fell on a letter-size envelope addressed to him in handwriting that more resembled a scribble, one of those ominous dispatches that gives off bad vibes before it's even read. He yanked open his top drawer and lifted out a switchblade, illegal in all fifty states. Rick popped the blade. The razor sharp chromium shone like white fire even on a bitter, gray day. The Marine stabbed the envelope and slit it open. One clean cut.

It was not uncommon for readers to send Rick Beanblossom his own news articles with a note telling him to eat it. At first glance that appeared to be the case. But there was no note with this article, just an old twenty-dollar bill that bore a round yellow seal. Rick read the story.

ST. PAUL NORTH STAR PRESS

ANNE MORROW LINDBERGH DIES

Rick Beanblossom *staff writer*

Anne Morrow Lindbergh, author, aviatrix, loving wife and mother died today at a convalescent home in Darien, Connecticut. She was 93. Mrs. Lindbergh had been in failing health for several years. One of her last public appearances was here in St. Paul in 1985 when she attended the dedication ceremony on the capitol grounds of the Paul Granlund sculpture of her famous aviator husband, Minnesota's own Charles A. Lindbergh.

When the history of the twentieth century is written Anne Morrow Lindbergh will undoubtedly be listed among the great women. Sadly, at her passing she may be best remembered for the kidnapping and murder of her first son, Charles Lindbergh Jr., stolen from his nursery at their country estate in New Jersey in 1932. Her death comes only a week before the March 1 anniversary of the kidnapping . . . .

The story was a week old. It had come across the wire shortly before deadline, a simple obituary piece the newsman cranked out before he went home that night. Most of the background info was culled from the AP story. Next day another reporter was assigned to write a feature piece on the life and times of the woman who had married Charles Augustus Lindbergh. Rick Beanblossom had to confess he knew little about the Lindberghs—other than the fact that young Charles, from Little Falls, Minnesota, had flown solo across the Atlantic in *The Spirit of St. Louis* in 1927. And that several years later the national hero known as the Lone Eagle and his wife Anne Morrow had their first-born son kidnapped and murdered. It was one of the most sensational news stories in American history. Crime of the century and all that stuff. A German carpenter named Bruno fried for it.

Again he searched the envelope for a note. There was nothing. But the twenty-dollar bill was an interesting touch. Rick sat at his desk. He stashed the switchblade and pulled out a magnifying glass. He magnified Andrew Jackson's face, then the writing below. "IN GOLD COIN PAYABLE TO THE BEARER ON DEMAND." It was a gold certificate. A collector's item. "SERIES OF 1928." Rick put the gold note to his nose. It had a musty smell to it, wet, earthy. What to think? He reluctantly put the twenty aside and opened the rest of his mail.

For years Rick Beanblossom lived alone in a high-rise condominium overlooking Lake Calhoun in Minneapolis. At times it seemed more of a cave dwelling in which he was hiding. Andrea Labore lured him out of his cave and out of his shell. Marriage took them back to Rick's hometown of Stillwater, Minnesota, once a sleepy river town, now a trendy suburb. Then came Andrea's new multimillion-dollar contract. She said the long commute from Stillwater to the newsroom atop the IDS Tower in downtown Minneapolis was killing her.

After the baby was born, legendary publisher

Katherine Howard personally offered Rick a job with the *North Star Press* in downtown St. Paul. Going stir-crazy at home as a writer and a house-husband, Rick accepted the offer. But he wanted to stay planted in Stillwater. Andrea wanted to move back to Minneapolis. They compromised.

Rick Beanblossom and Andrea Labore with their newborn child settled into a Romanesque-style mansion on St. Paul's historic Summit Avenue—a street F. Scott Fitzgerald once described as "A museum of American architectural failures." The Beanblossom "failure" was built of red sandstone in 1887, three stories tall with a peaked tile roof over a skylighted attic. The back porch served up an incredible view of the Mississippi River. The front windows offered up Cathedral Hill. Carved stonework of classic nudes topped a dramatic entrance arch. Rick thought the Victorian mansion was so tacky it was cool. Neighbors swore the old place was haunted. That sealed the deal. His own ghost. The family fortress. Lord of the manor. Andrea was twenty minutes from her job—the lord could walk to his.

The wind increased to a howl. Daylight fading fast. Rick was watching the worsening weather outside his climate-controlled office when Andrea called. She was feeling better. Little Dylan was fed. Andrea was bouncing him on her knee. The housekeeper was home with them.

"How are you getting home?"

"I'll get a ride. Don't worry about me."

"I love you."

That call was at 5:45 P.M. Rick set his work aside. He sat at his desk staring out the window. Easiest thing in the world. More snow. More wind. More winter. He picked up the mysterious twenty-dollar bill. Seemed the worse the weather got the more suspicious the bill became. He scanned the article again.

> Her death comes only a week before the March 1 anniversary of the kidnapping . . . .

Rick checked the day calendar on his desk. **Monday. March 1.** He looked at the gold note in his hand. Again at the article. The wind kept rattling the window. Rattling his nerves. A chill crawled up his spine. He shook it off. The incurable newsman stared long and hard at his telephone.

The old man would be at home. He was near retirement. Christ, he was near death. Emphysema. Kept threatening to move to California and live with his daughter. But as long as the Bureau of Criminal Apprehension, the state police in Minnesota, provided the old man with an office and a telephone he would be forever a cop, forever searching for one last case. Rick hated to bother him. He expected to be writing his obituary soon.

By this time it was dark outside. In the morning the paper would read, OFFICIAL SUNSET: 6:01 P.M. Rick Beanblossom hit the remote on his desk. The television set popped on. Channel 7.

Schlocky music was playing over videotape of his wife smiling into the camera. The news began with the announcement that Andrea Labore was home sick. Katherine Thompson-Jones, known in the Sky High newsroom as Katie Tom-Jon, was filling in. Her coanchor tonight was the regular guy, Stan Butts, known in the same newsroom as the "butthole from Cleveland," a.k.a. "Frankenanchor." It was a lovely business. The lead story was a blizzard warning. The Twin Cities were sitting on the eastern edge of a massive storm system.

Rick clicked the sound down to a whisper on his former employers and reached for the telephone. He punched in a number he knew by heart.

"What have you done for me lately?"

"That's my line. How goes the battle?"

"Feels good to be working for a newspaper again."

"I knew you'd be back. You've got newsprint for blood."

" So they tell me. Watching the news?"

"You bet. Where's Andrea?"

"Home with a cold."

"So what do you want? . . . the weather's on."

"Aren't you a coin collector or something?"

"Coins and stamps."

"I've got an old bill sitting on my desk here. I'm wondering its value."

"Coins and stamps, Masked Man."

"Well, you must know something about bills."

"Shoot."

"Twenty-dollar gold certificate. Series 1928. Slightly worn. Fair condition."

"Roosevelt recalled them in 1933 when we went off the gold standard, but a lot of people hoarded them as a hedge against inflation. It was the Depression, you know. Not being in mint condition, it can't be worth a whole lot."

The old boy sounded pretty damn good. Much better than Rick had expected. The hard-to-retire cop wouldn't be the first two-pack-a-day smoker to cheat the Grim Reaper. Rick Beanblossom took a deep breath and tried to sound nonchalant. "Could you run a check on the serial number for me?"

It didn't work. There was an icy silence on the far end of the line, a dramatic pause Rick had come to know well. He could hear the sound on the old man's television set go dead. *"I'd have to run that through FBI computers."*

Now it was Rick's turn to dish out the silence, a game they had played often over the years—played it with crooked politicians, with local yokel mobsters, and with a serial killer known as the Weatherman. After allowing for the seriousness of the request to sink in, Rick Beanblossom chose his words carefully.

"And could this routine check of serial numbers be done without setting off alarms at the FBI building?"

A sharp smoker's cough could be heard at the other end of the phone. His death rattle. *"I might choose to do it that way. Worth the risk?"*

"Yeah, worth the risk."

"Give it to me."

* * *

Rick Beanblossom's story has been told before, but it deserves mentioning here again how he came to meet the old man who would become his mentor, the cop who would become his unimpeachable source for both information and inspiration. It was during the recovery years, after Vietnam but before the thought of being a journalist crept into his head. He seldom ventured out back then, mostly down to the burn center at Ramsey Medical. The ugly incident took place at a park on St. Paul's East Side, up the bluff from the hospital. It was a glorious, spring day. The view over the capital city was incredible. The Mississippi River was raging with snow melt, near flood stage. A warm breeze told him winter was over. No more snow. Rick stood on a retaining wall, hands in pockets, forgetting for the moment there was anything different about him. He was as caught up in the optimism of spring as anybody that day.

They came up behind him. The two cops shouted not to move and he almost fell off the wall. He was ordered to put his hands in the air. He still stuttered back then and this war wound rendered him speechless. They ordered him down from the wall and up against it. "Feet spread!" He mumbled and stammered but the words would not come. Their questions went unanswered. He clung, shaking, to his new mask. Despite his uncommon valor in war he was now treated like a cruelly deformed puppy. The cops handcuffed him and led him to the squad car.

At the booking center they pulled the mask from his head. He avoided their eyes. They gasped in horror. He tried to bury his head between his knees. He was three hours in the county jail before they figured out they had a war hero in custody, not a burglary suspect. An aging detective with a nasty smoker's cough came into his cell. Offered him a cigarette. Apologized profusely. Gave him a ride home.

Three hours of writing later his phone was ringing. He hoped it was some answers about the mysterious twenty-dollar bill. Rick checked the clock: 8:45 P.M. Now it was snowing hard. Long white spirals. He stored his work on the computer and picked up the phone.

"Beanblossom."

"Have you found a ride home yet?"

He grabbed hold of the picture of Andrea on his desk. A rare smile broke across his blue mask. "Haven't asked. How's the baby?"

"I worry about him catching my cold. I put him to bed about an hour ago . . . fell right to sleep. You know he's over a year old. Soon we won't be able to call him our baby anymore."

"No. He'll be our little boy."

"So when are you going to find that ride home? The weather is getting pretty bad."

"People don't start heading out until ten or eleven."

"I know, but it wouldn't hurt you to . . . just a minute. . ."

"What's that, hon?"

"I thought I heard something . . . a noise . . . the wind is going crazy out there."

"Yeah, down here too. Is Jasmine there?"

"She's downstairs."

"Good. Then get some sleep. Everything is okay."

"First I have to call my sister . . . then I'm off to sleep. I love you. Bye-bye."

"I love you," he muttered. But she'd already hung up the phone.

When the monster stood the ladder up to the side of the house the temperature had already dropped below the freezing point. It was the peak of snowfall season. Increasing flurries moved across the yard in a northwesterly wind flow. Low visibility. Good cover. Up in the nursery at the southeast corner of the big house, the dim glimmer of a night light shone—maybe a low-watt bulb, maybe light from the hallway. Further down was the flickering glow of an incandescent light in the master bedroom. These were the only lights on the second floor. The young housekeeper would be on the first floor at the other end of the house. A light was burning in her room, as well as in the kitchen.

The monster was huge. Grotesque. A scarecrow ballooned out of all proportion. There were cloth sacks wrapped around its boots. Black pants. Thick black arms and black leather gloves. A black down vest hung over a black coat, the collar turned up. In the flickering flames of light coming from the house one could see a gunnysack pulled over its head. The sack was tied at the neck with a rope. A pair of dark glasses, perhaps night goggles, were stuck in the middle of the mask. Served as eyes. A floppy black hat held everything together. The extension ladder was made of soft wood in hopes it would be noiseless. Up this silent ladder the monster crept, lifting one foot past the other, as a firefighter would do. On the top rung, at the nursery window, it was shielded from the nasty weather. The biting winds of March were playing eerie tunes through the trees. The icy river to its left could barely be seen as it ran beneath the bluffs. To its right was the dome of a church ablaze in lights, still visible through the irregular columns of snow. A gnarly oak tree stripped of its leaves hung over the baby's window, its dark branches and sharp, pointed fingers reaching down for the ladder like frantic arms.

The window slid open surprisingly easily. No need for the chisel. The monster entered the house, set its left knee upon the windowsill and carefully and quietly maneuvered through. Once inside the monster paused a moment, allowing its glasses and its eyes to adjust to the subtle shades of darkness. Evil framed in frosted glass. The nursery door was three-quarters open. The light seen from below was spilling in from the hallway. A muffled voice could be heard not too far away. Someone on the phone. Maybe a radio was playing.

The room was hot and smelled of Vicks Vaporub. It was smaller than expected. And older. A step back in time. The ceiling was high. The open door was tall and narrow, with a glass transom. A small fireplace was bricked into the wall. The furniture was antique, carefully selected, good wood, the kind of thing a carpenter would appreciate. Taped to the wall was paper sunshine to help ward off the grim, winter days. In the corner the monster could see the crib.

The baby was asleep, right where he was supposed to be—tucked snugly and securely into his blankets. The top blanket was white with gold lions on it. Cartoon characters. The sheets matched the blanket, as did the pillowcase. The child was lying on his back, face up. He was dressed for the night in a one-piece sleeping suit with enclosed feet and a zipper up the front. In the semidark the elfin outfit looked maroon. It was red. The monster put a gauze bandage over its victim's tiny mouth and pressed it flat beneath the nostrils to ensure the child could still breathe.

Then in what has to be the worst crime known to woman, known to man, the baby, still fast asleep, was lifted from his crib. Snatched. Carried out the window into the freezing air, into the raw winds, into the flying snow, and dropped feetfirst into a burlap bag. The church bells beneath the dome began to chime, ringing out through the winter storm. The monster almost forgot and hurried back to the crib. As the bells were tolling the hour a note was tossed on top of the covers among the sleeping lions.

The first time Andrea Kay Labore walked into the Sky High newsroom Rick Beanblossom was thunderstruck. Hate at first sight. The man without a face had developed a sharp eye for beauty and she was so beautiful he hated her. Her back was to the glass walls on the fifty-seventh floor of the IDS Tower. Nothing behind her but sunshine and blue sky. She was a slender, athletic young woman, just a few pounds short of skinny, with big, brown, bedroom eyes. The girl of his dreams, an angelic figure he was convinced he could never have. Beauty he could never possess. So in the beginning he hated her. Perhaps all men find their way to love this way. Hate. Envy. Jealousy. Love.

Andrea was a former policewoman who left the force to earn a Master of Arts degree from Northwestern University's prestigious Medill School of Journalism. Rick was a former Marine with no college and no face. He had only one advantage over the golden girl from Minnesota's Iron Range. She wanted desperately to learn the news business—and he knew the news business. When Andrea told him she hoped to be an anchor someday, Rick said to her, "Learn reporting . . . anchor is the last job on the way out the door."

His phone was ringing. Rick placed the photograph of his wife back on the desk. Outside his window the snow was shooting by like white tracers in a firefight.

"Beanblossom."

"Where'd you get it?"

"What've I got?"

"It's ransom money from the kidnapping of the Lindbergh baby . . . but then you already knew that, didn't you?"

"Tell me more."

"Where'd you get it?"

"It came in the mail today along with the obituary I wrote on Anne Morrow Lindbergh."

"Yeah? I met her once before the war. She was a saint. The Lindbergh farm wasn't far from ours. Never cared much for her husband, or his old man for that matter. Tell me more."

"I don't know . . . it arrived in a plain, white envelope. Letter sized. Address was handwritten. Postmarked St. Paul, February 28." Rick picked up the envelope and held it to the light. "You'd be better at this than I am, but studying the handwriting . . . it's very strange."

"How so?"

"Beautiful, but sloppy. Somebody who used to know how to write. I'm guessing . . . senior citizen . . . maybe a cripple . . . paralyzed . . . something like that."

There was a thoughtful pause at the other end of the line, as opposed to his dramatic silence.

"The kidnappers were paid fifty thousand dollars . . . fives, tens and twenties. That was quite a chunk of money back in those days . . . remember, you could buy a full-course meal for less than a buck. The Secret Service provided the cash in gold certificates so it would be easier to trace. Most of the ransom money was never recovered. Some of the smaller bills started showing up in the New York area almost immediately, and then eventually around the country. But all told, those bills only added up to a few thousand dollars. Bruno Richard Hauptmann, the man eventually convicted and executed for the kidnapping, was arrested a couple of years later in New York City with fourteen thousand dollars of the ransom

money hidden in his garage . . . leaving more than thirty thou unrecovered . . . most of it in gold certificate twenties."

"Did any ransom money show up here?"

"A couple of banks in Minneapolis came across the smaller bills and turned them in. The only twenty that ever showed up here was in St. Paul in 1932. Police took it off a reporter who was working on a story about the kidnapping."

"What was his name?"

"Says here, Grover Mudd." He spelled it out. *"M-u-d-d."*

Rick jotted down the name. "That byline rings a bell." He underlined *Mudd.* "Ever heard of him?"

"Nope. Before my time. According to this he worked for the St. Paul Frontier News."

"That newspaper died fifty years ago."

"Sixty."

Rick glanced at the day calendar on his desk. **March 1.** Almost to himself he asked, "Why would someone send me a Lindbergh ransom bill on the anniversary of the kidnapping . . . ?" His eyes fell on the picture of his baby boy.

> *"I know, but it wouldn't hurt you to . . . just a minute. . ."*
>
> "What's that, hon?"
>
> *"I thought I heard something . . . a noise . . . the wind is going crazy out there."*

Rick Beanblossorn froze, a fight or flight reflex the Marine had not felt since that fiery day in Vietnam. The day of the napalm attack. He slammed down the receiver. Cut off his source. He called home. One ring, then voice messaging. Christ Almighty, she was still talking to her sister. "Get off the phone, Andrea," he screamed. "Get off the phone!" Again he slammed down the receiver. He grabbed his jacket, stuffed the obituary and the hot twenty into his pocket, tore through the newsroom, and hurdled down the stairwell and out the lobby door.

He slipped on the icy stairs and fell to the snowy sidewalk. Bruised his knee. He climbed to his feet fighting the crazy wind. Out of the corner of his eye he caught an old lady watching him from the skyway that bridged Cedar Street. Rick ran—up Fifth Street and across Wabasha, across St. Peter Street. It was a weeknight. The sidewalks were deserted. Through swirling snow the bank building on the corner flashed the time: **8:58**. Then the temperature: **29°**. He swore he was being silly, but there was that burning feeling in the pit of his stomach, that feeling he wasn't going to make it. He was scared. Rick Beanblossom ran.

He took the first few blocks with the speed of the halfback he once was, but at Rice Park his age and his bruised knee caught up with him. It was while bent over holding his leg that he noticed a pair of bronze shoes awash in white. Rick looked up. Standing before him, hat in hand, ghost in a storm, was one of his heroes—F. Scott Fitzgerald. The statue of the hometown boy had only recently been erected amid controversy. Memorial to a drunk. The inscription was from

Gatsby: *"So we beat on, boats against the current, borne back ceaselessly into the past."*

The streets of wedged brick were a foot deep in the frigid white stuff. Between the new walls of the Ordway Theatre and the ancient stone of the Old Federal Courts Building, Fifth Street formed a wind tunnel. Rick headed straight into the bluster, the silver crystals tearing at his mask, assaulting his eyes.

Dylan Labore Beanblossom is what they had christened their child. He had his father's dark, curly hair, back when he had hair, and his mother's big, brown eyes. The baby was just learning how to walk, how to run. Andrea was teaching him how to say, "Mamma." Rick was teaching him how to say, *"Semper fi."* Marriage had not been easy for either one of them. Beauty and the beast. Their relationship was as hard to tackle as a swirling snowflake. Dylan was the glue that held them together.

As he emerged from the teeth of the wind onto Kellogg Boulevard, Cathedral Hill appeared before him like a mirage. Not even winter's fury could darken the light of the great church. He could make out the dome atop the hill, and the cross atop the dome. Rick followed the iron fencing up the boulevard to the archdiocese park. Again he slowed to a stumble. Trying to run through this city built on hills was killing him and now before him lay the steepest hill in town. Stairway to the Cathedral of St. Paul. Gateway to heaven.

He had seen this church a thousand times from a thousand angles in all kinds of weather. But tonight was different. Strange. Disconcerting. As if removed by one degree from actuality. Something felt out of proper place and time. Rick climbed the stairs. The gusts down from the summit were blinding. The carillon bells at the top of the hill began their hourly hymn. Westminster chimes. *"I summon the living, I mourn the dead."* Then the carillonneur tolled the hour. It was 9 P.M.

At the top of the hill, at the foot of the great church, Rick Beanblossom doubled over to bag his breath, to rub the pain from his aching knee. He'd been out in the blizzard less than five minutes, still he couldn't shake the haunting feeling that he had made this ghostly run once before. As the nine bells from the cathedral faded into the sounds of silence he thought he heard a bewitching voice crying in the storm, but he couldn't tell where it was coming from or what it was screaming.

With his back to the church and his face to the wind Rick ran, caught his second breath, and sprinted straight down Summit Avenue. At this stage it was a race through snow hell. His eyes were watery. The night was a blur. He knew it was going to be close so he prayed—prayed it was all for nothing, that he was being paranoid, a severe case of new father syndrome. He tore by the monster gates of the James J. Hill Mansion, once home to the railroad baron. The Empire Builder. The street lamps were useless. Then down the avenue he could see his own house, mostly dark, but there was a hint of light, a ray of hope spilling out the nursery window.

His front yard was a blanket of blowing snow. Rick

swept up the stairs and through the entrance arch. He pushed through the oaken doors. The heat was cranked up. The house was hot. He flew up the grand staircase taking these wide steps two at a time.

"Andrea!"

Rick stumbled down the hallway and almost fell into the nursery. He slapped the light switch. The room was bright. But the crib was empty. A small pocket had formed under the blankets where the child's body had lain. A folded note was on top of the gold lions.

Andrea Labore hurried into the room. Could see the fear in Rick's eyes. "Where's my baby?" she asked in a frightened whisper.

"Jasmine," Rick yelled.

Footsteps were heard rushing down the hall. The young housekeeper, who was studying nursing, appeared in the doorway. "What is it, Mr. Beanblossom?"

"Do you have the baby?"

"No," she answered, defensively. "He was in the crib sleeping."

Cold and snow were pushing into the hot room. "Where is he?" Andrea demanded to know.

Rick Beanblossom limped to the open window. Yellow blades of dead grass led the way. Chunks of dirt lay on the floor. He stuck his head into the storm. The branches of the oak tree were blowing furiously. In the woods behind the house Rick thought he saw a giant shadow stumbling through the trees. "They've stolen our baby."

"What?"

Rick tore out of the nursery. "Don't touch anything."

Andrea, her face waxen, was on her knees peering under the crib. She searched the closet. "Where's my baby?" she screamed.

That anguished cry from the child's mother, over and over, was the only thing Rick Beanblossom heard as he raced down the back stairs. He cut through the kitchen, grabbed a large knife from a wood block and pushed through the back door.

The woods behind the house rolled down a hill to a narrow street below. The Marine flayed through the brush using the knife as a machete, just as he had once done as Master Sergeant Beanblossom in Vietnam. Everything was happening fast. Too fast.

This narrow street below the woods was more of a back alley. In the old days it serviced the carriage houses and the servants' homes erected beneath the mansions. In recent years it was home to an eclectic pairing of yuppie scum and starving artists. Point-blank headwinds whipped through the alleyway. Visibility was nearing zero. Rick stood frozen, trying to sense which way to run in the streams of snow. Then off to his right a pair of brake lights blinked in the blizzard and slid around a bend.

Again he was forced into the blinding whiteness. The snow was over his ankles and getting deeper every second. Rick hurtled through the drifts in defiance of the weather. He chased around the bend until the alley dumped onto Ramsey Hill, a steep street leading back up to the avenue. Near the top he could see a pair of taillights fishtailing toward Summit. The car was losing its grip. The Marine steeled himself for one more battle. He charged up the hill. But the footing was slippery for him too. He fell to his side, his blue mask caked in white snow. The knife went flying. The taillights above him were waving back and forth. Then they waved good-bye.

Rick Beanblossom grabbed hold of the knife, struggled to his feet, and wearily legged it to the top of the hill. Just a pair of little red lights, like a rat's eyes, disappearing down Summit Avenue. Fading to black in the white gloom.

The only thing visible was the great dome of the cathedral. Rick heard a siren muffled by snow. Already somebody had called the police. Probably an old man who shared his fear. He fixed his angry eyes on the blessed cross atop the dome, weathering yet another storm. "Don't you do this to me," he begged. "I have suffered." The Marine raised his voice to the cross, raised his voice to God in heaven. "Don't you do this to me!"

The man without a face turned away from the church and dropped to his knees where the wind and the snow were conspiring to erase the tire tracks. Obliterate the trail. He stared into the abyss, tears in his eyes. Snow. Nothing but snow. Silent snow. Secret snow. "Give me back my son," he choked out. "You give me back my son."

Mrs. Howard

The first time she married she was only fourteen years old. Her betrothed was nearing thirty. Her father hastily arranged the marriage after an unexpected pregnancy. The Great War had just begun. Her fiancé expected to be drafted. She wanted a new pair of underwear for their wedding night so she walked down to the village store. Shortages were common. Strict rationing was enforced. All that was left was men's underwear. One size. One price. The bride-to-be faced another difficult decision forced on her by an imperious father. She bought the men's underwear.

On their wedding night her husband thought she was just being shy. The truth was she was embarrassed to be discovered wearing a brand new pair of men's underwear. That first night he complained that she was too damn loose down there. There was blood and she didn't want her new underwear stained, so she folded them neatly and went without. Then the first time they were washed he stole them from her. The marriage was a disaster. He drank. He beat her. He went off to the war. Her baby daughter was born. He came home on leave. When police found her husband floating in the river with a fractured skull after a night of heavy drinking, she pretended to be sad. But mostly she was relieved. She liked to tell people he was killed *during* the war. A widow and a mother at fifteen.

To friends and employees Katherine Howard's true age was something of a mystery. She was of a generation of women who did not like to divulge their age. Some said she was ninety. Others claimed she was closer to one hundred. If she was the widow of legendary editor Walt Howard, her second husband, she'd have to be right around the century mark. Still, she did not look a day over seventy. She was in fact a healthy and handsome woman. She had bright blue eyes, piercing and wise, and not even the wrinkles and the lines could mar the purity of her skin. She maintained a slender figure. Sturdy and erect. Must have been a beautiful girl.

Few people at the paper even knew her first name. She had always been Mrs. Howard, owner and publisher of the *St. Paul North Star Press*. She was the kind of woman men liked working for. The motherly type with balls. She was an original board member of the Howard Foundation, a charity she and her late husband created with just a few thousand dollars shortly after they were married in 1938. Now it was one of the largest foundations in the Midwest, making grants to institutions and individuals in education, humanities and the arts, and health.

Walt Howard had become a local hero and a national leader in the newspaper world when, as editor of the *St. Paul Frontier News*, he launched a controversial front page cleanup campaign during the gangster era of the 1930s. When the *North Star Press* bought the *Frontier News* and subsequently closed it down, he became an editor at large at the paper. It was then that his first wife died, after a lengthy illness. He was still a man in mourning when Katherine came into his life. This time she married for love.

In 1939, with the country still in the throes of the Great Depression, the *North Star Press* found itself in trouble. On the verge of bankruptcy. Walt Howard put together a group of local investors and bought the paper. As the newspaper prospered during the Second World War, he bought out his silent partners.

Then in the fall of 1948 Walt Howard, the great crusader, was killed in a hunting accident. After ten years of marriage Katherine Howard found herself widowed again. Her advisers urged her to sell the paper while it was doing well. She refused. She assumed control. Learned the newspaper business. She exercised some common sense, showed unusual business savvy, and transformed herself from doormat to corporate mogul. She took the *North Star Press* to new heights, acquiring other newspapers and several radio stations along the way. Despite a heart condition, Mrs. Howard was still at the helm, still calling the shots half a century later.

One of her more recent shots was to hire Rick Beanblossom. Pay the masked man what he wanted. Let him write whatever he wanted to write. She offered him his own column, but he thought the paper already had a strong lineup of columnists. The newsman without a face opted instead to write special features and investigations. Political scandals. Unsolved murders. Kidnappings.

Jasmine

By 11 P.M. the scene outside the Beanblossorn mansion resembled a macabre Christmas mass. By midnight the crime scene was as bright as the northern lights. The March winds had subsided but the snowfall had only increased, whitening and brightening every light on Summit Avenue. Twirling red lights. Blinking orange lights. Streetlights. Flashlights. Headlights. Taillights. Searchlights and klieg lights. Minnesota's first illuminated snowstorm.

Squad cars arrived within minutes, chains on their tires. Canine units were sniffing through the snow behind the house. Television news crews out covering the weather heard the *"possible kidnapping"* call on their police scanners. The newspapers were right behind them. The FBI arrived within the hour, as did the state Bureau of Criminal Apprehension. US West was called in to install emergency phone lines. A giant satellite truck pulled up to the snowy curb. Two more satellite trucks were on their way. When the kidnapped child belongs to the queen of the evening news, a circus is guaranteed. Whether Rick Beanblossom and Andrea Labore cared to admit it, the horde now at their doorstep was for the most part their friends. Their news family.

Couldn't leave them sitting outside in the storm. So Rick turned the first floor of the stately house over to his colleagues in the media. Law enforcement commandeered the third floor. That left Rick and Andrea the second-floor bedrooms and the attic office.

Dylan Labore Beanblossom, instantly dubbed "Baby Dylan," had been gone from his crib less than two hours, but already the show had begun. Producers were busy pounding out their A.M. broadcast. Cue schlocky music. Roll intro. Headlines off the top.

"Good morning. A shocking story leads our news today. The fourteen-month-old baby boy of the Twin Cities' most popular newswoman was kidnapped from her St. Paul home last night. The kidnapping occurred at the height of the blizzard . . ."

The ransom note left in the crib read like a cruel joke.

Dear Sir!
Have 500,000$ redy. 400$ in 100$ bills. 50$ in 50$ bills. 50$ in 20$ bills. In 24 hours we will inform you through U.S. Mail were to deliver Mony.
We warn you. No polise. No FBI. No TV.
Your child is in gute care with nurse.
Indication for all letters is signature and seal below.
))) EKS

With squinted eyes Rick Beanblossom stared at the ransom note laid out on his rolltop desk. An FBI agent with a pair of tweezers had placed the item in a clear plastic evidence bag. It was the same sloppy scrawl as the handwriting that appeared on the mysterious envelope delivered to the *North Star Press*. Difficult to read. Rick's obituary of Anne Morrow Lindbergh and the gold certificate were bagged, tagged, and lined up beside it. The master bedroom was crowded with people. Mostly cops. FBI Inspector Stephanie Koslowski, on the phone, was the agent in charge. Rick had seen her often on the news, mostly commenting on the infamous Wakefield case, but they had never before met. She had come with her own special team. Trained negotiators. Criminal profilers. Technical wizards. Her people worked fast. The telephones were tapped. Surveillance cameras were installed. On the floor above, a communications center was being wired into place.

Koslowski had just finished briefing Washington. "Our lab people are in the nursery now," she told the Beanblossoms as she hung up the phone. She had a husky voice, strong and decisive. "Within hours every blade of grass, every morsel of dirt and fiber on that floor will be at our laboratories in Washington. Your son is being given top priority."

Andrea Labore was seated on the edge of a four-poster of antique cherry wood in the Victorian bedroom. She was sitting in silent disbelief. In most cases, television personalities are not quite as pretty, or as handsome, in person as they appear on the luminous tube. Andrea Labore was the exception. Not even the most powerful camera lens could capture her God-given beauty. The news anchor appealed to Stephanie Koslowski, "Why did they steal our baby?"

"Because you're on television, Andrea." The inspector spoke with a tincture of regret in her voice. "We had a television anchorwoman raped and beaten in Texas. In Iowa, we've got an anchorwoman still missing, the contents of her purse found spilled across a parking lot one morning. And those are just the cases that made the headlines. Most stalking of television personalities is handled quietly by local police." She addressed both of them now. "You can expect the kooks to come out of the woodwork on this one. The soothsayers, the hustlers, the cranks, the mental patients, the con men . . ."

Rick turned to Andrea, "And that's just the people with press credentials."

For the first time that evening some laughter rippled through the room. The inspector smiled, glad some of the tension had broken. "All of them will have a plan to save your child. All of them will want to talk to you personally." She went on. "Kidnap for ransom is rare. Since passage of the Lindbergh Law in 1932, the FBI has investigated more than four hundred kidnap cases. Only four of them remain unsolved. The time to catch kidnappers is when the ransom is exchanged. Pay the ransom."

"I don't think this crime is about money," Rick told her.

"I agree." She picked up the evidence bag with the ransom demand. "This note looks like a poor knockoff of Bruno Hauptmann's handwriting . . . a German immigrant trying his best to write English. We also found an extension ladder lying in the woods, right where you'd expect it to be. Fifty thousand dollars in 1932 would be roughly equivalent to five hundred thousand dollars today. Someone has gone to a lot of trouble to recreate the Lindbergh kidnapping."

Rick Beanblossom had reached the same bizarre conclusion. "My wife is not Anne Morrow, and I'm not Charles Lindbergh. We're reporters."

"Kind of ironic, isn't it?"

Rick put her age at fifty. Koslowski was tall for a woman. Seemed proud of it. But she had an ungainly appearance. Her hair was cut short, and she wore glasses so thick it was hard to believe she'd passed the bureau's eye exam. Tonight a phone call had yanked her out of bed. She'd dressed in a hurry. A flannel shirt and khakis. Her navy blue parka had a big yellow FBI stamped on the back. Still, the Marine would much rather have been dealing with a G-man. Maybe she was good. But just maybe she was affirmative action. It was hard to tell these days. Police work had changed. And so had the faces. Rick Beanblossom showed her again the Anne Morrow Lindbergh obituary and the gold certificate he had received in the mail. He pointed out the March 1 anniversary of the Lindbergh kidnapping. He told her how he had soon suspected the twenty-dollar bill *might* be Lindbergh ransom money. But not soon enough.

Stephanie Koslowski carefully examined the evidence. "And this arrived at your office today?"

"Yes, I already told you that. Where are you originally from, Inspector?"

"Chicago."

"Grow up there?"

"Yes, I did."

"Northwestern?"

"Yes. Law." She studied the envelope the articles came in. "What time did you go in to work today?"

"As I said earlier, about four. Are you married?"

"No. I'm not."

"Children?" Rick asked.

"No," she answered, "but I come from an FBI family. My father chased Soviet spies. My grandfather chased gangsters. My great-grandfather was one of the 'Untouchables,' and his father was a Chicago cop before there was an FBI."

"That must be one hell of a family album."

"Perhaps one day you can put it all in a book for us, Mr. Beanblossom." She pointed to the note left in the nursery. Offered up some history. "We still study the Lindbergh case at the academy. It was a remarkable investigation considering the limited resources police had back then."

"But wasn't the Lindbergh baby murdered?" The terrifying possibility spilled from the lips of Andrea Labore.

The inspector seemed to appreciate the opportunity to turn her attention away from the inquisitive reporter in the mask. "Yes, but investigators believe he may have been killed unintentionally. The ladder broke on the way out of the nursery. It's believed the baby was dropped and his skull fractured on the window ledge below. Your kidnappers know that. Killing your child would be senseless. They want to recreate a kidnapping, not a murder. If they want the ransom, and they do, they know they're going to have to prove to us your son is alive."

"What about where it says no cops, no press, no FBI," Andrea asked anxiously.

Stephanie Koslowski kept her attention focused on Andrea. "It's bluster. Why else would they pick a television personality? I suspect they know a thing or two about manipulating the media. Who else has access to your house? Keys?"

"Just Jasmine Allen."

"The housekeeper?"

"Yes." Andrea explained. "We have a maid service that cleans the house once a week, but they have no keys. Jasmine lets them in and shows them out."

"And how did you come to hire Jasmine?"

"She was recommended to us by the Howard Foundation. They have a program for minority youths."

"Troubled youths?"

"Yes, some of them have had troubles."

"Is Jasmine a local girl?"

"No. She's from Camden, New Jersey. She's here on a grant studying nursing."

"Have you had any problems with her?"

Rick Beanblossorn watched this interrogation from across the room. Andrea came off strong on television. Brimming with confidence. Now sitting on the edge of the bed Rick could not get over how frail and vulnerable his wife appeared as she tried to answer the inspector's questions. He chose to interrupt. "Jasmine is a trusted member of our family. She's cared for our son as if he were her own."

The inspector turned. Seemed to get the message. "Yes, of course." Perhaps the time had come to give the exhausted couple a break. Clear the room and let them rest. They had just lost their baby. Nerves were frayed.

"What's the best book written on the Lindbergh kidnapping?" Rick asked her.

"That would be *The Lindbergh Case* by Jim Fisher. Rutgers University Press. It's the text used at the academy. Mr. Fisher was an FBI man."

"And Mr. Fisher's conclusion?"

"He concluded, and I concur, that Bruno Richard Hauptmann acting alone kidnapped and murdered the Lindbergh baby."

"But that's not what others believe, is it?"

"It's easy to be a conspiracy nut, Mr. Beanblossom. All you have to do is raise questions. You never have to provide the answers. The kidnappers of your son have done their homework. They know the mistakes Hauptmann made. They're not bound to repeat them."

"I've noticed you always use the plural . . . kidnappers . . . as in more than one?"

"Yes. My gut instinct tells me there are several persons involved in this."

"But just a second ago," Rick reminded her with a little too much verve, "your gut instinct told you that Bruno Richard Hauptmann kidnapped the Lindbergh baby, all by his lonesome."

"Rick." The sharp admonishment came from Andrea sitting on the bed across the room. "I'm sorry, Inspector. My husband doesn't function well without an adversary."

A heavy silence fell over the scene. The tension was back. A vintage clock could be heard ticking on the mantel above the fireplace. A couple of agents shuffled from the room. Stephanie Koslowski cleared her throat. "The kidnappers are our adversaries. They want to play mind games with us. A chess match of sorts. The advantage is ours. The FBI has played this game before. Many times. They haven't."

"If they have Lindbergh ransom money," Rick said to her, picking up the plastic bag with the gold certificate, "they've played this game at least once before."

At the same time Inspector Koslowski was questioning Rick Beanblossom and Andrea Labore in their second-floor bedroom, other agents of the FBI were leaving the first-floor bedroom of Jasmine Allen. Much like Andrea upstairs, downstairs young Jasmine was seated on the edge of her bed. Shaking with fear. But for different reasons. Not only had Baby Dylan been stolen from the house while she was there, but it was obvious from the agent's questions that Jasmine was a suspect. Perhaps their chief suspect.

"Exactly where were you in the house when the baby was taken?"

"And what were you doing in the kitchen?"

"Mr. Beanblossom usually works days. How do you suppose the kidnappers knew he decided to work tonight instead?"

"How do you think the kidnappers knew in exactly what room to find the baby in a house this size?"

"Were you ever in trouble when you lived in New Jersey?"

"Would you be willing to take a lie-detector test?"

It was all black and white to them. Black girl. White cops.

For Jasmine Allen it had all begun as a dream come true. First came the grant from the Howard Foundation. With the grant came the chance to study nursing in Minnesota. Land of ten thousand clinics. To help with expenses she was placed in a housekeeper's job in a St. Paul mansion the likes of which she had only seen on magazine covers.

But most of her dream job had to do with Baby Dylan. Jasmine wanted to be a nurse who worked with children. Pediatrics. Dylan gave her the kind of training no school could offer. Though a thoughtful and caring mother, Andrea Labore was a career woman. Between the newsroom and her personal appearances she kept a nearly impossible schedule. When the new mother was at home she was often tired. Dead tired.

Jasmine cared for the baby. Her bond with the child grew stronger every day. Jasmine was growing to love Dylan Labore Beanblossom as if he were her own.

She was only nineteen, had the figure of a doll and the face to match. Her skin was as fair as Whitney Houston's, and she wore her long hair pulled back around her neck. Showed off more of her winning smile that way. In the old Camden neighborhood the boys called her "hot." So hot she could even attract the rich boys from the university. Jasmine Allen wasn't a flirt. Far from it. But she had enjoyed all of the attention, before the trouble.

The housekeeper with the hourglass figure pulled herself off of the bed and walked to the dresser. Lit a candle for Dylan. Picked up her jewelry box. Turned off the lights. She put the flickering flame in the window, the arctic wind still blowing snow against the pane. Jasmine opened her scuffed jewelry box. She'd had the box since she was a child. For years it housed only colored strings and plastic gems. Then she inherited the tiny silver thimble. She treasured it the way a bride treasures her diamond. She lifted this precious piece of silver from the box and clasped it between her hands as she whispered a prayer. A prayer for Baby Dylan.

Suddenly, in the middle of her prayer came the strangest noise. Not frightening. Nor startling. But eerie. Disembodied. Somebody had called her name, as if the wind singing through her window had clearly pronounced "Jasmine." This time she had to know. But through the glass shone only snow.

People on the avenue said the old place was haunted, and Jasmine had sensed early on that a spirit really did roam the halls of the Summit Avenue house. Sometimes, alone at night with the baby, she could hear a strange voice. Then she would see a shadow out of the corner of her eye. Once while taking a shower she saw the silhouette of a young woman standing outside the frosted glass. When she mentioned her fears to Mr. Beanblossom, he kind of grinned, as close as she'd ever seen him come to a smile. He too had heard stories about ghosts. He said they had probably gone into hiding because he scared the hell out of them. Rick told her there were scrapbooks and papers about the history of the house up in the attic office. He hadn't had time yet to go through them. Maybe if she looked she could find a spirit or two. She was welcome to try.

Jasmine Allen was going to need a kindred spirit. She rubbed the silver thimble through the palms of her hands. Already she had lied to them.

"Were you ever in trouble when you lived in New Jersey?"

She did not tell them about the baby.

Andrea

In the Twin Cities of Minneapolis and St. Paul, with a population three million strong, Andrea Labore was family. She came into viewers' homes five nights a week at 6 P.M. and 10 P.M. They listened to her honey-like voice as they sat down to dinner. They watched her smile and wish them a "good night" before they shut off the lights and fell off to sleep. She was every man's wife, every woman's sister, every child's mother. So when tragedy paid a visit to her home on that stormy winter night, Andrea Labore unwittingly committed the cardinal sin in journalism. She *became* the news. For in spite of her saintly face, despite her congenial disposition and her sky high Nielsen ratings, there were still people out there who hated her guts. Andrea had it all. And she had it on television. From the day she took over the coveted chair at the anchor desk, there was hate mail. There were phone calls. If you're a woman and you anchor the news, it comes with the territory. She never really understood the phenomenon, but she had learned to accept it.

Now it was the wee hours of the morning. Through the tall arched windows the queen of the evening news could see that the blizzard was abating. The snow had leveled off to a white mist. For what little remained of that hellish night Andrea Labore stayed seated on the edge of the bed. Edge of a cliff. She had been sitting in that exact same spot for hours. It was as if she could talk, she could reason, but she could not move. Rick Beanblossom knelt prayerwise beside the bed, beside her slender legs. He rested his hands on her knees. The sound of police chatter was ever present outside their door. Every now and then a searchlight would sweep past the window. Soon the sun would be up.

Before she left them alone, the inspector from the FBI had left the distraught parents with these words: "All of the people involved in the Lindbergh case are dead. Anne Morrow was the last of them." Stephanie Koslowski paused before speaking again. Chose her parting words carefully. "Almost every mistake made in the Lindbergh investigation, and there were a lot of them, can be traced directly to the decisions made by the father . . . Charles Lindbergh. His heart was in the right place, but he wasn't a cop. Cops have the ability to think like criminals. The Lindberghs were just too good for that."

Rick had no reply. No response. All he gave the FBI woman in return was an icy stare. Minnesota smug. On many counts, take away the mask and he was typical Marine Corps. Chauvinistic. Pigheaded. Out of step.

An anachronism. A wounded soldier from another time. Nobody knew that better than his wife.

She listened patiently as her husband spoke in a voice filled with exhaustion. Frustration. "Do you think they're up to the job . . . the police . . . the FBI?"

Andrea rested her hands atop his. Gave voice to what he was probably thinking. "Wasn't she in charge of the Wakefield case?"

"Yes, she was," Rick reminded her. "From beginning to end . . . Inspector Stephanie Koslowski."

The kidnapping of Harlan Wakefield became the largest manhunt in state history. Twelve-year-old Harlan Wakefield and his identical twin brother, Keenan, were popular Stillwater boys with a paper route. Much of their popularity stemmed from their freakish intellect. At age twelve they were already testing out of high school and preparing for college. Their remarkable talents had been displayed on local TV news and talk shows. One morning in late spring Keenan Wakefield rode home from the paper route alone. He was in shock. Scratched and filthy. Through tears he told authorities, he told the press, a big man wearing a ski mask had stepped out of the woods with a handgun and kidnapped his twin brother. Keenan turned to help, but the man fired a shot into the air. The boy rode home. Within hours a massive search was launched. Harlan's bicycle was found on the side of the road along with a spent bullet. A farmer along the paper route reported a gun stolen from his car. The FBI was called in. Inspector Stephanie Koslowski put together a special task force of local, state, and federal officials that at one time numbered more than a hundred full-time investigators. But four years and four million police dollars later the boy genius remained missing, and nobody was arrested. Night after night Inspector Koslowski could be seen on the evening news explaining her latest efforts. But as the months dragged by without a trace of the boy, the special task force dwindled and Koslowski's efforts began to sound more and more like excuses. The Wakefield case was eventually solved when what was left of the boy's body washed ashore in a flood. But it wasn't the FBI who brought the alleged kidnapping to a close.

Andrea Labore bowed her head to the cotton mask she so often held to her breasts like a security blanket. "Do you trust her?" she asked.

Rick Beanblossom took his wife's hand in his, squeezed it in that reassuring way that he had. "She got burned on the Wakefield case . . . it's she who doesn't trust me. Did you notice how I got asked everything twice?"

"I'm sure all of the men in masks that she's dealt with in the past have been on the other side of the law."

Her husband allowed an ironic laugh to escape. "Let me talk with Mrs. Howard," he said. "Between her and the paper, plus your station, we have incredible resources."

"Tell me about this forty-eight-hour rule."

Rick cleared his throat. Turned away. "It's one of

those unofficial, unwritten rules among cops, and crime reporters. If a missing child isn't found within forty-eight hours . . . chances are that child will never be found alive."

Andrea lifted his chin. Looked him straight in the eye. "You still have that police source, don't you?"

"He's kind of retired."

The mother without a child forced herself off the bed. "Call him out of retirement." She made her way across the room. Never in her life had she felt so weak, so totally empty. Her baby was gone. She felt physically ill. Worse than the night she had . . . .

"What are you suggesting, Andrea . . . that we investigate this ourselves?"

"Isn't that what you've already decided?"

"More or less," Rick answered, "but . . . ?"

"But what? Am I supposed to sit at home for forty-eight hours and wait for the mailman? " The plethora of lights on the new fallen snow poured through the thick glass, nearly blinding her. Andrea shaded her eyes with her hands. There were more police vehicles and news equipment in front of her house than there were for most Olympic ski events. Never before had she seen the news from this angle. She had fallen through the looking glass. With a bitter voice she pointed out the window. "Today they have a hundred investigators on the case. Tomorrow they'll have fifty. The day after that . . . twenty-five. You know how it works. Too many children have disappeared, never to be seen or heard from again. Some of them right here in Minnesota. Christ, Rick, we write their stories."

Once before Andrea Labore had *made* the news. She'd killed a man. Shot him through the chest at near pointblank range. From the day her big brown eyes landed on television for Sky High News the ugly incident was told over and over, told in every feature piece ever written about her.

The same semester the swimming champion from the Iron Range was being handed her degree from the University of Minnesota, the city of Minneapolis hired a new police chief to upgrade its aging police force. This new chief made the recruitment of women and minorities a high priority. Andrea joined up, winning a top spot in the chief's first graduating class. With a badge, a blue uniform, and a gun she went to work in a squad car patrolling the high-crime district of North Minneapolis. One night in late autumn—the time of year when the leaves are off the trees and the Minnesota air is on the bitter side of cool—Officer Andrea Labore stepped from her squad car on a routine burglary call. She drew her service revolver and ordered the suspect to freeze. He pointed a gun at her. She instinctively squeezed the trigger, just once.

Once was all it took. The suspect collapsed in the wet leaves along the gutter. He was pronounced dead on arrival at North Memorial Hospital. She'd been a cop less than two years. Internal Affairs ruled the shooting justified. Like a proud father, the chief of police pinned a medal to her uniform. The local media made much of the gorgeous and courageous policewoman. But the shooting haunted her. Four months later Andrea Labore resigned.

"This is different, Andrea. This time it's our son. Whether I like Koslowski or not, what she said about Lindbergh is true. The man made mistakes . . . he couldn't stop thinking like a father."

"What do you want to do, Rick, walk out there and face the cameras every day, hand in hand? Thank everybody for their cards and letters? For their prayers? Become the latest celebrity victims? Start a foundation? Give lectures? Shed tears on *Oprah*? Fuck that. I want my son back!" Andrea seldom used foul language. Again she pointed out the window. "What do you think police are finding out there?" She didn't wait for an answer. "Snow . . . nothing but snow . . . that's what they're finding. I was a cop once. You're an investigative reporter. Let's find our son."

Rick joined her at the window. Brushed a few strands of disheveled hair from her face. "And where would you like us to begin?"

Andrea Labore was slowly pulling herself back together. Her wits, and her strength, were returning. She'd been a swimming champion. She'd been a Minneapolis police officer. She was an award-winning journalist. In fact in her whole life, the most self-doubt she had ever entertained was about being a mother. A good mother. "Koslowski thinks it was an inside job. Besides the baby, only three people live here. The kidnappers knew the man of the house wasn't home.

They knew I was in bed with a cold. They knew exactly where to find the baby . . . at exactly the right time. No, I don't believe for a minute Jasmine was in on it, but Jasmine might have said something by mistake to the wrong person. My God, I might have said something." She ran her fingers through her hair. "When I turned off the nursery light, was that their signal?"

"And do you suppose these kidnappers have an incredible sense of snow?" Rick asked her. He motioned to the weather. "Did they really know there was going to be a blizzard on the night of March 1, to cover their escape. For starters, I think we're giving them too much credit. Whoever kidnapped Dylan knows us, or they know somebody who knows us . . . but I don't think a whole lot of planning went into this. They had exactly one week from the day I wrote that obituary. That's not a lot of time to plan a kidnap for ransom."

Andrea Labore turned to the magnificent window that graced the avenue. Forty-two panes of glass over forty-two panes of glass. She stared through the intricate web of ice that decorated each and every pane, stared with violent intensity at the rotating police lights dancing on the street below. "Okay, this is what we do," she said. "You start with the kidnapping of Charles Lindbergh Junior and work your way forward. I'll start with the kidnapping of Dylan Labore Beanblossom and work my way backward. Together we'll find him."

He paused. "I've already got a lead."

"What kind of lead? " Andrea asked with surprise.

Rick turned to her, his back to the winter scenery. "In 1932, a reporter in St. Paul was working on the Lindbergh kidnapping. Police took a ransom bill from him, same as the twenty-dollar bill that was sent to me. This reporter may have had contact with someone involved in the kidnapping."

Andrea was incredulous. "But those people are all dead . . . 1932 . . . they have to be gone."

"Yes, they're probably dead . . ." Rick ticked off the possibilities. ". . . But their children may be alive, or their grandchildren, or some criminal element out there who once knew someone involved in the Lindbergh case. This reporter might have written something that we can use . . . left something behind."

"Why didn't you tell this to the inspector?"

"Hell, it's in their files. If she's any good she'll know it by tomorrow." Rick Beanblossorn turned back to the icy window. The blizzard was spent. All that remained were tiny, crystalline flakes that floated to earth like gleaming mites of dust.

Andrea watched him there, ghost in a storm. Over his shoulders the flashing blue lights of snowplows caught her attention as they rolled along in synchronized harmony, throwing great billows of snow in celestial arches off of the interstate that snaked beneath the cathedral. She listened to the Westminster chimes, and then the first seven bells of morning. A ray of light stabbed the clouds. The sun was coming up on thirteen hours of snow. In an hour the saintly city would be blinding. It would be heaven, and it would be hell. She knew the man without a face had seen some incredibly dark days in his time, but this day, the darkest day of his life, the first day without his son, would begin in a world painted white. "And what are you going to do with this so-called lead?" Andrea asked.

Rick Beanblossom gazed up and down the historic avenue. "Follow it."

Angelbeck

As so often happens in this winter wonderland, a cold wave blew in behind the storm. The Tuesday morning temperature was 9 degrees below zero. The windchill factor made it feel like 21 degrees below. Diamond dust hung in the air. Arctic blue sky. Freezing sunshine. Spring was three weeks away and nowhere in sight. Snow blanketed the city like a holy shroud. The two apostles carved into the walls of the great church gazed out on a land of paralyzing beauty.

City plows couldn't get their winged blades down Summit Avenue because of all the vehicles parked in front of the Beanblossom house. The ruts were a foot deep. Any car leaving the scene needed a push to the center of the street. The local yokels camped at the Victorian mansion had the technology to generate a media event with as much skill and verve as any communications center in America. Three television network affiliates were outfitted with all of the bells and whistles that advertising money can buy. There was also an independent television station in the Twin

Cities, plus a public television station, both staffed with sanctimonious newsrooms that liked to hype the fact that they covered the news without the hype. These local shrills stormed Cathedral Hill with all of the purpose, and equipment, of a fully armed mountain brigade. But for the most part, coverage of the kidnapping stayed local. The three national networks were content to live off of the feeds of their affiliates. CNN was covering the abduction as a regional story. AP alone fed the nation's newspapers. Andrea Labore may have been queen of the evening news in the Upper Midwest, but to the rest of the country she was just another pretty face who stared lovingly into a camera and read the TelePrompTer.

In the blinding light of morning Rick Beanblossom escaped out the back door. He beat a footpath down the hill and disappeared into downtown traffic that was tied up on snow-packed streets.

Rick entered the lobby of the *North Star Press* and stomped his feet, knocking the heavy snow from his boots. He pulled a cell phone from his coat pocket and checked the battery. Commanding the wall before him was an oil painting of the great lady—Katherine E. Howard greeting all who entered her domain. The portrait was commissioned in 1958, by which time the gutsy woman was well on her way to becoming a newspaper legend, in the spirit of her late husband. The painting portrayed a strikingly elegant woman, comfortable in her age and her profession. Her face wore the countenance of wisdom. A life filled with learning. Yet even as she neared her sixth decade on earth, she had maintained for the artist a certain allure. Pizzazz. Sexiness.

Rick half waved to the security guard at the desk then caught an elevator to the executive offices on the seventh floor. The man without a face was used to being stared at, but not at his own paper. Today was different. Nobody expected to see him at work. He avoided eye contact all the way to Mrs. Howard's office.

She welcomed him with a hug, tears in her eyes. Closed the door behind him. Outside it was freezing but inside her office it was sunny and warm. Lots of glass. Books and art. Rick Beanblossom slipped out of his jacket and scarf. She brushed the snow from the clothes as if he were a sick child in from the cold, then hung the items in her closet. Rick pulled the boots from his feet. At her insistence, he seated himself in an overstuffed chair directly in front of her mahogany desk. It reminded him of a seat in the principal's office at Stillwater High School.

"Richard, I can't begin to tell you how awful all of this is. How's Andrea? Poor girl. My God. How can I help?"

Besides his own mother when she was mad at him, Katherine Howard was the only person he ever knew who called him Richard. Coming from her it was a compliment. Mrs. Howard took her chair behind the desk. She really was a work of art. A brilliant white mane graced her head. Hair white as snow. Her glasses framed a pair of enchanting blue eyes that over the years must have scoured a million headlines. And when she smiled, which was often, she showed off a mouthful of perfect teeth. It was amazing to Rick how much she still resembled the portrait in the lobby, painted more than forty years ago. Blessed with the figure of a young woman then. Still counting her blessings today.

"We're almost certain the baby is alive," Rick told her. "There's nothing to suggest otherwise . . . this is a kidnap for ransom. It's very rare."

Mrs. Howard pushed her long graceful fingers under her glasses and wiped the sadness from her eyes. Her manicured nails remained unaffected by the tears as they raced over a sheer cream polish and melted into the palms of her hands. She cleared the lump from her throat. Then she got down to business. "Now, Richard, tell me what exactly can I do to help?"

Rick paused a moment, remembering what his wife had said about investigating the kidnapping themselves. He knew Mrs. Howard wanted a straight answer. "Andrea and I talked . . . we don't want to sit on our hands and wait for the mailman to deliver another ransom demand. On a story like this . . . if we want answers, we have to move fast. We have a tremendous amount of resources here at the *North Star Press* that I'd like to take advantage of, though I am concerned for you and the paper about a conflict of interest."

"Oh, conflict of interest, my fanny." Mrs. Howard scolded him like a school boy. "That stuff is for college professors and journalism schools. This newspaper operates in the real world. Your son has been kidnapped. We have teams of reporters all over this. What else can we do?"

Rick Beanblossom pushed on. "I know this is a strange question, Mrs. Howard, but if you don't mind . . . ?"

"Yes, Richard?"

"Who was Grover Mudd?"

The owner and publisher of the *St. Paul North Star Press* removed her eyeglasses and pinched the bridge of her nose. "My God, there's a name I haven't heard in decades. Why on earth do you ask?"

"I understand he covered the Lindbergh kidnapping for a St. Paul daily."

"Yes, he was a columnist for my husband at the *Frontier News*. I met him once or twice when I was young. He was a very sick man."

"How do you mean?"

"I mean, he was always sick. Physically ill. In poor health. Ask old Swede. He runs our press room in the annex building across the street. Been with us forever. I'll bet Swede could tell you about Grover Mudd."

"What can you tell me?"

Mrs. Howard sighed as she thought back. "Oh, he was one of those colorful reporters that people in this business can't stop talking about . . . after they're dead and buried. Of course when they were alive . . . they were more trouble than anything. That was Grover Mudd, to hear my husband tell it. Uncouth. Unkempt. Grover never knew when to stop. He was a character right out of an old detective novel. He got the *Frontier News* in hot water on more than one occasion. I think my husband put up with him a lot longer than I would have."

"Do you remember much about the Lindbergh kidnapping case, or Grover Mudd's role in it?"

"I didn't know Grover had a role in it. But heavens, yes, I remember that case. It was the talk of the nation . . . talk of the world. Is that what this is all about?"

Rick explained as best he could. "Dylan's kidnapping . . . appears to be some kind of re-creation of that one. After I wrote the obituary for Anne Morrow Lindbergh, I got a twenty-dollar gold certificate in the mail. Series 1928. The police have confirmed it's Lindbergh ransom money. Then of course, last night during the blizzard . . . "

Mrs. Howard went into such deep thought Rick could almost see the years fading away on the brow of her troubled face. Suddenly, she pushed out of her chair and made her way to an overstuffed bookcase with more grace than any senior citizen had a right to. She removed a hardcover book from a top shelf. Then as she returned to her seat, Mrs. Howard placed a hand over her heart, as if it pained her. She handed the book to Rick. "People couldn't get enough of the Lindberghs," she said. "I've never again seen anything like it."

Rick appreciated her resourcefulness. Her thoughtfulness. He rested the book on his lap and read the title aloud through tired red eyes. "*Hour of Gold, Hour of Lead.* Anne Morrow Lindbergh. *Diaries and Letters 1929–1932.*"

"Yes. Those are Anne Morrow's letters and diaries from those days," Mrs. Howard explained, "when her son was kidnapped. Her words. Her thoughts. She was a brilliant woman. A real pioneer. Nothing like these media stars today. I think you might want to see how Anne handled things. It would seem to me that book would be invaluable to Andrea. As long as she holds it in her hands, she'll never be alone."

On the sky-blue jacket cover was a black-and-white photograph of the most beautiful, sad woman Rick Beanblossom had ever seen. It was beauty different from that of his wife. Pictured before him was a noble presence, an innocent melancholy. The photograph of the young heiress with the almond eyes was taken in the year after the kidnapping and murder of her son. If they snapped a picture of Andrea Labore a year from now, is that how she would look? Black and white? Her once radiant eyes drained of life? Rick opened the book. "And you say you've never again seen anything like the Lindbergh kidnapping? Not even the O.J. trial? Television?"

"Peanuts," said Mrs. Howard. "Not even close to the Lindbergh mania. And nowhere near the suspense. The kidnapping . . . the ransom payoff . . . then the baby found murdered . . . the arrest a couple of years later. Then came the trial . . . oh God, the trial." She spoke as if she'd been a juror. "It was after the outrage over the Richard Hauptmann trial that American newspapers began to clean up their act."

Rick shuddered at what he was hearing. A dead baby. An arrest. A trial. Still, he pushed on. "And Hauptmann was the man convicted and executed for the murder of the baby?"

"Yes. Bruno Richard Hauptmann was his full name. He was an out-of-work carpenter from Germany . . . here illegally."

"Do you think he did it? " Rick asked, slowly turning the pages of the book.

"Oh, I believe he was guilty as hell. We all did. The evidence against him was overwhelming. But the man didn't get a fair trial. It was a circus. Cameras in the courtroom. Overflow crowds standing and talking while the court was in session. Spectators posing for pictures on the witness stand. The actual chair had to be nailed to the stand so it wouldn't be stolen. There were mobs in the street outside the courthouse. Hot dog vendors. People hawking souvenir ladders like the one used to kidnap the baby. It was an old-fashioned lynching without the rope."

She went on, growing excited as she told the story. "The trial was held at the county courthouse in Flemington, New Jersey. Walter Winchell came down for the trial. Alexander Woollcott was there. Damon Runyon, H. L. Mencken, Fannie Hurst, Edna Ferber . . . they were all at the trial. So were the New York society ladies, in mink coats, no less. They were like the knitting women at the base of the guillotine in Paris. It went to the very heart of Americans and their sense of fairness. It wasn't too long after Hauptmann was put to death that the Lindberghs began to lose their halos."

Rick Beanblossom listened intently as Mrs. Howard spun one fascinating story after another about this bygone era. The quintessential baby boomer had always believed himself to be an anachronism. He should have been born in the year 1900. That lost generation. At seventeen he would have dropped out of school and enlisted in the Marine Corps. Fought in the trenches of World War I, instead of the jungles of Vietnam. Then would have come his days as a struggling novelist and expatriate in the decadence of postwar Paris. Followed by toilsome years as a hard-bitten, unapologizing newshound with a cigarette dangling from his lips in prohibition America. Bootleggers and G-men. Al Capone and Elliot Ness. After that he would have penned poignant tales of the Great Depression. Would have covered the great battles of World War II as a war correspondent. Then back to a brilliant writing career until the assassination of President Kennedy. By the time he arrived in Vietnam he would have been a jaded old man typing dispatches about foolish old men sending innocent young men needlessly to their deaths. That's the life he should have lived.

"Who's in charge of the investigation?" Mrs. Howard's question snapped him back to the present.

Rick fished out one of Stephanie Koslowski's FBI

cards. "She's in charge, I guess." He handed the card to Mrs. Howard.

"Oh dear God, didn't this woman handle the Wakefield case?"

"Exactly. Andrea and I are concerned we might be reading the same press releases . . . if you know what I mean."

From the frown on her face Mrs. Howard seemed to know exactly what he meant. She examined the business card in her hand. Raised an eyebrow. "I'll see what I can do if you know what I mean."

Rick Beanblossom sensed their talk was over for now. He got up to leave, but just as he rose from his chair Katherine Howard clutched her chest. Her face looked pale. She was scared. She quickly pulled open the desk drawer and fumbled with a bottle of pills.

"Richard . . . please . . . ?"

Rick Beanblossom grabbed the bottle from her trembling hands and flipped off the cap. Chalky white pills spilled across the desk. She grabbed one and popped it beneath her tongue. Then she sat back in her chair, still gasping for air.

"Are you all right?" Rick had never seen the great lady with so much as a hair out of place, much less this.

"My heart pills," she told him. "Nitroglycerin. You don't get to be my age without a few complications. But I'll be fine."

There was work to do. In just a matter of minutes Mrs. Howard had given him more help than he could have imagined. And a slight scare. She stood. Firm and erect. Put her arms around him. The combination of snow and sun reflecting in the windows was painfully bright. Stung Rick's eyes. He adjusted his mask. He was tired. His head ached. There were so many unanswered questions in a news story like this that he almost wanted to forget the story involved his son. If this was somebody else's kid, a senator, a movie star, some billionaire, he'd be thinking like a textbook on criminal investigations. But his mind was mush. Where do you begin when the kidnap victim is *your* son?

Within an hour of Rick Beanblossom's leaving Mrs. Howard's plush office, Captain Les Angelbeck took a seat in the stark examination room of the Ramsey County morgue, just a few blocks away. There was a newspaper on his lap. In his shirt pocket beneath his heavy green parka was his ubiquitous pack of Marlboro. In the other pocket was an inhaler. Breath in a bottle. On the payroll at the Minnesota Bureau of Criminal Apprehension he was listed as a consultant. But the boys still called him Captain. He wondered if behind his back they still called him the Marlboro Man. Now much of his day, or the half day he usually put in, was spent reading the newspaper.

LABORE BABY KIDNAPPED
FROM HOME
TAKEN FROM CRIB DURING
WINTER STORM
STATEWIDE SEARCH UNDERWAY

Les Angelbeck followed the fine print with trembling fingers. He was old. Death-in-sight old. Retirement came and went, several times. But he couldn't stay away. It's retirement that kills, not emphysema. This case was big. And personal.

His younger self would have been all over it. St. Paul police, the FBI, the BCA, all of them would have politely stepped aside and bowed to his experience. He'd walked a beat in Minneapolis, been an investigator for the county sheriff's department, and a police chief in a sleepy suburb. He even taught law enforcement at a community college. But it was with the BCA, the state police, that he became a legend among detectives. The Marlboro Man. Now the old boy had been put out to pasture. Given a gold watch. Awarded a proclamation from the state legislature and signed by the governor. It thanked him for fifty years of service. In particular, it cited him for the arrest, the conviction, and the execution of Minnesota's most famous killer. The Weatherman.

He had glaucoma. Wore sun visors flipped down over his glasses to protect his eyes from the blinding snow. The examination room was equally bright, so he kept the shades on. Angelbeck finally looked up from his paper. "Suicide?"

"Looks that way. But then again, some gangs are executing their victims this way. Make them suck on the gun, then pull the trigger."

On the aluminum table beneath the bright lights was a naked young man with winter white skin. The top of his head was missing. Blown out. His tongue could be seen through the crown of his skull.

"The angle's wrong," Angelbeck told her. "It would have taken out the back of his head, had it been an execution."

"Thank you, Sherlock, I never would have figured that out." The sarcasm came from Dr. Freda Wilhelm. She was the Ramsey County chief medical examiner. A forensic pathologist. "Maybe you'd like to guess the caliber?"

"A simple thirty-eight," he told her. "Smith and Wesson."

"Exactly." She was a disconcertingly large woman. Almost six feet tall. Weighed in at more than two hundred and fifty pounds. Her dark, graying hair was more frizz than curls, having been dyed and permed one too many times. She wore a military nurse's uniform, much like the navy vice-admiral uniform worn by the U.S. surgeon general. Designed it herself. It was white with blue striped shoulder boards and a gold-braided infantry rope looped ceremoniously over her right shoulder. Seldom was she seen out of uniform. The pretentious outfit and her imperious demeanor made the doctor an easy target for the media. Most reporters thought she was a joke. Some thought she was mad. Still, most cops found her deadly accurate. She had four years of college, four years of medical school, five years of residency, and two years as a fellow in forensic pathology. She was one of the few women in the country who had mastered the art of forensic science. But her salary was half of what most doctors earn. Every payday was resentment day. She often talked about job offers in Florida.

Freddie glanced up at the clock on the wall, a little too conspicuous for Angelbeck to ignore. "Do you have to be somewhere?" he asked.

"I go home for lunch."

"Since when?"

"I'm on a special diet. I'm going to lose a hundred pounds."

Les Angelbeck laughed and coughed at the same time. "Yeah, and I'm going to quit smoking."

"You're right. We're both doomed."

"I'm not afraid of dying," Angelbeck told her, struggling to his feet. "The only thing that haunts me is the thought of lying on that slab, with you hovering over me. Going to make damn sure I die in California." He cleared his throat. Held up the newspaper. "What do you make of this?"

"Are you back in the game?" Freddie wanted to know.

"A friend of the family called, asked me to look into it."

Captain, we need your help."

"Anything for you."

"Rick Beanblossom just left my office. Seems he and Andrea are going to conduct their own investigation into the disappearance of their son."

"That's ridiculous."

"So I thought, at first . . . but guess who the FBI has placed in charge?"

"Who?"

"Stephanie Koslowski . . . out of their Minneapolis office."

"I thought they quietly shipped her out of town after the Wakefield debacle?"

"Well if they did . . . then they quietly shipped her back. Can you help?"

"I'll make some calls . . . see what I can find out."

"Thank you, Captain, I owe you one."

The M.E. set aside a pair of blood-specked tweezers and peeled the latex gloves from her hands. She stared at the headline splashed across the top of the newspaper. "It's sweeps week. Those TV stations will do anything for ratings." Besides taking care of St. Paul and its suburbs, Ramsey County also provided forensic services to more than thirty rural counties in the Upper Midwest. When Freddie began the job she was doing three hundred autopsies a year. Guns, drugs, and AIDS, not to mention a serial killer, had pushed that number past five hundred. Few people knew death as intimately as Dr. Freda Wilhelm. That's what brought cops like Les Angelbeck calling.

And Freddie had another release from the pressures of death. Spiritual. A heavenly calling few people knew about. She was the organist at the Cathedral of St. Paul. Every Sunday morning she proudly took her seat in the choir loft and played her heart out at a three-manual, thirty-rank Ernest Skinner organ. When combined with the organ in the sanctuary, which she could play from her console, she commanded seventy-one ranks, eighty stops, sixty voices, and 4,560 pipes. She also helped lead a fund drive to replace the eighty-four-year-old copper roof of the cathedral dome. It creaked and leaked. Black rubber patches dotted the copper. Much of the original scaffolding had been built with untreated lumber. A major fire hazard. It would cost twenty million dollars to replace the roof and bring the magnificent copper dome up to code. The archbishop was tending to the big donors while Freddie and her committee collected the smaller gifts.

Les Angelbeck was one of the few people outside the church who knew about her role at the cathedral. But then he'd always made it his job to know the little things about people. "Tell me more," the police captain implored as he folded the newspaper headline in two.

"It doesn't make any sense," she told him. "Kidnap for ransom is almost impossible to pull off in this country. And if you were going to steal a baby, keep it for your own, sell it, whatever . . . you wouldn't steal from a high-profile couple like that."

"Which leaves . . . ?"

"Murder. That kid was murdered, Captain. Died last night. He's under ten feet of snow, and all is quiet."

"Just like the Lindbergh baby?"

"Exactly. The little guy will be found in the spring, or maybe in the fall when the hunters take to the woods. I just hope he's found in another county. I don't want him in here."

Angelbeck was skeptical. "I don't know, Freddie . . ." He looked down at the suicide victim laid out on the table. ". . . it's a lot easier to hide a live baby than it is a dead one."

Dr. Freda Wilhelm killed the bright lights above the corpse. "You came down here for my candid opinion. That's my opinion. You're not looking for a baby, Captain. You're looking for a killer."

Swede

The three offset presses that cranked out the *North Star Press* were located in the Mechanical Annex Building across the street from the newspaper. A tunnel under Fourth Street connected the two. The two-level pressroom had the cacophony of a firefight. Machine guns. Tanks. Warning bells that sounded every minute. The presses were running full bore, a prepress daytime run for the Sunday edition. Everybody wore headphones to protect their eardrums. Rick Beanblossom winced at the noise. The place was all grease and grime. Smelled of ink and oil. The workers, all men and not used to visitors, gave him the requisite stare he'd grown accustomed to. Rick stood like a statue beneath a tall arch of newspapers moving along a conveyor. He checked his watch: 9 A.M. His son had been missing twelve hours. Rick spotted the man he was searching for on a metal balcony above the rolling presses. Caught his attention with a wave.

Swede Bjorenson was surprised to see the masked newsman. They'd only met once at a social function for the paper. He gulped a last swig of coffee from his Styrofoam cup, then tossed the remains on the floor. He started down the stairs and signaled Rick into a control room. They slipped inside and closed the soundproof door. The quiet was heaven.

Swede Bjorenson had been with the *North Star Press* as long as anybody could remember. He was a heavy-set man with a round red face and a healthy glow. A beardless Santa Claus in bib overalls. He ran the presses. His father had had the job before him. One of his sons was working under him now. Swede took off his headphones and stuck a finger in his ear. "Between the boys and the machinery, I don't know which is worse." He wiped his mouth with a dirty, red hand-kerchief. "When I first started at the paper we would stuff cotton in our ears. Long time ago."

Rick smiled. A sad, but appreciative smile. "Mrs. Howard thought you might be able to help me."

Swede Bjorenson sat on a metal stool at a control console that faced a large window overlooking his presses. "Sure, Rick, anything I can do to help. I'm sorry about the baby. I'm sure he's okay. Who would hurt a little baby?" Swede had only the slightest hint of a Scandinavian accent, inherited from his parents who probably came straight from the old country. "I thought something must be up because . . . you know . . . we never get any reporters over here. Most of 'em ain't got the faintest idea how the paper gets out."

"I'm afraid that includes me." Rick pulled up a stool and sat beside him. On Swede's hearing aid side. It was obvious from his loud voice that the senior pressman was going deaf. Rick's father had been deaf in one ear. He knew the drill. Rick spoke up. Normal, but louder. "Who was Grover Mudd?"

"Grover Mudd? Golly, I ain't heard that name in years. He was the Rick Beanblossom of his day . . . a broken-down version. More like your evil twin."

"How do you mean?"

"Oh jeez, let me see . . . he was a friend of F. Scott Fitgerald's. Had Fitzgerald's self-destruct streak, but not his talent. They were part of a literary colony that hung around the Kilmarnock Bookshop down on Minnesota Street. It's gone now. Wonderful bookstore. Fireplace. Good coffee. Banned books." The Swede paused a moment. Gazed through his window. As he spoke he kept one eye on his rolling presses, one eye on the past. "Grover Mudd had a column for the *Frontier News* during the gangster days. 'Grover's Corner' it was called."

"Gangster days?"

"Oh yeah, Rick. Terrible days. Do you remember that old Jimmy Stewart movie, *It's a Wonderful Life*? St. Paul was like Bedford Falls had there been no George Bailey. Pottersville. Grover wrote some atrocious things. Of course, I was just a boy. My dad knew him well . . . used to read him to us every day. You either loved him, or you hated him."

"Did you love him, or hate him?"

"See the thing of it was, Rick, most people back then didn't want to own up to what was going on around town. And Grover, well, he got gassed in the war . . . the first war, that is. A Marine, I think. He had consumption. Drowned his agony in whiskey. Drugs too, they said. So he was more or less a drunk by the time he got killed."

"Did you say that he was killed?"

The old man cupped his ear. "Say what, Rick?"

Rick Beanblossom again spoke up. "When did he get killed?"

"Oh boy, was it 1935 or '36 . . . somewhere around there? My Esther Kay would know exactly when . . . she was a big Grover Mudd fan. I do remember Dad reading it to us. Grover had been out of work a couple years when they got him up by the cathedral one night."

"He was murdered?"

"You betcha. He stepped off the trolley with his little girl one snowy evening, and they cut him in two with a machine gun. The little girl wasn't hurt, but must of been a terrible sight. The murder was never solved."

Rick was shocked. "Mrs. Howard didn't mention anything about a murder."

Swede raised an eyebrow. "I'm surprised. Walt Howard spent the rest of his life badgering the police and the politicians for an arrest. Matter of fact, one of his very last editorials was a demand that the police solve the case, and that was some twelve years after the shooting. He called the unsolved murder of Grover

Mudd a lingering embarrassment to the St. Paul police department."

"Where's he buried? " Rick wanted to know.

"Grover? Might have been buried at Soldier's Rest in Oakland Cemetery . . . maybe Fort Snelling . . . I'm not sure."

"You said he was out of work . . . how did he lose his job . . . something he wrote?"

"Oh no . . . golly no. We bought out his paper. Closed it down."

"The *North Star Press* did?"

"Oh yeah, you bet. It was the Depression, ya know. Newspapers were going under all over the country. The *Frontier News* hadn't made money in years. We let them stay in business for another year under their own banner . . . mostly because they were running a cleanup campaign during the gangster days. But when the gangsters were through, so was the paper. And for the most part . . . so was Grover Mudd. He wrote for some of the little weeklies around town, but the *North Star Press* didn't want anything to do with him. The Minneapolis papers wouldn't touch his stuff. You see, after the gangsters were gone, he went after the politicians. Grover always said you can't have an underworld without an overworld. Must have been what got him killed, is what I always figured."

The man in the mask thought about all of this for another precious minute. Again he checked his watch. Outside the window workers were inspecting the newspapers as they rolled off the presses. "Well, if the

North Star Press bought the *Frontier News* . . . then we'd have all of their back issues, their photo collection, all that, right?"

Swede Bjorenson perked up. "Oh yeah, we got the whole kit and caboodle across the street there in the morgue . . . or the 'Library' I guess they call it now. Probably got all their financial records too. We've certainly got all the 'Grover's Corners.' " The old man suddenly remembered something and raised a finger. "Matter of fact, Rick, I saw his typewriter down in storage a few years back."

"Grover Mudd's typewriter?"

"Yes, sir. A big, black Remington. Had MUDD scratched into it with a nail. They did that sort of thing back then."

There was no ribbon in it. The thing was shot. Typed to death. The gilded trim and the Remington name once artistically etched in gold had slowly chipped away and the black iron was charcoal dull. Rick Beanblossom set the heavy typewriter on his desk, right atop the welcome note from Mrs. Howard. He pulled a tissue and wiped the dust from his hands. He ran the tissue over the battered face of the ancient machine and slowly exposed the letters *M-U-D-D*, now barely visible. The Marine took his chair, staring intently at this writing tool from another era. He felt strangely connected. Touched. Confused in an inexplicable sort of way. He glanced up at the picture of his baby boy. Whereabouts unknown. What kind of a man cannot protect his own family? A lump swelled in his throat and he turned away. The wounded veteran of Vietnam gazed upon the World War I poster of the doughboy with the rifle. JOIN THE MARINE CORPS. Rick swallowed the lump in his throat and got back to business. "All right, Grover . . . Marine to Marine . . . talk to me."

"Beanblossom."

"What have you done for me lately?"

"Somebody stole my son last night . . . somebody that was somehow involved with the Lindbergh kidnapping. Give me something . . . anything."

"You've made a lot of enemies over the years, Masked Man. You've got forty-eight hours to find your kid, then they dump him."

"Tell me something I don't know, goddammit."

"Who's running the show?"

"Koslowski . . . but then you already knew that, didn't you? The only good thing is she does seem to know a lot about the Lindbergh case."

"She damn well should."

"What does that mean?"

"As a student she had an article published in the Northwestern Law Review. *It was called, 'Kidnapping and the Law: A Legal Review of the Lindbergh Case.' "*

"Is that a coincidence, or are you implying something?"

"Let me tell you something about kidnap for ransom . . . in this day and age the only person who could pull it off would be a cop. Your son's kidnapping was an inside job."

"Inside the FBI?"

"Let's just say, you wouldn't be the first person to question her integrity."

"My son is missing . . . I don't have time for your riddles."

"But this is a good one. In 1971, right out of the academy, she gets assigned to the Seattle office. Do you know what her first big case is? Northwest Orient Flight 305, Portland bound for Seattle."

"Skyjacked. D. B. Cooper."

"Correct."

"The case is still unsolved."

"Correct again. Years later she's promoted to inspector and assigned to the Minneapolis office . . . and the first investigation she heads up . . . ?"

"The kidnapping of Harlan Wakefield. She leaves it unsolved."

"No, worse, Masked Man. You solved it. Made a fool out of her within the bureau. The FBI is not kind to its women. It's even less kind to its failures. Whatever you do, don't let Koslowski deliver the ransom. Do it yourself, or get someone you trust."

"And who do I trust?"

"You can trust me, and you can trust your wife. Nobody else."

"Tell me more."

"Charles Lindbergh paid the ransom without any proof his child was still alive. Don't you do that . . . no matter what the Feds tell you. Make a public announcement for the kidnappers . . . make it splashy, and make it today . . . before

any ransom is paid you want a Polaroid snapshot of your baby lying awake beside the front page of tomorrow morning's North Star Press . . . *Metro Final."*

"Andrea will do it . . . that'll get their attention. Did you find out anything more on that reporter you told me about . . . Grover Mudd?"

"Just what I told you last night . . . arrested with a ransom bill . . . released . . . no charges. After that . . . he disappears from police records, until he's murdered in 1936."

"Unsolved."

"Yes, unsolved."

"Turns out the *North Star* has all his writings. I'm going to start pulling his articles about the Lindbergh case. What else can we do?"

"Bring in an electronics expert. Someone private. I'll give you some names. Have him check your work phone to see if it's been tapped. Then check the walls for listening devices."

"Who would do something like that to me?"

"You've made a lot of enemies, Masked Man."

"Give me your best guess . . . where are they keeping my little boy?"

"Under your nose."

"What do you mean?"

"I doubt he was taken out of the city. If he was grabbed by somebody you know . . . I doubt he's even left the neighborhood. He's right under your nose. Bet on it."

Stormy

Summit Avenue. Tuesday. March 2. One P.M. Baby Dylan has been missing from his crib for sixteen hours. A massive ground search of the Cathedral Hill neighborhood has turned up no clues as to his whereabouts. Four satellite trucks line the curb. They are flanked by news vans numbered like billiard balls. Police vehicles surround them. The winter sun is low in the sky. Everything in sight is buried in snow. White and bright. Viewed from a wide angle the Victorian avenue shows like a Currier & Ives snowscape. A crowd of reporters forms a semicircle on the snowy lawn in front of the brick mansion. Beneath the entrance arch a dozen microphones are fastened to metal stands and reinforced with electricians' tape. The photographers complain about the lighting. At the last minute the battery of microphones are moved three feet further away from the entrance so that the mother of the missing child will be seen stepping out of the shadows of the house and into the bright winter sun.

The afternoon soap operas are put on hold for the

press conference, which will not really be a conference since Andrea has made it clear she will not be answering questions. If the kidnappers know a thing or two about manipulating the media, Andrea Labore and her husband could write a book on the subject. In Atlanta, CNN has agreed to live coverage if Andrea can keep the announcement under ten minutes. No problem. Andrea has decided that for maximum coverage and maximum effect, the announcement will be short and bitter. To personalize the crime she will stand alone at the microphones. The police, led by Inspector Koslowski, will line up on the steps behind her. She will say what she has to say. Take no questions. Turn and walk away.

It is 1:02 P.M. The anchors back in the studio have had their mandatory two minutes to warm up the audience. The big oak doors of the house are thrown open. Andrea Labore walks calmly onto the porch, through the arch and down the stairs. She is dressed casually—jeans, a white blouse, and a drab but comfortable sweater she would never wear on the Sky High news set. No coat. A dozen men and women from various law enforcement agencies follow her down the stairs. She pauses before the multitude of microphones. The only sound is the whirling of a hundred fast-speed cameras snapping a thousand pictures of a gorgeous face that is not moving.

To all those who know her, and to those who watch her on television night after night, Andrea Labore looks decidedly different on this side of the news. She wears little makeup. Her normally bright eyes are tired and sad. There is no hint of a smile. She appears slightly disheveled. Suddenly, to everybody watching, she looks like a mom. Just a mom. Andrea begins:

"Today, on behalf of my husband and myself, and the law enforcement community throughout Minnesota, I would like to address directly the persons who stole my son . . . Dylan Labore Beanblossom."

In the freezing air, her breath is visible as it rolls out before her. Her voice is not the mellifluous voice viewers are used to hearing. Instead, it is cold, edgy.

"You have demanded from us five hundred thousand dollars for the safe return of our baby boy. We now have the money, and we have the money in the specific denominations that you requested. We are fully prepared to follow your instructions for delivery of this ransom money."

Here Andrea stops. Swallows hard, as if she is trying to control her temper, not her tears.

"But let me make myself perfectly clear . . . we will not give you one single penny of this money unless we have proof that our son is alive and well. Before any money is released, you must provide us with a Polaroid snapshot of our baby, Dylan, lying awake alongside tomorrow morning's front page of the *St. Paul North Star Press*. Metro Final. If this photograph does not accompany your instructions, we will be forced to conclude . . ."

In mid-sentence the mother of the missing child runs out of breath, out of words. She stares into the snow at her feet. Then Andrea Labore takes a deep breath, regains her composure, and finishes what she has to say.

". . . we will be forced to conclude that our son is dead . . . and we will no longer negotiate with you. There will be no exceptions to this demand. Good-day."

Andrea turns. Parts the sea of cops. She walks with bold determination up the stairs and through the doors of a magnificent house that she has no intentions of apologizing for.

Jasmine Allen watched Andrea's announcement from the privacy of her room, which was on the first floor of the mansion, just off the kitchen. It had probably been servants' quarters since the first railroad baron, or lumber baron, or cattle baron, or flour baron, or whatever-the-hell-baron who helped build Minnesota first moved into the place. From what Jasmine had read about St. Paul's past, it was probably a whore-house baron.

When the hubbub from Andrea's appearance died down, Jasmine slipped out of her room and crept up the back stairs, past the master bedroom, then up another flight of stairs past the FBI. On the fourth floor she stole into the attic space Rick Beanblossom had converted into an office library. The large room of books hadn't been used in days. It was cold and day-time dark. Ice could be heard cracking on the roof over the vaulted ceiling. The young girl from New Jersey had grown accustomed to living and working in a house where things go bump in the night. Where on cold winter nights the stairs creak and the walls crackle. Where a noisy furnace worked double overtime to heat a house seemingly built with a hundred fireplaces a hundred years ago. She came to the attic for answers. She came for help.

Jasmine was scared to death, but not because of any supernatural spooks that might be wandering the halls. Early that morning the all-too-spooky FBI had driven her over to their Minneapolis office to look at mug shots. Or so she was told. Mostly they questioned her. For hours they questioned her. The lady FBI inspector had it in for her. Somehow that woman knew about the baby. They kept reminding Jasmine that she was not under arrest, but it didn't matter. She was too frightened by the agents to ask for a lawyer. She told them everything she could. They were unsatisfied. Said there would be more questions later. It was well after noon when the FBI lady drove her home. Jasmine ran to her room in a panic. She was a suspect in the kidnapping of Baby Dylan, she knew it. She moved to her dresser for her childhood charm. Something to protect her from the evil spirits now encircling her. But her silver thimble was missing. Her room had been searched. That is why the FBI ran her over to Minneapolis. To get her out of the house.

Through the attic window at the peak of the house Jasmine could see the great church, and beyond that the state capitol building. It was a quaint city. It was two quaint cities. But few of her kind lived here. Minnesota was a land of white people.

Mr. Beanblossom had told her the papers on the history of the house were in the old trunk beneath the picture window. *"Maybe if you look, you can find a spirit or two. You're welcome to try."*

Jasmine Allen flipped open the musty smelling seafarer's trunk and found it filled with yellowing papers. Newspaper articles. Letters. Crusty notes and receipts. She grabbed a handful at random, closed the trunk and took a seat on top of it. Then ignoring the world around her, she got lost in the writings and workings of people long since dead. Every now and then while she searched the forgotten documents for spirits unknown, a sharp chill would overtake her, a chill so acute she could see her breath. Then she would stop her reading and listen to the icy wind, a wind that all too often sounded like a crying baby. She could easily imagine the man in the mask happily wandering the spooky halls of the big house, but Jasmine couldn't imagine what a woman of Andrea's grace and charm was doing in this Victorian museum—any more than she could imagine how a woman of her style and beauty could marry a man without a face.

"What are you doing?"

"Mr. Beanblossom said there were papers about the house up here . . . said I could look through them."

Andrea Labore calmly strolled into the library and took a seat in an antique wooden office chair she and

Rick had found in the river town of Red Wing. They had filled the house with antiques. But now with her son missing, they were just things. Worthless things. "What kind of papers?" she asked the startled Jasmine.

"Newspaper stories, and papers about house repairs, and some letters that were written a long time ago."

Every time Stephanie Koslowski told her the housekeeper was hiding things, that Jasmine Allen was the chief suspect in the abduction of her son, Andrea was inclined to believe her. And then every time Andrea confronted the young girl, stared her straight in the eye, she found the scenario impossible to believe. Andrea only hoped that Rick was having more luck with Grover Mudd than she was having with Jasmine Allen. "This has all been so crazy, Jasmine, such a nightmare that I haven't had the time to really speak with you. I guess I should have come to you earlier."

"Did you have a talk with that dragon lady?"

Now the bitterness in Jasmine's voice reminded Andrea a little of herself. Too mad to cry anymore. "Inspector Koslowski? Yes, we had a long talk."

"And what did she tell you . . . did she say that I did it?"

"Not in so many words."

"I don't know what that means, Andrea. But it wasn't me stole your baby . . . but I know everybody thinks it was me."

"Let's you and me make a deal, Jasmine. I'll tell you

what the FBI told me . . . then you share with me what you didn't tell the FBI."

For the longest moment, Jasmine Allen said nothing—a tacit admission that the housekeeper had a lot more to say. "Okay, I guess."

"Okay." It was the ray of light Andrea was hoping for. The anchorwoman didn't want to talk to Jasmine the way a reporter talks to a cop, but she more or less did, passing along the information Inspector Koslowski had shared with her. "They think the ransom note was written by a woman. It looks like German script. The ladder used in the kidnapping came from a national hardware chain. One of a million. No fingerprints. The snowstorm swallowed all of the footprints. All of the tire tracks."

"What does all that mean?"

"It means that you didn't write the ransom note . . . you're not German. It means there is no physical evidence that you were actually involved in the abduction."

"I wasn't . . . so why did they search my room? Why did they steal my jewelry?"

"What jewelry would that be, Jasmine?"

"It was a thimble made of silver. It wasn't much, but I'm not a rich lady like . . . it meant a lot to me."

"Where did you get this silver thimble?"

"It was given to me when my grandfather died."

"And where did he get it from?"

"I don't know."

"It's not a thimble, Jasmine. The FBI searched your room with my permission. The silver piece they found is probably what they used to call a baby's thumbguard. Mothers would put them on their baby's hands to keep them from sucking their thumbs. When you were growing up in New Jersey, were you ever told the story of the Lindbergh baby?"

"We heard some stuff about it in history class . . . that's all."

"He was kidnapped from his crib in 1932 wearing a pair of thumbguards. Baby Alice Thumbguards, they were called. One of the thumbguards was found in the Lindberghs' yard a few days after the kidnapping. The other one has never been found. The thumbguard the FBI found in your room fits the description of the missing thumbguard. It's being sent overnight to the FBI office in Philadelphia, and tomorrow morning agents there are going to take it to the Lindbergh Archives at the New Jersey State Police Museum in Trenton, New Jersey. Once it is there, your little sliver of silver will be compared with the other thumbguard. Do you understand what that means?"

"If it belonged to the Lindbergh baby, then I am going to be in trouble?"

"Jasmine—you may be in a lot of trouble. It's just too much of a coincidence that you would have the missing thumbguard living in a house where another child has been kidnapped." Andrea had raised her voice a bit more than she had wanted to. She tried to soften her tone. "Don't you agree?"

Jasmine shuffled the musty papers in her hands. "I

found what I was looking for . . . I thought I might. Her name was Stormy Day. She was murdered."

Andrea was baffled. "Who was murdered?"

"It's in the newspapers here with all the papers about this house. Somebody cut it out and saved it."

Not really sure what the girl was talking about, Andrea held out her hand. "May I?" she asked. Jasmine handed her the article. It was a small headline, tucked away in a corner of the newspaper reserved for small stories.

NEGRO GIRL FOUND IN RIVER
BODY FLOATING OFF HARRIET ISLAND

Jasmine explained. "It says she was a hotel maid who cleaned houses on weekends . . . a Negro girl is what it says. One of the letters I found said she cleaned this house every weekend. The girl in the letter talks about how sad she is that Stormy got murdered."

"That is terrible, but it was a long time ago . . . 1934, it says. Why does it interest you so much?"

"Folks all over town say this house is haunted."

Andrea had heard the stories. "Nonsense."

"Maybe. But maybe not."

"And if this house is haunted . . . you think Stormy Day is the resident ghost?"

"I knew in my heart there's been somebody trying to warn us about something bad gonna happen. And then it happened."

Andrea handed back the article. Disappointed.

"And is that all that you want to tell me, Jasmine? Murdered maids? Ghosts?"

"I guess so."

Andrea Labore checked her watch. Her baby had been missing now for almost eighteen hours. She stood. Again her anger was rising. The FBI was right. The girl was hiding something. "Jasmine, it wasn't a ghost who crept up that ladder and stole my son. That monster is all too real." Andrea Labore turned to go. Made it halfway to the door when Jasmine stopped her.

"Andrea . . . ?"

" What?"

"I . . . I had a baby in New Jersey. Was a little baby boy."

Dylan

One rainy night in late March of 1932, Anne Morrow Lindbergh, pregnant with her second child, was roused from bed at 3 A.M. The man knocking at the front door was a special assistant secretary of labor from Washington, D.C. Her husband was not at home. This government official insisted he could solve the mystery of her missing son within forty-eight hours. He ordered her to run upstairs to the child's nursery and walk around. His theory was simple; it was impossible for a kidnapper to climb into the nursery without being heard downstairs. Since the man was a federal official, Anne cooperated. Then he ordered her to show him the furnace. Mrs. Lindbergh led him down to the basement where, before her horrified eyes, the man pantomimed the act of throwing a dead baby into the furnace. As if that was not enough, he then picked up a poker and began sifting through the ashes in search of bone fragments. This lunatic's inference was plain—that the Lindberghs had killed their own baby and burned the body.

Nearly seventy years have gone by, and people are still throwing the baby into the furnace.

In the twenty-four hours since his abduction a million words had been written about the kidnapping of Dylan Labore Beanblossom, but not one more word was heard from the kidnappers. It was just past 9 P.M. The temperature had dropped with the sun. 7 degrees below zero. 20 degrees below the average. Storm clouds were once again on the prowl. More snow was expected. Lights blazed throughout the Summit Avenue mansion. But up on the second floor, the only visible light glowed ever so gently from a Tiffany lamp in the Victorian bedroom. The eye of the hurricane.

Andrea, lying beside her husband, could not bring herself to get out of her clothes and crawl under the bed covers. Nevertheless, she had drifted into a troubled sleep. On the night stand beside Andrea stood *Hour of Gold, Hour of Lead* by Anne Morrow Lindbergh, the pages as yet unturned. Andrea had stood the book on end so that the melancholy photograph of the young author faced her side of the bed, as if it were that of a loved one.

Beside Rick, on the bedside table with the antique lamp, was a separate stack of Lindbergh books, the pages having been turned over and over again: *The Trial of Bruno Richard Hauptmann*, by Sidney B. Whipple; *Kidnap: The Story of the Lindbergh Case*, by George Waller; *Scapegoat: The Lonesome Death of Bruno Richard Hauptmann*, by Anthony Scaduto; *The Airman and the*

Carpenter, by Ludovic Kennedy; and *Lindbergh: The Crime*, by Noel Behn. But most important was the book balanced on his lap, the one recommended to him by Inspector Koslowski: *The Lindbergh Case*, by Jim Fisher. She was right about one thing, the book was excellent—the kind of research a Pulitzer Prize-winning reporter admires. He was paging through it for the second time.

Like the Fisher book, George Waller's work was exemplary, as was Sidney Whipples's 1937 account. But the other books were nothing but bullshit conspiracy theories. The authors had formed their conclusions first and then worked backward—Bruno Hauptmann was innocent, they claimed, and facts that suggested otherwise were either explained away or simply ignored. Some went so far as to implicate the Lindberghs in the disappearance of their son. Only a moron would believe such nonsense. Only a hack would write it. Still, the photographs displayed in all of the books were gut-wrenching. Keeping the books company was a small green bottle of Excedrin and a half-empty can of Mountain Dew. After hours and hours of reading the Minnesota newsman had reached one unremarkable conclusion—Bruno Richard Hauptmann climbed the ladder that night in 1932 and kidnapped the Lindbergh baby. Mrs. Howard was right, the evidence against him was overwhelming.

But could the German carpenter have had an accomplice?

Rick Beanblossom thought about that as he sat on

the four-poster in blue jeans, white socks, and a weathered sweatshirt. The near silent ticking of the mantel clock seemed like a drum beat. For the hundredth time he checked the hour. Then he returned to his books.

Across the Amish quilt lay a dozen photocopies of the long deceased *Frontier News*, crisp black-and-white copies made from yellow and brittle newspapers. The headlines were bold, but the print was extremely fine and difficult to read. The papers were scattered from Rick's folded knees to the gentle curve in Andrea's sleeping back. There were also rolled-up sheets of *The New York Times*, copied from microfilm. The *Frontier News* coverage of the Lindbergh kidnapping was sensational all right, but the locals weren't reporting anything other newspapers of the day weren't reporting. That is until June of 1932, two months after the fifty-thousand-dollar ransom was paid. One month after the baby was found murdered. Rick kept returning to one page in particular:

ST. PAUL FRONTIER NEWS

* Page One * Tuesday, June 14, 1932 * Two Cents *

ST. PAUL WOMAN QUESTIONED
IN LINDBERGH KIDNAPPING

More Ransom Money Shows Up Here

by Grover Mudd

A young German woman now living in St. Paul was questioned and later released by police after paying for a new dress with a ransom bill from the Lindbergh kidnapping. Employees at the Golden Rule Department Store said the woman passed the twenty-dollar gold certificate on Saturday afternoon after trying on a dress. Suspicious clerks called police. The woman was taken into custody while waiting at the trolley stop on Seventh and Wabasha. She was released several hours later after police determined she had come by the bill innocently when she cashed a check at a Minneapolis bank on Friday.

To date most of the ransom bills recovered from the March 1 kidnapping and subsequent murder of twenty-month-old Charles Lindbergh Jr. were recovered in New York City. The baby, son of famed aviator Charles Lindbergh and Ann Morrow Lindbergh, was snatched from their country estate in Hopewell, New Jersey. His badly decomposed body was discovered in woods near the home on May 12. The case remains unsolved.

The woman questioned told police her name was Esther Snow, age 22, of the Bronx, New York, now residing on Grand Avenue in St. Paul. However, police identified the woman through immigration records as Esther K. Trinka, age 32, of Leipzig, Germany. Officials at the U.S. Department of Immigration were notified of the slight discrepancy before the woman was released without conditions . . . .

They let her go. Rick Beanblossom read it over and over. St. Paul cops catch the woman red-handed spending ransom money from the crime of the century, and they let her go. They catch the woman lying to them about her identity, and they let her go. She also chopped ten years off her age. The masked newsman couldn't believe it. Apparently the cynical newshound who wrote the story couldn't believe it either: "... were notified of the slight discrepancy ..." Rick tore through the papers on the bed and found the other headline that had grabbed his attention:

THE NEW YORK TIMES
"All the News That's Fit to Print."
New York, Wednesday, March 2, 1932, Two Cents

LINDBERGH BABY KIDNAPPED
FROM HOME
Child Stolen in Evening
Woman Believed Involved

Through the night, the faceless reporter sat on his bed surrounded by shadows of the past. And everything kept coming back to a mysterious woman. He rubbed his weary eyes. He scribbled desultory notes, rambling thoughts, on a yellow legal pad:

Esther Snow, St. Paul, a.k.a Esther K. Trinka, the Bronx via Leipzig, Germany ... Grover Mudd, Frontier News ... both found holding $20 gold certificates in St. Paul ... connection ... Mudd contacted her???

Even corrupt police wouldn't have returned the hot $20 to her ... did she have more ransom money ... is that where Mudd got his $20???

Rick Beanblossom swallowed two more aspirin and chased them with a swig of Mountain Dew. There was no way in hell he was dozing off. An irritating wind kept crying through the windows. Andrea stirred restlessly in her sleep. Before she had drifted off he shared with her everything he'd discovered since his talks with Mrs. Howard and Swede Bjorenson. About Grover Mudd. The *Frontier News*. St Paul's gangster days. Even the rusting typewriter. The one thing he didn't share with his wife was his newfound suspicions about Lindbergh expert Stephanie Koslowski.

Rick paused to reflect. Stephanie Koslowski? Jasmine Allen? Either way, the kidnapper could be in the house. He slid a hand across his wife's shoulder. She was curled up in a fetal position, her arms folded tight. She wore a white sweater. Black slacks. Light, white socks. He ran his fingers through her silky hair, a sensuous feeling he never tired of. Then he returned to his scribbling:

> *Bruno Hauptmann, Kamenz, Germany, immigrates Bronx, NY . . . Esther Trinka, Leipzig, Germany, immigrates Bronx, NY . . . Get dates! . . . L. baby kidnapped March 1, New Jersey . . . B. baby kidnapped March 1 St. Paul . . . both ladder through 2nd story window . . . A. Lindbergh and housekeepers in house . . . C. Lindbergh was not supposed to be home that night, but was . . . A. Labore and housekeeper in house . . . R. Beanblossom was not supposed to be home that night, but . . .*
>
> *L. baby, 50 thou ransom . . . B. baby, 500 thou . . . L. baby murdered night of kidnapping . . . B. baby . . .*

Andrea woke with a scream. Rick fell back against the headboard. His pen and legal pad flew through the air, hit the lamp, and knocked it to the floor. Now the only light in the room spilled beneath the bed. The room itself was semidark and shadowy.

Andrea continued to scream. Rick grabbed for her, but she was out of the bed and racing for the door. "Dylan! Baby!" She ran down the darkened hallway, stumbling, clawing her way to the nursery door.

Rick tried to catch her, but she was swift as a ghost. "Andrea!" At the door to the nursery he tripped over her in the dark and they both tumbled to the hallway floor. Rick threw his arms around his wife and held her tight.

Tears were streaming down her face. "Why is he crying?"

"Andrea, he's not in there. You've had a bad dream."

"I can hear him crying. Rick, can't you hear him?"

"It's the wind, Andrea honey, it's just the damn wind."

"He's crying . . . my baby is crying and they're ignoring him."

"No, Andrea, no." He kissed her forehead. "They're taking good care of him. They want money . . . that's all. He's with a nurse, remember? " He stroked her hair.

Andrea calmed herself, more awake now. She struggled to her feet, Rick helping her. Then she pushed gently away from the caring arms of her husband. She peered into the empty nursery. Andrea Labore strolled weakly down the hall to the railing over the grand staircase. Rick followed her. She leaned on the polished wood for support and took a deep breath. Reporters were gathering below. The overnight shift. FBI agents stepped to the staircase above.

"You give me back my baby!" Her angry demand echoed through the mansion.

Rick was right behind her. "Andrea, please, there're people in the house."

Twenty-four hours of grief and frustration had finally caught up with his wife. The tears in her eyes were tears of rage. From the balcony the mother of the missing child addressed the gathering throng below and above her. "You hear me and hear me good . . . if you hurt my baby, I'll put a bullet right through your head. I'll put two bullets through your head . . . one for me and one for Anne Lindbergh. " As sound bites go, it was a classic. She stormed into the bedroom collapsing on the bed, folding a pillow around her ears to shut out the windswept cries of the baby.

Rick Beanblossom stood alone at the top of the grand staircase. The reporters were stirring below, uncomfortable. More lights were popping on all over the house. St. Paul police were at the front door. On the stairs leading up to the third floor, Stephanie Koslowski and her team of FBI agents stood like zombies staring down at the man in the mask. Telephones were ringing. A grandfather clock was playing hourly chimes. The father of the missing child held up his hands in a vain attempt to turn uproar to silence.

"Everybody relax . . . she had a bad dream, that's all. She didn't mean it. Everybody leave us alone . . . we'll be okay." The man without a face, without a son, calmly strolled past the carved oak panel and quietly closed the bedroom door.

It was in those nebulous moments of consciousness just before sleep takes hold that the missing baby came crying on the wind. At first Jasmine Allen believed that Dylan was back home. Prayed it was so. Then came that awful scream. A scream not of joy, but of terror. There was running upstairs. Tumbling. Weepy voices pleading for help. And through it all Dylan kept crying. The young housekeeper lay in bed with the covers up to her chin. It was just that horrible wind, she told herself. She was confused, not quite awake. But there was no mistaking what Jasmine Allen heard next.

"You give me back my baby!"

It was a voice overflowing with hate, the raging hatred a mother shows only to those who harm her children. The mother's deadly threat set Jasmine to shivering. Now she would welcome a ghost.

Jasmine Allen knew nothing about a thumbguard from the Lindbergh kidnapping. For all she knew the sliver of silver her grandfather had left to her could have been a Monopoly piece. She felt herself a victim of the ghost that still haunted America—racial prejudice. Never in her life had she been surrounded by so much hideous whiteness. White land. White people.

And what of her own prejudices? How was it she could openly admire white men, but she could barely contain her contempt for white women?

Back in New Jersey she had put her own baby up for adoption. Not once was she allowed to hold the child in her arms, so fearful were they of her motherly instincts. If it had been the child of a black man and black woman, she probably would have kept *him*—or so she told herself—but this was the child of a black woman and a white man and she was told to get rid of *it*.

Then came the grant from the Howard Foundation. She never applied for it. Had no idea who it was that recommended her. The money to study nursing in Minnesota appeared out of thin air.

Jasmine Allen crawled out of bed, the warm covers still wrapped securely around her shoulders. The baby was still crying. And again, she heard the wind calling her name. "Jasmine." She dropped to her knees and pulled the blanket over her head. Now she could hear two babies crying. She covered her ears.

Suddenly, a shaft of cold air enveloped her, cut right through the blanket around her shoulders. Then like the abrupt end to a thunderstorm, all was quiet. And in that silent moment, Jasmine knew.

It was snowing again. A quiet snow. Precursor to another storm. Candles were glowing in windows up and down Summit Avenue. Standing behind a windowpane trimmed with frost, Jasmine's black skin beneath the white gown gave the young housekeeper the benevolent appearance of the ghost of Christmas past. And like that all-knowing spirit Jasmine knew that if the baby was crying, the baby was still alive. The true ghost that haunted the house on Cathedral Hill had carried the baby's crying home on the wind. Jasmine heard it.

Jasmine Allen turned and gazed around the room with an at-peace smile. "I know that you are here, Stormy," she said softly. "I heard the baby crying . . . I know what it means . . . thank you."

Esther

Day two. Wednesday. The third of March. Thirty-six hours into the kidnapping. Clouds thick as thieves were dark and ominous. The morning temperature struggled to just above zero. Winds were gusting to 20 mph. At 9 A.M. the National Weather Service made it official. Another blizzard was in the Twin Cities forecast—eight to twelve hours away, depending on the track of the storm.

The first break, and heartbreak, in the abduction of Dylan Labore Beanblossom came at roughly the same time as the blizzard warning. At 9:05 police received a 911 call from the Ramsey Medical Center. A young woman from the pediatrics ward had run screaming from the lobby with a baby in her arms. On her way out the door she babbled that the baby belonged to Andrea Labore. St. Paul police located her on West Seventh Street and chased her on foot all the way to the High Bridge. Halfway across the steel-arched span she climbed a snowbank to the railing and, still holding on to the baby, threatened to jump.

At the mention of Andrea Labore, the FBI was alerted at their command post in the Beanblossom mansion. The bridge was clearly visible through the windows at the rear of the house.

As bridges go the High Bridge is not a work of art, but it is impressive, spanning two river bluffs with breathtaking views. Forever a part of the cityscape, the original bridge had recently been dismantled, and with much fanfare and many photo opportunities, a sleeker, more elongated High Bridge slowly took its place over the water. But this new bridge proved to be just as lethal as the old. In San Francisco, the despondent ritually throw themselves into the bay from the rustic rails of the Golden Gate Bridge. In St. Paul, they make an equally dramatic plunge into the Mississippi River from the wrought-iron rails of the High Bridge. At a free-fall speed of about seventy-five miles per hour, the drop of two hundred feet is almost always fatal.

The north wind flew down the river like a warrior's spear. Cut right to her bones. Inspector Stephanie Koslowski slipped between the St. Paul squad cars blocking the Smith Avenue entrance. The police department's critical incident response team had also responded. State police put a chopper in the air. Koslowski pulled her gloves tight and buttoned up. The inspector was dressed in a long wool coat, navy blue. Light boots. Still, her clothes were no match for the icy winds of March. Shivering, she walked half the length of the long bridge where she was met by a trained negotiator.

"Inspector, I'm Kathy Giles, St. Paul police." Commander Giles was a handsome, no-nonsense woman, bundled up to her chin in her winter uniform.

"Stephanie Koslowski, FBI. How long has she been up there?"

"About twenty minutes. Water rescue is working into position, but they are going to need a few more minutes. They've got a ton of ice to push through."

The coatless young woman was standing on the frosted metal railing hugging the aluminum pole of an arc light with one arm and holding a baby in the other. Her eyes were glassed over. She seemed immune to the cold. The baby she was clutching was wrapped in a single white blanket, hardly adequate for the weather.

"Any idea who she is?"

"We can't get a name out of her," Giles told her, "but she claims she's holding the Labore baby. She shut down about ten minutes ago. Hasn't spoken a word since. The hospital doesn't seem to know much more . . . nameless, ageless female with infant, waiting for an examination." Commander Giles scanned both ends of the bridge. Shook her head in wonder at the swiftly gathering army of news photographers as they took up choice positions along the bluff tops. "It's all the damn media coverage," she swore. "Drives people crazy."

"Then perhaps I should talk to her."

Stunned by the sound of the smooth, familiar voice, Koslowski and Giles turned at the same time—turned so fast they almost wrenched their necks.

"Andrea," Koslowski asked, "what on earth are you doing here?"

The newswoman wore a brown suede coat over her slacks. Thin leather gloves. She had hurriedly slipped on a pair of loafers. Her voice betrayed no hint of panic, in stark contrast to the previous evening. "I could see the commotion from the house." Andrea Labore should have been out of breath from hurrying to the bridge, but a preternatural calm had settled over her. A supernatural calm considering it was possibly her baby that was now dangling over the river.

"Where's your husband?" Koslowski asked.

Andrea quickly searched the crowd with a reporter's eye, then she broke the news. "Postal inspectors delivered a second note from the kidnappers, just after you left. Rick read it and tore out of the house. I thought he might be here."

"Did he take the note with him?" Stephanie Koslowski had the panicked countenance of someone suddenly losing control of her own investigation. She glanced over her shoulder at the baby on the bridge. She stared at the rear ends of the mansions that ran along Summit Avenue—people so arrogantly rich they had built with their backs to the river so their homes could face one another. "Andrea, I warned you, the kooks come out of the woodwork on these cases. Chances are that's not your baby out there."

"But there's a chance it might be."

"We have people trained for this sort of thing," Giles told her.

"Yes, I know that, but please let me talk to her." Andrea Labore poured all of her persuasive skills into one single word. "Please . . ."

The second break in the case came only minutes after the first. A postal inspector hustled up the front stairs and into the house. He handed Rick Beanblossom a note discovered that morning at the downtown office. A thousand cards and letters had poured into the Beanblossom-Labore address, making the search for another ransom demand extremely difficult. But with hundreds of postal workers volunteering overtime, they'd found it. The man in the mask read the note. Then he put the contents together with everything he had learned in the past twenty-four hours. He was convinced he had the kidnapping of his son all figured out. It was an inside job all right. Inside the *North Star Press*.

Rick Beanblossom escaped the media horde through the back door and, working alone, story of his life, found the house he was searching for on a steep street in a rundown neighborhood not far behind the State Capitol Building. He had no idea that his wife had also hurried out of the house.

For more than a hundred years the neighborhood

hidden behind the majestic dome of the capitol had been one of the poorest sections of the city. White trash. The houses were small clapboards nailed together on small lots. Scandinavian immigrants had passed the homes on to impoverished Germans. The Germans had left the houses to the Irish. And now, although descendants of all three ethnic groups could still be found living there, the downtrodden neighborhood had for the most part been passed on to blacks, American Indians, and refugees of Southeast Asia. But there remained a strong sense of pride in the dilapidated neighborhood. Its people, like those before them, no matter how low their jobs, still got up in the morning and went off to work.

The steep street was extremely narrow, almost impassable, made worse by the mushrooming snowbanks. Most people parked their cars at the curb in front of their houses. The street was seldom cleared. Plows just wound around the cars, burying them. Then people shoveled out their cars and threw the snow back into the street. Rick stepped around mounds of snow and crept up the icy stairs to the door. He glanced up at the sky. The clouds were gun-metal gray. More snow on the way. He pulled his hands out of the pockets of his leather flight jacket and took another peek at the note. Then he knocked hard at the door.

Across the street a mailman was trudging through his route. Another day. Another bag of mail. For all the jokes about postal workers, it was the men and women of the United States Postal Service who had come through for him. Rick knocked again. Harder this time.

Swede Bjorenson answered the anxious knock at the door. The man whose job in life was to roll the presses at the *North Star Press* was astonished to see the newsman standing there. "Hello, Rick. What a surprise. Is there any word on the baby?"

"Swede, I need to talk to your wife . . . Esther Kay. You said she could tell me about Grover Mudd."

Swede was dressed in his bib overalls, same clothes he wore at work. His round face was a constant red, but still he seemed flustered by the request. "Jeez, Rick, I told you everything. I don't know what it is my Esther Kay could add . . . though I did come to remember when it was that Grover was killed."

"April 3, 1936," Rick told him, matter of fact. "The same day Bruno Hauptmann was electrocuted for the kidnapping and murder of the Lindbergh baby."

"Yes, that's right. They shared the headlines that day."

"I'd still like to talk to her about him . . . it's important, Swede."

Bjorenson leaned into the freezing air. "See the thing of it is, Rick, she's not well. I don't think she'd be up to talking today."

"Swede, my son is missing. Your wife might know something. Some little thing she doesn't even know she knows."

The old man seemed suddenly nervous. He put a finger to his hearing aid, doing more stalling than adjusting. "She can't help you, Rick . . . and as sorry as I am about your boy, I don't like you coming to my house like this. We really don't have visitors. We're private people at home here. I hope you understand that."

A cold breeze came between the two men. The reporter famous for his Minnesota cool, his Minnesota smug, stood on the steps and stared right through the elderly Swede. "I don't give a good goddamn about your privacy, old man. I want to come in and talk to Esther Kay Bjorenson . . . or whatever the hell she's calling herself these days."

Suddenly furious, Swede Bjorenson blocked the doorway the way a winter cloud blocks the sun. "Don't you talk to me like that, Rick Beanblossom. I am not one of your interviews."

"My son has been kidnapped and every bone in my body tells me your wife knows something about it."

"How can that be?"

Rick swallowed his anger. "Grover Mudd wrote about a woman named Esther K. Trinka, an illegal immigrant from Germany also known as Esther Snow. In 1932 she was arrested in St. Paul for spending a ransom bill from the Lindbergh kidnapping. Yesterday, I learned that a man who has been working forever at the *North Star Press* is married to a woman named Esther Kay . . . who it just so happens was a big fan of Grover Mudd. *'My Esther Kay would know exactly when he was killed.'* That's what you told me."

He may have been well into his senior years, but he

was still a big man, fit and ruddy. Swede Bjorenson took a step outside, as if to clobber the impudent son of a bitch planted before him. "You come to my home and dare suggest that my wife stole your infant son . . . and the Lindbergh baby, to boot?"

Rick Beanblossom held his stare. "Then this morning," he continued, speaking slowly and distinctly, trying to restrain his fury, "postal inspectors handed me this note from the kidnappers of my son." He dangled the note before the pulsating face of Swede Bjorenson as if it were a search warrant:

> Dear Sir!
> We warn you for making anyding public or notify polise. Now you suffer consequences. As we have to change our plans the amount we want in return is 700,000$. Don't mark any bills or record serial numbers. 100$ bills. 50$ bills. 20$ bills.
>
> Don't be afraid about the baby. He is care for day and night.
>
> So now we will at random pick polise officer to deliver the Mony with our instructions. This polise will soon come to you.
>
> But he will not do so until FBI are out of the case and news people are quiet. This kidnapping has been in redy for a year. We are prepared for everything.
>
>))) EKS

Rick lowered the paper, no longer making any attempt to mask his hostility. "It's almost a duplicate of the second ransom note sent to Charles Lindbergh in 1932," he told Swede. "And it's signed the same as the original ransom note that was left in my son's nursery. *'EKS.'* Esther Kay Snow. FBI experts told us these notes were probably written by a woman trained in German calligraphy. Is your Esther Kay a German?"

Swede Bjorenson seemed shocked at the sight of the note, suddenly more wounded than angry. It was as if after all these years some kind of truth had just been shoved into his face. He stepped back into the small house. Held open the door. "Come in."

The heat was on high. The stuffy rooms were neat and clean. For a moment, perched on a threadbare rug, Rick was reminded that he was not born and raised in a Summit Avenue mansion. He was raised in a small river town among working people, in a modest house, not all that different from this weather-beaten cottage.

Swede Bjorenson said nothing, merely walked wearily down a narrow hallway coated with layers of crusted wallpaper. Disappeared into a corner bedroom. Rick Beanblossom followed him.

The bedroom reeked. The heavy smell of medicine. The faint odor of urine. Shades were drawn against the brightness of winter snow. The lighting was forty watts poor. The wallpaper in this back room was once white with red roses. Now the walls were yellow and the roses had faded to black. Water stains had formed circles on the ceiling.

Esther Kay Bjorenson, skeletal and decaying, was lying in bed. Buried under four layers of blankets. Beside the bed an IV bottle hung from a hook. A tube ran into an arm that was no thicker than a bone. A bucket of ice stood on the night stand, alongside a pharmacy of medicines that had long ago given up the fight. Her hoary white locks had been brushed that morning, giving her even more of a hideous appearance. She had the sunken cheeks of a corpse, with skin so pale her facial bones were not only visible, they were countable. On the tips of her wretched hands were fingernails extraordinary in length. Graceless. Vulgar. They were painted *Fire and Ice* red. The wrinkles on her face had, over the years, all melted into one another, but the lines around her mouth, where the skin was yellow and flaking, were particularly deep. The face of a lifelong smoker. Must have been a hard life, too. It was probably her favorite nightgown she was wearing, but it more resembled an old wedding dress. Off white. The color of her head. Miss Havisham in a coma, just lying in her death bed until God got around to her. The dying woman had to be past ninety. She was the right age, all right, but she was in the wrong state of health.

"How long has she been like this, Swede?" Rick's voice was soft.

"Almost two years. A nurse comes in every day."

"Is that why you've never retired?"

Swede didn't answer him, just stared in grief at his wife of more than fifty years.

"Did she come over illegally?" Rick wanted to know.

"I guess so, yes."

"Any family here?"

"No. She had a sister in Germany."

"What was her maiden name?"

"Before we married, she was Esther Kay Smith."

"A German woman named Smith? Did she use any other names? Esther Snow? Esther Trinka?"

"I've never heard those names before."

"Did she move here from New York?"

"She came down here from Little Falls. She lived in New York before that."

"Where in New York?"

"She was smuggled off Ellis Island. That's all I know."

"Did she ever talk about the Lindbergh kidnapping?"

" Never."

"Did she know Grover Mudd?"

Swede shrugged his heavy shoulders. His burden. "From the way she sometimes talked of him, and she didn't talk about those days a lot, my guess would be that she knew him back then."

"And you and your wife have lived in this house all these years?"

"Yes, and we still don't own it. Had to take out a second mortgage to pay the doctor bills."

"How old is your Esther Kay?"

"I don't know. Older than me by a few years, I guess. I never asked . . . isn't that funny?" Swede spoke softly. Ruefully. "You have to understand the times, Rick. The war was on. They were going to deport her. I was a young man in uniform. She was an older woman . . . and quite a beauty. I know she just married me to stay in the country, but I like to believe she grew to love me."

Rick sat on the edge of the bed, at the feet of the comatose Esther Kay Bjorenson. The Marine had had it all figured out. He'd charge through the front door and rescue his son. Now this. Heartbreak replaced the certainty in his eyes. He was the reporter who won the Pulitzer Prize for investigative reporting. He was the television news producer who broke the story of the Wakefield twins—a boy genius who shot to death his twin genius and then tried to cover it up by dumping his brother's body in the river. Rick Beanblossom was the published author who followed serial killer Dixon Bell to his fiery death. Now he sat confused, dazed, frustrated by his inability to solve the kidnapping of his own son. Maybe the FBI woman was right.

"Almost every mistake made in the Lindbergh investigation . . . can be traced directly to the decisions made by the fatber . . . he wasn't a cop."

Rick examined the callused hands of Swede Bjorenson dangling before him, years of newsprint ground into the fingertips. Working hands. The kind of hands his father had. He stared up at the old man's gray hair. His red eyes. "Your wife's life is over, Swede. For all intents and purposes, so is yours, . . . maybe even mine. But my son is only a year old. I don't think he should have to die because some ancient criminal wants to rewrite history."

Swede glanced down at him, contempt written all

over his gnarled, red face. "Maybe, Rick, while I'm at work she gets out of bed, climbs ladders, and steals little babies from their homes . . . sneaks back here and bakes them in the oven. Maybe, but I don't think so. Now, shouldn't you be at home with your wife? Because I'd like to be alone with mine."

Rick stood, more sad than mad. "She knows something, Swede. I was led here. I'll be back."

"Are you going to tell the police?"

The father of the missing child paused in the doorway. Glanced down at the ermine skeleton peeking out of the bed covers. Silent Esther. "Tell them what . . . that the mastermind of my son's kidnapping is a white-haired old lady lying in a coma?"

"Maybe you'll want to check the oven on your way out. Might be another Pulitzer in there for you."

The river below the bridge was a witch's brew of black water and white ice. Snow needles rode the north wind downstream. Like the crazy girl on the bridge, Andrea Labore was ill-dressed for the weather. Cautiously, she approached the girl on the railing. Over the river bluff to her east, Summit Avenue rolled down Cathedral Hill to the heart of St. Paul. On the western bluff, restored Victorian homes skirted a mile of park land along Cherokee Heights. To the south lay the outlines of bridges across a river still raging with ice. Trees along the bluff tops were brown and bare. The crowds at both ends of the bridge had grown.

The closer Andrea Labore inched to the baby in the

crazy girl's arms the sicker she felt. Then angered. And then, in the end, heartbroken. Her motherly instincts told her the baby was a boy, but it was those same natural instincts that convinced her beyond a shadow of a doubt that the baby on the bridge was not hers.

The child was about the same age as Dylan, but Dylan had eyes like saucers and dark curly hair. This baby was light-haired, with little peepholes for eyes. He wasn't crying yet, but he appeared as befuddled as a baby can possibly be. The young woman seemed determined to jump; of that Andrea was sure. But would she take the baby with her? Over the years the anchorwoman for Sky High News had read such stories to her viewers. She would shake her head in sad indignation and then move on to the next story. The next tragedy.

"My name is Andrea Labore," she told the girl. "I live in that big house on the bluff." She pointed. "Third one down. Can you see it? I saw you from the windows . . . and then they told me you wanted to talk with me."

The young woman glanced up at the stone mansions. She had short, oily blond hair, and a long face apple red with cold. Her oversized sweatshirt bore the name of an East Side bar, and it draped a figure skinny to the point of sickly. She had firm hold of the baby boy, but like Summit Avenue's relationship with the river, she didn't seem to have any connection to him.

"Is that my baby you're holding?" asked Andrea.

The wind went quiet. Clouds froze in the sky. Even the baby seemed poised for an answer. But there was no answer. The girl was absent. Living life in another world; a world Andrea had nearly crossed into the evening before. "What is your name?" she asked simply.

The crazy girl seemed to stare right through Andrea. Below her the river was still three-quarters ice. Above her the state chopper circled like a vulture. Andrea moved a foot closer. City crews had yet to clear the bridge. A bank of snow lay up against the rail. She stepped into the dirty white pile and felt the icy cold creep into her feet.

Andrea held out a hand, more of warning than of help. "Listen," she said, masking her own grief, "I won't play games with you. I want my baby. You've got no right to risk the life of my baby." Andrea could not help but notice how the girl's eyes flickered every time she used the words, *"my baby."* They were the only words getting through to her. "Please give me my baby, and then we'll talk."

It was working. The more Andrea said *"my baby,"* the more the girl emerged from her stupor. "He's such a pretty little boy," Andrea told her. "I'm very proud of him. Maybe you could come to our house and visit. I think my baby would like that."

Nothing is colder than a polar wind down the river. Andrea Labore would remember that morning over the Mississippi River as the coldest day of her life. The one ray of warmth in the entire day came in that frenzied instant, that frantic, fleeting moment, when the suicidal young woman slowly held out the baby.

Maybe in Andrea Labore the troubled girl saw perfection. Or maybe she wanted only to be the hero in a story she saw unfolding on television. Who is to know what their last coherent thought is before the mentally ill fall from reality—before they leap from the real world?

Just like in the movies, it all seemed to happen in slow motion. Andrea Labore saw the girl step off the frosted railing, the baby still in her arms. She could see the girl leave the railing and push the baby away from her body as she toppled backward into the freezing air. Andrea went straight for the child. Saw the baby's little head disappear over the railing. Over the water. Andrea dived. Like the champion swimmer she once was, she went over the railing head first, and with the cold world spinning around her in slow motion she grabbed the baby's tiny wrist with her outstretched right hand. But her weight took her up and over the railing, and with her free left hand it was all Andrea could do to grab hold of the bottom rail at the foot of the walkway.

Andrea Labore was dangling from the High Bridge, her left hand barely holding on to the bottom railing along the walkway, her right hand firmly grasping the soft wrist of a terrified baby. Commander Giles was scrambling to help, reaching over the railing, clawing at her glove. Inspector Koslowski was desperately trying to get a piece of her slippery, leathery coat. But Andrea Labore was losing her grip. Slipping out of her glove. Literally hanging on by a thread. She watched in horror as the crazy girl fell like a rock into the blackened water below and disappeared beneath the ice flow of the Mississippi River.

Two patrol boats shot out from beneath the bridge. Divers in wet suits jumped into the frigid water.

The baby was screaming in terror. Andrea listened, heartsick. She saw one of the boats below pushing out in front of her, forcing its way through thick streams of ice. The rescue team had their arms stretched out to her, screaming to her. Beckoning. Andrea knew that she, like the girl, was going for a swim. She had neither the strength nor the grip to pull the baby back to the bridge. A chill not associated with any wind overcame her. Death come calling.

But death might have to wait. With all of her might she swung the baby back and forth, a rocking motion. She whispered a prayer. She swung the baby a second time. Made her peace with God. Then on the third swing she let the baby fly gently out over the water.

With the baby falling free Andrea's hand finally slipped from the glove. She fell away from the clawing hands above her. Away from the bridge. And with a primal scream the proud girl from the Iron Range fell two hundred feet into the icy river below. But on her way down, just before she crashed through a sheet of thin ice and disappeared beneath the freezing water, Andrea Labore was sure she could see the baby falling like a tumbling snowflake into the waiting arms of St. Paul's water rescue team.

Koslowski

When Rick Beanblossom left the Ramsey Medical Center at 4 o'clock Wednesday afternoon, the snow was just beginning to fly. Andrea's condition had been upgraded. Serious, but stable. She was suffering from hypothermia. She had a concussion. Her left eardrum was punctured, and a permanent loss of hearing in that ear was a distinct possibility. She was wrapped in a heating blanket. Woke up complaining about the cold. Then she was sedated. Fell back to sleep. The baby she had thrown to the rescue team was resting right where his adventure had begun, back in the pediatrics ward. Satisfactory condition. A search for his identity was underway. The hospital was inundated with offers of adoption.

The same water rescue team that had saved Andrea's life was dragging the ice-strewn river for the life they were unable to save. Rescue workers and reporters alike marveled at how accommodating the great river could be—returning to the surface those with the will to live, and swallowing without a trace those who wished to die.

Rick Beanblossom rode the mile home in icy silence. He felt blessed that his wife had survived. The fall should have killed her. Must have been an angel on that bridge. But their son was still missing.

Daylight was doing a slow fade. The roads had begun their slippery surrender to the winter weather. Rush hour traffic was clogged. Inspector Stephanie Koslowski was behind the wheel. Rick knew the FBI lady was furious about being denied immediate access to the second note. But she had gone to the bridge, and she was smart enough not to pick a fight with him. Together they would return to the mansion and wait for the so-called random cop mentioned in the ransom note.

"We know both notes were written by a woman of German descent," Koslowski told him. "This woman once had some training in German calligraphy. Now does that coincide with this Esther woman you visited?"

Rick found the sound of her voice grating. "I told you, she's comatose. It was a long shot. I took it."

"So maybe there is no Esther Snow. The kidnappers are just using the initials as a cover. Even if there was an Esther Snow, she could have been dead for years."

They inched across an overpass above a labyrinth of intersecting freeways called Spaghetti Junction. State trucks were already salting and sanding. The inspector went on, the anger in her voice slowly building. "The thumbguard we found in Jasmine Allen's room turned out to be a perfect match with the thumbguard the state police have in New Jersey. There is a ninety-nine percent chance it's the missing thumbguard from the Lindbergh kidnapping. What an incredible coincidence." They started up Cathedral Hill, snow building beneath the unmarked cruiser. "Do you know how your housekeeper came by this thumbguard?" Koslowski answered her own question. "Her grandfather gave it to her. She told me his name was William Allen. It turns out the black man who found the Lindbergh baby dead in the woods was also named William Allen. So let's assume they're both the same William Allen, and Jasmine Allen is his granddaughter. Now, she just happens to be employed in a home where a baby has been kidnapped in an amazingly accurate reenactment of the Lindbergh kidnapping. Are you making sense out of all of this, Mr. Beanblossom?"

Rick held his tongue as they drove by the great cathedral with the leaky dome and started down Summit Avenue. He thought of that famous line about the tangled web we weave when we practice to deceive. Only an expert on the Lindbergh kidnapping could orchestrate the crime that had robbed him and Andrea of their son. Stephanie Koslowski was high-minded and bold, and she was smart. But was she devious? Jasmine Allen appeared young and innocent. Damn near angelic. But was it all pretense? An act?

"One more thing," Koslowski added, as if he were

actually conversing with her, "do you know a Captain Les Angelbeck . . . with the BCA . . . they call him the Marlboro Man . . . he's semiretired?"

The question stunned the Marine, but Rick Beanblossom kept his cool. "I've talked to him on the phone a few times over the years. Why do you ask?"

"I was just curious . . . his name came up today."

Just curious, my ass. The newsman in him wanted to know more, but he also knew better. Whatever the inspector was up to, be it good or evil, would have to play itself out.

Traffic was backed up a block as they approached the three-ring media circus that surrounded his home. Reporters had been respectfully asked to leave the house while they waited for a message from the kidnappers. But they didn't leave the yard. Live shots were the order of the day, mostly from in front of the red sandstone mansion on Summit Avenue. When it was all over, no matter how it ended, there would be no more living here.

The snow was increasing by the minute. Stephanie Koslowski hit the wipers switch to clear the windshield. "If the payoff is tonight, we're in trouble. We'll never be able to get a chopper in the air."

Rick Beanblossom shielded his eyes with his hands as the news photographers on stakeout spotted their approaching car. "And I assume if this random cop is to make the payoff tonight, your people are prepared to follow him."

"That's the plan."

"And if I ask you not to follow him . . . ?"

"We'll follow him anyway. The time to catch kidnappers is when the ransom is paid. All we need is one person in custody, then we can find the baby."

The knock at the door came forty-five hours into the kidnapping. It was 6 P.M. Rick was upstairs in the bedroom, standing before a television set watching the local news. The kidnapping of his son and the hospitalization of his wife were competing with the blizzard warning for the lead story. Suddenly, there was a commotion downstairs. He stepped into the hallway. At the bottom of the wide stairway, Inspector Koslowski and her team of agents had someone surrounded—the random cop? Rick heard a thousand questions being fired when they finally noticed the man in the mask standing on the landing. All went quiet. Then the agents stepped aside, just far enough aside for Rick Beanblossom to see the cop.

He had on his winter parka. The hood was up over his head, protecting him from the weather. Snow outlined his sagging shoulders. He was stuffing his thick leather gloves into the parka pockets. Then he unzipped the warm coat and tossed the hood from his head.

Rick was dumbfounded. For just that one moment he was certain Inspector Stephanie Koslowski had set the whole thing up. He wanted to kill the bitch right where she stood. But that wouldn't get his son back.

"Mr. Beanblossom," she said to him as he started down the stairs, "this is Captain Les Angelbeck of your state police. Apparently, he was sent here with a message for you."

Les Angelbeck stuck out his hand. "Mr. Beanblossom . . ."

Rick took the hand in his. It was a big hand, yellowed and callused from years of smoking. Still, he had the firm grip of an ex-GI, despite all of the years that had gone by. "Captain Angelbeck," said Rick, greeting him.

"Mr. Beanblossom, I've always admired your work. I'm sorry that we have to meet like this." The police captain cleared his throat, as if stifling a cough. "Another nasty night out there. Hard on my chest."

"Do you have something for me? " Rick asked him, trying with all of his might to maintain his composure.

"Yes . . . yes, I do. I was just showing it to the inspector here. A taxi driver dropped the envelope off at our headquarters, then disappeared. We're trying to track him down." The old cop handed Rick a handwritten note, the writing both frightening and familiar.

Dear Sir!
Here is your picture you ask for. Look hard masked man. No funny stuff or we'll do the job. We have notify you already what kind of bills. Put it in a knapsack. Give Mony to polise officer and him only. Instructions will come to your house. We warn you not to set any trap in any way or cause more troubles. After we have Mony in hand we will tell you where to find your baby. Have a airplane redy it is about 150 miles away.

)))EKS

Then Captain Les Angelbeck reluctantly handed Rick Beanblossom a Polaroid snapshot of that morning's *North Star Press*. Front page. Metro Final.

There was virtually nothing in life that scared the burn victim. Rick Beanblossom had had fear torched out of him. But the photograph of his baby boy lying awake atop the newspaper with his cherubic little face pressed up against a can of lighter fluid and a book of matches set the man in the mask to shaking, trembling with fear and anger. For a moment, he was thankful Andrea was hospitalized, did not have to see this.

Angelbeck spoke first. "As horrible as that looks, he's still alive. And he looks in good health."

"The threat of harm is actually a good sign," Koslowski added. "It's the absence of a threat that we have to worry about. There were no threats in the letters Bruno Hauptmann sent to Charles Lindbergh. Why? Because the baby was already dead."

Rick handed the note and the photograph over to Stephanie Koslowski. "Captain, I'd like to speak with you alone, please."

Koslowski interrupted. "Gentlemen, we don't have a lot of time here."

Rick Beanblossom ignored her, turned his back on the inspector from the FBI and walked through the long dining room, toward the kitchen.

"Why did the kidnappers pick you? Strange coincidence, don't you think?"

"Maybe you haven't been as confidential as I've been led to believe."

"That's bullshit. My wife doesn't even know about you."

"But the kidnappers do?"

"We're being set up here," yelled Rick.

"Keep your voice down . . . don't you think I know that? The question is, who? Did you have your office checked for wire taps?"

"Not yet."

The kitchen was the one room in the house both he and Andrea hated. The appliances were modern, but the decor was outmoded and worn, the lighting was poor. The room was scheduled to be remodeled. Rick Beanblossom grabbed the forehead of his mask and squeezed, thinking he could somehow force out all of the answers "It's Koslowski . . . she's on to us. She asked me about you earlier."

"So what?"

"You said yourself she was a suspect."

"No, I said her ass is on the line. It won't hurt her to close this one. The last thing the Feds want is a local cop solving their kidnap cases . . . not to mention a reporter." The hard-to-retire detective broke off, coughing. Wiped his mouth with a dirty handkerchief. "You're going to laugh at this, Masked Man, but during the Weatherman killings . . . I actually believed for a while that you were a suspect."

"And do you now suspect that I kidnapped my own son?"

"I wish you had. I can deal with you."

In Rick's eyes Les Angelbeck had grown incredibly ancient. He had emphysema. Glaucoma. He was hobbling about without the aid of his walking stick. "Where's your cane?" Rick asked, changing the subject.

The captain pocketed his handkerchief. "I stopped using it. It hurt my hand more than it helped my leg. Besides, it made me feel old."

Rick had to laugh. "How are you going to do this? They could run you all over town tonight . . . and in a blizzard, no less."

"Maybe that's one of the reasons they picked me. The go-between in the Lindbergh case was seventy-two years old. A total stranger to the family. He met the kidnapper. He made the payoff. His testimony was crucial in the conviction of Bruno Hauptmann."

"But the Lindbergh baby was dead."

"Yes, the baby was already dead."

Jasmine Allen stepped into the kitchen from her back room. She seemed as surprised to see them as they were to see her. March winds rattled the old house and shot a cold breeze through the room. Rick did not have the time to figure out what she had heard. "Jasmine," he said to her, "they could use some more coffee out there."

"Yes, sir."

Les Angelbeck nodded her way as the young girl brushed by him and left the men standing alone in the kitchen. "Suspect number two, I presume."

"Yes," Rick acknowledged. He waited a second to make sure she was well through the door, then went on. "This Grover Mudd you told me about . . . in June of 1932 he wrote an article about a woman taken into custody in St. Paul for passing a twenty from the Lindbergh ransom money."

"There's no record of that."

"Police let her go . . . said she got it from a bank. Her name was Esther K. Trinka, also known as Esther Snow . . . supposedly thirty-two years old . . . probably an illegal from Germany. I think that's where Mudd got his twenty from. I also think those are her initials on these ransom notes."

Now it was Angelbeck's turn to laugh. "Well, if it's Esther Snow I'm going up against, at least it'll be a fair fight. She's got to be a hell of a lot older than I am." He pulled a receiver the size of a matchbook out of his coat pocket. "Here, take this."

"What is it?"

"It's a homing device. The transmitter is in my car. Just follow the beeps."

"And Koslowski?"

"They're hooking up their own gadgets to my car. Don't worry, I'll short them out. It's going to be just you and me out there."

"And how many kidnappers?"

"Just one. They'll only send one."

"Where's this going to end up?"

"At a cemetery," Angelbeck told him. "They'll lead

us to a cemetery. Same as Lindbergh. Do you have a gun?"

"Do you really want me to have one? " Rick asked.

"Maybe not." Angelbeck nodded toward the door. "Let's get back out there before they get even more suspicious."

But Rick had another question. "One more thing, Captain. On the phone the other night, you said something about not liking Charles Lindbergh. Why?"

"Because he was a goddamn Nazi, that's why. Just before the war, I climbed up the water tower in Little Falls and helped paint over his name."

"I met an old woman today who was from Little Falls," Rick mused. "So Lindbergh was that despised?"

"I can't think of another man in American history who fell so far from grace."

"And then flew back again?"

"Yes, I suppose. History is funny that way." Les Angelbeck paused a moment. "I'm sorry there hasn't been a chance to ask . . . how's Andrea?"

"She's going to be okay."

"That's good. I miss her." The old man was of course referring to television. The two had never met, and yet it was obvious Les Angelbeck considered Andrea Labore a friend, if not a member of his own family. "Come. Let's get your son back."

There wasn't a knapsack big enough to hold that kind of money. Instead, the ransom money, all seven hundred thousand dollars, was packed into a maroon and gold hockey bag, one of those oversized, floppy gym bags hockey players stuff with equipment. It was virtually all of the money Rick Beanblossom and Andrea Labore had. Their broker had sold their stocks, cashed their bonds. Like the Lindberghs before them, Rick and Andrea had too much pride to let others put up the ransom. Or even help. Rick dropped the heavy bag in the foyer, at the feet of Les Angelbeck. Then he started up the grand staircase.

Stephanie Koslowski was right on his heels. "Something is wrong . . . why would they pick a police officer? First they tell us to keep the cops out of this . . . then they want a local cop to deliver the ransom. Are you buying into this, Mr. Beanblossom? " She followed him like a scolding mother, up the staircase to the landing on the second floor. She glanced over her shoulder, made sure Les Angelbeck was out of earshot, but still in sight. "They're going to kill him, Rick. And if they'll kill him, they'll kill the baby. It's imperative that we take them at the payoff. Now what is going on here?"

It was the first time the inspector from the FBI had called him by his first name. Her voice had changed. It rang with a passion, as if the time had come for Rick to believe they were both on the same side. They argued in intense whispers. "Why don't you tell me, Inspector?" Rick asked. "You haven't exactly been up front with me, have you?"

"I have been more than up front with you . . . and patient. I've answered every one of your snide little questions. And I've put up with your Lone Ranger act. But the hour is at hand. I want to know what was said in that kitchen."

Rick Beanblossom gazed down the stairs at the old man standing in front of the door, for years his unimpeachable source for both information and inspiration. Seven hundred thousand dollars was sitting at his feet. Rick turned back to Koslowski, a cop he wouldn't trust with his car keys. "I simply wanted to know if he was healthy enough to make the payoff. My son's life is at stake. Now, Inspector, if you'll excuse me, I won't be bothering you tonight with any more snide questions." Rick started for the master bedroom.

"Interesting thing about this Captain Angelbeck that you've talked to on the phone a few times over the years . . . seems that he has an obsession with the Lindbergh case."

That stopped him. Stopped him dead in his tracks. "How's that?" Rick asked.

Koslowski looked down at Angelbeck, then back at Rick. She kept her voice low, but at the same time made damn sure every word was getting through to him. "In 1982, fifty years after the kidnapping, the governor of New Jersey ordered the Lindbergh case archives opened to the public. It took the New Jersey State Police five years to catalogue everything . . . two hundred thousand documents, besides the physical evidence. Crime scene photos, the kidnap ladder, the fifteen ransom notes, the baby's garments, even interviews with the original police investigators that were taped years later."

"Make your point," Rick demanded.

"The New Jersey State Police housed the entire Lindbergh case archives in a state police museum open to the public. It's in West Trenton. Our agents checked the museum's visitors logs when they were there with the thumbguard. It seems that a Captain Les Angelbeck of the Minnesota Bureau of Criminal Apprehension was there when it opened in 1986. He was there again in 1987. And again in 1992. The museum also has several letters from the captain requesting information about the kidnapping . . . specific details. According to the St. Paul Public Library, Captain Angelbeck has, at one time or another, checked out every book ever written on the Lindbergh kidnapping. Turns out, he even obtained a published article I wrote on the case while I was in law school."

Rick Beanblossom could not believe what he was hearing. He peeked over the balustrade at Les Angelbeck, who was staring up at them both.

Koslowski went on. "It's not all that unusual, really. A lot of cops fixate on famous cases. My father was that way with the Rosenbergs. He worked on that case. I prefer the D. B. Cooper skyjacking. I worked that case as a rookie in Seattle . . . still check out leads when they come in. But as far as we can tell, Captain Angelbeck never worked on the Lindbergh case. So what's it to him?"

Through the windows at the front of the house Rick

Beanblossom could see the snow being whipped into a blizzard. He was feeling claustrophobic. But the chill running up his spine had nothing to do with the weather.

Jasmine Allen walked into the foyer below with a tray full of coffee. She stopped suddenly, as if by order. Maybe, Rick thought, it wasn't a tangled web they wove. It was a perfect triangle. The plane ran from Jasmine Allen to Les Angelbeck. Then up the stairs it went to Stephanie Koslowski. Then back down the stairs to Jasmine Allen.

FBI Inspector Stephanie Koslowski followed the same triangle with her eyes before she spoke. "So what do we do now?"

The faceless Marine thought of his baby boy lying across the front page of a newspaper, a can of lighter fluid and a book of matches propped next to him. He struggled to find his voice, a voice fraught with confusion and fatigue. And fear. "I guess we wait for instructions."

Colonel Snelling

The state of Minnesota lies at the center of the North American continent. The weather is a crapshoot. An unusual combination of an arctic high pressure system over the Rocky Mountains and a low pressure system over the Great Lakes created the conditions for the second late winter storm in as many days. It was a quarter before the hour of nine on Wednesday evening and snowing hard when a taxi arrived at the Summit Avenue address—forty-seven hours and forty-five minutes into the kidnapping.

The police had warned cab companies to alert their drivers to such a request. It was the same tactic Bruno Hauptmann had used to extort money from Charles Lindbergh—pick a cab driver at random, hand him a note and pay him to deliver it. Comply completely, the drivers were advised. Remember everything. While the taxi driver was being grilled by Inspector Stephanie Koslowski and her team of FBI agents, Captain Les Angelbeck, money in hand, headed out the door and into the weather. He had precious little time. The instructions were crystal clear.

> Go to St. Paul public library. See Silent Snow Secret Snow by Conrad Aiken. Hurry library closes 9 P.M.

Bad weather is the natural ally of bad people. From the moment the kidnappers of Baby Dylan put the ladder up to the house, good luck and bad weather had been on their side. In a state where people are obsessed with the weather, few people were more cognizant of the elements than Les Angelbeck. He was always dressed for the worst. At the BCA, his raincoats, his umbrellas, and his bulky winter coats had become legendary. He'd lost his father to the weather. The Armistice Day Blizzard. November 11, 1940. In 1945 he'd fought through the Battle of the Bulge in brutal weather. During the Weatherman slayings, he almost froze to death when he got stranded in a snowstorm. All that saved him was the proper clothing.

The police captain followed snow emergency routes downtown to Rice Park. The routes had been plowed, but already some side streets had become impassable. He reached the library only five minutes before it closed. Lugging the ransom money, he had to scramble. Turned out "Silent Snow, Secret Snow" was a short story, not a book. With the help of a patient librarian, they found a copy of *The Collected Short Stories of Conrad Aiken* perched on a bookshelf. Les Angelbeck, still chasing his breath, flipped the pages until he found the story. Found the instructions.

> Cross the High Bridge to 13. Drive 13 to the heights of Mendota. Do speed limit. You are being watched. St. Peter's Church on the bluff. Below the steeple. 30 minutes!

If he'd had the breath to sigh, it would have been a sigh of relief. Les Angelbeck knew the two-lane highway well. It was an old fishing route. He knew St. Peter's. Two cemeteries lay nearby. If they played it smart, and so far they had, they'd keep it simple. One stop. One drop. Grab the payoff, release the kid, and be done with it. In this kind of weather, too many things could go wrong.

Les Angelbeck was back on the road, rolling through the downtown streets of St. Paul in a big Chevy cruiser. The old man knew these streets like the back of his arthritic hand. He liked St. Paul. At heart, it was still a village. Brick roads. Noble buildings aging with grace. Strong neighborhoods. Good cops. The crime rate here was a fraction of what it was across the river in Minneapolis. But Les Angelbeck wasn't dealing with St. Paul cops. He was dealing with the FBI. The veteran cop popped the car's cigarette lighter. He stuck the burning red coils into the tracking device agents had planted in the front seat. After a few electrical sparks, for all intents and purposes, the FBI's case went up in hot smoke. Angelbeck rolled down the window to clear the air. Now it was just him and the masked man.

Rick Beanblossom should have gone down the backstairs and through the hilly woods behind the house to the street below, where his car was waiting for him. "Stay a mile back," Angelbeck warned him. "Stay alert."

In the West Seventh Street neighborhood, the police captain hung a left onto Smith Avenue and started across the High Bridge. Here the burgeoning storm was at its worst. Strong winds down the mighty river coupled with blowing snow created near-zero visibility. The long span was slick and icy. He could feel the tires slipping beneath him. On a bright day he could have seen the bluffs of Summit Avenue in his rearview mirror. Maybe even the Beanblossom place. On this night the only things visible in his mirror were preternatural flashes of snow. If anybody was following him, he'd have a hard time spotting them. He turned the heater on high.

Suicides were common off this bridge. In his research on St. Paul's gangster days, Captain Angelbeck came across a news story about a giant Norwegian cop who was thrown from the High Bridge after struggling with a gangster's moll. Must have been one hell of a woman. It was rumored that back then St. Paul cops used the bridge for interrogation purposes. He believed it. And it was on the infamous High Bridge, only hours earlier, that Andrea Labore risked her life to save the life of a child not her own. As he sat before his television set night after night, the old man often wondered what it would be like to be married to such a woman. Bold and beautiful. Sexy and smart. Seemed there were few women of that kind when he was young. Today they were reporters. Lawyers and doctors. And cops.

Captain Les Angelbeck followed Smith Avenue as instructed. Then he veered onto Highway 13, a pioneer road older than the state itself. The road followed the bluffs that followed the river. West, then south. In winter weather the winding stretch was dark and dangerous. When they told him to do the speed limit, did they account for blizzard conditions? To make St. Peter's Church in only thirty minutes would be a challenge. Yet even in these conditions, Angelbeck let just one hand control the steering wheel while with his other hand he fished out a pack of Marlboro and again fumbled with the car's cigarette lighter. That was probably how the beloved GIs of World War II would be remembered by their children—barreling down two-lane highways in their big Fords and Chevys with a cigarette stuck between their lips, and only a wrist to guide the steering wheel.

As Les Angelbeck slowed the car to round a tree-lined curve, damned if he didn't glimpse a pair of headlights in the rearview mirror. Just a glimpse. Then they were gone. He prayed it was the man in the mask and not the FBI. He checked his watch.

Snuggled into the bluffs along the snowy route was the tiny town of Mendota, a narrow stretch of highway littered with beer joints and hardware stores. It was a twist of irony that the first area in Minnesota to be settled was today one of the least developed of the Twin Cities. Les Angelbeck guided the big Chevrolet through Mendota and up the hill toward the church, the big rear end of the unmarked cruiser fishtailing in the wind. He wasn't sure he was going to make it to the parking lot without getting stuck. But momentum and willpower carried him up the slippery hill. Then he cranked the wheel hard right. Off the highway he careened, into the snow-packed parking lot. There he slid to a stop.

Now nothing lay before him but snow. Nobody had been there in hours. Again he checked his watch. Three minutes to spare. The car behind him was gone. Still, his ailing heart sank a bit. It was too poor a place for the payoff. There was only one way in. One way out. But it was the perfect spot to be given more instructions. Even in blizzard conditions, the quaint little church on the bluff with the tall steeple could be easily viewed from three directions.

It was a storybook church constructed of limestone quarried from the river and roofed with pine shingles. Built in 1853, it was the oldest surviving church in Minnesota. Still in use. Services every Sunday morning. The church grounds were surrounded by mountainous snowbanks. To the captain's left, just south of the Mendota Bridge, a 727 ablaze in red and white lights floated toward earth through gusts of falling snow. It sailed across the river and settled onto the runway at the international airport. Soon the weather would put a stop to all flights.

Angelbeck rolled the car forward toward the church. When the snow got too deep, he stopped again. He swung the hockey bag with the money over his shoulder and climbed from the car. A wind with teeth of cold steel bit his face, grabbed the cigarette from his mouth, and sailed it to Wisconsin. The gust of icy air pushed the windchill to 20 degrees below zero. He turned his back to the cold roar. Across Highway 13 a pine-laden cemetery ran up the bluff and over the hill. That, he believed, is where they'd be watching him.

Through snow already a foot deep the old cop slogged his way to the main doors below the church steeple. His arthritis was teaming up with his emphysema. The one-two punch was killing him. He was almost on his hands and his knees before he reached the tall double doors. They were locked tight. Another note was stapled to the wood, like Martin Luther posting his 95 theses on the castle church door.

> Drive the Mendota Bridge. Follow signs to historic fort. You have 10 minutes. You are being watched.

Les Angelbeck set his sights on the Mendota Bridge, with its mile of arc lights strung over a series of concrete arches. In the storm the lights appeared as a parade of fireflies following the jet planes that sailed across the Minnesota River and Fort Snelling State

Park. They had chosen their route well—connecting rivers and connecting highways midway between Minneapolis and St. Paul. Great vantage points. Numerous escape routes. And a keen sense of Minnesota history.

The old man returned the ransom money to the car, and then he returned the car to the heart of the blizzard.

Rick Beanblossom picked up Les Angelbeck coming out of the St. Paul Public Library. A homeless man stood on the corner at Rice Park. Across the street at the Ordway Theatre another man was shoveling the sidewalk. On Fifth Street, a burly snowplow driver was standing on the side of his truck, scraping ice from the window. Every one of them could have been exactly what they appeared to be, but more likely they were FBI. Rick followed the big Chevy out West Seventh Street in his new Camry. He saw Angelbeck swerve onto Smith Avenue, obviously headed for the High Bridge. Visibility was nearing zero. In a way, this was good. The television news stations would not be able to get their three-hundred-thousand-dollar, infrared, gyro-stabilized, helicopter cameras into the air. Rick wasn't as sure about the FBI. God only knew what they had in their arsenal. He trained his eyes to shades of white. He tuned his ear to the constant beeping of the homing device. By today's standards, the device was crude, something out of an old James Bond movie. But it worked.

Inspector Stephanie Koslowski had done the seemingly impossible. She had lifted the weight of suspicion from herself and placed it squarely on the aging shoulders of Captain Les Angelbeck. As he slowly made his way across the bridge, Rick didn't want to dwell for one minute on what had happened to his wife here six inches of snow ago. Instead he transferred all of his energies onto the back of the legendary cop who was his friend.

"Interesting thing about this Captain Angelbeck . . . Seems that he has an obsession with the Lindbergh case."

How did Les Angelbeck run a check on serial numbers from the Lindbergh ransom money without setting off alarms at the FBI building? Simple. He already had a list of the serial numbers. They were published in every major newspaper in 1932. But that meant he'd lied about not knowing anything about Grover Mudd. He'd had to know Mudd from the newspapers of the day. He had to have read of the woman who called herself Esther Snow. But as old as Angelbeck was, he was too young to have personally known Grover Mudd. He didn't become a cop until after World War II. By then Grover Mudd had been dead ten years. Then there was the note from the kidnappers: *Look hard masked man*. Only one person was ever allowed to call him *masked man*.

There was virtually no traffic after the bridge; blowing snow had wiped the landscape clean. As he inched his Camry through the wind and the snow toward Highway 13, he again tried to set aside thoughts of the victim being his son. Work the story as news. Cold, hard news.

"According to the St. Paul Public Library, Captain Angelbeck has . . . checked out every book ever written on the Lindbergh kidnapping."

Up until the assassination of President Kennedy, the Lindbergh kidnapping was the crime of the century. Perhaps it was the big case Les Angelbeck had always wanted to solve. So he restaged the whole thing. Not for the money, but for the glory. Or maybe the old man did it all for Andrea—a woman he fell in love with on television. The hero syndrome. Steal her baby, then come to the rescue. At the hour of the kidnapping, Angelbeck had Rick chatting on the phone. But wait, wasn't it Rick who had called him?

Beanblossom theory number two: Esther "Snow" Bjorenson kidnapped the baby, just as she was once accused of kidnapping the Lindbergh baby. The coma was a ruse. The theory was probably a ruse too.

Theory number two and a half: Swede Bjorenson kidnapped the boy to pay off his medical bills. To avenge his wife's accusers.

But theory number three was still hard to surrender: Inspector Stephanie Koslowski kidnapped the baby. She was Les Angelbeck in drag. She didn't do it for the money, but for the glory within the bureau, to continue the proud family tradition of crimebusting. Or maybe, like Angelbeck, she too had fallen in love with the queen of the evening news.

And what of Jasmine Allen, a young woman with a

direct link to the Lindbergh kidnapping? She had to be the key. No, she wasn't the brains behind the abduction, but she was the inside source. Was she working with Angelbeck, or Koslowski?

And theory number four: none of them kidnapped the baby. The real kidnapper was still out there, jerking all of them around. Puppets dancing on strings.

Rick Beanblossom followed the beeps onto Highway 13, the answers to the mystery no more clear than the road in front of his mask. He turned the heater up a notch.

The closest Les Angelbeck could get to the original stone fort was a deserted parking lot beside a decrepit barracks. The ugly brick building had been constructed as a training facility during World War II. Now it was abandoned. The aging police captain gazed out at the snowstorm. He'd grown up on a farm in the center of Minnesota. He'd grown up fast. He had lived his entire life with a tremendous amount of respect for the weather, and just the right touch of fear. As a boy, he'd found his father's body buried in a snowbank, blindsided by a blizzard while out hunting. The captain caught his precious breath. He zipped the heavy parka up to his chin and tied the fur-trimmed hood tight around his head. Pulled on his gloves. He grabbed the hockey bag with the ransom money and climbed out of the big Chevrolet. Left the doors unlocked and the engine running. The pane-glass windows of the brick barracks standing forlornly at attention before him were broken. Crusty gray paint was peeling off the frames. But there was no graffiti. No broken bottles. No trash. It was a corner of the Twin Cities so deserted the vandals had yet to discover it.

On top of his other ailments, Les Angelbeck had glaucoma. The wind was still on the rise, sweeping threads of finely spun snow into his rugged face. He could barely make out the pentagonal outline of the historic fort. Across immense windrows of snow, he spotted the Round Tower at the southwest point. A bare flagpole was planted on top of it. A rusty chain that once hoisted Old Glory was flapping in the wind. The Round Tower's walls were six feet thick, with musket slits that faced inside the fort as well as outside. At the foot of the fort's massive exterior walls were steep bluffs that dropped down to the river's edge. Two rivers. The Mississippi River to the north, and the Minnesota River to the south. Colonel Josiah Snelling had strategically placed his fort at the very edge of the tall bluffs where the two rivers joined forces.

This was it. The payoff. They would make their escape through the woods. Three interstate freeways and an international airport were within spitting distance. Once again the weather was on their side. If something went wrong, below the bluffs were miles of park land in which to hide, to escape. Criminally brilliant.

Les Angelbeck plodded his way across the snowy

field to the nineteenth century fort. Its tall, imposing walls stood out like icebergs in the ocean, challenging all who came before them. In its long history Fort Snelling was never attacked. Not by the British. Not by the French. Not even by the brave warriors of the great Sioux uprising. Standing at the foot of the great walls the police captain could easily understand why. Only a fool would mount an assault on such a well-built fortress. A fool or the weather.

Les Angelbeck half-circled the Round Tower and followed the rough limestone walls to the gatehouse. Here the long walls reached their lowest point, but still they could not be scaled without tall ladders. At the foot of bluffs he could see a black river running through the white storm. Huge ice chunks raced by like speedboats. But it had been decades since the captain had tramped around the venerable fort. In the blowing snow he was confused, cold, and tired, didn't know exactly which river it was he was looking at.

The gatehouse to Historic Fort Snelling appeared common barn lumber, weathered with age. By 1825, 300 soldiers, 105 cannon shells, and 1,000 pounds of gunpowder stood guard over the Minnesota Territory from this very point. Yet on this frigid night a rusty padlock was all that secured the fort. Not a footprint in sight.

Les Angelbeck spotted the bloody message right away. Tacked to a small door on the entrance gate, just above the padlock, was a plain white sheet of copy paper with crimson lettering smeared across it. A great wind was tearing at the note.

> Throw Money inside the Fort.
> You are being watched!

The note was colder than the windchill. Written in blood. Cold blood. The dark red handprint of a baby was stamped just below the exclamation point.

The old cop studied the top of the wall. Might as well have been the top of a mountain. A split-rail fence led up to the wall, undoubtedly erected to keep soldiers and visitors from toppling down the bluffs and into the river.

Doctors had told him to get an oxygen tank, pull it around with him on a cart like a child with a little red wagon. He refused. They told him to move to Arizona, California, or New Mexico. Get out of Minnesota. The weather would kill him. He refused. If he was dying, and he was, Les Angelbeck was going to die his way.

The cheeks on his face were sickly red. His milky white eyes were hurting from the strain. Too much reading. Too much driving. Too much weather. He doubled over to collect his thoughts, collect his strength. When he'd rested, when he had bagged his breath, he took hold of the seven hundred thousand dollars in ransom money and with all of the might he could conjure up, he heaved the heavy hockey bag high into the air.

It almost made it. Almost cleared the wall. But the

bag with the money hit the top stones and dropped straight down into the snowbank in front of him.

His second toss was even weaker. It hit the wall like a sack of potatoes and fell back to the snow with a silent thud. The law of diminishing strength. A third throw would be useless.

He shouted at the top of his tortured lungs, "I can't throw that high. I'm an old man, goddamn you."

But even swearing was exhausting. Was anybody inside, or was he yelling at the wind? And if they were inside, could they hear him? As he gasped for more air, his mind was working. Rick Beanblossom was right; he couldn't possibly have been picked at random. Somehow the bastards knew. And if they knew of his secret links to the masked man, then they had to know of his age. And of his health. And of his long interest in the Lindbergh kidnapping and its Minnesota connection.

"Damn you," he muttered once more. "In my day I'd have you in handcuffs by now . . . the whole lot of you." But he knew in his weakening heart his days were nearly over. Why on earth had they picked him? Christ, a child's life was at stake. And what exactly had Koslowski told the man in the mask as they stood arguing at the top of the stairs?

He searched the blizzard for a shadow of help. None was in sight. Les Angelbeck picked up the money and slung the icy hockey bag onto his shoulder. It weighed a ton. Once again he was a dog-tired GI marching through a snowstorm in Belgium. He stuck his foot onto the split-rail fence and grabbed hold of a stone jutting out of the wall. With every ounce of strength he could muster, he pulled himself to the top of the fence. Balanced there in the heavy winds. One of his gloves fell off. He was choking on the flying snow. His breath came in spurts. That was the thing with emphysema, you can breathe air in, but you can't get it back out. Can't exhale. The lungs have lost their elasticity—makes the heart work overtime. Pull double duty. And if the wind is in your face . . . ?

From where he now stood atop the fence the proud old man could almost reach up and touch the top of the wall. For a young man it would be a simple toss. Into the air and into the fort. For him it appeared a near-insurmountable hurdle.

Captain Les Angelbeck let the hockey bag slide from his shoulder to his gloved hand. One last breath. All he needed was one last breath. One heroic heave. He put his face into the stone wall and prayed for the wind to subside. It was the winter of his life and he was teetering on a fence. Then, just as he cocked his arm to throw the money into the fort, a loud shot cracked the storm. It may have been a gunshot, or it may have been only a breaking tree branch—whatever it was, it shot to the very heart of Les Angelbeck. Instinctively, he clutched his heart and squeezed his chest muscles with all of the strength he had mustered for that final throw.

But there would be no throw. His heart was exploding inside of his chest. The pain was unbearable. Again he squeezed with all of his might, only to find little might left inside of him. Little life. He was dangling from the stone wall by one hand when his heart finally gave up the fight. The bag with the ransom money fell to the snow beneath him, and Les Angelbeck fell away from the fort wall—toppled backward through the snow and then dropped over the deadly bluffs. Like a human snowball he rolled down the embankment, through the trees and the bramble, over the sharp rocks and down to the river's edge. He ended up flat on his back at the shoreline, one shoulder in the icy water, the rest of him resting on the snowy riverbank in this snow-laden land that he had loved so much.

All was deathly quiet now but for the great tearing wind, the stealth currents of the Mississippi River. The snow falling silently on his weather-beaten face. He felt strangely warm. Liberated.

Death is funny that way, especially when it calls on the elderly. At the very end all of the ailments melt away. Now the captain's bones were free of pain, and the hearty air he breathed filled his lungs, then let it out again. Even his eyesight returned to normal. From his deathbed of snow and water the pride and joy of the Minnesota Bureau of Criminal Apprehension could see up the bluffs to the stone walls. The blizzard's attack on the fort was exacting a toll. More stones fell away from Colonel Snelling's masterpiece, rolled down the bluff and into the river. And at the foot of the fort walls, right where the ransom money lay, Captain Les Angelbeck was sure he could see the tortured face of a young man hiding behind a mask.

* * *

By the time Rick Beanblossom found Angelbeck's car at Fort Snelling the snowfall was crazy. Horizontal and stinging. Sub-zero winds were gusting to 50 miles per hour. He took shelter beneath the venerable walls and followed the boot prints to the gatehouse. There, with the aid of a flashlight, he read the bloody note tacked to the door.

> Throw Money inside the Fort.
> You are being watched!

A few feet from the gatehouse was a split-rail fence, and lying at the foot of the fence, in the deep drifts, was the maroon and gold hockey bag. Rick picked it up, felt the heft of the seven hundred thousand dollars in ransom money. The padlock was still rusted to the gate. The snow beneath the gate was undisturbed. Nobody had entered the fort at this point. Something was wrong. Angelbeck's fast-disappearing boot prints led up to the gatehouse—then they stopped. Rick peered over the fence, saw the sharp drop to the river. He put his hands to his face to shelter his eyes from the storm. He could see that the snow there had been broken, as if parted by a toboggan. Rick threw the bag over his shoulder and leaped the fence. Then the Marine half-climbed, half-slid his way down to the river's edge.

The snow was painted red. Then he saw the captain. The old man was bleeding from the head and mouth, his lungs and throat weathered and shredded like old newspaper. Rick Beanblossom dragged his mentor out of the water and cradled his head in his arms. He brushed the icicles from his face, a face even whiter than the snow. And yes, a face with death written all over it.

The police captain forced open his gray eyes and damned if he didn't manage a smile. "What have you done for me lately?" he croaked, barely audible.

"Where's my son?"

"I figured it out, Masked Man. Damnedest thing. While I was climbing that wall up there . . . I figured it all out."

"We know about you and the Lindbergh case . . . now, where is he?"

"We've been double-crossed. The both of us. She knew I was on to her."

"Who knew?"

"Esther. . ." he mumbled. "Esther Snow."

"No. I've seen her. She's a puppet in a coma. Somebody's pulling her strings. Tell me where my son is."

The Marlboro Man managed to expunge one more cough. One last throat-clearing, blood-spitting, hacking cough. "She's got him," he wheezed. "The old witch had to get rid of me first. Now she'll come for you."

"Who's got him?"

But it was not to be. Les Angelbeck whispered two unintelligible words. One of them may have been "snow." Then the legendary police captain was gone.

The Marine brushed the icy flakes from the cop's

lifeless face. "Oh God, don't die on me, old man. We've got a case to solve . . . one last case." But it was doubtful even God could hear him over the roaring wind.

Captain Les Angelbeck was laid out on a riverbank of snow and ice. In an hour his body would be buried by the blizzard. Rick Beanblossom struggled to sling the hockey bag over his shoulder and wearily climbed his way back up the bluff, one snowy foot at a time.

The father of the missing child rested beneath the stone walls. He glanced down at the river, then he shouted over the gatehouse. "I've got the money. Do you hear me? I've got your goddamn money!" With a strength born of anger and sorrow, the Marine heaved the hockey bag into the wind, up and over the wall and into the historic fort.

Rick waited for some kind of sign that they had received their package. Their blood money. But what kind of sign could there be?

"They're going to kill him, Rick. And if they'll kill him, they'll kill the baby."

The Marine leaped to the top of the fence. Caught his balance in the wind.

"The time to catch kidnappers is when the ransom is paid . . ."

Rick couldn't remember the last time he'd scaled a wall. Probably boot camp at Parris Island. He stuck his foot onto a jutting stone, grabbed hold of another stone, and climbed—climbed through the wind and the snow. Climbed knowing his son's life lay in the balance.

He found himself on a rooftop inside the fort. From there he leaped into a snowbank, got to his feet, and brushed himself off. The hockey bag was gone. A single pair of boot prints led across the yard to the fort's pinnacle. The Round Tower.

Armed only with a flashlight, Rick followed the large prints to the tower's musket slits. It was [illegible] inside the Round Tower the monster h[illegible] watched [illegible] and waited. He followed the deep footprints around the stone walls to the double doors.

The doors to the tower were wide open. A simple padlock had been pried off and left lying in the snow. Rick stepped inside. With walls six feet thick the storm was locked out, but flurries had forced their way through the slits. The tiny white crystals swirled through the air like crazed spirits. The building, deadly silent, had an earthy, musty smell that Rick's sharp senses recognized from the gold note sent to him on the anniversary of the Lindbergh kidnapping. A spiral staircase built of stones quarried from the river led upward. He let his flashlight survey the path. Up and down the walls. Up and down the stairs. Nobody. Nothing. But the snowy boot prints led downward. Stairway to hell. Rick crept quietly down the stairs, the only noise being the wailing wind through the musket slits.

He half expected to find his baby boy. Prayed he would. But upon reaching the basement level he found no signs of life—or death. His flashlight swept over the dirt floor. That's when he saw it. Between two wooden barrels was a black hole in the earth. There the boot prints disappeared, as if the devil himself had come for the ransom. It was what soldiers call a rabbit's hole. In constructing his fort, Colonel Josiah Snelling had not missed a trick. If the fort was overrun, he and his men would retreat to the impregnable Round Tower where, with plenty of food and ammunition, they could hold out for days. And if the Round Tower should be overrun, the conquering horde, be they British, French, or Sioux, would find not a soul. The Americans would have silently slipped away, out a secret tunnel that led down to the river, their canoes hidden in the woods. But Fort Snelling was never attacked. And so the tunnel had never been used. Until tonight. Like the wily colonel, the kidnappers had not missed a trick.

They had their money. They'd made their escape, just as they had escaped Charles Lindbergh so many years ago. The Marine stood there numbed not by the cold, but numbed instead by the cruelty of these monsters. Andrea Labore would no more have her son returned to her than Anne Morrow Lindbergh. This ransom was never meant as an exchange for the baby. This ransom was meant to kill Les Angelbeck.

"She had to get rid of me first . . . now she'll come for you."

Rick Beanblossom wound his way up the spiral stairs, perhaps the oldest staircase in the Midwest. On the very top stair he put his shoulder to the log door and pushed through an angry gale to the roof. There the Marine stood, frozen like a statue at the zenith of the fort on the peak of the bluff where two great rivers and two great cities came together. Through the harsh weather the distant lights of St. Paul glowed like the northern lights, while to the west the downtown lights of Minneapolis were blurred in the storm. But most of all what Rick Beanblossom saw from the tower of the historic fort that night was snow. Nothing but snow. Silent snow. Secret snow. What would he tell the baby's mother?

"Sorry, Andrea, they got away."

The kidnappers of Dylan Labore Beanblossom, and maybe even the kidnappers of the Lindbergh baby, had disappeared into the white night. Sailed on the wind. Vanished, like ghosts. Once again the mysterious Esther Snow, be she real or myth, had outwitted the best detective minds in the country—including the legendary Marlboro Man. Now this old witch would come for him, using his son as bait. For what reason, Rick did not yet know.

He turned his attention to the distant lights of St. Paul. The literary souls of Sinclair Lewis and F. Scott Fitzgerald still walked the streets at night. But to Rick Beanblossom, the most haunting soul of all was that of a newspaper hack who had never written a book, a local reporter who had spent his life exposing the skeletons of others while fighting a losing battle with the ghosts of his own past. Grover Mudd was the man's name. And if this Marine, this wounded veteran of Vietnam, was going to get his son back alive—he was going to have to learn everything there was to know about that wounded Marine of World War I.

Saber-rattling winds unremittingly battered the face of Rick Beanblossom, turning his blue mask so white he too seemed to vanish in the storm. He could no longer see through the blizzard, but nor could he be seen. An invisible man, vanishing quite slowly in the winter weather, disappearing, fading away, until all that could be seen were the darks of his eyes, and all that could be heard was the wind and the whirl, and the silent but relentless pounding of the snow.

Anne

Andrea Labore lay in her hospital bed and stared out the window at the Cathedral of St. Paul. The bells in the tower rang out the hour. Westminster chimes, muffled by the blizzard. It was 10 P.M. Never before had she seen the church from this corner of the city. At times the great dome up on the hill disappeared altogether in hellish bursts of white. But always the blessed church reappeared, reminding the queen of the evening news that God Almighty was here to stay. Andrea Labore was not a religious woman, but she envied those who were.

Commander Giles of the St. Paul Police Department had gone out of her way to keep her informed. Ransom instructions had been delivered to the house. A police officer had set out to make the payoff. The FBI followed. No word yet. Rest, they told her. Try to get some sleep. Her husband's whereabouts, they said, were unknown. But Andrea Labore knew. Rick would follow the ransom to the gates of hell, of that she was sure.

A watery echo haunted her aching ear, as if a seashell were clamped to her head. Everybody in the hospital talked with a hollow voice. She had a severe muscle tear in her left arm. Her back hurt. Andrea could count the myriad aches and pains up and down her body, but they were nothing when compared to the pain she was feeling in her heart.

Maybe God was doing this to her to remind her she'd been a terrific career woman, but a lousy mother. A mediocre wife. One public appearance after another. Make a speech. Cut a ribbon. Rush to the station. Into makeup. Read the six o'clock news. Host a debate. Rush back to the station. Read the ten o'clock news. Drive home and kiss a sleeping baby. The truth was that before the abduction, Dylan had spent more time in the arms of a housekeeper than he had in the arms of his mother. Now God only knows whose arms he was in.

Anne Morrow Lindbergh had her first baby, a boy, and then flew around the world with her husband. Made aviation history, then got home and wrote a book. *North to the Orient*. Was she the superwoman of her day? That afternoon Rick had brought her other book to the hospital, the book Mrs. Howard had given to him.

"It would seem to me that book would be invaluable to Andrea. As long as she holds it in her hands, she'll never be alone."

On the window side of the bed a table lamp was glowing, just enough to read by. Andrea Labore picked up the book with all the reverence of the Holy Bible. *Hour of Gold, Hour of Lead*. She studied the sadness in the face of Anne Morrow Lindbergh. The photograph that graced the cover had been taken in the year after the kidnapping. Her beautiful countenance seemed drained of all emotion. She looked quiet and composed. Noble, almost saintly. Does a saint cry? Did she scream? Did she bleed? Did Anne hurt the way Andrea hurt?

Again Cathedral Hill was lost in the storm. Endless white. Hell hath no fury like two Minnesota blizzards in two days. As winter raged with unending anger outside her window, Andrea Labore paged through the diary until she found the date she was searching for. She rolled into a position where her back hurt the least and held the pages beneath the lamp. Watched as the light spilled over the words. It was Anne Morrow Lindbergh writing to her mother-in-law.

Wednesday, March 2, 1932

Dear Mrs. Lindbergh,

(Better destroy after reading)

. . . At 7:30 Betty and I were putting the baby to bed. We closed and bolted all the shutters except on one window where the shutters are warped and won't close. Then I left and went downstairs and sat at the desk in the living room. Betty continued to clean the bathroom etc. until some time between 7:45 and 8:00, when she went in to the baby again to see he was covered. He was fast asleep and covered. Then she went downstairs to supper . . .

At ten Betty went in to the baby, shut the window first, then lit the electric stove, then turned to the bed. It was empty . . .

BOOK TWO

1932
THE RANSOM

Time has not continued since that Tuesday night. It is as if we just stepped off into one long night . . .

—Anne Morrow Lindbergh
May 18, 1932
Hour of Gold, Hour of Lead

Grover

The morning rain tasted of acid. The air reeked of rotting flesh mixed with the sour smell of mustard. The young Marine lieutenant wrestled a gas mask over his head and staggered back through the charred forest. But the mask had a hole in it the size of a nickel. He plugged it with his finger and dropped into a trench. Separated from his men, the only sound he could hear was his own heavy breathing. He was suffocating. He spit the dry rubber from his mouth and ripped the mask from his face. The yellow-green mist rushed in. His head throbbed. His nostrils burned. His throat was rasping hot. Tears like acid burned his eyes and he rubbed until the skin below them was raw. On hands and knees he tried to vomit the Great War, but the counterfeit mustard had robbed his stomach. The young Marine urinated into a handkerchief then placed it over his nose and mouth, used it as a mask.

The Corps had their orders. Take St. Mihiel. Smash the Hindenburg Line. But this Marine would never see

St. Mihiel. For him the war was over. Mustard out. He collapsed and slept in the rain.

The Marine woke when the foul weather abated. It was dusk. Red streaks of the setting sun shot through the storm clouds and fell across the trench. The yellow-green mist had drifted away, but the unforgettable odor of the gas lingered on. He sat up. His chest felt on fire, his mouth bloated and dry. He itched all over. His hands were blistered.

Then came the haunting feeling he was not alone. Only three feet away another wounded soldier sat slumped against the sandbags, staring at the Marine. His uniform was gray. The sodden coat read, *Hauptmann*—German for *captain*. His hair was dark, made even darker with blood. His round, mud-spattered face was eighteen at most. His arms and legs were lifeless. A stringless marionette. It was only the flicker in the German boy's watery eyes that betrayed death. He seemed far too young for an officer, but then things weren't much better on the other side of the trench.

The American Marine braced himself and stared back. A rifle lay between them. The Marine reached for it, slowly, and dragged it back into his arms. He cradled the stock against his ribs and pointed the barrel at the Hun's face. The German *Hauptmann* did not move. Days of fighting through the Argonne Forest and this boy soldier, this baby-faced enemy was all he had to show for it. Suddenly, he felt old. His guts were telling him to squeeze the trigger, but his heart said no, and that annunciation men call death had hold of his brain.

When the whistle sounded that morning he had been able to shake it off. Lead the charge. Now it had the best of him. He could feel it there, making a home for itself at the base of his skull. He lowered the rifle.

It had begun like a kidney punch in the hour before dawn as he sat shivering in the cold drizzle waiting for the order to attack. He'd tried to rub it out, but it crawled up his spine. It was not like the lice that camped in the seams of his uniform, but more like a predatory animal. The dreaded scorpion of fear. Cowardice. Death. He had seen it in other men. It stung their pride, their reason, sucked the courage from their bodies. Now after so many battles, it had moved in on him.

"Don't run, Marine."

Why now, he asked himself? His stripes were earned in combat. In the trenches outside Verdun. During the stand in Belleau Wood. With the taking of Soissons. There was talk of medals, of official letters home to the local newspapers detailing his heroism.

"Don't run, Marine."

The American Marine got to his feet and peered over the sandbags into the woods. There was a river back there where he could cleanse himself. He tried to climb out, but slipped on the slimy boards and landed on his ass in the manner of a circus clown. He scrambled for the rifle and turned to defend himself from the back-shooting Hun. But the German captain's only assault was a breathless chuckle. The Marine left him behind.

It was a small river, narrow and knee-deep, not like the mighty waterway where he had played as a child. He lay on his belly and drank the cold water until he was nauseous, his head euphoric. His ears rang with voices: a stew of accents, homesick stories of small towns tucked away in parts of America he couldn't imagine—orders, more orders, counter orders, the sound of mail call a fortnight ago:

"Harbold?"

"Dead!"

"Alvarez?"

"Dead!"

"Walker?"

"Dressing station."

"Erickson?"

"Dead!"

"Mudd?"

It began to rain again and he wanted to pray, but when the green rockets that warned of a gas attack invaded the heavens that morning, God deserted him.

"The lousy bastard."

So the wounded soldier prayed for home, that sainted city on the Father of Waters where life was good, the air was fresh, and the fight for the right was always won. The newspapers said so. He heard his daddy scream and saw train cars buckling over a raging river. He dreamed of a girl he was fond of. The Marine lieutenant doused his head in the cold, muddy, bloody water. His lungs were scorched. His innocence shot. And the river washed away his youth.

* * *

Grover Mudd turned away from the window, away from the noise and the traffic from the street below. He dropped the newspaper with his front-page story onto his desk and slouched into the sagging springs of his dirty leather chair. In Minnesota's theater of changing seasons it was hot. Hellish hot. The heat wave was into its third week; the crime wave was into its sixth year. In St. Paul, gangsters can fuck in the street. The average, everyday, law-abiding citizen can't, but gangsters can. Nestled above a sweep of white sandstone bluffs on the Upper Mississippi is a magical little city where, if you're a gangster, you can fuck the blond-haired, blue-eyed beauty of your choice right in the middle of the goddamn street. Fifty years ago, it was unthinkable. Fifty years from now, would anybody believe it?

His suspenders were sweating through his white shirt at the shoulders. His tie was off. He peeled his back away from the sticky brown leather and pulled a handkerchief from his trouser pocket, ran the soiled cloth around his neck. Grover's divorce had finally come through. The grand old wedding, two children, a big fat mortgage, and a divorce. If it weren't for the kids, he'd shoot the lousy bitch. But at least now Grover Mudd was free—free to join the gangsters on the street and fuck until his eyes watered. The former Marine Corps officer jerked his hand to his mouth and coughed. It was a hacking cough, with nails that tore deep in his chest. Just another summer cold he told himself, brought on by the heat. Earlier in the winter he'd wrestled with a bout of pneumonia, brought on by the cold. Grover had a lie for every season, and with every passing season the lies grew bigger and bigger. He reached for a Lucky Strike. Struck a match and lit up. Blew smoke across the room. He wiped the water from his eyes and stared again at the headline as it emerged through the cigarette smoke.

ST. PAUL FRONTIER NEWS
* Page One * Tuesday, June 14, 1932 * Two Cents *

ST. PAUL WOMAN QUESTIONED
IN LINDBERGH KIDNAPPING
More Ransom Money Shows up Here
by Grover Mudd

Grover looked out at the newsroom. The *St. Paul Frontier News* . . . was it possible? Could this money-losing newspaper in this gangster-infested hick town break the crime of the century wide open?

Grover's little corner didn't amount to much: a wall half of plaster, half of pebbled-glass, a doorway with no door, a broken-down desk that must have been built in because it was too big to get out, and a black typewriter with gold trim—a decent Remington he'd bargained for at a pawn shop up on Seven Corners. He'd carved his last name into it with a nail. Times were hard. Theft within the newsroom was rampant.

Back copies of the *St. Paul Frontier News* were stacked everywhere. Crumpled typing paper carpeted the floor. The latest edition of that rag called the *North*

Star Press was stuffed into the wastebasket, and the wastebasket was stuffed under the desk. In a solitary corner a secondhand fan with a frayed cord was blowing the hot air around—but then people on the street were saying the same thing about Grover Mudd and the *Frontier News.*

"There ain't no gangsters here, they just make 'em up to sell newspapers."

Tacked to a wall of flaked paint above his desk was a myriad of newspaper articles on the kidnapping and murder of the Lindbergh baby. Paramount among the clippings was a news photograph of Anne Morrow Lindbergh, the most recent taken. It may have been the saddest photograph Grover Mudd had ever seen. Her large oval eyes shied away from the camera. The gentle smile that once framed her delicate mouth seemed lost forever. A noble melancholy. It seemed hard to believe that a woman of her frail beauty was an accomplished pilot, navigator, radio operator, world explorer, wife, mother. Some of the clippings surrounding the photo were months old. Others, like those about the ransom money, were more recent. The crime of the century remained unsolved, and America's thirst for news about the case remained insatiable. Turning a deaf ear to the noisy traffic outside, Grover picked up his story again and read.

> . . . A young German woman now living in St. Paul was questioned and later released by police after paying for a new dress with a ransom bill from the Lindbergh kid-

> napping. Employees at the Golden Rule Department Store in downtown said the woman passed the twenty-dollar gold certificate on Saturday afternoon after trying on a dress. Suspicious clerks called police . . .

Grover Mudd wiped the perspiration from his receding hairline and shoved the red engineer's handkerchief back in his pocket. He last heard 92 degrees, 5 degrees cooler than the day before. The long sleeves of his shirt were scrunched up above his elbows. St. Paul's pugnacious reporter yanked a bottle and glass from the top drawer of his desk. Poured himself a shot of moonshine. He picked up the newspaper and shuffled back to the open window.

> . . . The woman questioned told police her name was Esther Snow, age 22, of the Bronx, New York, now residing on Grand Avenue in St. Paul. However, police identified the woman through immigration records as Esther K. Trinka, age 32, of Leipzig, Germany. Officials at the U.S. Department of Immigration were notified of the slight discrepancy before the woman was released without conditions . . .

Grover shot the whiskey. Stearns County 13. Best booze in the Midwest. He wiped the moonshine from his lips, stole one last drag from the cigarette, then flicked the burning butt out the third-floor window. He stared at his own writing. Digested the facts. Then slowly and sardonically he read her alias aloud, one silly syllable at a time.

"Es-ther 'so-called' Snow."

He often wondered what it would be like to be married to a truly beautiful woman. Perfection incarnate. He glanced over at the photograph of Anne Morrow Lindbergh. The envy of every man. Wasn't going to happen with the shape his mug was in. Grover Mudd was sneaking up on forty. He looked older, felt older still. His black hair was thinning. His eyes were stony gray with creeping lines of red. Shadows crisscrossed his face in a way that made him look mean. He wore a scowl, seldom a smile. In his football days at the university he was a sight to see. Swift and fleet of foot. Golden halfback for the Golden Gophers of Minnesota. Big man on campus. Now he was a wreck. Broken first by war. Then by marriage. Then by whiskey.

Grover coughed into his fist. He tucked the day's newspaper under his arm and shoved his hands into the deep pockets of his baggy brown trousers. He stared out the window, something he was good at. Dames. Lots and lots of dames. He searched the city for a woman who could fulfill his dreams; dreams of uninhibited sex in city parks. Sex in the back of a trolley car. Sex for breakfast and sex for lunch. Sex in the middle of the goddamn street.

In his articles for the *Frontier News* Grover Mudd had told the story often; how St. Paul, Minnesota, had come to be a "safe city" for America's gangsters. It was called the "O'Connor System." At the turn of the century the Democratic machine that controlled city hall was run by Richard T. O'Connor, alias the Cardinal, who was one of the Big Four in national Democratic Party circles and a close friend of President Cleveland. His older brother, John J. O'Connor, alias the Big Fellow, was the police chief. It was the Big Fellow who put out the word: St. Paul is a "safe city" for gangsters. Only three rules. Check in with Dapper Danny Hogan at his place on Wabasha Street. Spend money. And all crimes are to be committed outside the city limits. The Cardinal handled the political fix. For more than a quarter of a century the system worked.

Then one morning back in '28, Dapper Danny Hogan stepped on the starter of his shiny new Paige coupe and was blown to smithereens. Due to failing health, John J. O'Connor resigned as police chief in 1920 and moved to California. He died there in 1924. Richard T. O'Connor suffered a stroke in 1926. He laid in a hospital bed for four years. Finally died in 1930. The O'Connor System was still intact; but the rules of sanctuary were no longer obeyed, and there were no Cardinals or Big Fellows to enforce them. The only solace for people like Grover Mudd, who was born and raised in St. Paul, was the fact that these three men, O'Connor, O'Connor, and Hogan, were now roasting in hell.

> ... She was released several hours later after police determined she had come by the bill innocently when she cashed a check at a Minneapolis bank on Friday ...

The gangsters still came to St. Paul, and the cops were still letting them go. Grover Mudd slapped the newspaper against his leg. "Es-ther 'so-called' Snow," he said again. A cop friend of his at the station house put him on to her Grand Avenue address. Most cops just wanted to put a bullet through his head. It was time to pay Miss Esther a little visit.

Miss Trinka

Esther K. Trinka was already a worldly woman when she sailed for America as a stowaway. Postwar Germany was chaos, poverty, and debauchery. Good men were hard to find. Jobs, even harder. In fact, there was only one job a woman could make any money at. Desperate after the unsolved murder of her famous aviator father, she tried it. Found she was good at it. Since the end of the war, many of her countrymen had sailed for America. Swayed mostly by Hollywood movies, Esther dreamed of following them. Land of the free, home of the brave, and all that stuff.

From stowaways who'd been caught and shipped back to a life of prostitution, Esther Trinka learned the rules. Choose an American ship rather than a German ship. The American ships sailed from Hamburg. Hide in plain sight. Mix with the passengers. Keep clean. Literally. Wash every day. Most of all, avoid contact with the ship's officers. And when you arrive in New York harbor, stay away from Ellis Island at all costs. Lie, cheat, swim, do whatever you have to do to reach the shores of Manhattan, but do not let them take you to Ellis Island.

Pretty little Esther had been the brightest student in her school, outshining even the boys. Her English as a second language was excellent. Once established in America and earning a living, she would send for her baby sister.

Through her nightly encounters Esther nearly saved enough money for the trip from Leipzig to Hamburg. She robbed pockets for the rest. No sooner had she stepped off the train when she learned the SS *James Madison*, recently rechristened the SS *Charles Lindbergh*, was boarding passengers for New York City.

Smuggling aboard the *Lindbergh* was easy, but going undetected proved more difficult. Three days out to sea, a ship's officer asked to see her ticket. Esther batted her sea-blue eyes and told him the truth. He could have taken her to bed and had the time of his life, but instead he took her to see the ship's captain. And *he* took her to bed.

Captain Horatio James Smith was a burly old salt from the nineteenth-century school of shipping. In calm seas he was known to his men as Hor Smith. In rough seas they just called him the Hor. These days found him in a particularly salty mood. The whole idea of having his ship renamed for an airplane pilot set his sea legs to wobbling. He still referred to his bold vessel as the *Madison*.

The captain's quarters were luxurious. The bunk was made of solid oak and was larger than most hotel beds. The food and drink were delicious and plentiful. But then so was the captain's demand for sex.

Esther had learned at a young age that her beauty could be used as a weapon against men to get her the things she wanted. But as she grew older she learned tough men required sex. Like her aviator father, the sea captain was a tough man.

In the first days and nights she could handle him well enough. He was a big boy with a heavy ass so she tried to stay on top of him. Whenever she could, she got away with just a juicy blow job. But sometimes when he was drunk, his dick was stiffer than he was and too often she found herself pinned to the bunk, smothering, while Captain Horatio James Smith bounced up and down on top of her, in perfect rhythm to the convulsions of the sea.

The North Atlantic is cold and rough and the crossing grew as hard as the captain's dick. Seasickness overcame her, though Esther tried to hide it. Sometimes when the captain would leave for the bridge she would spit the come from her mouth and then vomit the food and drink. All that kept her going were his promises, and those were as plentiful as the sex.

Esther had explained her situation to the noble American sea captain. He was more than understanding. Not only could he get her safely off the ship and onto American soil, but he could introduce her to the right people in the heavily German Yorkville section of Manhattan. He also promised her a hundred dollars and a place to stay until she could afford to live on her own. All she had to do in return was keep the captain's cabin warm and inviting throughout the long voyage.

One day she awoke at dawn and the seasickness was gone—and so was the Captain. The air smelled of land. Passengers scurried by the porthole pointing with awe. Esther washed, dressed, and joined the officers on the quarterdeck. It had been nearly a week since she'd been outside during the daylight. The rising sun stung her eyes. Wisps of morning fog still lingered in the air, but on the horizon the great lady with the torch could be seen standing proud as a goddess. There was nothing but silence among the immigrants. Men removed their hats. Women wiped away their tears. Esther Trinka did not speak, nor did she cry. She had made it to America. God bless.

With the Statue of Liberty in plain sight, Esther Trinka was quarantined in the captain's cabin and examined by the immigration doctor. She was declared in excellent health. Still, she found herself locked in quarters while the ship sailed up river and docked at Hoboken. She grew nervous. Out the porthole she could see the tall buildings of Manhattan glide by like icebergs on the ocean, a million sheets of glass reflecting the sun.

After the ship's passengers disembarked, Esther was unceremoniously hauled from her quarters and placed in line with a dozen other stowaways. The captain with the big dick and the big promises never returned. The stowaways were marched down the gangplank and put aboard a small steamer. Ordered to sit. As it left the pier, Esther realized her worst fears had come true. The boat of stowaways was a ship of fools, and Esther Trinka was the biggest fool of them all. They were not bound for Manhattan. They were bound for Ellis Island. There, they would undoubtedly be branded illegals and put on a slow boat back to Germany. Esther Trinka had been double-crossed. *Betrogen!*

Acting on impulse, Esther did a swan dive over the rail and into the water. When she emerged, the whistles were already blowing. Then came the screaming sirens of the harbor patrol.

To swim the Hudson River in the light of the day would be futile, so Esther swam beneath the pier and clung like a barnacle to a slimy pole. She clung to that pole in the filthy, icy water for more than ten hours, until the sun had completely disappeared from the Manhattan skyline. At times she got so cold she nicknamed herself Esther Snow.

With contrasting emotions the young stowaway from Germany swam the Hudson River that night, toward the bright lights of New York City. She was afraid of being caught, as the harbor patrol seemed relentless. But her hatred for the ship's captain, another man who had betrayed her, kept her swimming. The city lights grew so near she could see the silhouettes of people passing beneath the street lamps. She felt the cold, so frigging cold there were times Esther "Snow" began to pray the harbor patrol *would* find her. Pick her up and wrap her in a blanket. But the harbor patrol passed her by, and just after midnight, the German stowaway crawled freezing onto a dock in lower Manhattan and collapsed. Curled into a ball. She lay there all night, shivering. In the morning, warmed by the sun, she got back on her feet and began her new life.

Captain Horatio James Smith was to sail the SS *Charles Lindbergh* back to Hamburg after a two-week refit in Hoboken. But he only made half the voyage. The night before he was to hoist anchor, the good captain was found castrated on the oak bunk of his luxurious cabin, his head bashed in while he slept, his testicles removed with a razor and stuffed into his mouth. His men buried the Hor at sea, his balls tossed in after him. But as was the case with a famous German aviator, the murder remained unsolved.

Miss Snow

It was the middle of the afternoon in the middle of June. The sun was as hot as an Irish boiler. Grover Mudd caught the Selby–Lake Line trolley out of downtown. The going home traffic had just begun. He dropped a nickel in the fare box, flopped into the rear seat, and rode the car to the dark tunnel that ran under Cathedral Hill. The great church growled at him like a giant bulldog as he disappeared beneath the ground. The coolness was heaven.

The summer days were long and hot all right, but the politics of the day were even hotter. Republicans spent the summer months praying for the president. But the economic depression was only growing worse. Herbert Hoover needed more than prayers. Democrats were spending the summer organizing, picking a presidential candidate for the November election. Looked like they were going again with Al Smith, the former New York governor. A Roman Catholic. A sure loser. Grover shook his head.

In Minnesota, the young Farmer–Labor Party was on

fire. As a viable third party they had a good shot at deposing both the Republicans and the Democrats. Floyd B. Olson was their man for governor. The newspapers were backing him as a real crime fighter. Prohibition was supposed to end crime, but all it had done was organize it. Blood was spilling faster than whiskey. Even the worsening economy was overshadowed by the fear of crime—and the crime of the century, the kidnapping and murder of the Lindbergh baby, hung over the struggling nation that summer like the oppressive heat.

Think about it. Grover Mudd did. He had a son less than two years old. Shadowy figures in the cover of night crawled from the woods like bogeymen, stole up a ladder, entered the home of the most famous man in the world, and silently spirited away his infant son. Bashed in his head. And ditched the tiny body. Then, with the baby already dead, the monsters demanded ransom money. And they got it. Common sense said it was a two-person job. *The New York Times* reported a woman was involved. For the killers of Charles Lindbergh Jr., there seemed only one hitch—how to spend fifty thousand dollars in gold certificates.

The banana-yellow trolley emerged again into the vile heat. The growl of the great church was behind him. The grass and shrubs along the boulevard were beginning to show the effects of the drought. Everything was pale green. Droopy. Grover hopped off the clanger at Dale Street, hoofed it down to Grand Avenue, and found the address he'd been given. It was a so-so neighborhood at the end of a busy street. Mostly apartments. Some rooming houses. The Scots lived on Grand along with the Irish. The rich lived up on Summit. The darkies who served them lived up on Rondo.

Grover ducked in out of the heat. As apartment houses go, it seemed an okay place. Elms on the avenue kept the building cool. The hallway rugs were thick and bright. The walls smelled of fresh paint. A much better redoubt than the musty hole-in-the-wall he'd taken refuge in after the divorce.

The German girl, *E. Snow*, was listed as living upstairs. Apartment 2B.

"Two B or not two B, that is the question . . ." Grover mumbled to himself. He draped a tie over his sweaty shirt and wrestled on his rumpled suit coat as he climbed the stairs. He looked as if he'd just wandered through a Turkish bath. Then walking down the hall, he warbled a little ditty that was going around town. *"Ten thousand Jews are making booze in endless repetition, to fill the needs of a million Swedes who wanted Prohibition."*

Grover gave the apartment door a good hard rap in that way that cops know how to do. Immigrants fear the sound.

"Yes? Who is it, please?"

It was a woman's voice, kind of smoky, pleasant enough with not much concern in it, considering what she'd gotten away with. "Esther Snow, my name's Mudd. Grover Mudd. I'm a reporter with the *Frontier*

News. Got some questions for you. Open the door so we can talk."

"Go away, thank you."

Grover chuckled, *"Go away, thank you."* She was a polite dame. There followed a long silence on both sides of the door. The man from the *Frontier News* didn't budge. He was sure he could hear her breathing on the other side, her ear pressed to the wood. He made sure she could hear him. "Still here, thank you."

"Go away," she said again. This time her voice was louder, more emphatic, with no "thank you" to punctuate the end of the sentence.

Grover Mudd lit a cigarette. Blew out the match and flicked it down the hall. "What do you say you answer a few of my questions, Esther honey . . . and then I'll try and restrain myself from going down to that little immigration office they got at the federal courthouse . . . and raising questions about you." He bent over and blew a stream of smoke through the keyhole.

More silence. Dead silence. Then she unlocked the door. Kept the chain on. Peeked into the hallway.

The first thing Grover saw was one great pair of eyes. Big eyes, more blue than green. They were the kind of eyes that make men fall in love. It wasn't hard to guess why the cops had melted before those puppies. "You Esther? I'm Grover Mudd. Did a little piece on you in our paper today. Maybe you saw it?"

"What do you want?"

"Glass of cold lemonade would be nice . . . little whiskey in it, be even better."

"Whiskey is against the law."

"So is kidnap and murder. Open the door. We'll talk."

She removed the chain and let the door swing open. Turned her back on him and walked away. The body matched the eyes. Stunning. She was wearing one of those white lacy things high society dames run around the house in after dark. It ran to the floor, had long sleeves with frilly cuffs and padded shoulders. She lit a cigarette of her own, didn't bother to ask Grover for a light. She poured a Scotch into a tall glass. Then she turned to face him. "Leave the door open and get to the point . . . what do you want?"

Surprised wouldn't be the right word for it. Grover had seen beautiful women before. Saw them every day. Next day he'd already forgotten what they'd looked like. But there would be no forgetting the face of Esther Snow. Had that movie star look to her. Not quite real. Like she was always back-lit. She had white-blond hair that began as a wave then turned to long curls as it dropped over her high cheekbones. The fine, gold hair framed her sculpted face, like the sun through a cloud. She had a patrician nose, with a complexion cool as cold cream. Her cupid's bow lipstick was ruby red. But it was those eyes that did men in. The brows were pencil thin, opposing comets. Her sweeping lashes were black as midnight. The whites of her eyes were snow white, like her new name. All in all, the kind of eyes men kill over. Or maybe for.

"A get-to-the-point kind of girl." Grover kicked the

door closed with his heel. "I like that in a woman, Esther Trinka . . . Snow . . . or whatever the hell your name is."

"This is America. I can be whatever I want to be . . . true?"

"True enough."

She spoke English well, leaving behind only a hint of her German accent. "I choose to be Esther Snow."

His guard was up. Blondes were dangerous. "Yeah, and I'm Santa Claus, and I choose to believe you've been a bad little girl who ain't here on the up-and-up."

"And this 'up-and-up' means what . . . Santa?"

"Means you're here illegally doing illegal things. *Verstehen sie?*"

"Yes, I understand."

Grover browsed the room. Sized up the place. Decent space. Nicely furnished. A huge floor-model radio housed in a fine wooden cabinet sat in the corner. A Philco. Top of the line. "Do you work?"

"I'm looking."

"Pretty fancy digs for a woman who's looking for work."

"Are you married?"

The question took Grover by surprise. "Kind of."

"She *dumped you*, ya?" She had a cocky look on her face. For all her femininity, she was as tough as bricks. "Is that not the American term?"

"The term is *divorced*." It had been a while since a woman had cracked-wise with him. "You're a smart woman, Esther. I like smart women. But let me give you some advice. St. Paul is a small town. Don't get too smart." Grover covered his mouth and muffled a bad cough. He half turned away out of embarrassment. Put his cigarette out in an ash tray she had on the table.

Then she was next to him, close, snubbing her cigarette out beside his. Her hands had a bewitching kind of style. She was obviously proud of her long nails. *Fire and Ice* red. Liked to show them off. "You cough like a friend of mine . . . you too were in the war?"

Grover pulled out his wrinkled hankie and wiped the froth from his lips. "I saw Belleau Wood. What's your friend's name?"

"Richard."

"Richard what?"

"Just Richard."

"Is Just Richard around town?"

"No. New York."

"When did you arrive in St. Paul?"

"A month ago."

"And before that you were living in New York, like Just Richard?"

" Yes."

"Where in New York?"

"The Bronx."

"You married there . . . in New York?" She didn't answer. On the table Grover noticed a German newsletter sticking out from her mail. He'd learned enough of the language during the war to translate the banner: *Friends of the New Germany*. "How about

Leipzig . . . you married there?" Again she didn't answer. So he got to the point. "You must have wanted that swanky new dress pretty bad. You could have paid for it with any shopworn twenty. But not you. Nope, you pulled out a clean, crisp gold certificate. Meanwhile, the whole country is on the lookout for those golden beauties. You're either the gutsiest woman in the world . . . or the stupidest. Which is it, Esther Snow?"

"You are such a clever man . . . you tell me."

"Funny thing happens then. Cops run a check on the serial number and, low and behold, it's the hottest twenty ever to hit this town . . . ransom money for the Lindbergh baby. Of course, the kid is already dead."

"I read all that in the newspaper, Santa Claus. The *North Star Press*."

That stung. This bitch was sharp. Razor sharp. "Maybe. But what you didn't read in the *North Star Press*, or any other newspaper, was the sob story you laid on those cops when they got you downtown . . . " He leaned into her. ". . . Or maybe a good-looking dame like you laid something else on them."

She slapped his face. Slapped him hard. He grabbed her arms and pulled her tight. She stiffened, braced herself like a dog that had been beaten before and knew what to expect. She was sprinkled with cheap perfume, but wild, whorehouse wild, the kind of fragrance that toys with a man. Grover was mad. He didn't care for being toyed with. Or slapped. "Let's have it, sister . . . what did you tell the cops? Why did they let you go?"

"I told them I got the bill from a bank in Minneapolis."

"Sell it to someone else."

"It is true."

"What were you doing in Minneapolis? That's a long ride just to cash a check."

"It was the Bank of Germania. The one in St. Paul was closed during the war and never opened again."

"So this check you supposedly cashed came from Germany?"

"It came from New York . . . drawn on a German bank."

"Did you and your friend Richard ever get over to New Jersey? Hopewell? Princeton? Sourland Mountains . . . that neck of the woods?"

"I don't know those places."

"But you must have read about them in the newspapers . . . little boy back there went missing?"

"I heard Santa Claus came down the chimney and got him."

He threw her down on the couch. She was sexy that way. Lying across the couch. Roughed up a little. Anger flashing across those eyes. "My name is Mudd. Grover Mudd. Don't ever forget it again. And the baby's name was Charles Lindbergh, Junior. Don't ever forget that again, you German bitch." Grover caught his breath as he felt another cough coming on. He suppressed it, wiped his mouth with his sleeve.

Straightened his tie. "Got any more?" he asked, looking around.

She composed herself. Sat up, the anger lingering across her brow. "Any more what?"

"Gold notes."

"That was the only one they gave me."

"Let's pretend the bank gave you five of them . . . all twenties. You spent one on the dress . . . and I'll buy one from you. That'll leave you three to hang yourself with." Grover pulled a wad of bills from his pocket and counted out twenty bucks. He dropped the bills on the table in front of her.

"I'll check." She got up and searched her purse. It was a hell of an act. "Is this one?"

Grover snatched the gold certificate from her hand. It was folded lengthwise, then folded again. Then again. He flattened it out. Eight sections. "Why don't you tell me, Esther, is this money from the Lindbergh kidnapping?"

"I got it from the bank."

He pocketed the bill. "That's okay, we've got a list of the serial numbers down at the paper. I'll be in touch." He walked to the door. Opened it. "One more thing, Esther honey . . . what was the name of the ship you sailed on to America?"

She closed her purse. Brushed her angelic hair from her eyes. "It was named the *James Madison*."

"The *James Madison* . . ." Grover wondered aloud. ". . . Ain't that the ship they renamed the *Charles Lindbergh*?"

Esther Snow put her hands on the curve of her hips and stared defiantly at his war-weary face. "Yes, I believe it was."

"Don't go anywhere."

"You think you are a policeman?"

"Worse, honey, I'm a reporter . . . and when it comes to dealing with your ilk, reporters are smarter than cops and less merciful. Your days in St. Paul are numbered . . . all of ya's."

Grover Mudd slammed the door behind him. He pushed out of the building and started for the corner. Stopped at Dale Street for a cigarette. His blood was boiling, and it wasn't from the heat. There was something about Esther Snow that stuck in his craw. She was that unique type of woman so delicious to a man that the mere thought of her face haunts him for days at a time. The impulse goes beyond sex. Beyond love. It's damn near hate. She's usually tall and slender, and married to someone else. Legs from her hemline to her neckline. Eyes to kill for, and pouted lips daring you to steal a kiss. Esther Snow was such a woman. She was gorgeous. That dangerous kind of gorgeous.

Despite the tussle, the interview had actually gone better than he'd anticipated. When pushed, she gave it up easy, maybe too easy. Yes, she was still hiding things, but he got a gold note out of her without swallowing her line about German banks. Esther Snow had come to America on the *Charles Lindbergh*. Is that where the seed was planted? She had men friends in New York, slash, New Jersey. Scene of the crime. She was living there at the time of the crime. She arrived in St. Paul with her hot twenties soon after the ransom was paid. While other immigrants were standing in bread lines, she was leading a life of leisure and comfort. And she was in this country illegally—he had that on her. Nothing seemed to move her, except the threat of deportation. Was she in town to wash that money? Or was she just another immigrant in the land of ten thousand lakes fishing for a sucker to marry?

Grover pulled the gold certificate from his trouser pocket. Examined it. He glanced back at the apartment house, at her second-story window. The curtain moved. Was she watching him from behind the glass? Hard to say, the afternoon sun was in his eyes.

Esther Snow was one for the books all right. But was she a baby killer? A woman born without a soul? That crack about Santa Claus stealing the Lindbergh kid was particularly cold. Not even the newsroom gang, infamous for their gallows humor, made jokes about the kid. You could still lay into Charles Lindbergh as a pompous ass with an airplane—son of a Socialist and son of a bitch. But Anne Morrow Lindbergh was every man's wife. Every son's mother. She was off limits. And so was the kid.

Mr. Howard

Grover Mudd hopped off the trolley and hurried to work. Again he'd overslept. He bounded down sloping Fourth Street and up the worn stairs of the Frontier Building. Just before he went in he shot a contemptuous glance at the competition, the *North Star Press,* across the street.

The green marble lobby was empty. The elevator doors slid open. Deserted. The operator had been laid off. Grover thought about the stairs. Then he thought about his lungs. He stared at the grimy walls of the elevator. Took a deep breath. He drew the safety gate closed and punched bronze button number three. The elevator jerked up one and a half floors and stopped. "Son of a bitch!"

Grover slammed his foot into the alarm button and added profanities to profanities about Elisha Otis and his goddamned invention. He slumped into the corner. Loosened his tie. A hot elevator in a hot building, on yet another hot day. He knew from experience the wait would be ten to fifteen minutes. Grover was going to suffocate. The eternal fire that camped in his chest flared up. He swallowed a cough. With no whiskey to douse the flames the former Marine Corps officer had to resort to mental discipline. Think of a cold, rainy night, he told himself. No problem there. Alone on the floor of the steamy elevator Grover Mudd closed his watery-red eyes and ran the facts of the case through his reporter's mind.

Tuesday, March 1. It is dark outside. Extremely dark. It rained all day. Clouds hide the moon and the stars. The air is cold. The ground is muddy. The fourteen-room house has just been completed. It is located in a remote area of New Jersey, on the road to Princeton. Just a dirt road through the backwoods, really. Here the most famous couple in the world hope they can escape the reporters. Get away from the autograph seekers, the nuts and the cranks.

At eight o'clock Anne Morrow Lindbergh and the nursemaid, a young Scottish woman named Betty Gow, put the baby to bed in the upstairs nursery at the southeast corner of the house. Mrs. Lindbergh closes and locks the window shutters, except for the shutters on the southeast window. They are warped and cannot be brought together tight enough to close. The nursemaid sits with the baby until he falls asleep. Then she goes down to the servants' quarters for dinner.

At 8:30 Charles Lindbergh returns home after forgetting about a speaking engagement in New York City. The famed aviator is not supposed to be at the house this evening. He's in time to have dinner with his grateful wife. After dinner, they walk into the living room and sit on the sofa. It is nine o'clock. Lindbergh says that while sitting there he hears a noise that sounds like slats of an orange crate falling off a chair in the kitchen. He thinks nothing of it.

Ten o'clock. Charles Lindbergh is working in his downstairs den, directly beneath the nursery. Anne Morrow Lindbergh is upstairs drawing a bath. Nursemaid Betty Gow decides to look in on the baby. She opens the nursery door. It is freezing. In the dark she can see the southeast window standing open. She lights the stove. She places her hands in the crib. Nothing but blankets. The baby is missing. A small white envelope is lying on the windowsill.

> Dear Sir!
> Have 50,000$ redy 2500$ in 20$ bills 15000$ in 10$ bills and 10000$ in 5$ bills. After two to four days we will inform you were to deliver the Mony.
> We warn you for making anyding public or for notify the polise the child is in gute care. Indication for all letters are signature
> and three holes.

For obvious reasons police were withholding the signature and a description of the three holes. Grover was hoping to get his hands on the note. Study the handwriting. Show it to an expert at the university. Photographic copies of the ransom note were already on the black market. A few phone calls, a few bucks. . . . The note could have been written by a woman, but it sounded more like a man. An immigrant.

The consumptive reporter extended his leg and again slammed a foot into the alarm button.

The first police report released to the public said the kidnappers consisted of a party of two or more persons. They are believed to have driven a car to the vicinity of the Lindbergh home and parked as close as possible without being detected. At least two members of the party proceeded on foot to the east side of the Lindbergh residence and assembled a three-piece homemade ladder, which they brought along. The ladder was then placed in position against the east side of the house so that one of the kidnappers was able to enter a window of the victim's nursery on the second floor. Apparently one person climbed the ladder, removed Charles Lindbergh Jr. from his crib, and left with the victim in the same manner. The ladder was then taken apart and thrown some distance southeast of the house. End of report.

When police found the ladder, it was broken. Grover speculated the shabby ladder held the weight of the kidnapper going up, but when he came down with the added weight of the baby, the ladder split. The lousy bastard slipped. Did he drop the baby? Was that the noise Lindbergh heard? Is that when the child died? When police arrived at the scene they found the baby's blanket had not been turned down. It was still pinned to the mattress. That meant the baby had been lifted from his crib by his head.

Saturday, April 2. The baby has been missing for more than a month. Lindbergh finally gets instructions from a kidnapper who calls himself "John." This John communicates with the Lindberghs through a Dr. Condon, a fat seventy-two-year-old publicity-seeking buffoon who lives in the Bronx. For good measure John sends along the baby's one-piece sleeping suit. Lindbergh and Dr. Condon are to bundle the ransom money and then wait for instructions. Lindbergh insists there be no police interference.

9:30 P.M. Lindbergh and Condon are led to St. Raymond's cemetery on Tremont Avenue in the East Bronx. They get out of the car and wait. No rain, but it's cloudy and cold. The sidewalks along Tremont are deserted. The cemetery is pitch black. Then Lindbergh says he hears a man's voice come from the tombstones. "Hey Doctor! Over here! Over here!"

Dr. Condon, out of sight from Lindbergh, reportedly meets John in the cemetery and hands over the ransom money—fifty thousand dollars, most of it in gold certificates, the serial numbers recorded. In exchange for the money Condon is given a small white envelope, which he turns over to Lindbergh.

> The boy is on the Boad Nelly. It is a small boad 28 feet long. Two persons are on the boad. The are innosent. You will find the Boad between Horseneck Beach and gay Head
>
> near Elizabeth Island.

April 3. The search begins. Charles Lindbergh spends the next five weeks searching by air and by sea for a boat called the *Nelly*. The search is futile. He is out to sea without a radio on Thursday, May 12, when a truck driver stops along the Mount Rose road, less than two miles from the Lindbergh estate. It is 3:15 P.M. Cool. Rainy. He slips into the woods to take a piss. By 7 P.M. the whole world has heard the news. The Lindbergh baby is dead. Been dead all along. Murdered, probably the night of the abduction. Ditched in the woods near the house. Police inform the child's mother.

"How could I have been so hopeful?"

Ironically, one of the few persons in the world who doesn't hear the news that day is Charles Lindbergh. Still out to sea. Searching.

Grover heard footsteps above. Someone was playing with the cables. He got to his feet. Wiped the sweat from his brow. The motor kicked in and the elevator jerked upward. Grover Mudd rose through the air, toward heaven, but his mind was still in New Jersey.

Suspects: Dr. John Condon, the go-between. A perfect stranger to the Lindberghs. Supposedly picked by the kidnappers because he wrote about the case in a letter to the editor, published in a neighborhood newspaper in the Bronx.

Betty Gow, the nursemaid. An immigrant. Young and pretty. She knew the layout of the grounds, the baby's routine, and the Lindberghs' schedule. But the Lindberghs believed she was clean. So did the police.

The housemaid and the groundskeeper. An older married couple. Same story as the nursemaid.

Then there was the mysterious Violet Sharpe, a maid at the Morrow estate, where Charles Lindbergh was supposed to stay after his speaking engagement the night of the kidnapping. Under police questioning, the British immigrant told a hundred different stories about her activities on the night of the crime. Was repeatedly caught lying. Shortly after the baby was found dead in the woods, she committed suicide. Drank cyanide chloride, a substance commonly used to clean silver. Did she kill herself because police were closing in? Or was it, as friends and coworkers said, that she had a date with the loony bin long before the baby was snatched.

Finally, Esther Snow, an illegal immigrant from Germany. Nabbed in St. Paul for spending a gold note from the ransom money. Released. Found with a second note stuffed in her purse. Too many newspapers had been burned on the Lindbergh case. Reporters had become reckless. A backlash was growing among readers. Now Grover Mudd was going to his editor, Walt Howard, with his suspicions about the cold but beautiful Miss Snow. If he ever got out of the infernal elevator.

The elevator doors opened. Should have been a breath of fresh air, but it was only less hot air. The temperature was flirting with 100°. In the newsroom, a dozen fans blew the sultry air around. Visible dust particles hung in the air. Got under everybody's skin.

Another round of layoffs had visited the paper. Another round of pay cuts awaited those who had survived. Before his divorce Grover Mudd was earning four hundred and eighty dollars a month. Damn good money for a reporter. With the latest pay cut, he was down to two hundred and forty dollars a month. "What's news, Fuzzy?"

"Mostly Lindbergh stuff."

"Good. Let's have it."

Fuzzy shuffled the wire copy in his hands. "London newspapers are saying cops hounded Violet Sharpe to her death. Innocent girl, disgrace to American justice and all that rot."

Fuzzy Byron was a dirty old man, literally. Unkempt. Unshaven. Unclean. Short and frail. The spectacles, precariously balanced on his permanently inflamed nose, were thicker than Coke bottles. If he did not die in total darkness he would die in a fuzzy world. He hung around the paper during the daytime, a copy boy, a messenger—a harmless old man Walt Howard paid out of petty cash. Most in the newsroom knew him best as Grover Mudd's drinking partner. He was ugly and incorrigible, and Grover could stare at the broken blood vessels in Fuzzy's red face and see a reflection of himself in twenty years. They crossed the newsroom and squeezed into Grover's corner office. "What else?"

Fuzzy tried to focus on the wire copy. "Well, mostly it's just second-guessing. Police chiefs and detectives around the country are sounding off . . . asking why the woods around the Lindbergh estate were never searched in the first place. No bloodhounds, no search teams, no Boy Scouts, nothing. Why weren't police there when the ransom was exchanged? Why was the ransom paid without proof the baby was still alive? Why wasn't a lie-detector test given to all of the servants? Why aren't New Jersey State Police sharing evidence with New York City Police, or the FBI?"

"Too late now, the trail is cold."

"Yes, sir," said Fuzzy, "and just about everybody is demanding the resignation of that guy who runs the state police there . . . what's his name?"

"Schwarzkopf," Grover told him. "Colonel H. Norman Schwarzkopf. Military man. West Point."

"Do you know him?"

Grover slumped into his chair. "I met him once in the hospital. He was a battery commander in the Third Army Division. He got gassed." Grover cleared his raspy throat. Wiped his mouth. "I've got to brief Walt Howard in two minutes. What did we find out about *Friends of the New Germany*?"

Fuzzy removed his spectacles and used his shirt to wipe the sweat from the thick glass. "*Friends of the New Germany* is an American Nazi group based in New York."

"Where in New York?"

"The Bronx."

"The Bronx," repeated Grover. "Everything keeps coming back to the Bronx, doesn't it? So . . . did Esther

Snow come to St. Paul to spread the cause, or did she come here to spread that money?"

"Well, Grover, I think she's here to spread that money."

"But why did she pick our fair city?"

"Because there's nothing fair about our city. Crooks wash their money here. You wrote an article about it . . . remember?"

Grover remembered. St. Paul was the fencing capital of the Midwest, much of the money linked directly to the Chicago syndicate. Millions of dollars of hot money was exchanged for cool money. But it was a slow process. Wash money too fast and you end up like Al Capone. Behind bars.

Grover stood. He checked his engineer's pocket watch. Time to see the boss. He pulled the bottle of moonshine from his drawer and stole a quick swig. Offered it to his partner in crime. "We have to tread lightly here, Fuzzy my friend." He picked up his notebook and grabbed a stubby pencil. "This is one dangerous woman."

The editor's door was open. Walt Howard was standing behind his desk, talking on the telephone. Grover knocked.

Walt Howard hung up the phone. "Come in, Mudd." He was a tall man. Slender. His hair was passing from premature gray to that distinguished shade of silver. He wore wire-rimmed spectacles, spectacles that had witnessed a thousand news stories and had perused a million newspapers. A picture of his wife was on his desk. They'd been married twenty years. "Sit down, Mudd."

Grover sat in the chair in front of the desk. The editor's office was the antithesis of Grover's corner. Spacious. Neat. Comfortable. A new copper fan humming in the window was trying to keep things cool. The papers were neatly arranged and weighted down. Grover leaned forward so as not to stick to the leather chair. "There's a rumor the paper is for sale."

Walt Howard took his chair. "We don't report rumors."

"But this one is interesting. Rumor has it the interested buyers are our friends across the street."

"There's a depression out there, Mudd. Newspapers aren't above its effects. Dailies are going under all over the country. The *Frontier News* hasn't made money in years."

He was the editor now, a man in charge of a dying newspaper. But it was Walt Howard, the reporter, who had come to interview Lieutenant Grover Mudd after the Armistice.

FRENCH AWARD ST. PAUL MARINE
CROIX DE GUERRE
Survives Gas Attack

Returns home a hero, that kind of story—a profile piece with enough syrup on it to kill a pancake. Then the man went out of his way to land the wounded veteran a job at the *Frontier News*. Grover was never sure if Walt Howard made the connection between Mudd the war hero, and Mudd the old engineer who died in the Red River train crash. Fell asleep at the throttle. Vilified by every newspaper in the country.

"How would you like a shot at your own column, Mudd?"

"Pardon me?"

"Your own column. Shoot your mouth off in print the way you do in the newsroom. You can sit down there in your little corner and pound out your opinions on everything under the sun. Politics. Crime. Sports. You name it, you write it."

Grover Mudd was a news reporter, and a good one. He'd never thought about pontificating. Like every other reporter in America, he dreamed of one day writing the great American novel. The offer momentarily stunned him. "Why would you want me to do that? I mean, cops and robbers is what I do best."

"You can still write about cops and robbers . . . but do it in a column. This city is down to two newspapers, and there's not a city in this country the size of St. Paul that has only two newspapers. If we're going to compete with the *North Star Press*, as opposed to being swallowed up by them, we need a boost . . . an edge . . . spice things up a bit. I think you're the man for the job."

"You couldn't print the things I really think."

"I'll print everything you write, Mudd. That'll be your undoing."

"And when would you want this column to begin?"

"The sooner the better. I'll clear a daily space for you."

"You would want five columns a week?"

"No. Six."

Handling a heavy workload was not Grover's strong point, even when he managed to crawl out of bed on time. "Can I think about it? I'm chasing a hot story right now."

"I heard you were chasing a hot skirt . . . let's have it."

Grover flipped open his notebook. "I went to see this Esther Snow, she calls herself . . . the one who passed the gold note from the Lindbergh ransom down at the Golden Rule." He paused for effect. "I think she may be connected to the crime."

"Those bills are showing up all over the country. They've been plugged into the system." Walter Howard had a healthy touch of skepticism in his voice.

"That means they haven't washed the bulk of the money," Grover told him. "They're spending it, one dollar at a time. Besides, most of those other bills were fives and tens. This was a twenty."

"One bill does not a kidnapper make."

"She had another one in her purse. I bought it off her." Grover removed the gold certificate, pressed neatly into his notebook. He handed it to his boss. "Last night we checked the serial number against the list released by the Treasury Department. It's Lindbergh ransom money."

Walt Howard seemed suddenly intrigued. He was actually holding ransom money from the Lindbergh kidnapping, but he still sounded skeptical. "What does she look like . . . this Esther?"

"Like something you see in the movies. A real tomato. Young, gorgeous, beautiful, smart . . . those kind of adjectives."

"What . . . are you in love already?"

"You asked . . . I'm telling you . . . she's gorgeous."

"I can't wait to meet her. If I weren't a married man . . ." He pointed at the picture of his wife.

Grover ignored his sarcasm and went on. "Whoever wrote the ransom note was probably a man, but it's safe to assume the abduction was a two-person job."

"Not so safe. One person could have pulled it off. What if this guy works alone . . . totally alone?"

"A woman's footprint was found in the mud below the nursery window," Grover reminded him.

"And did police make a cast of this footprint?"

"No. It got trampled in all of the commotion."

"So the footprint could have belonged to Anne Lindbergh, or the nursemaid, or the housemaid."

"*The New York Times* reported a woman was involved."

"They were speculating . . . even the *Times* does that."

"So you're telling me I've got nothing?"

"No, I'm telling you you've got one hell of a story going here . . . but before it makes my newspaper, you have to nail it down."

Those were the words Grover Mudd wanted to hear. He had the ball, run with it. "One other thing," said Grover, "turns out this Esther Snow is a Nazi."

"Yes, and I'm a Republican, and you're a Democrat . . . so what?" Walt Howard returned the gold note. "I'll be needing an answer on that column idea."

Dr. Frankenstein

On June 22, 1932, a month after the Lindbergh baby was discovered murdered in the rainy woods of New Jersey, Congress passed a federal kidnapping law. Before that, in many states kidnapping was classified as a high misdemeanor, with a sentence of five years to life. With President Hoover's signature, kidnapping became a federal offense under the presumption the kidnappers had taken their victim across state lines. The crime now carried a mandatory sentence of life in prison. A year later the law would be made even tougher. If the victim was harmed the kidnappers could be sentenced to death. The amendment also allowed the FBI to enter a kidnapping case within twenty-four hours, in effect giving the Feds immediate jurisdiction. This new statute was called the Lindbergh Law.

Grover Mudd stood outside Memorial Stadium at the University of Minnesota. An awesome sight to a football fan. And to a veteran. Built of brick and iron after the Armistice, the hulking edifice was finally dedicated in 1924—dedicated to the soldiers who gave their lives in the Great War. The Romanesque stadium, they said, would stand for centuries. The acropolis of the university—a living monument to the young men who left school, left home, and went overseas to fight the war to end all wars. Grover found something poignant in the sappy rhetoric, and something simple and reassuring about the big brick house where on Saturday afternoons the golden boys of autumn lined up for battle.

He could remember when the spiraling elms and the tall cottonwoods on the pastoral campus were mere saplings. Grover crossed the shade of the old yard and climbed the elongated steps of the new Physics Building. Beneath the Roman columns he stomped out his cigarette.

He had come to the university to see an old teacher from his college days, Dr. Louis Schnacky, professor of psychiatry and the study of human behavior. His specialty was the study of the mind. More specifically, the criminal mind. In Grover's day, they called Dr. Schnacky "the Alienist." Today his students affectionately referred to him as Dr. Frankenstein because of his uncanny resemblance to actor Colin Clive, who'd portrayed the mad scientist in the Hollywood movie a year earlier.

Dr. Schnacky was a white-haired legend, a frequent guest lecturer at the famous Police School of Northwestern University. But to detectives on the street, Dr.

Schnacky was a different story altogether. When he dared venture into a real police station, he was usually mocked out the door with duck calls: "Quack, quack." The professor argued, quite convincingly, that criminals had shot their way into the twentieth century, while police were still wallowing in the nineteenth. Grover remembered an especially fascinating lecture the professor had given two decades earlier on London's most famous murderer, Jack the Ripper. Dr. Schnacky had predicted the Ripper would never be captured.

"Why did he stop killing?"

"Elementary, Mr. Mudd. He died."

The hall was summertime hot, but quiet. No students. Grover found Dr. Schnacky sitting alone at the foot of a lecture hall laboratory. Even on this, the hottest of days, the professor was adorned like a fruit cake in brown suit coat and red bow tie, as if he'd found some scientific way to beat the heat.

Grover carried his suit coat in his hand, his tie stuffed into his pants pocket. He was sweating and coughing. He carried a large envelope with him as he made his way down the steep stone stairs to the experiment table. There lay all the trappings of science, a Bunsen burner, beakers, test tubes, and a dirty sink. On the wall was a huge map of the human brain.

"Grover Mudd," pronounced the professor. "Yes, I do remember you. Good football player. Poor student. So now I'm to understand you're a news reporter?"

"Yes, the *Frontier News*." Grover glanced about,

admiring the new facilities. The small auditorium could comfortably seat two hundred students. Above an exit door was the Periodic Table of Elements. A chalkboard was scribbled over with a numerical equation. "A long way from the musty old hall we used to sit in."

"That musty old hall turned out some brilliant students," Schnacky reminded him.

"It sure did."

"You weren't one of them." Dr. Schnacky hadn't lost his bite. He was a wiry little man who had aged well. He enjoyed a good book, usually a mystery, and a good argument. "I believe I generously gave you an incomplete, as opposed to failing your lazy bones altogether. If my memory serves me correctly, and my memory is extraordinarily accurate, I'm still owed several term papers, including a paper on the history of, and the abolition of, the death penalty here in Minnesota."

Grover laid his coat across the table. "Sorry, Professor, a war broke out."

"You always had an excuse, didn't you?"

Grover couldn't tell if the wily old professor was joking or not. The college dropout pulled a pair of eight-by-ten photographs from the envelope and presented them to the professor, as if they more than made up for the delinquent term papers. "This is a photograph of the actual ransom note from the Lindbergh kidnapping," Grover explained. "The note was left in the nursery after the abduction." He pointed to photograph number two. "And this is a photograph of the note Lindbergh was given when the ransom was paid."

Dr. Schnacky appeared pleasantly surprised. Even impressed. "Where did you get these, if they are what you say they are?"

Grover tried to answer his question without giving out too many details about his connections with local mobsters and eastern reporters. "Lindbergh thought the crime might be the work of the underworld, even though cops and common sense should have told him it wasn't. So he invites this New York gangster named Mickey Rosner into his home. He's just a smalltime racketeer really, but he convinces Lindbergh he can work through the mob and get the kid back. Lindbergh orders the cops to share all their evidence with this lousy bum, including the ransom notes."

"That's the stupidest thing I've ever heard."

"Actually, our hero wanted Al Capone, but the Feds had a real problem with that."

"You're joking."

"Hey, the man's a pilot, not a detective. Anyway, that's where these came from. There're a hundred copies out there. Newspapers aren't printing them at the request of the police, as if their publication could do any harm now. For five bucks, I can get you a photograph of the dead baby lying in the morgue."

"That won't be necessary." Dr. Schnacky placed a magnifying glass over the photographs and lost himself in the ransom letters. "Without an attempt at analysis, one is immediately struck by the German phraseology."

"Real German, or fake German?"

The professor answered, "Real. He's still thinking in German, but he's trying to write in English. At times phrases appear to be confused, but that changes when one thinks of the sentence as a literal German translation. His custom of placing the dollar sign after the money amount is definitely German."

Grover Mudd didn't know much about the rules of grammar in English or German, nor did he care. He wasn't that kind of writer. "Are you sure it's a man's handwriting?"

"Yes, definitely. I suspect he used a German-English dictionary, or perhaps someone dictated the letters to him."

"Another immigrant who speaks English?"

"Yes, if it was dictated."

"What do you make of that so-called signature?" With the arrival of the photographs Grover Mudd had finally gotten a peek at the mysterious signature. Not really a signature at all. Instead, at the bottom right-hand corner of the ransom note was a strange symbol. It consisted of two interlocking blue circles about the size of a quarter. In the oval that formed where the blue circles overlapped was a solid red mark the size of a nickel. Three holes were punched into the circles.

"A bit devilish, isn't it?"

"Frankly, Professor, I was hoping for a little more than, 'a bit devilish.' "

"Yes," said the professor, "it would have been nice if he'd signed his name."

Grover pretended the sarcasm was not at his expense. "Paint me a picture . . . what kind of man would do this?"

"I'll have to study these . . . may I keep them?"

"Of course."

"To answer your question, Mr. Mudd, if we can believe what we read in the newspapers, and that's quite a leap of faith, he's a man suffering from dementia praecox."

"And that means . . . . ?"

"He believes himself to be omnipotent. All powerful. He has no feelings for others. He feels only for himself. In reality, he's a lowlife. Menial job, if he has a job. He whines a lot. Probably an immigrant who believes everybody in America is out to get him. Doesn't have much money, so he thinks fifty thousand dollars is a king's ransom . . . whereas your mobster friends would call it chump change."

"Why the Lindbergh kid?"

"Simple. Charles Lindbergh is everything he wants to be, but never will be."

"So you're saying this kidnapping wasn't about money?"

"Not entirely, no. You see, Mr. Mudd, he wanted the money, but more than that he wanted to strike at the heart of Charles Lindbergh and, in effect, at the heart of America. Our hats should be off to him. He did it. From a criminal standpoint, the crime was bold and brilliant. This kidnapping may be one of the few things he's ever succeeded at. Instead of feeling remorse, I suspect he's feeling pretty good about himself right about now."

The stagnant air in the lecture hall was suffocating. Not a window in sight. Grover cleared his throat. "Let's just suppose, Professor, that he had a partner in crime. A woman."

Dr. Schnacky laughed. "Interesting theory, Mr. Mudd, but if I could tell you what goes on inside the mind of a woman, I'd win a Nobel Prize."

"Let's pretend she's just another criminal in cahoots with our demented-something friend."

"Dementia praecox." The professor thought about that possibility. "Then the plot thickens. It wouldn't be his wife, not even a girlfriend. No, it would have to be his mistress. Maybe another man's wife. Someone he finds it truly dangerous to be with."

"What are we talking about here . . . sex in the elevator?"

"A very sexual relationship indeed. That would be the only way she could control a man like him. Remember, this is a man who believes he's omnipotent. God hasn't made the woman too good for him. The more beautiful she is, the more he would believe he was entitled to her."

"And the more he would go out of his way to prove his worth to her?"

"Yes, perhaps. But this is all theory. I really must

study these notes, and even after that, it'll still be all theory."

"I've always found your theories intriguing."

"Yes, as I've always found your sloth." The professor returned to studying the handwriting. After staring intently at the photographs Dr. Schnacky shot up, as if he had suddenly remembered something. "Where were you wounded, Mr. Mudd?"

Grover was taken aback. "I was gassed."

"Yes, but where?"

"In some woods near St. Mihiel on the Meuse. Why do you ask?"

"May I have a sample of your handwriting?"

"Now wait just a minute, I've got a damn good alibi for the night of the kidnapping. At least a hundred people saw me and Fuzzy Byron staggering down Wabasha Street near midnight."

The professor showed no appreciation for Grover's warped sense of humor. "I'm serious. I need a sample for a comparative analysis." He dug out a pen and paper. "Write the same notes for me. I'll dictate."

Ice Man

At the time Grover Mudd was scribbling ransom notes, Esther Snow was standing at her second-floor window over Grand Avenue waiting for the Ice Man. She was tired of the heat. Tired of being questioned. She was sick and tired of Grover Mudd. The *Frontier News* reporter had called her on the telephone with so-called follow-up questions. He was different than other men she had known. The cops were easy. They were no different in St. Paul than they were in New York, than they were in Germany. But Grover Mudd was a reporter. An American newsman, one of the most amoral species on earth. Every day she perused the *Frontier News*. How long before a reporter like Grover Mudd would once again put his suspicions into print?

The damn fly was back. All morning long, a fly the size of the Red Baron had been buzzing the apartment, driving the German beauty crazy. Then, just minutes before show time, the slimy creature had the nerve to land on the glass an inch from her nose. Esther Snow dropped her hand like a guillotine and sliced the fly in two with a long, red fingernail. Staring between halves of the dissected fly, she saw the Ice Man arrive.

He was a Bavarian giant. Tall as a church steeple. A bit on the skinny side, but sturdy and strong. But more than his nationality, more than his size, it was his attitude that had captured the attention of Esther Snow. She needed a man like him. His was the face of a criminal. In German brothels, Esther Snow had seen his countenance a thousand nights.

She watched him pull open the rear of the truck and drive the ice pick deep into the frozen block. Chips of ice splayed like broken bones. He glanced up. Saw her standing in the window. He flung the block of ice over his shoulder and started up the stairs.

Esther lifted her cigarette from the ash tray and stole one last puff. She splashed another dash of perfume across her neck. Brushed the wrinkles from her sleeveless dress. She slipped into a pair of shoes, felt uncomfortable, and slipped right back out. Then she admired her reflection in the mirror just as the Ice Man rapped at the door.

Esther Snow took her sweet time answering. She opened the door an inch and copped an attitude of her own. "*Was wollen Sie?*" she asked in German.

"Your ice," he answered, in tortured English.

Esther looked him up and down. He was sweaty and pale. Wore no shirt. His hair was greasy, wet, and dirty. His shoulders were cherry red from the sun and the ice. She swung the door open, but didn't move.

Made sure he brushed her shoulder as he ducked through the doorway and headed for the kitchen. She turned and walked the door closed with her back.

Standing alone with him in the kitchen, she could already see the bulge in his pants rising to full mast. The lanky Bavarian lifted out the old chunk of ice, what was left of it, and dropped it into the sink. Then he picked up the block of fresh ice and fitted it into the icebox.

Esther was impressed by how deeply imbedded the pick was in the ice. She approached him from the rear as he stood working the ice into the box. The door was wide open, the block of ice cooling the room. With the same fingernail she used to decapitate the fly, she ran it gently up his backbone to his neckline. The Ice Man froze. She traced his red shoulders while he stood there like a statue. She let her fingernail slide around his neck and pantomimed slitting his throat. He stiffened again, in more ways than one. Then Esther slid around in front of him, the curve of her back to the block of ice. When he bent his head into hers and tried to put his lips on her face, she turned her head away. Still, she pulled him close.

He ran his hands up the back of her dress, his fingers incredibly long and anxious. When his hands had worked their way under her dress and up the back of her smooth thighs, he realized she was wearing no panties. There was nothing under that dress but a woman the likes of which he had never before known. The Ice Man lost control.

He fumbled open his pants and rammed his dick at her thighs, missing every time, too excited to find the spot. Esther Snow threw one arm around his neck, and with her other hand she reached down, got a good hold on him, and guided him inside of her. She wrapped her legs around his waist as he slammed her into the ice block. It was rock hard and freezing cold, and Esther couldn't say which sensation was more arousing, the extra-long dick thrusting inside of her, or the ice slamming into her bare ass. When she felt him coming, Esther seized the moment, whispering devilish orders into his ear as her fingernails scarred his back with fine streaks of blood. In a matter of seconds it was all over, like a vampire claiming his nightly victim. Only this was a woman preying on a man, and the hot sun was shining through the window.

Spooks

Grover Mudd left the speakeasy on Seven Corners just past midnight. Not drunk, just feeling good. It had been a productive day. The photographs of the ransom notes had arrived, and even Walt Howard thought the money they cost was money well spent. The interview with Dr. Schnacky had also gone well, though Grover would have liked to have coaxed more out of him on the aspect of a female accomplice.

The trolley arrived. Last trolley of the evening. Grover boarded and dropped his nickel into the fare box. Then he damn near dropped his jaw. Seated mid-car was eerily the spookiest couple he'd ever seen. It was a man and woman dressed head to toe in black, as if they had just come from a seventeenth-century funeral. Her face was hidden behind a black veil. His face was shadowed by a wide-brim hat and a turned-up collar. Even sitting down, he was a big man. They rode the streetcar in silence. Stared lifelessly out the window. Grover brushed by them.

The lights in the car were dim and yellow, giving the

interior of the trolley the unearthly glow of a candlelit crypt. A colored man had the rear seat, the only other passenger on board, so Grover plopped into a seat near the rear. He slumped against the open window, his coat across his lap. Begged for a breeze. The heat was still hellish, stoking the fire in his chest. The great church up on the hill was ablaze in light. Sparks flew from the overhead wires as the car disappeared into the tunnel beneath Cathedral Hill.

"Nail it down," he was told.

"A bit devilish," he was advised.

Grover kept hearing their voices over and over again. But the two words that kept him company on the way home that night were "dementia praecox." The term denotes persistent and logically reasoned false beliefs. Delusions. Often of persecution or grandeur. A person with dementia praecox may lead a relatively normal life, since most aspects of general behavior are unaffected by delusions. Good luck explaining that to a cop. No wonder they thought Schnacky was a quack.

The colored man got off the trolley at Dale Street. The motorman reached up and rang the bell twice and they moved on. Down Selby Avenue. Grover Mudd and two spooks in the night. It was a sultry evening with little moonlight. No breeze. No noise but the click-clack of the steel wheels as they rolled over the tracks.

And what about the professor's bizarre handwriting exercise? Grover Mudd scribbling ransom demands for a dead baby, writing them over and over again, as if he were the chief suspect in the child's abduction. In the end, all of the psychological babble Grover was trying to digest was spent on the author of the ransom notes. Undoubtedly a man. But what kind of woman would be party to such a crime?

As interesting as all of the theories were, and as productive as the day had been, Grover Mudd was still no closer to proving that a woman was in on the kidnapping and murder of the Lindbergh baby. Nope, all he had was the mysterious Esther Snow and her gold certificates.

The trolley rolled across Lexington Parkway when something odd happened. Mrs. Spook got up, made her way to the front of the trolley, and stepped off at the next stop. Nary a word to Mr. Spook, her companion in black. But that was not all that caught Grover's eye. Something was hauntingly familiar in the way Mrs. Spook moved. A premonition of sorts. The Angel of Death.

Now Grover was alone, save for the motorman at the controls and the Grim Reaper. The only thing missing was his scythe.

They rolled through the Snelling Avenue intersection and into the residential part of town. Here the streets were quiet, poorly lit. Grover sat with his eyes fixed to the back of the black hat. Then suddenly the hat rose from the seat and floated toward the ceiling, rose in the manner of a storm cloud, like Count Dracula, until it nearly hit the top of the car. The spook moved into the aisle with malicious purpose. Grover was shocked to see not a scythe in his hand, but an ice pick. The giant shadow of a man moved catlike toward the motorman and before Grover could shout any type of warning, the spook had swung his lanky arm and hooked the uniformed motorman by the neck. Blood gushed from the wound. The spook yanked the motorman from the driver's seat and flung him through the folding doors and into the street. On his way out, the motorman left a foot-wide streak of his blood across the windshield.

The spook wrenched the motor switch forward and then swung the accelerator into the eighth hole. Locked it there. The trolley picked up speed. Ice pick in hand, the shadow of death turned to face his prey. Grover stepped into the aisle, nowhere to run, too scared to scream. He was the tallest man Grover Mudd had ever seen. He had a bony face with black eyes, and white alabaster skin. The spook stormed down the aisle toward Grover, and along the way he used his ice pick to smash the overhead light bulbs. By the time he was within striking distance, Grover Mudd was crouched in the dark facing an immense shadow.

Illuminated only by passing street lamps, the spook raised the ice pick and attacked. Grover Mudd stuck his head down and charged forward. He hit the spook mid-stomach and drove him backward down the aisle. He felt the point of the ice pick rip into his shoulder. His chest caught fire.

The spook struggled to right himself, but before he

could gain fall height, the ex-football great had his suit coat over the bastard's head. Grover tried to stay low and work behind him. The spook swung the ice pick like a wild man, hooking steel bars, gashing the rattan seats. Grover could see from the corner of his eye that the trolley was racing out of control. The cross streets were flying by like telephone poles. When they were both on their feet and free again, it was Grover at the front of the car and the man who would murder him toward the rear.

Now the spook had flames dancing in his eyes, as if his orders to kill had come straight from the devil himself. His nostrils flared. His dark hat was on the floor with Grover's coat. His hair was stringy black, and parted down the middle. His white scalp made it look as if he were scarred, his head once split in half. The apparition moved toward Grover slowly this time, the ice pick poised to strike.

Grover could feel the blood running down his back, soaking his shirt. The sensation infuriated him, but at least this was something he knew. This was war. He reached into his trouser pocket and pulled out his necktie. The former Marine Corps officer wrapped the tie around his fists and pulled it tight. A garrote.

For a second, and it was only a second, the giant assassin seemed flustered. He lunged toward Grover, the ice pick nicking a corner of his ear. Grover ducked and came up behind the spook. He had to literally leave the floor to secure the tie around the giant's neck. The son of a bitch fought like a sturgeon, but Grover had him. He dragged the spook backward, trying to choke the life out of him, but it was like strangling the living dead.

Then the Marine's wounds began to catch up with him. His bloody shoulder was weakening. His head went numb. Blood from his ear was running into the corner of his eye. The anger that raged inside of him was no match for the fire that *lived* inside of him. He was sick with cough. He didn't have the strength to finish the job.

The trolley was at runaway speed, 60 miles per hour, but Grover knew he had no other choice. He wrestled the struggling, choking spook to the wood floor. Then he released his grip and ran. He sprinted down the planks and threw his good shoulder into the rear exit. The folding doors burst open. An alarm sounded. A red light flashed.

Grover hit the bricks. He rolled shoulder over wounded shoulder until he flopped face down in the street. Instinctively, he crawled forward two feet and lifted his head just in time to see the streetcar clip the rear of a delivery truck and jump the track. The overhead wires came down in an explosion of sparks and chased the trolley across the boulevard, where it buckled against an oak tree unimpressed with rail travel. The collision was deafening. Sirens were screaming in the distance.

Sparks ricocheted through the smashed streetcar like gunfire. An electric inferno. Whoever was inside, or whatever was inside, was surely dead. And so was

Grover Mudd, or so he felt. He lay face down in the middle of Selby Avenue. A breathing corpse. Tortured breathing. Only one eye working. He kept it open just long enough to read the street sign on the corner. Cleveland Avenue. Grover had a good laugh just before he lost consciousness. It was his stop. He was getting off here anyway.

Chief

Esther Snow read about the streetcar attack on the front page of the *Frontier News*. The article was written by Grover Mudd. But the vivid account was in the third person; it never mentioned he was on the car. The motorman was upgraded to serious condition. He was going to live. In fact he was going to be quite a hero. Mudd had sketched colorful prose about the operator's valiant hand-to-hand combat with the midnight monster. The fight was so bloody and ferocious the operator would probably not be able to recall it. As Esther furiously turned the pages of the St. Paul daily she couldn't help but wonder if there wasn't a way to gain some measure of control over America's cherished free press.

The German beauty was nursing a scotch and soda in the elegant bar of the Commodore Hotel. It was a small bar teeming with class, from the mirrored walls to the black lacquered ceiling. Artesian wells kept the foyer air-cooled. Piano music waltzed out of the lounge. The stately bar reminded her of the best of

Berlin. The best of New York City. The Commodore was once the home of F. Scott Fitzgerald and his wife Zelda. Esther Snow didn't care for Fitzgerald's pretty American stories. She much preferred the dark, haunting works of Joseph Conrad and Conrad Aiken. But for now it was the work of a hack named Grover Mudd that was haunting her.

Perhaps she was going about this all wrong. He was a rather attractive man, in a rundown sort of way. If he was the kind of man who would not take money, would not take a beating, what would he take? What exactly would it take to bend a man like Grover Mudd her way? Would he melt before her as easily as Richard had? As easily as the Ice Man? No, she was being foolish. During the war Grover Mudd was on the other side of the line. Now he was on the other side of the law.

As much as she liked St. Paul, her stay was growing increasingly frustrating. Thanks to Grover Mudd and the *Frontier News,* Esther Snow was suspect in a crime so heinous that not even America's most hardened gangsters would touch her money.

You can't have an underworld without an overworld. Her appointment showed up, walked into the lobby like he owned the place. At the very least he had a piece of the booze action or he wouldn't have set the meeting here. He was a big man. Barrel-chested. He hid his girth under a dapper set of threads. A white felt hat. A Chesterfield coat. She liked his no-nonsense style. This was the man she had dealt with after her arrest. The Ice Man had failed her. Now she would turn to the best friend a criminal could have in the city of St. Paul.

"So, Esther, we meet again."

"Hello, Mr. Police Chief."

"Actually, I've been demoted. I'm now the Assistant Police Chief."

Esther smiled. "I think we can still work together."

Dr. Schnacky

Stabbed, cut, bruised, and beaten, Grover Mudd was stitched up and released from the hospital after only a day. He limped out of the hospital looking like Frankenstein's monster, and not moving much faster. But the most frightening aspect of the streetcar incident was that police found no body inside the fiery wreckage. There was a seven-foot specter walking around with one hell of a stiff neck. And he was carrying an ice pick with Grover's name on it.

Dr. Schnacky was startled by the look of his former student. "My God, Mudd, what happened to you?"

"I fell off a streetcar. Have you studied the ransom notes?"

To stay cool Grover and the professor walked in the shade of the old yard, then ambled west, toward the river bluffs. The sun was high in the white-hot sky. The noontime temperatures were nearing 100°. The university lay behind them.

Despite the heat, the wizened professor was still

dressed in a dark wool coat and a bow tie. He edged into the shadow of a red oak before answering Grover's question.

The gangsters of the day did not interest Dr. Louis Schnacky. The Al Capones of the world were no mystery. They killed people for money. Wanton greed. It was the deviant criminal that intrigued Dr. Schnacky. Jack the Ripper. Elizabeth Borden. Leopold and Loeb. "The ransom negotiations covered a period of thirty-two days," he reminded Grover, "over which time fourteen notes were written to Charles Lindbergh by the kidnapper. Keep in mind I had only two of those notes to work with."

"And your conclusion?" Grover asked anxiously.

"Simple physics, Mr. Mudd. If you know the stimulus, you can always predict the reaction. If you want to know the criminal, study the victim."

"The baby?"

"No, no, Mudd, damn you . . . think. Get out of the sun."

Grover stepped into the shadow of the oak.

"Charles Lindbergh was the intended victim here," Schnacky went on. "Physics, Mr. Mudd, as applied to magnetism . . . opposites attract and likes repel. The criminal sees himself as Charles Lindbergh, thus he would see the real Charles Lindbergh as his enemy. And how would he bring his enemy, the great Charles Lindbergh, to his knees?"

"Through Charles Lindbergh Jr., " Grover answered tentatively.

"Correct. The most devastating blow to the virility of a parent that can be struck is through an attack on the child. Don't kill the man . . . kill the man's son."

Grover Mudd was back in college now, being scolded like a schoolboy for not exercising his brain. "Do you mean they intended to kill the baby all along?"

"Yes. But there is no *they.* The perfect crime can be committed by only one person. Get others involved, and sooner or later one of them will make a mistake."

"You sound like my editor, Professor."

"Then your editor is a very smart person. Only a lone man would do something like this. A mentally ill man. The fifty thousand dollars ransom was way out of proportion to the enormity of the crime. It was just enough to satisfy his practical need for money. I stand by my diagnosis of dementia praecox. Omnipotent."

"Okay," Grover argued, "tell me more about your so-called lone man theory."

"His initials are *B-R-H,* but not necessarily in that order."

"How could you possibly deduce that?"

"By that colorful symbol he signed with. The two large blue circles represent the letter *B*. The red circle in the middle represents the letter *R* . . . I suspect his middle initial. And the three holes are the letter *H*."

"C'mon, he probably made up that symbol on the spot."

"We do nothing at random, Mr. Mudd. Our subconscious is always at work. His decision to use a symbol instead of a false name was made on a conscious plane, but his choice of that particular symbol was made by his subconscious."

"No wonder the cops think you're a quack. What does he look like?"

"Since he's envious of Charles Lindbergh, he's about Lindbergh's age. But he's envious of the younger Lindbergh, so I put his age about the same as yours . . . past thirty-five, nearing forty. From the unusual distance between the rungs of the ladder, we know he's an athletic man, but again, he's envious of the taller Lindbergh. About your height, I would guess. The ladder was built in a hurry, which explains its shabby construction, but it was designed remarkably well. It could reach a second-story window, but could be easily folded and fitted into the backseat of a car. The kidnapper's occupation, when he worked, involved a great deal of mechanical aptitude. This, coupled with the fact he sees himself as a latter-day Jesus Christ, means we can hypothesize that he too is a carpenter."

"Well, that's one for the books, all right. Mr. Howard will love me when I hand him this piece. Anything else?"

"Yes. Tell Mr. Howard the kidnapper's handwriting bares a striking resemblance to your own."

Grover laughed, disbelieving. "I don't know if it's the heat or all the psychology, but that tears it . . ."

"Wake up, Mr. Mudd. He was gassed. Same as you. You both have definite signs of a marked tremor in your handwriting. You both consistently transpose letters and omit words. When you showed me the photographs of the ransom notes, at first I believed it was his trouble with the English language. Then I suddenly remembered the note you sent, asking to see me. You did not write like that before the war."

"You remembered my writing?"

"Don't flatter yourself, Mr. Mudd. Your essays, the few you managed to complete, are still on file. I pulled them for analysis."

The memory of being gassed left Grover Mudd devoid of wisecracks. Suddenly the professor's theories began to make some sense. Walt Howard was constantly badgering his star reporter about his poor spelling. His missing words. "*Where in hell did you learn how to write, Mudd?*"

On a dirt path above the river two university athletes, dressed only in shorts, sprinted past like Greek gods. Their golden bodies were being shaped and chiseled for the rousing season of football that lay ahead.

Dr. Schnacky softened his tone. "It's important the suspect be arrested away from his home, out on the street, because he'll be carrying a ransom bill on his person. He carries one with him at all times. That way whenever the opportunity presents itself, he can convert it to clean money. He folds the ransom bills in a distinct manner, so that they can be readily distinguished from his other money. But more important, I believe, he carries a ransom bill with him to remind him of his great crime, of his power over Colonel

Charles Lindbergh. Every shred of evidence is important, because this man will never confess. The more you confront him with evidence of his guilt, the louder he will scream his innocence."

Grover watched the two athletes disappear around a bend in the river, carrying with them the sunshine that glistened on their backs. He played his trump card. "I have reason to believe our kidnapper had a female accomplice."

Now it was Dr. Schnacky's turn to laugh. "Sorry, Mr. Mudd, but as you newspapermen would say, 'I'm not buying it.' He acted alone."

Grover boarded an east-bound trolley headed out University Avenue. He still had to stop at Montgomery Ward and pick up a birthday present for his daughter. But he left the university feeling uneasy. If the renowned Dr. Schnacky was to be believed, the man who had kidnapped the Lindbergh baby bore a striking resemblance to Grover Mudd. Grover wiped the sweat from his brow, the dust from his eyes. Thank God he didn't live in New Jersey. He'd be under arrest by now.

The wounded veteran found a window seat near the rear. He searched the car for any mysterious characters. Grover Mudd, forever looking over his shoulder. When he felt comfortable, he lifted a newspaper clipping from his shirt pocket. It was a photograph of Anne Morrow Lindbergh, which he examined self-consciously. Then he carefully slipped the photo back into his shirt pocket, directly over his heart. Grover pulled the gold certificate from his trouser pocket. Noted the way Esther Snow had folded it. Three times. Lengthwise first. Eight sections. He thought about the things the professor had told him, substituting just one key word.

"She carries one with her at all times. That way whenever the opportunity presents itself, she can convert it to clean money. She folds the ransom bills in a distinct manner, so that they can be readily distinguished from her other money."

But still the pieces would not fit. Was Esther Snow gassed? Did she have signs of a marked tremor in her handwriting? Were her real initials *B-R-H*? She sure as hell wasn't a carpenter. The reporter laughed aloud at the thought of the shapely German girl with the *Fire and Ice* fingernails pounding together a wooden ladder. But his laughter was cut short by a hacking cough that ripped through his lungs and tore up his throat. Now other passengers were staring at him. Using the sleeve of his shirt, Grover wiped away his spit. Then he closed his eyes and cursed the blistering heat as the trolley rolled down University Avenue.

"She carries a ransom bill with her to remind her of her great crime, of her power over Colonel Charles Lindbergh. Every shred of evidence is important, because this woman will never confess. The more you confront her with evidence of her guilt, the louder she will scream her innocence."

Myslivecek

The sun had finally set on yet another sizzling day: 94°. Grover Mudd was nursing a whiskey at Bo Kelly's place, a speakeasy on Seven Corners. Before Prohibition it was a tavern and a reporters' hangout. Things hadn't changed much with passage of the Eighteenth Amendment. Since the father of Prohibition, Minnesota Congressman Andrew Volstead, had his office in the federal courthouse right across the street, the proprietor thought it might be a good idea to board up the windows. The sign out front was taken down. Other than that, it was still Bo Kelly's. Above the bar hung a huge painting of blood-red Lucifer, pitchfork in hand. He bore a striking resemblance to the two detectives who marched through the door. Made their way to Grover.

"Hello, Mudd."

"Hello, dick." Grover had a way of saying hello so that the *D* in Dick was not capitalized. He noticed Myslivecek had a copy of the *Frontier News* stuffed under his arm.

Dick Myslivecek, a big round cop with an unpronounceable name, was a former police chief. Now he was an assistant police chief. In the press room Assistant Chief Richard Myslivecek was shortened to Ass Chief Dick Head. The veteran reporters shortened it even more. Over the years the fat Czech had gone from Officer Dick Head to Chief Dick Head. Now he was working his way back down. "I'm guessing that's soda pop in that glass," Myslivecek said to Grover.

"It sure is, dick, and the moon is made of green cheese."

In St. Paul the office of police chief was a political appointment. The top cop was handpicked by the mayor and removed by the mayor. With a mayoral election every two years, St. Paul had been cursed with twenty-four police chiefs in the past twenty years. Under civil service rules these police chiefs could not be fired. So they were simply demoted. St. Paul had more ex-police chiefs than most towns have police. Every officer in the higher ranks had a goon in plainclothes who followed him around. Brainless muscle. Myslivecek's muscle was named Wally. The muscle man grabbed Grover's drink from his hand. Tried a swig. "That's not soda pop, Chief. I think it's whiskey."

Grover wiped the perspiration from his bruised and battered face. It had been a long, hot day. He wasn't in the mood for this crap. He just wanted a quiet drink. Catch the streetcar home. Maybe sleep late in the morning. "You owe me a drink, dick."

Myslivecek laid the *Frontier News* on the bar, the newspaper open to Grover's follow-up piece on the streetcar attack. The article went on to castigate the St. Paul Police Department as "worthless" when it came to catching criminals. Even seven-foot criminals wearing a neck brace that said "arrest me" were invisible to St. Paul cops, it said. Grover had also included a few choice words about the release of Esther Snow. He had crossed the line into editorializing. Shades of columns to come.

"Tell you what I'm going to do, Mudd . . . you empty your pockets onto this rag here, and if you've got less than twenty bucks on you . . . I'll buy you that drink."

Grover, well aware of what kind of money he was carrying in his pocket, kept both his hands on the bar. But then big Wally poked him in the ribs with a finger that was hard as a gun barrel.

"Empty 'em, Mudd." Grover, angry now, dug into his pockets. Slammed his cash on the bar.

"What's this, Mudd?" Myslivecek asked.

"Looks like a twenty-dollar bill to me," Grover answered.

"Looks like a gold certificate to me."

"It was still legal tender last time I checked."

"Last time I checked we had a flyer on these honeys." The assistant police chief examined the gold note more closely. "Yes sir, said right on it, watch for the bills with the little yellow seal on 'em. Especially the twenties." He showed it to his lackey. "Is that a gold twenty, Wally?"

"That's a gold twenty, Chief."

"This is a gold twenty, Mudd. Where'd you get it?"

Grover shrugged his wide shoulders. "Must have been in the change they gave me when I bought those two tickets to the policemen's ball."

Myslivecek laughed, a mean, nasty laugh. "I got to check this note with my list, Mudd." Then a troubled expression crossed his chubby face. "Seems I might have you on some serious charges."

Grover Mudd rolled his eyes. "What do you really want, Chief ?"

Myslivecek lowered his voice until it was barely audible. "I want you to walk out that door and get into the squad. I'm taking you down to the station house and running a check on the note here. And if it shows up on the list I think it's on, you're going to spend the rest of your life getting corn-holed in Leavenworth."

A black Hudson sedan was parked at the curb pointing the wrong way. Another detective was perched on the running board. When he saw his partners emerge with Grover Mudd in their hands, he reached over and pulled open the back door. More like a kidnapping than an arrest.

They moved out West Seventh Street to Smith Avenue, where they hung a left. Away from the station house. Grover, sitting erect and somewhat agitated in the backseat, was squished in the middle. Between a fat cop and a tall cop. Between a rock and a hard place.

He'd been caught red-handed with one of the hottest bills in America. The fat dick had come looking for it.

It was late. All of the windows in the squad were rolled down, allowing the steam off the pavement to roll in. Grover was sweating. The heat made his throat go dry. His lungs were catching fire. He knew how much trouble he was in. Smith Avenue led over the High Bridge. He choked down a nervous cough.

The tall, iron bridge was erected between two bluffs. It connected St. Paul to its wayward West Side, which was cut off from the rest of the city by a sharp bend in the river. There was no reason Grover could think of to be crossing to that side of the river. It only led out of town.

As they rolled onto the bridge Grover could see the dingy downtown lights off to his left. Beneath the High Bridge the tracks of the Great Northern Railroad followed the river, and just for a moment the engineer's son was reminded of his daddy bringing home the trains. Then about halfway across the long span the black sedan crossed the center line, slowed to a crawl and coasted along the sidewalk side of the bridge. In the shadows between two street lamps, the squad car rolled to a stop. One of the street lamps was out. They turned the engine off.

Every reporter in town had heard the stories about the bridge being a popular spot for eliciting confessions, but none of them had actually been witness to an interrogation.

"Where'd you get it?" Myslivecek asked, rolling his copy of the *Frontier News* into a club.

"What have I got?"

"It's ransom money from the kidnapping of the Lindbergh baby . . . but then you already knew that, didn't you?"

"Tell me more."

"Where'd you get it?"

"I came by it innocently through a Minneapolis bank."

Myslivecek crashed his elbow into Grover's temple. Grover doubled over, only to catch Officer Wally's knee in his forehead. It was like being sandwiched with bricks. The driver stepped out of the car and opened the back door. The three cops hauled Grover from the back seat and hurled him at a wrought-iron railing that narrowly protected pedestrians from the river below. They were two hundred feet above the water. About eighteen stories. Grover crashed into the rail and dropped to his knees. It wasn't as bad as being corn-holed in Leavenworth, but he knew he was in for one hell of a beating. How far would they dare go?

"Listen, you rummies," Grover managed to mutter, "this kind of shit might work in the movies, but . . ."

Grover felt the steel heel of a shoe slam into his kidney. It carried the pain of a gunshot. He slumped to the sidewalk.

Were these goons working for Esther Snow?

They kicked him in the pit of the stomach. Stomped on his head. He covered his face with his hands.

Or maybe they were just good and pissed off about his reporting.

They put the boot to him again. Grover deflected most of the kicks to his back and his shoulders. Then Myslivecek began beating him over the head with the *Frontier News*. Grover had never realized how much a newspaper could hurt.

Maybe, and this was a bit of a stretch, but just maybe these cops wanted to solve the Lindbergh kidnapping. Perhaps they innocently believed be really did have some of the answers.

But then their integrity as honest cops came into serious question. Wally and Myslivecek hoisted the newsman into the air by his clothes and heaved him headfirst over the bridge. Grover grabbed the bottom rung of the wrought iron railing and tried to push himself up, like a handstand, but the cops kept forcing him down, like a toilet plunger. Never before had he seen the mighty Mississippi River from this angle. It was a remarkable view, in a frightening sort of way. The water was black as coal and as daunting as the jaws of a shark. In all the stories he'd written about the suicides who'd thrown themselves from the bridge, he'd always wondered why they didn't just pop to the surface. Swim back to shore. Now he knew. From the High Bridge, the Father of Waters was the mother of all suicides. There could be no surviving such a spill.

Grover's stomach was in his throat. His eyes were

bulging from their sockets. He couldn't cry for help. He couldn't even breathe. If the cops were faking it, not really going to let him fall, it was one hell of an act.

Then Myslivecek was yelling at him. "You're a two-bit rumor-monger, Mudd. A washed-up reporter for a washed-up newspaper. My toilet paper has more use."

Grover was blacking out. He heard something about toilet paper and two-bit rumors just before they hauled his ass back over the rail. Next thing he knew they were slapping him to on the sidewalk. He had to look around to make sure he was still on the bridge. The three cops forced him to his feet. Back into the black Hudson he went. Headfirst. He was on the floor for this trip. All things considered, it was more comfortable than the ride out. At least he was lying down.

The son of a bitch Myslivecek was good to his Czech word. Grover Mudd was hauled down to the police station on Steep Street. Ordered to sit on a steel chair beneath a bare light bulb. Handed a glass of water and a soggy towel. He wiped his face while he waited. Sure as it snows, his gold certificate showed up on the Treasury Department's list of Lindbergh ransom bills.

"Book him, Wally."

Grover's fingerprints were inked for the record. He was cleaned up, then lined up in front of a camera where his mug was shot twice for posterity. Front and side. He spent the rest of the night in a jail cell. Tried to sleep on a mattress stained with urine. At five in the morning, just as dawn was breaking, Grover was kicked awake. During the night all charges had been dropped. Lack of evidence. His gold certificate was confiscated. He was free to go. Standing in the morning light of Steep Street the former Marine Corps officer and Great War veteran had a bitter laugh, and a nasty cough, at his new place in American history. For one hot summer night he was a bona fide suspect in the kidnapping and murder of the Lindbergh baby.

Grover Mudd spit blood onto the sidewalk in front of the police station. He wiped his mouth clean and started up the hill for the paper.

Fuzzy

In the past few days his head had taken more hits than a baseball. Three of St. Paul's finest had dangled his reporter's ass from the tallest bridge west of Brooklyn. A seven-foot spook had tried to decapitate him in a streetcar. As if that weren't enough, the weather was still trying to kill him. The mercury shot right past 90, headed for 100. It was in the middle of this reign of heat and terror that Grover Mudd was to begin writing a daily column for the *St. Paul Frontier News*. But as he studied all of the crimes in all of the news articles that were tacked to the wall above his desk, none of the atrocities could long divert his attention from the grainy photograph of Anne Morrow Lindbergh.

"Who was the first child kidnapped for ransom in America?" Fuzzy Byron asked, fairly sober. The part-time copy boy, and full-time wino, was seated on a stack of newspapers piled high on the office floor.

"Let's see," said Grover, removing his necktie and rolling up his sleeves. "That would have been poor little Charlie Ross. In Philadelphia . . . 1874, 1 believe it was. Before that the crime was almost unheard of in the United States."

On the afternoon of July 1, 1874, four-year-old Charlie Ross disappeared from the front of his house in the exclusive Germantown neighborhood of Philadelphia. Charlie's father, Christian K. Ross, was a wealthy retail merchant. After two days of frantic searching for his lost son, he received the first in a long series of bizarre letters.

> Be not uneasy you son Charlie be all writ we is got him an no powers on earth can deliver out of our hand. you will have to pay us a big mony if you regard his lif . . .

The story soon leaked to the newspapers, and all across America poor little Charlie Ross became a household name. But the publicity only complicated negotiations with the kidnappers. On July 6, they sent a second note demanding $20,000.

> If yu love money more than child yu be its murderer not us . . . if we get money yu get him live if no money yu get him ded.

But look at the two ransom notes. In the first note the word "you" is spelled properly throughout. In the second note it is consistently misspelled. The reverse happens with the word "money." Philadelphia police and the Pinkerton Detective Agency quickly surmised the mistakes were intentional, that the kidnappers were hardly the illiterates they pretended to be.

Up in New York City the chief of police had an even keener observation. The only person who could pull off a kidnap for ransom would be a cop. Acting on a tip, New York detectives soon matched the handwriting in the note to a local burglar named William Mosher. Mosher's brother-in-law was a New York policeman named William Westerveldt. The two men commonly worked with another burglar named Joseph Douglas. Over the next four months the police and the Pinkertons set several traps for the trio of kidnappers, but they never showed their faces. In December, burglars Mosher and Douglas were shot and killed during a burglary in Brooklyn. Douglas confessed to the kidnapping before he died. Officer Westerveldt was arrested and convicted of conspiracy and extortion in the disappearance of Charlie Ross. He served seven years in prison, but he never revealed the whereabouts of the missing child. Christian K. Ross and the boy's mother spent the rest of their lives searching for their kidnapped son, but poor little Charlie Ross, America's first kidnap victim, had vanished from the face of the earth. And it was never learned what became of him.

Fuzzy Byron stared into the rays of hot sun streaming through the dirty glass. "But the Lindbergh case is different," he said. "The ransom was exchanged. The baby's body was found. Why no arrest?"

Grover Mudd and an entire nation were pondering the same question. Grover tried to stitch it all together. "What if two people had so much evil in common, they actually thought as one? That would fit Dr. Schnacky's 'lone man' theory that I told you about. Think about it . . . there were three men in on the kidnapping of Charlie Ross, right? And it was two men who grabbed Bobby Franks . . ."

By the time the Lindbergh baby was snatched, the world had long forgotten about poor little Charlie Ross. For an entirely new generation the crime of kidnapping was associated with a rich little Chicago boy named Bobby Franks. But this boy's abduction and murder was so notorious, so contemptible, that the names of the kidnappers became better known than that of their victim. Their names were Leopold and Loeb.

By the age of eighteen Nathan F. Leopold Jr. had graduated from the University of Chicago. He had an IQ near 200. At age seventeen Richard A. "Dickie" Loeb graduated from the University of Michigan. They were children of immense wealth, but social misfits. Homosexual lovers. Brilliant students. Moral imbeciles. On the afternoon of May 21, 1924, this pair of geniuses set out in a rented sedan to test German philosopher Friedrich Nietzsche's concept of the superman. They would use their superior intellects to commit the perfect crime. The supreme thrill. Murder. Then they would mock authorities by sending a ransom note and collecting money for a victim who was already dead. Shortly before the abduction Loeb wrote Leopold the following note:

> The superman is not liable for anything he may do, except for the one crime that it is possible for him to commit—to make a mistake.

So cold was their disregard for human life that on the afternoon of the abduction they had yet to select a victim. They were driving around their fashionable Hyde Park neighborhood for an hour when the Harvard Preparatory School let out for the day. Fourteen-year-old Bobby Franks was walking home. Leopold and Loeb pulled alongside. Loeb knew the boy from tennis and said that if Bobby wanted a ride home, he had a new racket to show him. Bobby Franks climbed into the backseat. Richard Loeb got in beside him. They hadn't driven very far when Loeb grabbed a chisel and violently stabbed Bobby Franks in the head four times. At nightfall they drove to the edge of a swamp on the outskirts of town. Leopold and Loeb stripped the boy of his clothes and poured hydrochloric acid over his face. Then they dragged his body to a culvert, but in doing so the two intellects made the first in a series of stupid mistakes in their so-called perfect crime. When Leopold removed his coat to stuff the body into a drain pipe, his eyeglasses fell from his coat pocket and landed on the ground near their victim.

A railroad worker found the body of Bobby Franks the very next morning. Police found the eyeglasses. By the time the first ransom note arrived at the Franks' house, Jacob Franks, a multimillionaire box manufacturer, already knew that his beloved son had been bludgeoned to death. And so did the newspapers.

The eyeglasses were special order. Only three pair had been sold. One of them had been sold to Nathan Leopold. After a night of interrogation by cops a lot smarter than the two supermen, Leopold and Loeb signed full confessions.

"What if . . ." Grover asked, "what if the Lindbergh baby was stolen by a lone man, and a lone woman? Like Leopold and Loeb, but different, more as one. Sounds strange . . . but let's go over this one more time." He swung around in his chair to face Fuzzy. "Doctor Schnacky says the man's initials are BRH."

Fuzzy leaned forward to catch the breeze of the whirling fan. "Esther has a friend in New York named Richard."

"But Schnacky seemed convinced the *R* was his middle initial."

"Though not necessarily," Fuzzy reminded him.

"Schnacky says the man was gassed, like me."

"Esther says Richard has a cough, like yours."

Grover Mudd wiped the perspiration from his face. "She has the personality for it, but what if she didn't do it? What if *that* was Esther's game . . . to lead men to believe she was involved in this crime or that crime, the more sensational the better?"

"Esther Snow got caught twice with Lindbergh ransom money. Once by the cops, once by you. And may I remind you, my friend, that several people are trying to kill you."

In his heart Grover knew there weren't several people trying to kill him. There was only one. Esther Snow wanted to raise the stakes. The beat-up reporter pushed out of his chair and limped over to the open window. Grover Mudd badly wanted a drink, but the whiskey would have to wait. He turned to his partner in crime. "You're a wise man, Fuzzy. Is there any doubt in your mind that Esther Snow came to St. Paul to wash money from the Lindbergh kidnapping?"

"I was a wise man, many years ago," Fuzzy told him. "Now I'm blind as a bat. Most of the time, drunk as a skunk. But I can see this, Grover . . . Esther Snow is up to her pretty little neck in the Lindbergh kidnapping. And you may be the only man willing to prove it."

Big Fellow

Esther Snow had a corner table overlooking the stage that overlooked the dance floor. A colossal chandelier, with lights flashing a rainbow of colors, hung over her. The Hollyhocks Club was packed. Stripper Sally Rand was to be featured at midnight, performing one of her famous fan dances. Up on stage Fats Waller was on the piano wailing, "Ain't Misbehavin." Waller's music and slap-happy style brought a smile to every crook in the place. Freddie Barker and creepy Alvin Karpis were there. St. Paul was their favorite city. George "Machine Gun Kelly" Barnes was there along with his lovely wife, Kathryn. So was famed bank robber Frank "Jelly" Nash, as well as Al Capone's enforcer, Fred Goetz, alias "Shotgun" George Zeigler. Shotgun George was best known as the mastermind and executioner of Chicago's St. Valentine's Day Massacre.

Esther Snow was enjoying the headline-making company. She was enjoying the excellent music and a fine glass of champagne. In fact the only thing she wasn't enjoying about St. Paul was the damn newspaper. The illegal immigrant from Germany had the *Frontier News* folded to the back page. Circled in a corner was a piece by Grover Mudd. Straining her eyes in the rainbow of lights beneath the chandelier, she sipped her champagne and read the article one more time.

DID A WOMAN KIDNAP THE LINDBERGH BABY?

by

Grover Mudd

First off, let's do away with the myths. The Lindbergh baby was not kidnapped by a gang. Any of our local yokel mobsters will tell you the minimum ransom for a snatch like that would be two hundred thousand dollars—not a measly fifty. Besides, mobsters have ethics. They don't kidnap rich children. They kidnap rich children's fathers.

There is another theory circulating in police circles, only this theory has the added weight of one of America's top psychiatrists. He calls it the "lone man theory." In his scenario a real nut case acted totally alone to kidnap the kid. He's even drawn up a profile of this kidnapper. Boils down to a little German fellow who thinks he's God. Seems to be a lot of that going around these days.

But there's another theory out there. Let's call it the "lone man theory—plus one." This theory holds that it was indeed a man who climbed the ladder that rainy night last March—but waiting for him at the bottom of that ladder was a woman. A man would have kidnapped Charles Lindbergh, not Charles Lindbergh Jr. This crime has female written all over it.

By coincidence, a woman was recently arrested here in St. Paul for spending a ransom bill from the Lindbergh kidnapping. But she batted her eyelashes and the cops let her go.

Let me draw a profile of the woman involved in the Lindbergh kidnapping. For starters, she's knockdead gorgeous. She's an illegal immigrant who has come to the land of the free to be whoever she wants to be. Change her name. Change her looks. Change everything but her ways. She's a smart woman. The first thing she did after the ransom was paid was flee New York. The second thing she did was come to St. Paul. She knows the fix is in here with the cops.

Why did she choose Charles Lindbergh to be her victim?

Because this is a woman who detests men, especially the smart ones. The admired. The decorated. The heroes. Not only will she eventually outsmart them. She will, in the end, humiliate them. If that doesn't work, she will kill them. The issue with her is not money. The issue is power.

It was this woman, a woman in love with the idea of power, who is responsible for the death of the Lindbergh baby. And she may be right here in St. Paul.

"Interesting reading, isn't it, Esther." Assistant Chief Richard Myslivecek wheezed into the chair beside her. "I mean, it's more editorial than news." His girth filled the entire chair, blocked her view of the other patrons. He unbuttoned his coat so that his pistol was showing. Scratched his belly. The sweaty tuxedo made him look like a giant penguin just out of water. "Word is, the

Frontier News is going to give Mudd his own column. Another Walter Winchell. Be shooting his mouth off every day."

Esther Snow folded the newspaper. "Yes, it is interesting, considering the man who wrote the piece is supposed to be dead."

Myslivecek yawned, a long, phony yawn. "We kill a gangster . . . we look good. We kill a cop . . . we control the investigation. We kill a reporter, especially a crime reporter . . . all hell breaks loose. Not smart. We've got no control over the newspapers."

"This is one part of America I do not understand."

"What part is that?"

"The newspaper part."

"They keep us honest . . . and besides, the funnies are great."

A waiter rushed over to serve the giant cop. Myslivecek ordered a ginger ale with a shot of bourbon. A round of applause erupted for Fats Waller and his band. Then the jazz stride pianist was singing "Black and Blue."

"What would be his editor's name?" Esther asked.

"It would be Walt Howard," the cop said, mimicking the woman. "A real square shooter. Straight as an arrow."

"Is this square shooter married?"

The waiter returned. Set the ginger ale and bourbon in front of the man who once ran the entire police department. "Walt Howard? Yes, but I understand his wife is in and out of the hospital a lot."

Esther Snow gestured toward Grover's column. "What are you going to do about this?"

The big Czech didn't bat an eye. Kept the smile on his face as he swayed to the music. "Run you out of town."

"I beg your pardon?" Esther could not believe what she had just heard.

"Look, lady," Myslivecek explained over the music, "I don't know if you were in on the Lindbergh snatch, and I don't care. We got a sweet thing going here in St. Paul. Ain't nobody in this town going to touch Lindbergh money." He leaned into her face, crossed a line Esther Snow didn't want crossed. He talked soft, but serious. "There's only one thing the gangs in this town fear. The Feds. The Feds are the only ones with the resources to keep up the chase. So far, they ain't been much of a factor here . . . not like in Chicago. But Feds are like grasshoppers. They start out a pest, then turn into a swarm."

He came even closer. Close enough to steal a kiss. "Blondie, you ain't as safe here as you think. Too much pressure comes down, lot of the boys here be willing to turn you in . . . or maybe do you in. You might want to think about getting out of town for a week or two. Let Grover Mudd make his next move . . . see what he stirs up."

Then the round, red face of the crooked cop lit up, as if the idea had just popped into his head. "So happens, I got a cabin up north. Big place. Real nice. I had a player piano brought in by boat. Thirty-five miles of water before you even reach sight of it. It's raid proof. Some real good fishing. It's pretty up there. You'd like it."

"Where is Little Falls, Minnesota?"

Myslivecek seemed surprised, like she wasn't catching his drift. Esther Snow also noticed the cop had yet to touch his drink. She slipped open her purse.

"It's up the river," he answered, more than a bit miffed.

"I'd like to see it."

"What the hell for? Ain't nothing up there."

Esther suddenly smiled. Pointed across the room. "Is that Clark Gable, from the movies? I love him."

Myslivecek swung his fat frame around in the chair. "Is he in town? Where?"

"Do you know him?" Esther asked.

Myslivecek was straining his thick neck to peer through the crowd. "Sure, I know Clark. He likes to fish up in Brainerd. I don't see him."

Esther laughed, her foolish, little laugh. "I guess it wasn't him."

The cop eased his fat ass back into a comfortable position. Rested his suspicious gaze upon the sparkling blue eyes of Esther Snow.

"You ain't going to Little Falls, Esther. You're going exactly where I tell you to go. That is, if you want to get out of this town alive. Is that understood?"

Fats Waller wrapped up his set to thunderous applause. The master of ceremonies bounded on stage to introduce the next act, a buxom stripper hired to warm up the crowd for Sally Rand. Another man replaced Fats Waller at the piano. The show began.

Esther Snow feigned hurt. A shadow of defeat crept into her eyes. A lone dark tear, right on cue, rolled down her pure Aryan cheekbone. "I have to powder my nose," she sniffled.

Dick Myslivecek reached for his drink. "You go right ahead, Esther Snow. Powder your pretty little nose." Then he raised his glass in salute. "Here's Mudd in your eye."

They were the last words out of his mouth.

Miss-liv-e-check. The name means "small game hunter." The assistant chief was proud of that. He was born for detective work. The big Czech began his career under Chief O'Connor. It was the Big Fellow himself who taught him his craft. Together they'd solved a lot of mysteries over the years. Now this. Grover Mudd wasn't the only person in town suspicious of the German beauty. What if Esther Snow really *was* in on the Lindbergh snatch? The crime of the century would also be the arrest of the century. Solve this mystery and he'd once again be chief of police. Hell, he'd be elected governor.

The rotund policeman sat back in his chair and rested his hands over his ample belly. Up on stage the zaftig girl began her act. Note by note, piece by piece her clothes went flying through the air. The joint was howling.

Myslivecek now had two ransom bills from the

Lindbergh kidnapping in his possession. One he'd taken off Esther Snow at the department store, and the other he took off Grover Mudd. But there were problems. Two of them. He'd already publicly swallowed Esther Snow's sob story about getting the gold certificate from a Minneapolis bank. And Grover Mudd wouldn't admit that his note came from Esther Snow—though Myslivecek knew damn well that it had. If he was going to make the arrest of his life, he was going to need a lot more dope on the mysterious woman. But first things first. He glanced over his shoulder at the powder room. The detective was going to make damn sure she gave him the fuck of his life. Esther Snow in the north woods.

The lace brassiere came off the stripper. The Hollyhocks Club was roaring.

Dick Myslivecek finished his drink. Almost gagged. It tasted like poison. That was the problem with Prohibition, you never knew if the moonshine you were getting was good or bad. Not even at a class joint like the Hollyhocks. He reached for Esther's champagne. Gulped it down.

The stripper had her thumbs in her panties. Her tits were bouncing around stage like ripe melons. Myslivecek was getting hot. For several reasons. First off, the strippers had been warned about going too far. Anything below the waist was too far. This town had morals, and damned if the assistant police chief wouldn't enforce them. She inched her panties over her thigh. Myslivecek's dick was rising. He began sweating profusely. The place was packed. The humidity was hell. He couldn't wait for the cool of autumn. The stripper turned her back to the audience and one of her buns toppled out. Myslivecek was never so horny in his life. Never so angry. He was going to arrest the wench. Right after the show. Then her other bun popped out. Her bare ass was showing. Full moon. The big peach. The crowd was ecstatic. Dick Myslivecek had never seen anything like it. And just when the volcanic cop felt like he was going to explode, he did.

He began by coming in his pants. He jammed his fist into his crotch. Now he was urinating. Then his stomach cramped, the way a gut wound would feel. The fat cop doubled over. Tried to scream. He flew out of his chair, clutching his throat and knocking over the table. Patrons were stunned. Then suddenly they were screaming at the sight of his face. Myslivecek heard a gurgling noise in his ears. Saw a white foam spewing from his lips. He tried so hard to scream he spit up a stream of blood. Half the people around him were rushing to help, the other half were fighting to get out of his line of fire. Blood-soaked spitballs were shooting from his mouth. Some of the toughest gangsters in the country were gagging.

Myslivecek was forced back into his chair. He fought like a bull to stand, but the Hollyhocks waiters were holding him down. The pain was excruciating. Humiliating. He soiled his pants. Then a pair of beautiful tits was staring him in the face. The woman he wanted to arrest for indecent exposure was holding her panties with one hand and her nose with the other. "Pew! What did this pig eat?"

Finally, at death's door, the lifelong detective put it all together.

"Is that Clark Gable over there?"

The sultry German had slipped the big Czech the mother of all Mickey Finns. Cyanide chloride, commonly used to clean silver. The remaining undissolved crystals had spilled onto the dance floor along with his drink. The rainbow lights from the chandelier made the white crystals twinkle like heavenly stars. It was as close to heaven as the St. Paul detective would get. Assistant Police Chief Richard Myslivecek had solved his last murder. His own.

Eddie

It was a spooky old bridge that creaked with the wind. Robbed you of your balance. A tornado had once torn it in two. The city propped it back up. The wood planks of the walkway were weatherbeaten. Splintered. Full of gaps. The wrought-iron railing along the walk where the cops had dangled his head over the black water was rusting and loose. Stealing across the High Bridge, Grover Mudd kept his nose high in the night air, because with every step he could see that mean Mississippi River far beneath his feet sloshing against the piers.

He found the spot. At mid-bridge, the street lamp was still out, creating a long stretch of darkness. Nightmarish. The whole frigging span, from bluff to bluff, gave him the heebie-jeebies—dark, unpleasant memories that left him in vengeful spirits. Grover waited. He popped a Lucky Strike between his lips and fumbled for a match, recalling his conversation with the bartender at the Green Lantern Saloon the afternoon Myslivecek's fat ass was laid to rest.

"What's news, Eddie?"

"You write the damn newspaper, you tell me."

Grover shot his whiskey. Cleared his throat and signaled for another. "Says her name is Esther Snow. German gal. Lives up on Grand. She's in from New York."

Eddie's crooked face grimaced at the sound of the name. "Killer blonde," he said. "Says she's got some bills to move, but she never puts up."

"What's the going rate on stolen bills these days?"

Eddie shrugged his shoulders. Poured Grover another drink. "Depends on what you're peddling."

"Gold certificates."

"Tough ones. Nice to have, hard to fence. Forty to sixty cents on the dollar, depending on how hot they are."

Grover Mudd chucked another drink. "Let's just suppose the kidnappers of the Lindbergh kid chose to wash their ransom money here in our fair city. What do you think they'd get for that kind of money?"

"Squat," Eddie told him, "that's what they'd get here. That money comes from a dead baby. Nobody in this town would do something like that."

"Not even Esther Snow? Word on the street is, she mixes a killer martini."

Eddie, an ex-boxer, leaned over the bar. The words spilling from the corner of his crooked mouth were soft, but intense. Near fear. "Thing is, Grover, people are scared of her. She ain't just bad . . . she's evil. What if she did poison Myslivecek? What if she hired some palooka to take your head off in that streetcar?"

"You heard about that, huh?"

"Yeah, I heard. I also heard about your ass dangling from the High Bridge. Let's say she was behind all them things . . . and the Lindbergh snatch, to boot. That would make her the most unholy character to ever hit this town. I just hope she stays the hell out of here."

"Can you get a message to her?"

Eddie glanced over his shoulder. "I'll put out you're asking to see her. Might take a few days. Word is, she's laying low up in Little Falls. Stop back in."

Grover was shocked. "Little Falls?"

The apex of the High Bridge may have been the coolest place in a hot town. The breeze off the water carried the aroma of autumn, with a wisp of winter. The great church on the hill was ablaze in lights. The mansions that straddled the bluffs along Summit Avenue were ablaze with life, the rich going about their parties as though the city's problems were not their problems. Cloud to cloud lightning flashed in the sky, but far to the east. A cleansing shower had again passed them by. The intrepid reporter blew a stream of smoke into the summer breeze. Checked his watch.

His children came to mind. They were on his mind the night he was attacked on the streetcar. They flashed across Grover's eyes the night the cops wrestled him onto this bridge. It was fair to say that his daughter and his baby son would be the last two thoughts he ever entertained on this earth. He was growing particularly fond of his little girl. She never seemed more happy than when she was riding the streetcars with her daddy. They could live without him; they'd already proved that. But how do parents go on living without their children? How were the Lindberghs to cope with such a loss?

More and more, Grover Mudd believed in his heart he had one of the answers. Bring the kidnappers to justice. To date, Dr. Schnacky had been right about everything except the kidnapper's sex. Square pegs. Round holes.

"She would be very methodical and extremely cautious, with full confidence in herself but no real confidence in those close to her. This caution would make it very difficult to apprehend her since, considering everybody an enemy, she would be constantly on guard."

Grover never saw the car that dropped her off. Never saw the shadow she emerged from. She just appeared at the high end of the bridge, like a ghost, walking his way. It was Esther Snow, all right. She had that fearless gait. That gorgeous figure. She was alone. Meeting a man who hated her guts in the middle of a tall bridge, in the middle of the night, didn't seem to bother her one bit.

As she came closer, Grover could see a string of pearls bridging a low neckline. The long sheath dress she wore was formal, black as the night. Her scarf, white as new-fallen snow. It was the kind of outfit a society dame would wear to a fancy club. Esther Snow strolled straight up to his face. Stopped and fished a cigarette from her bag. "Do you have a light?"

Grover struck a match. In the glow of the fire he was once again awed by her spectral beauty. Her smoky voice. Smoke from hell. "I heard you wanted to see me."

"How was Little Falls?" Grover asked.

"Little. It reminded me of my home as a child in Germany."

"What did you think of the water tower?"

"What water tower?"

"The one that has 'Home of Charles Lindbergh' painted on it."

"I took no notice."

"Tell me, Esther . . . what is it about Lindbergh you hate . . . no, better yet . . . what is it about this country you hate? I know you're a damn Nazi."

"Always with the questions. American newsmen. Take, take, take . . . and they give us nothing. Why do you do it?"

Grover flicked his cigarette butt to the river below. Fished out another. Took his time lighting it. The evil bitch wanted to play games. He looked out over the city. His city. Small, provincial St. Paul. "Sometimes," he said, "I think all that you can do is take care of your little corner of the world. You're standing on my corner."

"Tell me, do you read poetry, Mr. Mudd?"

"Just the stuff on toilet stalls."

She laughed, but it was a forced laugh. "I have become particularly fond of an American poet . . . Conrad Aiken. Have you heard of him?"

"He won a Pulitzer Prize for something or other. Don't know his work."

Esther Snow held her head high and waxed poetic over the river, as if the High Bridge were a stage. "*Ah, but just wait! Wait till we are alone together! Then I will begin to tell you something new! Something white! Something cold! Something sleepy! Something of cease, and peace, and the long bright curve of space.*"

"Yes, that's very pretty, Esther honey, but just tell me something about your friend Richard . . . the friend with the cough like mine."

"What is to tell . . . he lives in New York."

"Where in New York?"

"The Bronx."

"Surprise, surprise . . . tell me more."

"What is more to tell?"

"Is he German?"

"Yes."

"Does he speak English?"

"Not well."

"Does he enjoy climbing ladders?"

"You know, now that you mention it . . . he does enjoy carpenter work."

"How did the baby die?" Grover asked.

"And what baby would that be?"

"The baby in New Jersey. Anne Lindbergh's baby."

Esther paused. Smiled that wicked but alluring smile of hers, as if she'd just learned a secret. "You have fallen in love with her . . . have you not?"

"Fallen in love with who?" Grover demanded to know.

"With the Lindbergh woman." Again she smiled, just short of a smirk. "And all of this time I thought that your affection was being saved for me."

"You're a sick soul, you know that."

"I am sick, you say? You fall in love with a picture in your newspaper . . . and you say I am sick."

"Tell me about the kidnapping."

"I tell you, Grover Mudd, the same thing I tell your police. I know of no babies in New Jersey. I got the gold bills from a bank in Minneapolis where I go to cash a check."

"Was that check from Richard?" Again, she turned cold as ice. In the dark of night, her eyes were more green than blue. Grover pointed across the river. "The day they brought you in . . . what was the name of the cop who questioned you at the station house?"

"It was Polish name, or Czech . . . I could not pronounce it."

Grover enjoyed a good, sarcastic laugh. "How do you do it, Esther . . . control men like that . . . kill men like that . . . cops, crooks, crooked cops?"

"Men want only two things . . . sex and money. And they only want more money so they can have more sex. When I have to, I can offer both. What is it I can offer you?"

"The quid pro quo being . . . ?"

"Do not write about me anymore. I am shy."

"Yeah, you're shy like the Mata Hari."

"And do you think I could not control an American newspaperman?" Her sculpted face carved its own space in the night. Her hair seemed to glow in the dark. The breeze carried her perfume into his face. "Are you a real man, Grover Mudd? Or did you maybe lose your manhood in the war? I have seen such wounds, you know. It hangs between the legs, but it serves no purpose."

Grover turned white. "You two-bit lousy whore." He raised his hand to strike her, then thought better of it.

"Are you going to kill me, Grover Mudd? Throw me from the big bridge? Is that why we meet here?"

"Isn't that what you paid to have done to me . . . or were they just supposed to scare me?"

"No, they were supposed to drop you."

Grover tossed his smoke and smacked her hard across the face. Her cigarette went flying from her mouth, the lighted end falling like a star to the black water below.

She shook the hair from her eyes. Checked her lips for blood. Found none. She pulled out another cigarette. "You roar like the lion, but you are only the kitten chasing his tail. Do you really believe that I am afraid of you?"

Grover knocked the new cigarette from her hand. "Yes, you're afraid I can get you deported." He watched her for a reaction. But there was none. The ice queen.

"Still, did you not lure me to the dark bridge to at

least have your way with me?" She hoisted herself up to the loose railing. Sat there straddling it. Perfectly balanced, her ankles crossed, her toes pointed outward. The prima ballerina. The push of a finger would send her toppling backward into the Mississippi River.

Grover stuck his finger into her face. "I lured you to the bridge for some answers."

Esther threw back her head. Addressed the stars in the sky. *"It was as if, in some delightful way, his secret gave him a fortress, a wall behind which he could retreat into heavenly seclusion."*

Again with the poetry. Grover inched forward. "If you're harboring the secret I think you're harboring, you're going to burn in hell, Esther Snow."

"And knowing that, what have I left to lose?"

"Your life. We harbor killers here in Minnesota, but in the state of New Jersey they electrocute them. Strap them into a chair and throw the switch."

She dropped her head. Stared him seductively in the eye. "Come now, Grover Mudd. Show me how it is done here in the great Middle West." Esther Snow swayed with the wind, so graceful there were times she seemed to be defying the laws of gravity. Any mortal woman would have fallen into the drink.

"Get off the rail," he ordered.

Esther Snow dropped her heels. Dangled her long legs before him. Ran a toe up the inside seam of his trousers. "There is an old English word made more popular here in America. The word is 'fuck.' Sadly, there is no translation to German."

The whores in Europe had said the word joyfully. Playfully. Sometimes, in need of food, desperately. But Esther Snow was mocking him.

"It is the kind of word you can only use with a woman you love, or a woman you do not know. Fuck me, Grover. Here. Now." The more she spoke, and the more seductive she became, the more the German crept back into her accent. "Would you like me to turn around for you? Spread apart my legs? Close my eyes?" Esther Snow slid off the railing. Turned her back to Grover Mudd. Stood over the railing with her long, slender legs spread slightly apart. "Come now, Grover Mudd, pretend I am the Lindbergh woman."

It was too much. Grover wanted to grab hold of her gorgeous legs and flip her over the railing. Watch her fall. Watch her tumble and scream to the water below. He wanted to stare into her eyes as she met death.

Instead, he spun the German beauty around and grabbed her long, white-blond curls with both his fists. He pulled her face so close to his they were sharing breath. She spit in his face.

Grover hit her again. And again. But she struck back. Her fingernails tearing the side of his face like a fork. Grover was furious. Murderous. His face was bleeding from where her nails had ripped open his skin. The blood had reached the corner of his mouth. His lungs were on fire, but the fires of passion were burning even hotter, hotter than Grover Mudd had ever dared to dream. And when it came to women, Grover Mudd dreamed a lot.

"Fuck me, Mr. Newspaperman. Do you know how?"

His hands had never brushed such fine hair. Such fine clothes. He ripped the dress from her shoulders, exposing both her breasts. They were perfectly rounded, flawless, with large dark nipples. When she saw that he'd gotten an eyeful, that he marveled at what he saw, she slapped him again. Caught him off guard. Sent his bleeding head reeling. He raised his arm to strike her, to knock that smug beauty right off her shoulders. But Esther Snow wouldn't cower. In fact she was smiling at him, that enchanting, accursed smile.

"Fuck me, newspaperman. Do you know how?"

He ripped her dress even further. Stripped her to the waist. Her stomach was smooth and as flat as batter. Her smoky voice was syrup.

"Do you know how?"

Grover Mudd snapped, decided then and there to fuck the German bitch. He lifted her high into the air. Again her backside was precariously balanced on the railing. Only this time she was counting on the newspaperman for support. The slightest nudge would send her reeling.

Grover ran his hands up the back of her dress, up the back of those long legs. He wasn't surprised to find her wearing no panties. Just garters and silk stockings. He stripped them from her legs.

It was all a nasty, violent game to Esther Snow, and she played it well. She wouldn't stop him from stripping her. Hell, she would help him. But whenever he paused to enjoy what he had uncovered, to touch her breasts, to taste her flesh, she would whack him upside the head. "Do you know how?"

Grover slapped her back. Harder and harder. He was practically beating her. He undid his pants only to find her helping him. Then, as he jammed it between her thighs, she hit him again, the hardest yet. "Do you know how?"

Grover was dizzy. Sick to his stomach. Hard as a rock. With no help from her, but with no opposition, he thrust his way inside of her. As deep as he could push it.

Esther Snow threw her arms around his neck. Ripped open the back of his shirt with her fingernails. Grover fucked her as hard as he'd ever fucked in his life, but there was no controlling the woman. She dragged her fingernails across his back until Grover could feel the skin opening. The blood running. He slammed her into the rail. Now her arms were dangling freely from the bridge. Her golden hair was waving over the water like a white flag. She was only a dick-length away from a watery grave, but she was laughing. Braying. An ecstatic cackle. How could something that tasted so sweet be so goddamned depraved?

Grover gripped her waist with both of his hands. Now he could have it both ways. Fuck her, then drop her. She had to know this. But she made no attempt to fight him. She was too busy enjoying the *friken* fuck.

Sooner or later it had to happen. A car was coming. And so was Grover. He could see the headlines in the *North Star Press.*

FRONTIER NEWS REPORTER NABBED ON HIGH BRIDGE
Grover Mudd Caught with Pants Down
Woman Believed Involved in Moonlight Encounter

The headlights fell over them. Illuminated her hair like a flaming torch. Highlighted the malicious joy in her face. Exposed her breasts to the light. Then the car horn exploded, same time as Grover. Esther Snow screamed with delight.

It was the fuck of his life, but his career as a crusading reporter was probably over. He would be exposed to the world as a fornicator. But then, like the two hate-filled lovers on the bridge, the car did not stop. Just kept on going. The red taillights fading away with the sounds. Another fucking night in St. Paul.

Grover Mudd and Esther Snow were left alone in the dark. Their fate consummated. Their passions drained. Their secret safe. Their hearts were torn in two opposing directions—opposites attracting, likes repelling—good and evil dangling from a bridge that dangled over a river that cut through the heart of a city.

Mudd

The summer of 1932 was fast rolling to a dry, dusty end. And the Lindbergh story, once hotter than the coals that burn in hell, was running out of steam. Walt Howard had taken a leave of absence. His wife was ill. The other editors rolled their collective eyes at the mention of the unsolved case. It wasn't that nobody cared, but in the newspaper world, stories have a life. Even the most sensational stories have to be constantly fed and nourished lest they wither away on the vine.

On the East Coast there was little left to report. Under pressure to cut the state payroll, the governor of New Jersey took advantage of the lull in Lindbergh news to lay off fifty state troopers. It was widely believed the kidnappers lived in New York City. Three overworked detectives there kept busy tracking the ransom bills that were turning up regularly, most of them in and around the Bronx. The FBI went back to chasing gangsters. The Secret Service went back to chasing bootleggers. All the city of St. Paul had on the

Lindbergh case was two ransom bills, and Esther Snow.

She had kissed him gently on the cheek that night. Then she'd walked away. Disappeared into the murky shadows of the High Bridge. Didn't say a word. Didn't have to. For in that one little kiss was an unapologetic admission of complicity. Conspiracy. It was the cold kiss of death. And it was a kiss good-bye.

In his mind's eye, Grover Mudd saw it all now. How she picked up the baby at the foot of the ladder. Wrapped his bloody head with the burlap bag. Smothered him with her hand. Carried him to the waiting car. She squeezed his tiny body to her breast as they bounced over the dirt road through the dark woods—Esther Snow holding in her arms the stolen baby of the most famous wife and mother in the world.

"They went this way with the body of my boy, looking for a place to hide it. Why not here? Too near houses. That river? Too easily found. Through quiet Hopewell past all safe homes, past orphans' home, up that lonely hill . . ."

The shadowy Richard is behind the wheel. Her lover? Her stooge? Her husband?

"Jst er tot?" Richard wants to know. *"Is he dead?"*

"Ya," she answers.

Then into the woods. She kisses the lifeless baby on the cheek and lays his body into the shallow grave along the Mount Rose road. If he isn't found, they can still get their money.

* * *

She left him a letter before she left town. Grover found it tacked to the door of his room one night. He stood in the dim yellow light of the hallway and read:

> *"The little spiral was still there, still softly whirling, like the ghost of a white kitten chasing the ghost of a white tail, and making as it did the faintest of whispers."*
>
> *Goodbye, Kitten. Some day may we meet again. Esther*

It was obvious from the beautiful handwriting that the woman had been trained in German calligraphy. He read it again. He stared at the little missive until his eyes blurred. Tried to make sense of it. Then he stuffed the note into his pants pocket and unlocked the door. Esther Snow was gone.

Assistant Chief Myslivecek had seized both of the ransom bills. And he was dead. Now only God knew what had become of them.

Grover Mudd slumped into his favorite chair. Actually, the only chair in the room. The scratches she'd left across his face were fading. The cuts on his back had mostly healed. But the stake she'd driven through his heart was still there.

The new columnist for the *St. Paul Frontier News* sat in the dark. For the first time in months a cool breeze drifted up from the street. The air smelled of rain. He felt frustrated, burned. Would one successful kidnapping be enough? Or would the mysterious Esther Snow strike again, in another place and time, under another new name? There had to be some way to document her role in the crime of the century, so that in fifty or a hundred years the next Grover Mudd, or the next Dr. Schnacky, could look back and say with a ray of certainty that the crime of the century was not unsolvable.

It was past midnight when the knock at the door came. Grover had been too tired to make himself something to eat. He'd downed two whiskeys and flopped on the bed. Fell asleep with his clothes on. The pounding on the door sounded like a fire alarm. He opened the door in a half stupor, more to stop the racket than to hear what package of fresh hell the caller might deliver.

"Are you Mudd?

"Yes, what do you want?"

The cab driver stuck a note in his face. "This is for you." Then he was gone.

Grover closed the door. Stumbled back to the bed. He flipped open the note.

I have what you are looking for
be at the church in the hour after midnight
in the stairs to the bell tower

Grover dropped the message between his knees. Buried his head in his hands. His body was half-dead. His mind was half-asleep. He knew her games. It was

Esther's handwriting, all right. But this note was different than her good-bye note. This note was plain and simple. Was she setting him up?

Grover grabbed the clock on the table. Stuck it to his nose: 12:30. In this town *the church* meant only one thing. The Cathedral of St. Paul. He had thirty minutes to get there. The streetcars had been put to bed. He'd have to walk. Hell, he'd have to run.

Saint Paul

Powerful rakes of lightning broke across the midnight sky, and for an extra long second the city of St. Paul seemed on fire. Hellish. Then it was black again, and thunder exploded with sound of bombs. Grover Mudd ran, trying to beat the rain.

The Marine veteran beat it down to Summit Avenue and took the first few blocks east with the speed of the golden halfback he once was, but by Lexington Parkway his age and his wounds had caught up with him. Grover doubled over to bag his precious breath. He tried to heave the whiskey shots from earlier that evening, but all he could wrench from his throat was a retching cough. Still fighting the war. Still trying to climb out of that trench. He knew in the end he'd cough up a lung. Then mercifully, it would be over. They could wrap his ravaged bones in old newspapers and toss them into Soldier's Rest at Oakland Cemetery. Lay a simple headstone on top of him. Say a prayer. Plant some grass. Only then could he get on with his death. Maybe some day start over again.

Grover Mudd pulled himself back to life, crossed the parkway and continued east on Summit. The avenue of churches. A multitude of steeples from a multitude of faiths sailed past the corners of his eyes. The rain began. A hard, heavy rain, more pestilent than refreshing. The streets of wedged brick were flooded in seconds, and the absolute feeling came over the ailing Marine that he had made this chilling run once before. Still, Grover ran. He believed in his heart the story of the century was coming to an end, and Grover Cleveland Mudd, crime reporter for the *St. Paul Frontier News*, was going to be there. As hard as he tried he could not escape the saintly visage of Anne Morrow Lindbergh staring into that empty crib.

"Everything is telescoped now into one moment, one of those eternal moments—the moment when I realized the baby had been taken and I saw the baby dead, killed violently, in the first flash of horror. Everything since then has been unreal . . ."

Grover ran with the thought of her husband, the stoic, heroic Minnesota Swede, standing over the black, leathery remains of his son at a New Jersey morgue.

"Colonel Lindbergh, are you satisfied that this is the body of your baby?"

"I am perfectly satisfied that it is my child."

That night, while the aviator's child lay on a slab in the county morgue awaiting cremation, a news photographer slipped in through a window, removed the shroud and snapped a picture of the baby's decomposing body. Sold on the street for five dollars apiece. It was one of those photographs that winds through the newspaper world, but never sees publication. But Grover Mudd had seen it.

The cathedral stepped out of the clouds into full view. In the south tower the church's only bell began its lonely chime. *"I summon the living. I mourn the dead."* It was 1 A.M. He was late. Grover tripped across Western Avenue and fixed his bloodshot eyes on the blessed cross atop the grand dome, weathering yet another storm. The brightly lit cathedral cast a deadly pall over the unsaintly city. The rain was beating harder, and the wind circled him like a crazed spirit.

Then a block from the Cathedral of St. Paul, the strangest thing happened. As Grover passed before a red sandstone mansion, he was halted by a preternatural light in a second-story window. A feeling arose from the depths of his subconscious. Unearthly. He used the moment to catch his breath. To regain his strength.

When they were kids, they called the place the house of the two naked ladies, because carved stonework of classic nudes topped a dramatic entrance arch. As children, they swore the dark house was haunted. The Victorian mansion had been built by a lumber baron, or a railroad baron, or maybe it was whorehouse baron. Point is, Grover had passed by the house all of his life giving it no more than a fleeting glance. But tonight he stopped. Stared. A sixth sense told him it had something to do with the kidnapping.

In a window situated on the southeast corner of the big house, he could make out the spooky dim of a night light, or maybe a candle, or maybe it was the glow from an oil lamp. A gnarly, old oak hung over this faintly illuminated window and in the wind its dark branches and sharp, pointed fingers were reaching down for the glass like frantic arms—made more eerie still the silhouette of a young woman standing behind the glass. It wasn't Esther Snow, but she had that same enchanting, out-of-place kind of beauty. Even in the dark. Even from a haunting distance. She seemed cloaked in the kind of sorrow no woman her age should experience. Was she staring back at Grover? It certainly seemed that way in the rain. Then lightning broke over the mansion and she was gone. The light went out. The feeling evaporated. And Grover ran on.

He stumbled past the colossal mansion of the legendary James J. Hill, founding father of the Great Northern Railroad. It was the largest house in the state of Minnesota. Home of the robber baron who had worked his engineers to death. The man to whom Grover's father had devoted his life. Eighteen-hour days and two million miles. Worked until the night he fell asleep at the throttle. Grover clung to the iron fence for support and made his way to the corner. Across the street stood the cathedral.

His clothes were soaked. His eyes were watery. His mouth tasted of spit and blood. Everything was happening fast. Too fast. The night seemed all but a blur.

Grover Mudd had seen this church a thousand times from a thousand angles in all kinds of weather. But tonight was different. Strange and disconcerting.

Grover searched the bell tower for a glimpse of her angel-blond hair, but there was nothing up there but bats and shadows. Lightning and rain. Face to face, he'd only met Esther Snow twice. Both times his emotions had seized his senses. This time, he swore, would be different. He crossed the street and started up the stairs to the immense doors of the cathedral. But under the great rose window, just out of the rain, he stopped. The window's theme was the Resurrection. At its center stood the lamb of God holding aloft the banner of victory over death. Grover Mudd had mixed feelings about God. Still believed the lousy bastard had deserted him. Left him in a bloody trench to fend for himself.

It was cold inside the church. Grover stood in the narthex adjusting his eyes to the dark. Candles were all that lit the way. He peered into the sanctuary.

Begun in 1906, the Cathedral of St. Paul was still under construction. Ten years of finishing work remained on the interior. Windows were missing. Walls of golden stone awaited the arrival of the chiseled apostles. Still, the size of the Renaissance masterpiece was breathtaking, even for a man with little breath. The capacious dome rose 186 feet from the floor, and not even a pagan like Grover Mudd could ignore the presence of a heavenly being. A priest knelt before the altar rail consoling a parishioner. A dozen souls praying for salvation were scattered among oaken pews that could seat three thousand.

Out of respect for the late-night worshipers, Grover successfully fought the urge to cough. Maybe it was being in out of the weather, or perhaps it was the church, but his chest settled down. His breathing returned to normal. Grover Mudd hadn't felt this peaceful since that first shot of whiskey.

The church had two towers, but only the south tower housed a bell. Grover moved stealthily through the candlelight shadows on the pink marble floor. Directly beneath the south tower a tall wrought-iron grille protected the baptistry. These words from John 3:3 were portrayed in the window: *"Unless a man be born again he cannot see the Kingdom of God."* Grover saw a large door to his left. He struggled with it, got it open. Slipped inside.

In the stairwell, Grover found the planks and rails of scaffolding among the dust and disorder. The chill of the brick walls was penetrating, slipping like sin through his wet clothes to his bones. The stone dust was making it difficult for him to breathe. From halfway up the steep stairs came the flickering glow of an oil lamp, along with its waxy smell. And there was the silence, that cold, hollow kind of silence that is intensely magnified by the low concussion of thunder and the drumbeat of rain. Then something strange. It might have been the rain, or maybe a parishioner inside the chapel, but for just an instant he could swear he was listening to the sound of a crying baby.

Grover wiped the raindrops from his face. He rested his aching back against the cold bricks and listened to the weather. He was aging faster than a dog. The church served only to remind him of his mortality. He kept his tired eyes on the door, and every once in a while he bent his shivering neck and peeked up the dark stairs that climbed toward the heavens. He ached for a cigarette, but smoking, though it stilled his nerves, seemed disrespectful somehow.

It occurred to him that maybe she was in the wrong tower. Could it be the Nazi woman was standing in the north tower, waiting for him as he waited for her? He was just about to find out when from out of the dark at the top of the stairs floated a message in the form of a gold note. It made its way down the stairs to Grover Mudd like one of those magic carpets he'd seen in the movies. And as it floated nearer and nearer Grover could see how rigid it was. Crisp and clean. It was money. He reached for it, but like all of the money in his life, it slipped from his hand. Zigzagged all the way to the floor. Grover leaned over and picked it up. He held it up to what little light there was and examined it. It was a twenty-dollar bill. A gold certificate. Three folds. Eight sections. Esther Snow, still with the games. He stuffed the gold note into his pants pocket alongside her good-bye note and started slowly up the tower. Hugging the walls. Moving cautiously skyward through the shadows that snaked up the wet stairs. Past the dim light of an empty loft built to one day house a choir and an organ. He felt like the prince, or maybe the frog, in some dark fairy tale. He felt like a reporter being played for a fool.

Grover Mudd wearily legged it one hundred feet to the top of the south tower. A trapdoor was ajar, bouncing open and shut with the wind, leaking rain down the stairwell. He could smell Esther's perfume in the air, and his mind raced back to that night on the High Bridge. He pushed open the trapdoor and climbed into the bell tower. Into the weather.

Even in the wind and the rain the view was incredible. In a city built on seven hills, built over ancient Indian graves, he was towering above the highest hill in the city. Below him the lights of St. Paul followed the bends in the Mississippi River until they faded into the bluffs off Battle Creek Park.

Grover jumped as the wind slammed the trapdoor closed. He turned and made his way around the cast bell, a miserly voice unworthy of such a grand edifice. A rope hung from the center. Biting raindrops whipped through the granite arches. He steadied himself against the gusts of wind by clinging to the ornate balconies that bordered the rectangular belfry. "Esther," he cried out. "Esther Snow." But in the storm it was hard to hear his own voice.

Suddenly, without warning, lightning lit up the night sky and Grover Mudd jumped back, startled. Fooled. Trapped. Standing on the balcony ledge, almost as tall as the arch itself, was an apparition straight out of the fires of Dante's hell. Dressed in black from head to toe, he looked seven feet tall. In this cathedral of God his ungodly frame was back-lit by the lights of the storm so that his face was not visible. In the wind his great coat flapped like a cape. His wide-brimmed hat seemed glued to his head. In one hand he held an ice pick, and with his other hand he waved Esther Snow's white scarf like a weapon, a pennant flying in the wind, unfurling, ready to engulf all those who got in the way. The faint fragrance of the German girl's perfume wafted through the tower.

The Ice Man's neck was horribly disfigured, swollen to the size of a goiter. The work of Grover Mudd. He could no longer speak so the giant spook made a slashing motion across his deformed neck.

"Where is she?" Grover yelled.

The Ice Man leaped down from the balcony. Grover held his ground. Had nowhere to go. Still, he was not prepared for what he saw next. In the flashes of light produced by the storm, the Ice Man's face, or what was left of his face, danced before Grover's eyes. Only the black, beady eyes remained intact. All his other facial features had been destroyed in the blaze. The electrical wires of the streetcar left raw streaks of burned flesh across his cheeks, burns so deep crisscrossing muscle fibers were exposed. The fire that followed the crash had blackened and blistered what remained of the man's face. His nose was gone. His lips were missing. Only three teeth were left dangling from his gums. In a way, Grover felt sorry for the scarred son of a bitch. No man could be expected to go through life looking like this. He should have died in the electric inferno.

In the night sky there was nothing subtle about the lightning or the thunder. It was war. The Ice Man crept slowly Grover's way. The trapdoor, the only way out, had slammed closed. A long leap away. Too long.

"Where is she?" Grover asked again, playing for time. "Is she down below . . . waiting for one of us to fall at her feet? She used me too, you know. That's what she does."

The Ice Man didn't flinch, just kept on coming, and for one horrifying moment Grover Mudd could perfectly picture the seven-foot monster bounding up a homemade ladder on the orders of Esther Snow. Emerging from a darkened window with a baby in his arms. "My God," he claimed, "are you Richard? Did she make you do that?"

The man without a face lurched forward, bringing the ice pick down across Grover's chest. The pick ripped open his shirt and drew blood, but Grover jumped away fast enough to avoid being stabbed, his back slamming into the cast bronze of the bell. Its two tons reverberated through the tower, momentarily stunning the Ice Man, who cupped his ears. It took only that one slice of the ice pick and the sound of the bell for Grover Mudd to size up his foe. He was slower than last time they had met. Weaker. Christ, he was barely alive. Grover slowly circled the bell, keeping his hands on the bronze metal.

Even in the wind and the rain, even with lightning

strikes igniting bursts of thunder, Grover could hear the Ice Man breathing. A slow, tortured breath, as if Grover's own troubled breathing were being played back to him on a phonograph record, and the needle was stuck. "I don't want to hurt you anymore," Grover pleaded. "I've been there. You belong in a hospital."

Though he stumbled through life with a thousand excuses, a cold, the flu, the damn Minnesota weather, Grover Mudd knew in his heart that his lungs were in no better shape than the Ice Man's face—two men whose lives had been burned beyond recognition.

"Where is she?" Grover demanded. "Show me where I can find her and together we'll make her pay. Then we can both get on with what little there is left of our lives." He pulled the twenty-dollar gold certificate from his pocket and held the note to the Ice Man's hideous face like a crucifix. "If you can show me more of these . . . we have her. We can put her away. We can put her to death, for God's sake."

But the weather ripped the gold certificate from Grover's hand. The only evidence he had in the kidnapping and murder of the Lindbergh baby was caught by the wind and sailed out of the tower.

The Ice Man thrust his elongated arm forward and this time swung the ice pick at Grover's head. But his aim was off. All the ice pick did was ring the bell. Again, with the tolling of the bell, the Ice Man cupped his ears. That was when Grover Mudd made his move, slipped around the bell and leaped onto the Ice Man's shoulder.

But it proved a mistake. The burn victim flung Grover over his shoulder like a block of ice and slammed him into the bell; Grover dropped to the floor.

Momentarily stunned, Grover couldn't tell if it was the church bell or his head that was ringing.

Then the Ice Man wrapped Esther Snow's perfumed scarf around his fists the way Grover Mudd had wrapped his tie that night in the streetcar. A garrote.

Before Grover could clear the ringing from his ears and get back to his feet the spook had the cloth around Grover's neck and he was strangling the life out of him.

The rain was in Grover's face. The wind in his ears. And whether he had much faith in God or not, Grover Mudd was on his knees praying. Praying for a miracle, or perhaps just a sense of fairness. He wasn't any more ready to die in this cathedral tower than he had been in that muddy trench, and if there was a God in heaven—and Grover Mudd truly believed there was—the lousy bastard owed him. Owed him big time. The time had come to pay up.

Lightning disappeared from the night sky. The thunder stopped. Rain continued to fall, but the Ice Man's grip on Grover's neck suddenly loosened. Just as Grover lacked the strength to finish off the Ice Man that night in the runaway streetcar, now the Ice Man lacked the strength, or perhaps the will, to kill Grover Mudd.

Grover tore Esther Snow's garrote from his neck and crawled like a child into a corner of the granite balcony. Sat there, gasping for life. The white cloth, stained with his blood and smelling of her perfume, he used to wipe the rain from his brow, and the red froth from his lips.

The Ice Man, exhausted, stumbled backward into the cathedral bell. It tolled only faintly. Then the tall faceless figure rested his frame against the bronze metal, as if nailed to it. A tear seemed to escape the corner of his eye. Or maybe it was the rain.

Grover Mudd was too beat to stand. Too choked to talk. He wanted only to be born again—for the rain to wash the blood from his mouth, and for the wind to replenish his lungs. The puzzle that was the Lindbergh kidnapping again fell to pieces. If the Ice Man couldn't bring himself to kill a local yokel newspaperman, the very man who'd left him to burn alive in a fire of electricity, he certainly couldn't kill a baby. No, in all probability Esther Snow had gotten some other weakling to climb that ladder.

In the end, the tall apparition, known only as the Ice Man, raised his watery, black eyes to Grover Mudd and caught the newsman's stare in a ray of light that spilled down from the illuminated cross atop the dome. He took a giant step toward Grover. Then his charred face and misshapen neck jerked sharply heavenward, and blood shot out of the deep burns of his forehead. In the storm it was impossible to hear the report of a rifle, but Grover Mudd had seen head wounds before. The man without a face stumbled silently backward, flew over the tower balcony like a bat, and vanished.

Grover struggled to his feet, climbed onto the ledge of the balcony and stood in the tall arch of the bell tower. He could see the long, black shadow sprawled face down on the grassy knoll at the foot of the church.

The shot could have come from anywhere below. From that distance, in this kind of weather, who's to say she wasn't aiming at him? Grover rose to full height, arms extended, waiting for her to finish her work. He drew every last bit of angry breath that he could muster and shouted from the top of his tortured lungs. "Go ahead, Esther, shoot! Take your best shot!"

But there was no gunfire. No bewitching voice. Only the sound of the weather, and the wretched cry of a wounded soldier coughing up his guts. It was as if the wind and the rain had conspired to erase her tracks. Yes, Esther Snow was out there somewhere, but she was gone.

The rain seemed to lessen some, but the cool, wet winds of autumn returned and brought the long, deadly summer of 1932 to a merciful close. Grover Mudd wiped his mouth with the back of his hand. He stood alone in the high arch of the great church. Ghost in a storm.

Silent Esther. Secret Esther. He pulled her good-bye note from his pocket. Read it one more time.

"The little spiral was still there, still softly whirling, like the ghost of a white kitten chasing the ghost of a white tail, and making as it did the faintest of whispers."

Goodbye, Kitten. Some day may we meet again. Esther

Esther so-called Snow may have been gone for now, but Grover Mudd didn't believe for one minute the evil witch was done with him. Or done with his city. "There will be another day," Grover managed to mumble into the storm. "There will be another day."

BOOK THREE

THE PAYOFF

Oh, what a terrible train of misery and sorrow this crime has pulled behind it. Will the consequences never never cease?

—Anne Morrow Lindbergh
June 10, 1932
Hour of Gold, Hour of Lead

Freddie

The temperature had dropped so fast and so far on the night of the payoff that it took two days for his frozen body to thaw. It was the very last place the great detective wanted to end up—on the examination table at the Ramsey County Morgue. Rick Beanblossom knew it. Dr. Freda Wilhelm knew it. With a twenty-one-gun salute, the old GI would be laid to rest at Fort Snelling National Cemetery, not far from where he had fought his last battle. But for now Captain Les Angelbeck was laid out for a preliminary examination, with the Ramsey County medical examiner hovering over his naked corpse. It was Friday morning.

The man in the mask sat on a stool nearby, avoiding the face of the dead cop the way most people avoided him. "Was he shot?" Rick wanted to know.

"Doesn't look that way," Freddie told him. "My guess would be congestive heart failure." The doctor shook her head in sympathy. "I'm very sorry, Rick. The man was a legend."

"I agree," said Rick, "but why are you offering your condolences to me?"

"Oh, I'm sorry, I heard you two were close."

"Where did you hear that?"

"Well, I mean, you did find his body . . . and he was trying to find your son out there . . . wasn't he?"

"You going to the funeral tomorrow?"

The M.E. glanced up at the clock. "I'll be in the organ gallery for the service."

"That's right, you play the organ for the cathedral. How did you get that job?"

"Your Mrs. Howard recommended me to the archbishop. He liked what he heard."

Rick watched as Freddie removed her military-style coat, folded it gently, and laid it across a gurney. She rolled up her sleeves, and Rick could not help but notice how graceful she was for a large woman. Her hands had the long lissome fingers of a musician, and despite her girth she seemed light on her feet. Yet always she maintained an aura of power.

"And how is your wife?" Freddie asked.

"Her name is Andrea."

"Yes, how is your Andrea?"

"She's home now . . . resting. She has a bad back, and an earache."

"Do you know how many bloated bodies come through here that went off of that bridge?"

"Ten times the number that survive."

"That's right, love. She's one lucky woman . . . your

Andrea. When is she going back to work? . . . I hate that other girl."

"After we find Dylan."

Freddie held another title among those who worked the crime beat. This title was unofficial. She was the county's chief gossip hound. Rumor control. More a funnel than a leak. But as Rick Beanblossom had learned years ago, too often her information was good, and her insights were invaluable. Trouble was, Rick never knew to how many others the woman was feeding the same information. Today Freddie was more surly than insightful. "You're a damn fool, Rick Beanblossom. Worse, you're a damn Marine."

"Why a fool, because I believe my son is alive?"

"No, because you should have been down here four days ago." Now she was mad. The examination room was white and sterile and smelled of antiseptic. The lights were bright. Glass cabinets and aluminum sinks lined the walls. A digital scale sat on the counter top. In neat rows on aluminum shelving above the sinks were hundreds of bottles of formaldehyde, each glass jar keeping alive a tissue specimen or a body part.

Rick Beanblossom loosened his tie and stuffed his gloves into the pockets of his flight jacket. The morgue was freezing. He leaned back and watched as the doctor stormed over to a cabinet and began lining up surgical instruments. "And four days ago you would have told me . . . what?" he asked.

Freddie slammed the instruments into a straight line along the counter top. "I would have told you to stuff a sock into the mouth of your Barbie doll wife . . . instead of turning her loose on live television. I would have told you not to pay the ransom money until you literally had your eyes on the baby. I would have told you to stay at home with your wife while the police talked a suicidal maniac off of the bridge . . . while the FBI delivered the ransom. But no, it had to be you and Angelbeck, didn't it? One amateur sleuth without a face, and one elderly cop without a clue." She turned to the table, pointing. "Well, now he's dead, your wife went to the hospital, and your son is . . . okay, let's say, still missing. Something tells me the kidnappers knew exactly who they were dealing with." One at a time she slammed closed the cabinet drawers. "A damn fool. You've made every mistake Lindbergh made. Didn't you learn anything?"

"Obviously you and Inspector Koslowski have had a long talk. Is she another one of the special friends you leak information to?"

"If you had listened to Stephanie Koslowski, you might be home rocking your son to sleep right now."

This wasn't the first time Rick had heard this line—or even the second. The newspapers were having a field day. Radio talk shows were merciless, television news was almost as bad. The message was the same everywhere. Rick Beanblossom and Andrea Labore had screwed up. The more the details of the payoff became public, the more the public displaced their sympathies. And there was another social phenomenon at work—backlash. Almost overnight Andrea

Labore went from being the All-American mother, to being a yuppie scum TV reporter pursuing career over family. A Minneapolis weekly went as far as to print her appearance schedule for the month leading up to the kidnapping. The implication was clear—there was little time left for raising a child.

Freddie walked into a closet space off of the E room. She lifted a white bucket from the floor and returned it to the counter top. "Did you at least mark the bills?" she asked.

"Yes, but this crime isn't about money," Rick told her. "There'll be no money trail to follow . . . not like the Lindbergh case. Now we're in uncharted waters . . . but so are they."

"So what's your next move?"

Researchers in the library of the *North Star Press* had compiled for Rick a complete book of everything Grover Mudd had ever written while at the *Frontier News*. Then they whittled it down to his writings on the Lindbergh case. Reporters at the paper had tracked down Grover Mudd's daughter, Grace Lee Hoff. She was a widow. Lived in Danbury, Connecticut. Rick and Andrea dispatched an overnight letter to Mrs. Hoff requesting any writings she might have of her father's that related to the kidnapping of the Lindbergh baby.

A private investigator was sweeping Rick's office for bugs and wiretaps.

"Are you familiar with the writings of a Doctor Schnacky," Rick asked the medical examiner. "University of Minnesota . . . 1920s, 30s?"

Freddie lifted a human brain from the white bucket, studied it as if the tissue mass was alive. Filled with answers. "He was the Sherlock Holmes of his day. Studied the psychology of killers. A pioneer in profiling. Today most of his writings seem dated, but back then it was pretty heady stuff. If I remember right, his theories on Jack the Ripper and the Lindbergh kidnapping were dead on. Where did you dig up his name?"

"Grover Mudd."

"Who?" Freddie raised her eyes quizzically. "Wasn't he on the radio, or something, way back then?"

"No, he was a St. Paul reporter. Worked on the Lindbergh story. Apparently he was consulting with Schnacky. He was also a Marine. Got gassed in World War One."

"Bad news," Freddie told him. "When I cut open our friend over there," she said, nodding toward the corpse of Les Angelbeck, "he'll have those same ravaged lungs . . . as if he'd been killed by mustard gas."

"The gas didn't kill Mudd," Rick told her. "He was murdered. Ambushed up by the church. Tell me something, Freddie, do you believe in reincarnation?"

"That's a strange question to ask a coroner."

"How so?"

Freddie set the brain down on the counter. It was dry and chunky, green and white with the texture of cauliflower. It had been sitting for days. "I see the reincarnated remains of human beings every day. The girl that leaps from the bridge. The teenager who overdosed. The old man with congestive heart failure. The child beaten to a pulp by his mother, or more often his mother's lover. Every day. The same people. The same death." The chief medical examiner pulled open a drawer and removed a knife the size of a machete. "And all of them," she said, "stare up at me from the examination table with the same sorry eyes and say the same damn thing. *'Maybe next time I'll get it right.'*" She turned to Rick, knife in hand, as if she were going to kill him. "Do you remember that girl with the baby that jumped from the bridge?"

"Yes."

With that the chief medical examiner expertly, but violently, chopped the dried brain in two, like a head of lettuce. One clean cut. "Come here," she said.

Rick walked over to the counter, his senses awash in fumes of formaldehyde.

Freddie began picking at the girl's sliced brain, chalky bits falling to the counter top, like dandruff. "Everything you put into your body goes to your brain. See that?" she asked. "Cocaine," she answered. "See that? Orange juice. See that? LSD. Gee, I wonder why she jumped?"

"Are you that good?"

She picked up the knife and chopped the brain into quarter slices. "I'll run some toxicology tests to make it look scientific, fill out some highfalutin' reports so it's official . . . but yes, love, I'm that good."

"And your advice now . . . ?"

"Like I told the captain over there when he came to

see me . . . stop looking for your son, and start looking for a killer."

Although history told him that child victims were usually killed after the abduction, it was still not the kind of advice Rick wanted to hear. In his heart he felt she was wrong. This case was the exception. But the good doctor was right about one thing. If it had been anybody but his son, if he had been thinking straight he'd have come to Doctor Freda Wilhelm first, not last.

Rick Beanblossom said his good-byes, pulled his gloves from his pockets, and walked to the doorway He stopped there. Deep in thought. Then he turned "You know, Freddie, for a long time, during the Weatherman killings, I actually considered you a suspect."

"That's funny, Rick, because a lot of people suspected you."

The Marine took a long last look at the stark white body of Les Angelbeck. "Yes, so I was told." He looked back at Freddie. "Are you still thinking about moving to Florida?"

"It could happen anytime."

Rick slipped the gloves onto his hands. "You once told me that serial killers were predominantly white males . . . that they preyed on white females. Do you believe there's a difference between men's crimes and women's crimes?"

"I most certainly do."

"And the kidnapping of my son, Freddie . . . is that man's crime, or is it maybe the work of a woman?"

Freddie ran the knife across her navy blue skirt, ꞌiping it clean of brain dust. "It's a woman's crime, .ick. You're looking for a woman. But then you lready knew that, didn't you?"

Grace

Where Summit Avenue melted into the intersta
below the cathedral, front end loaders were busting u
hard mountains of snow and scooping the frost
white remains into big orange dump trucks. It was th
final phase of the long, arduous, and very expensi
task of digging an entire state out of two consecuti
blizzards. Farther up the avenue, police cars still pr
tected the Beanblossom mansion, but fewer of ther
The FBI remained headquartered on the third floor
the house, but they too were fewer in numbe
Reporters were milling around out front, but most
the satellite trucks had vanished. Traffic on the avenu
had, for the most part, returned to normal. Dyla
Labore Beanblossom had been missing a mere fou
days, but even the most optimistic people in la
enforcement suspected they were now looking for
body, not a baby.

The reporters covering the story were speaking i
code. Journalese. They were throwing around clich
like "guarded optimism," and "hoping for the bes

ut preparing for the worst," and, when it came to the ansom, the favorite, stupid cliché of every TV eporter in America, "it raises more questions than nswers . . . Brad Dumbfuckbutgoodlooking . . . Sky ligh News . . . St. Paul."

Andrea Labore picked up the remote and killed the elevision set. Her initial rage at the abduction had urned to sorrow. Now her sorrow was returning to age. She'd been in bed for two days. One in the hos- ital. One at home. Today she was getting out of bed. n her silk pajamas she limped over to a tall dresser nd pulled open that drawer where husbands never o. Beneath the lingerie were hidden the poignant let- ers and the romantic trinkets of her school days. The ormer Minneapolis police officer reached past those hings, reached all the way to the back of the drawer nd pulled out her old service revolver. She limped ver to one of the wing chairs where her purse was ying open and she dropped the gun inside. Then the ueen of the evening news moved to the picture win- low and parted the curtain. The sun off the snow was linding. The air was freezing. A piercing draft slipped hrough the panes. She wanted to throw open the win- low and shout her side of the story. But Old Man Win- er would have none of that. The windows had been ealed for the season, and outside the cold and the now were as silent as the monsters who had kid- apped her little boy.

"What are you doing out of bed?" Rick Beanblossom ossed his jacket onto the chair with the purse. Noticed the gun. He lifted the handle between his fingers like it was a dead fish. "What is this?"

Andrea didn't answer.

"Is this the same gun that . . . ?"

"Yes, it is," she finally said, "and I very much hope to use it again."

"Well, that's the difference between you and me."

"What, Rick, that you wouldn't resort to violence?"

"No," he told her, "I'll kill them with my bare hands." He dropped the gun back into her purse and sunk into the other chair. Exhausted. A newspaper was on his lap.

Andrea was fuming. "You wouldn't believe what they said, on the air, at my own television station."

Rick glanced over at the dark picture tube. "Have you read a newspaper lately?" He held up the front page.

BABY DYLAN GONE FOUR DAYS
Police Fear Worst
Experts Say Payoff Was Botched

Andrea let the curtain fall. "How did I become the villain in all of this?"

"You're on television. You wanted it all. You got it all. Your kid paid the price. A simple morality tale to end the twentieth century." Rick tossed the newspaper alongside the purse and nodded toward the phone. "Did Mrs. Howard call?"

"We haven't heard from her since the ransom was paid. Why do you ask?"

"She wasn't at the paper, and I wanted to ask her about something I learned today about Fort Snelling."

"Do you mean about that escape hole?"

Rick explained what he had learned from other reporters at the *North Star Press*. "In 1959," he said, "the state wants to run a highway right through the middle of crumbling Fort Snelling. Historians and preservationists fight the plan. They win. The highway gets rerouted, and private money is raised to restore the fort to its original grandeur. Guess who the fort's biggest benefactor turns out to be?" He answered himself. "The Howard Foundation. Founded by Mr. and Mrs. Walt Howard."

"That helps," said Andrea. "Mrs. Howard would know exactly who did the work on the fort. What did Freddie have to say?"

"She says we should be looking for a woman."

Andrea lifted herself back onto the bed. Her back was killing her. "We have been looking for a woman. Maybe that's our mistake."

"I don't know. We've still got a pretty good suspect right under our roof."

"Jasmine had a baby."

"What?" said Rick, stunned.

"Jasmine had a baby out of wedlock," Andrea told him. "When she lived in New Jersey. The baby was put up for adoption. That's her big secret. She spends all of her time up in the attic looking for ghosts."

"How do you explain the thumbguard, for Christ's sake? She got caught red-handed with evidence literally taken off the Lindbergh baby."

"I don't know . . . I just think we're barking up the wrong tree."

"Okay, so let's eliminate Jasmine as the coincidence of the century . . . who does that leave us with?"

There was a knock at the door. "Come in," said Andrea, none too happy.

FBI Inspector Stephanie Koslowski pushed into the room, a red, white, and blue envelope in her hand. She paused, the realization that she had interrupted something. "I'm sorry," she said. "This package just arrived for you, overnight from Connecticut. I think it should be opened right away."

Andrea struggled from the bed. Took the Federal Express package. She tossed the newspaper to the floor and sat down in the chair, right between Rick's jacket and the gun in her purse. She read the name of the sender. *Mrs. G. L. Hoff*. Then she tore into it.

Rick stood. Crowded in behind her. Inspector Koslowski hovered over them both.

Inside the onion-skin package Andrea found a beautifully handwritten letter placed on top of a stack of photocopies. Even in their haste to hear what the woman had to say, the trio of investigators couldn't help but admire the noble appearance of a letter lovingly written by a generation that despised the typewriter for personal conrrespondence, not to mention the fax and E-mail.

Dear Rick & Andrea,

Though I've spent most of my adult life in Connecticut, and my children were born here, we still consider ourselves Minnesotans at heart. We always keep our ears open for Minnesota news. So we were shocked when your baby boy was kidnapped, and even more shocked when I received your overnight letter. Our prayers are with you.

I was very young when my father was murdered. Even younger when my parents divorced. Mostly I remember that a day with Father involved riding the yellow trolley cars. What a joy it was—to the parks, to the lakes, out to Como Zoo, always aboard the yellow trolleys.

One night Father and I stepped off of the trolley beneath your big cathedral. There was a sudden burst of noise. I remember ducking down. When I looked up, Father was stretched out in the street. I remember seeing a car drive away that night, and staring at me from behind the passenger side window was an incredibly pretty lady with white-blond hair. In my memory she seems almost angelic. That was in 1936. My father's murder was never solved.

I can't imagine how my father's name came up in your son's case, but since receiving your letter I have spent every hour digging through our Danbury attic for Father's papers. He left behind quite a few boxes (typical writer). My daughter and I searched for anything he wrote related to the Lind-

bergh kidnapping. Ironically, his very first column was on that kidnapping (photocopy enclosed). It speculates a woman kidnapped the baby. He appears to have had somebody in mind (maybe that Esther woman from the first article). His column wasn't called Grover's Corner when he first began writing it. That came later, probably because it appeared in a corner of the back page. Or maybe because Father had a corner office. I'm not sure.

Enclosed are all of the news articles I could find that pertain to the Lindbergh kidnapping. There is also the draft of a piece written shortly before his death. It concerns the upcoming execution of Bruno Hauptmann. It's a typewritten piece only, possibly because it was never published. I don't know. The Frontier News *had ceased publication, and Father was doing freelance writing in the last years of his life. He was also in very poor health. The mustard gas he breathed during WWI was killing him. I only mention his health because the piece doesn't always make sense (perhaps why it was never published).*

I also found a very curious note. I've made a copy. I'm sending you the original. It may mean nothing, but it was signed by a woman named "Esther." Even more curious, it was among the papers from the coroner's office. (Could he have bad it on him when he died?)

My phone number is at the top of the page, as is my daughter's. If you have any questions, call us day or night. God be with you both, and with your baby boy.

Sincerely
Grace Lee (Mudd) Hoff

P.S. Rick, I was thrilled to hear you found Father's typewriter. Please keep it. He'd be proud to know it fell into such wonderful hands.

Andrea handed the letter to Inspector Koslowski as Rick leaned over her shoulder and anxiously walked his fingers through the papers. Andrea knew exactly what he was searching for. She shuffled the news articles and found a separate envelope near the top.

"Here it is," she said, beating him to it.

The mother of the missing child lifted the curious note from the envelope and held it in her hands the way one would hold a butterfly, as if it might spread its wings and steal away if improperly handled. The paper was the yellow-gray color that comes with decades of storage, yet it had been folded and unfolded so many times that it now had the threadbare texture of cotton. This made the faded handwriting, beautiful handwriting, difficult to decipher. Still, Andrea Labore was able to read the note aloud, slowly and deliberately.

"The little spiral was still there, still softly whirling, like the ghost of a white kitten chasing

the ghost of a white tail, and making as it did the faintest of whispers."

Goodbye, Kitten. Some day may we meet again. Esther

Andrea was mystified. Quizzical. "What does it mean?"

Stephanie Koslowski spoke right up. "It means that we have a sample of her handwriting."

"Exactly," said Rick, seconding the motion. "Her first mistake in her flawless kidnapping." Ever so gently he took the note from Andrea's hands and held it before the eye-slits in his mask. "You got a little too cute, Esther."

Koslowski agreed, admiring the note. "I'll bet she doesn't even remember writing it."

Andrea was incredulous. "Yes, boys and girls, if she's still alive."

But her skepticism was a lonely voice. Perhaps for the first time in the investigation, Rick Beanblossom and Stephanie Koslowski seemed to be on the same page. They smelled a break.

Rick handed the note over to the woman from the FBI. "All right, Inspector, get your troops over to Swede Bjorenson's house. Kick his door in if you have to. Get a sample of that Esther Kay's handwriting, preferably letters from when she was young. Then get them off to your famous laboratories in Washington. Let's find out if that old lady in the coma is really Esther Snow."

Hauptmann

At first nothing is visible but snow. Heavy, swirling snow. The white ice has seized the night and erased everything in sight. Then slowly a trolley car emerges from the storm. It rumbles through the snow until it comes to a halt beneath the dome of the great church. The figure of a man and a little girl step from the trolley. A harsh, hacking cough can be heard over the roaring wind. Grover Mudd. His threadbare coat hangs on him as if it were merely a coat on a clothesline flapping in the wind. His face wears the contorted agony of a man who knows he is nearing the end of his life. He squeezes the hand of his little girl. Tucked under his arm is a newspaper. The *St. Paul North Star Press*. It is dated April 3, 1936.

HAUPTMANN TO BE EXECUTED TONIGHT

Appeals Run Out on
Lindbergh Kidnapper
Confession Unlikely

But why no confession? Why, the world asks, does a man so saturated in guilt take to his grave such atrocious secrets? Because he is innocent? Or because his utter lack of a conscience, his lack of a soul, allows for no remorse, no measure of redemption? Grover Mudd knows Bruno Hauptmann's secret, not that any newspaper cares to print it. That secret is Esther Snow, the smarter half of a pair of criminals so cold and heartless they fear only the failure of their mad schemes.

The trolley rolls away, into the white night. The winter wind that has stolen into spring catches the *North Star Press* in its jaws, rips it from the bony arms of the unemployed reporter and sends a flurry of newsprint sailing east. The little girl is scared. She clutches her father's hand as if he too might blow away.

She was smart, Esther Snow. No more gold notes had appeared in Minnesota since her disappearance. In fact across the country not one single gold certificate from the Lindbergh kidnapping had been discovered since the arrest of Bruno Hauptmann. No, the cold, calculating witch would wait until Hauptmann was executed. Fried. Dead and buried. Only when lover boy was safe in his grave would she cash in. Nobody would be looking for the bills anymore. And even if the gold notes began to appear again, the authorities would hush it up—refusing to admit the possibility that there was more than one kidnapper. So Grover Mudd writes, writes like a dying man, one article after another, implicating a woman in the kidnapping and murder of the Lindbergh baby. And all of them are returned to him. Rejected. The newspapers have their killer.

A pair of headlights appears in the storm, like a pair of ominous moons. They are attached to the shadow of a car that floats through the snow as if on air. It is floating their way, and Grover Mudd guides his daughter back a step to let the car pass. The headlights melt into the snowflakes and the brightness blinds him until all that he can make out as the car nears is a shock of white-blond hair.

Police figure there is still thirty thousand dollars in ransom money out there somewhere. Grover figures Esther has it hidden. But the man who had once gone toe to toe with the evil witch knows in his heart, and in his lungs, that he will not be around to see her dig it up. Or to see her fall.

The headlights pass. The passenger side window is down and it is snowing inside the car. Then from out of that snow emerges the barrel of a gun. Five flashes of white light. No sound. No sound but the voice of his little girl kneeling over him. *"Daddy don't die! Daddy don't die!"* He is on his back now. Five bullet holes ring his heart. Blood and saliva drip from his mouth and melt into the cold, white earth.

When he spews from his mouth his final cough, when the phlegm in his throat will not exit and the fire in his lungs will not die, Grover Mudd rolls to his side. With an infantile curl of his fingers he takes the hand of his little girl. He uses the snow as a pillow. The Minnesota snow as a casket. In the end there is a break in the storm, and to his left he can make out the archway of a sandstone mansion, two naked ladies dancing over the entrance. To his right stands the Cathedral of St. Paul, its massive dome hovering over him like a black cloud. He is dying on Summit Avenue. Halfway between sin and redemption. Heaven and hell. Then the peace that passes all understanding passes over him. In the end, death does what no opiate can. It frees him of all physical ills. Restores his soul. Replenishes his faith. Grover Cleveland Mudd meets death in perfect harmony. He is forty-one years old.

The blizzard returns to Summit Avenue with a vengeance. It acts like an eraser and begins to erase the memory of Grover Mudd. One minute the newspaperman can be seen lying dead in a snowbank, the next minute he is disappearing as fast as the ground. His head goes first. Then the swirling snow swallows his arms and his legs. In another instant his torso, his heart, his stomach, and his tortured lungs all whirl away, swept clean, like a pile of bloody dirt. Everything is white again, and silent. Then the swirling snow sets off down the avenue in search of another Marine.

Rick Beanblossom bolted up in bed. Woke in a freezing sweat. The swirling snow dissipated before his eyes. The sheets were soaked. This had happened often in the past. Vietnam nights. The sweat glands in his head had been destroyed in the napalm attack, and often in the early days his body would overheat in the middle of the night as his mind returned to the jungle. He had believed those nights were over, that age and marriage had cured him of his nightmares. He was mistaken.

Andrea moved in her sleep, but tonight her own demons were allowing her some rest. Rick pushed aside a wave of papers from a bygone era and crawled from bed, walked to the bath, and yanked a towel from the rack. He wiped the sweat from his chest as he made his way across the bedroom to the window that overlooked Summit Avenue. There was plenty of snow, but it was two days old. The sky was winter dark, but clear. On this night the only snow that had fallen had fallen in his dream. He looped the towel over his shoulder and leaned against the freezing glass. The cold was heaven.

There was the poster of the doughboy from World War I hanging in his office. The big, black Remington typewriter was on his desk. A gold certificate from the Lindbergh kidnapping had arrived in the mail. A thumbguard worn by the Lindbergh baby was discovered in his house. Grover Mudd was haunting him all right, but in a helpful sort of way. Most of the articles Grover's daughter had sent to them Rick had already seen, having been retrieved from the archives of the *North Star Press*.

The handwritten note from "Esther" was on its way to FBI laboratories in Washington. Inspector Koslowski had found Swede Bjorenson laconic, but surprisingly cooperative. He willingly turned over several letters that his wife Esther Kay had written to him during the war. He asked only that they be returned. The ransom notes sent to Rick were already in Washington. Koslowski was working fast. She didn't think Esther Kay Bjorenson had much time left.

Rick's mind was dust and ashes. With every passing day, with no word from the kidnappers, his ability to concentrate was ebbing.

"There is something very deep in a man's feeling for his son, it reaches further into the future."

Anne Lindbergh wrote that. Rick Beanblossom would have added, *"and it reaches further into the past."* Somehow, every bit of suffering and hurt, every bit of humiliation and degradation was erased on the day Dylan was born. Now Rick was facing a life without his son, and it was killing him. The Marine closed his weary eyes and whispered a prayer, before returning to the papers on the bed.

It was the typewritten piece Grover Mudd had written shortly before his death. There was no date on it, but judging from the subject matter it must have been written in the spring of 1936. Rick returned to the light of the window and read it again.

WHAT ABOUT THE OTHER KIDNAPPER?

by

Grover Mudd

Did Bruno Hauptmann kidnap the Lindbergh baby? He sure did. The evidence against him was overwhelming. He got caught with the ransom money. There's not a jury in this country that wouldn't have convicted him. Does the lousy bastard deserve to die? Yes, he does. Those questions have been settled.

The unanswered question is this, did Bruno act alone? Hell no. There was a woman with him. We've known that from the start. Coincidentally, a gorgeous woman by the name of Esther was arrested right here in St. Paul with ransom money from the Lindbergh kidnapping. I saw the bills. Held one in my hand. When the heat showed up, Esther actually had the temerity to run and hide in Lindbergh's hometown of Little Falls.

This woman wants power. The kind of power only men have. How to catch this murderer? Lure her to a cemetery with false promises, as she did Lindbergh. Better yet, lure the witch back here to St. Paul. Then give her what she wants. Power. Respectability. A big office all her own where she can give orders from morning till night. Then we all salute the German witch with the big red fingernails. But I think a lifetime of respectability will just about kill her. She's a born criminal. A very rare breed. She'll do it again. Watch your children.

To the untrained eye, it was desperate writing. Rambling, chauvinistic thoughts. But the Pulitzer Prize–winning journalist for the *North Star Press* recognized it for what it was—the first draft, the rough draft, of a newspaper column. Grover Mudd may not have been the most eloquent writer of his day, but he was better than this, even on his death bed. The piece was unfinished. Unpublished. Why? Because the man was killed?

Or because he was having doubts about the things that he was sure of?

Rick read the piece over and over. Esther Snow. Grover seemed almost obsessed with the woman. But were these clues, or were they just the arcane ravings of a dying man? And if they were clues, what was he telling Rick and Andrea? Go to Little Falls?

The writings of Grover Mudd had convinced Rick Beanblossom of one thing—Esther Snow was alive and well, and now the evil witch was jerking *him* around. More important, she was holding his son. She had mailed him the gold certificate. She had penned the ransom notes. She had lured Les Angelbeck to his house. Then she had lured them both to the fort. No, she didn't climb the ladder that snowy night, any more than she climbed the ladder that night at the Lindbergh house. She got somebody else to do that. Somebody else waited inside the fort. Escaped through the rabbit hole.

As he stared into the frosty night, Rick had two choices. Find her modern-day Bruno Hauptmann and he would find Esther Snow, who would lead him to his son. Or first find Esther Snow, who would lead him to her Hauptmann, who would lead him to his son. Rick Beanblossom glanced up at the dome of the great church. The bells rang out the hour. Midnight. Another day gone by. Another day without his little boy. As hard as he tried to live in the moment, the man in the mask could not escape the haunting feeling that he had passed this way once before—that if he thought about it long and hard enough, willed it to happen, it would all come back to him. Come back with a vengeance. "Keep talking to me, Grover," he said to the night. "Just keep talking."

Ghosts were working overtime that night on Summit Avenue. Downstairs, Jasmine Allen in her angel-white bathrobe moved through the darkness of the foyer, past the grand staircase and into the grand hall. They called it a dining room, but it was a long, lordly area off of the princely staircase. The young housekeeper was making her final rounds before retiring for the evening. A house this size had to be put to bed every night. The lights turned out. The fires extinguished. The radiators checked. The baby . . .

Jasmine swallowed a sob. She had been swallowing that same sorrow every night for the past week. She moved in front of the elongated table that graced the hall. Towering before her was a fourteen-foot fireplace that had been built of blue-gray granite from the Iron Range. The mantel was dark oak. There was enough room in the hearth to roast Joan of Arc. No screen harbored the flames like a modern fireplace, and sometimes when the huge fireplace was dormant, the winter wind would force snowflakes down the flue and into the dining room—giving the room the magical appeal of a snow dome. Even when the logs in the hearth were ablaze it was not unusual for a downburst to smother the fire and send red-hot embers airborne.

Tonight the sky was clear and cold. No snow. Then just before midnight, the wind again went on the prowl. Its haunting echo could be heard at the foot of each fireplace, but the breathing wind was loudest of all right here in front of her. Jasmine could hear footsteps upstairs in the master bedroom. Somebody walked into the bathroom, then back across the room to the window over the avenue.

The housekeeper tossed in another log to ward off the spooks in the hearth. Last log of the evening. The flames took hold of the dry wood and did a grateful jig high in the air.

The Minneapolis newspaper quoted the FBI woman as saying Jasmine would be taken in for questioning first thing Monday morning. A TV station reported that she'd be taken into custody. But now the *North Star Press* was raising questions about the FBI inspector herself. The paper said that she had bungled some famous cases in the past. At times it seemed like Dylan Labore Beanblossom was getting lost in the blame game.

Ice on the roof cracked with the nighttime temperatures and sent a rumbling shiver through the house. Shadows of the flames danced on the walls. Then the living wind called her name through the fire and Jasmine jumped back. This had happened before, this disembodied voice in the night, but she could never tell where the voice was coming from. But tonight, the cry was coming from the fire. Strange thing was, the higher the flames climbed, the colder the room got. Soon Jasmine could see her own breath.

Andrea Labore had rolled her eyes when Jasmine told her of the housemaid murdered in 1934. It was hard to tell what the man in the mask thought of the story.

"There was a girl that worked here. Her name was Stormy Day. She got murdered."

"Pretty name."

That was all he said. *"Pretty name."* He could say more with his eyes than any man she had ever met, but these days his eyes were red and tired, and difficult to read.

"Pretty name."

Again the wind through the fire called her name. Louder this time. Jasmine had heard enough. She breathed deeply. Was about to shout back. But then suddenly, the log on the fire exploded into flames seven feet tall. The room lit up as if it were high noon in hell. The flames began to take shape. Had it not been such a beautifully haunting figure emerging in the blaze, it would easily have been the most frightening thing Jasmine Allen had ever experienced.

Poised in perfect repose, the spirit in the fire, the sublime silhouette of a young woman, spoke to Jasmine in the softness and sweet innocence of a little girl's voice. Almost shy. Soothing, not frightening. *"The child is found in the church."* With that the apparition was gone. Vanished in the flicker of a flame. Disappeared so fast the black shadow may not have been there at all. The fire in the hearth returned to normal. The wind died.

Jasmine Allen was left trembling. But not out of fear. More the trembling of an epiphany. Her only fear, and a real fear it was, is that she would not be able to make sense of the message. *"The child is found in the church."*

Besides, who on earth would believe her?

Mrs. Traylor

Saturday. March 6. At the end of the day it was the organ music people would remember, a haunting, straining rendition of "Amazing Grace" played ad infinitum, piped through loudspeakers over the seven hills of the wintry white city. And then there was the endless procession of squad cars with their red swirling lights streaming down the snow-lined avenue. The skies were glass clear. The temperature reached 16 degrees. Sunny and cold. A good day to be laid to rest.

Among cops Les Angelbeck was a legend, but to the people of Minnesota he was just a police officer who died trying to rescue a baby. Perhaps nowhere in America do its citizens say good-bye to their men in blue the way they do in the Upper Midwest. From as far away as Canada, from the north woods of Wisconsin, across the prairies that sweep through the Dakotas, down through the farm fields of Iowa, and back up to the Twin Cities—a solid mass of uniformed police officers. Mounted patrols, noble cops on noble horses. Whimpering police dogs, and an occasional bark. And everywhere one looked, there were people. Thousands of them. On the snowy banks of the Cathedral of St. Paul, mothers clung to their bundled children. People crammed into the windows at the school across the way. From the foot of the great church to a mile down Summit Avenue people lined the snowy boulevards, many with their hands over their hearts, some with small American flags, while others simply held homemade signs that read Thank You.

Rick Beanblossom stood at attention beneath the entrance arch of his home and watched in awe as the Thin Blue Line escorted the flag-draped coffin of Captain Les Angelbeck down Summit Avenue. He saluted the hearse as it passed, rolling its way down to Snelling Avenue, where it would swing left, and then follow the Old Fort Road out to the cemetery. FBI Inspector Stephanie Koslowski stood beside him, hand to her heart. And then the organ music stopped, and there was silence. A lot of snow, a lot of people, and a lot of silence.

As cold as it was, he didn't feel like going inside. Rick pulled his collar up and then buried his hands deep into the pockets of his flight jacket for warmth. The crowd along the avenue began breaking up. Children stopped and pointed up the stairs at the man in the mask. Parents paused to look at the Victorian mansion where the baby was stolen, until police out front politely hurried them along.

Koslowski spoke first. "There's good news and bad news on the handwriting analysis," she told Rick.

The ice was melting between the two, but still the Marine listened to her warily. Les Angelbeck's suspicions about the tall, homely inspector were never far from Rick's thoughts. Esther Snow, whoever she was, was not acting alone.

That morning Koslowski had openly complained to Mrs. Howard about the kidnapping coverage in the *North Star Press,* about the unfair allegations of incompetence they were hurling at the FBI, and at her personally. Mrs. Howard, forever the diplomat, promised to speak to the editors. The great lady had stopped by the house on her way to the funeral. She had asked about Andrea and seemed slightly bewildered when Rick told her that Andrea had left for a little detective work in Little Falls. The owner and publisher of the *North Star Press* handed him a manila envelope that she had hurriedly stuffed with some of her late husband's papers. Rick had read so many documents from that era that they were beginning to blur together. Still, everybody involved, including Stephanie Koslowski, believed the key to the mystery of the missing baby could be found in words that had been put down on paper by people long since dead, or dying.

Standing in the freezing cold, her breath visible before her, the woman from the FBI tried to speak on a more personal level. No notes or documents. No official reports. One professional investigator to another. "Keep in mind handwriting analysis is subjective," she told Rick. "Even to this day nine handwriting experts will swear in a court of law that Bruno Hauptmann wrote the ransom notes to Charles Lindbergh. But at least one equally qualified expert will swear, just as emphatically, that he did not."

"What is your point?"

Inspector Koslowski carefully adjusted a pair of glasses that seemed too big for her face. "Our experts in Washington have concluded that the handwriting of Esther Kay Bjorenson, based on letters she wrote to her husband when she was young, matches the handwriting of the 'Esther' note that was sent to Grover Mudd."

Rick let the news sink in. "Then Esther Kay Bjorenson is Esther Snow?"

"It appears so."

His reporter's instincts had been dead on. The day that he had rushed to the Bjorenson house, the day the second *EKS* ransom note arrived in the mail, he knew that he was being led to Esther Snow—the same Esther K. Snow that Grover Mudd had unmasked a lifetime ago. But now she was comatose, near death. Somebody was using her.

"And the bad news," Rick said guessing, "is that the ransom notes sent to me don't match her handwriting."

"No," Koslowski said, correcting him, "the bad news is, they probably do match."

"What? That's impossible."

The inspector stated the FBI's case. "Keep in mind, the notes sent to you were written by an elderly woman. It's a difficult comparison, but our people in Washington are comfortable with their conclusions.

They added fifty years to the handwriting and concluded that all of the notes and letters were written by the same person."

Rick Beanblossom was incredulous. "Are you telling me that old lady is not in a coma?"

"Her husband won't consent to an independent medical examination," Koslowski informed him. "He says she's near death, and he doesn't want her disturbed. We'll try for a court order, based on the handwriting evidence. It's also possible that she slipped into a coma shortly after writing the notes. Maybe this crime was her last hurrah. We just don't know yet."

"Well, let's find out," Rick said, raising his voice, suddenly angry.

People on the street were staring up at them again. Koslowski stepped in front of the Marine, using her long winter coat to shield the conversation from onlookers and the ever present ears of the press. "You stay away from her, Rick. Even through that mask I can see your mind at work. Let us handle this. Whether you care to admit it or not, there are some things that we do well."

It is terrible to think of a senior citizen this way, but God, this woman was ugly. Wretched and misshapen. Mrs. Howard of the *North Star Press* was one of the oldest women Andrea Labore knew, but she still maintained a certain beauty and grace. But this crone was hideous. Andrea knocked the snow from her boots and, with only a slight limp, made her way into the library as if it were the proverbial house built of gingerbread in the middle of the forest. An obvious calcium deficiency had arched the old woman's backbone into a crescent moon. Her pumpkin head hung from the arch. Her nose seemed more of a parrot's beak, loosely attached to the fatty layers of dead orange skin that drooped over her bulbous skull. She appeared bloated, but frail. With books in her hands, she shuffled back and forth across the hardwood floors of the old town library like a malevolent gnome in a blowzy dress. She had no teeth, and her gums were clearly visible when she spoke. Actually, she didn't talk as much as she barked. "What do you want, child?"

It was Saturday morning. The highways had been reopened. Good traveling weather. Andrea had jumped at the chance to check out leads in Little Falls. Sitting around the house was driving her crazy. Rick would be attending the funeral of Captain Angelbeck. They agreed on a checklist, and then Andrea was off. Now seeing the elderly woman, Andrea took stock of her own sweet youth. Suddenly her back didn't hurt as much. "Mrs. Traylor, my name is Andrea Labore. I came up to Little Falls from St. Paul to tour the Lindbergh home. At the house they suggested you were the person to talk to about those days."

"And a lot of days before those days." Mrs. Traylor pushed the books into slots on the shelves, whether they actually belonged there or not. Later in the day one of the younger librarians would sort out the mess.

She looked Andrea up and down. "Skinny little thing, aren't you?"

Little Falls, Minnesota, is small town America. Midwest farm country more than two hours north of the Twin Cities. The town nestles up to the wild banks of the Mississippi River, still free of the plethora of locks and dams and industry that await the great waterway downstream. Little Falls is where the rich timberland of northern Minnesota meets the windswept prairies of western Minnesota. It was here that the "Lone Eagle" grew up. Set his moral compass.

"I'd like to talk to you about Charles Lindbergh."

"Which one?" asked Mrs. Traylor. "The Bolshevik congressman who ran for governor; the Nazi who flew his little airplane to Paris, big whooping deal; or the little boy who got kidnapped? They were all named Charles Augustus Lindbergh."

"The pilot," answered Andrea.

"Oh," sighed the old woman. "Why do you ask?"

"I'm a reporter. I'm working on a story."

"That's what the world needs. Another story about that worthless son of a bitch." Mrs. Traylor cut loose with a loud fart. It may have been her age, but Andrea suspected the vulgar woman could fart on cue. "People in this town still singing the praises of Charles Lindbergh. Been doing it for years. Did they tell you about the day we all climbed the water tower and painted over his name? 'Home of Charles Lindbergh.' I wanted to write 'Home of Lindbergher Cheese.' But we just whitewashed it. Let's see, then there was the night we strung Lindbergh up from a tree and burned him in effigy."

"Which Lindbergh?"

"Two out of three of them, that's which Lindbergh. Do you know how old I am?"

"No."

"Me neither. Damn shame to live this long. Seems the only thing in life I've ever forgotten was my age. I was his lover, you know."

"Which one?"

"Which lover, or which Lindbergh?"

"Which Lindbergh?"

"The congressman. His first wife died. Then came me. Then he married a certain schoolteacher drifted here from Detroit. Lazy hussy."

"Do you mean Evangeline . . . Charles Lindbergh's mother?"

"Yes, I suppose."

Andrea thought a minute about that last statement. "But if you were the elder Lindbergh's lover before he married Evangeline . . . you'd have to be almost one hundred and twenty years old."

"God, I'm not that old, am I? Maybe I came after the hussy." Mrs. Traylor finished stacking the books. They were standing in the children's section. "I was much prettier back then, you know. And I am talking beautiful, a real sex kitten. You think you're sleeping beauty, don't you? In my day a skinny little thing like you couldn't get a job selling cigarettes in a flophouse."

It had been a long time since anybody had talked

down to Andrea. Still, there was something honest and compelling about the old woman's crudeness.

"Come here, Rapunzel." She motioned Andrea over to a wall of brown and white photographs. The pioneer days. "See that picture?" Mrs. Traylor asked, pointing proudly. "That's me."

The faded photograph was dated circa 1919. An era of buxom women. The young woman standing in front of the library had a full figure. Very attractive. In youth the prominent nose gave her face an incongruous kind of beauty. Only in old age had it betrayed her.

Andrea searched the faces in the other photographs. "Do you happen to remember a woman named Esther Snow . . . it would have been around the time of the Lindbergh kidnapping?"

Mrs. Traylor shook her head in disgust. "You're going to have to do a lot better than Esther Snow if you're going to challenge my memory."

"You knew her then?"

"Yes, I knew Esther. German gal. I remember her because she was the only woman in Little Falls could claim to be as pretty as me. Mean little bitch, but a gorgeous woman. Had fingernails right out of Hansel and Gretel. She had a sister up here for a while. Well, she claimed it was her sister. I always thought it was her daughter."

"Her daughter? Why would she lie about something like that?"

"Well, honey, in those days you didn't have children

out of wedlock and boast about it. Not like these women today."

"What brought them to Little Falls?"

"To hear Esther tell it, she sailed over here on the SS *Charles Lindbergh* . . . I think they changed that ship's name back to the *James Madison* right about the time we whitewashed the tower. Anyhow, that's where she heard of us. When she got off the boat the only thing she knew about America was New York City and Little Falls, Minnesota. And we did have a sizable German population here. Personally, I thought Esther Snow was a born liar. She'd lie when the truth wouldn't hurt her. So there."

"What became of her?" Andrea wanted to know.

"What became of Esther Snow?" Mrs. Traylor shuffled back to the desk for more books. "Last I heard, and that was a normal person's lifetime ago, she married some man from the newspaper down there in St. Paul."

"Swede Bjorenson?"

"It might have been a Swede. She never came up here after that. Funny the things a person remembers, isn't it?"

"And the sister . . . what became of her?"

"She ran down to St. Paul when the war broke out. Apparently Esther found her a husband too."

"The FBI says Esther Kay Bjorenson wrote the goodbye note to Grover, and probably the ransom notes to ne. Koslowski's all but convinced she's Esther Snow. Vhat did you learn?"

"I learned a lot, but I don't know if it's worth anything. ;sther Snow had a sister up here in Little Falls, or maybe it ·as her daughter. That's what brought her up here."

"But, Andrea, Swede said her sister was in Ger- nany. Was he lying?"

"Maybe he didn't know. Apparently she brought her sis- ·r to America, probably illegally, and hid her up here in Lit- 'e Falls. When the war broke out she brought her down to t. Paul and found her a husband."

"So she sends her little sister to Little Falls, Min- ,esota, because that is where the great Charles Lind- ·ergh hails from . . . which may be the only thing she new about the place. She flees New York after the idnapping. Runs to her sister in Little Falls, then nakes her way down to St. Paul, only to find out the ity is a crooks' haven."

"Yes. Then she runs back here to Little Falls when the oing gets rough. But I don't understand why she wouldn't ave wanted her sister in New York with her. She obviously ·ved her very much. She smuggled her into America. She an to her when she was in trouble. She found her a hus- and."

"And then for sixty years she hid the fact that they vere related . . . even from Swede . . . her own hus- and? Why?"

"Mental retardation? Epilepsy? They did that kind of hing back then . . . hide children in the attic, in the base- ent . . . put them into so-called homes."

"There was no indication from Swede that Esth Kay's family suffered anything like that. And her on family was that sister in Germany."

"I was just thinking out loud. Mrs. Traylor suggested t sister may have been born out of wedlock . . . but hiding h is pretty drastic, even for those days. What?"

"You sound like a source I used to have . . . speakir of which . . . our electronics expert found a bug in m phone at the paper."

"Who would do that . . . the FBI?"

"I asked him that. He said a tap that sophisticate has to be installed with the phone. He thinks it's bee bugged all along. Dylan's kidnapping may have bee in the works for a long time."

"Rick, is it possible Esther's sister is doing this to us . or maybe her daughter?"

"Why would she want to reenact a crime Esther su cessfully committed over sixty years ago? And wh about the handwriting?"

"Maybe she got Esther Kay to write the notes before s lapsed into a coma. Or maybe she forged her sister's han writing."

"After reading what Grover Mudd had to say . she'd have to be an identical twin sister. Both of the diabolical."

"I didn't get diabolical out of Mrs. Traylor. The woman five hundred years old. The best I could do was 'mean litt bitch' and 'born liar.' County records weren't much he either. Those two, whoever they were, didn't leave a pap trail."

"Maybe they did, and we just haven't figured it out yet."

"What do you mean?"

"Mrs. Howard dropped off some of her late husband's papers this morning . . . you remember, Walt Howard, the crusading editor. Most of it's routine, but two things jump out . . ."

"What are they?"

"Do you remember that unpublished column Grover Mudd wrote just before he was killed . . . about Bruno Hauptmann's woman accomplice?"

"Yes . . . I remember you reading it to me."

"Walt Howard had a copy in his files. Grover must have sent him a draft. Then Grover was killed. The other piece I noticed was written twelve years later . . . October of 1948. It was an editorial written and published by Walt Howard, calling for a renewed investigation into the unsolved murder of Grover Mudd. But there was no follow-up. Walt Howard died in a hunting accident that weekend."

"And, Rick, all of this means . . . what?"

"What time is it?"

"Just past five."

"It means, come on home."

"I'm on my way. What are you going to do?"

"Me? I'm going to pay another visit to Esther Snow."

It was dark and extremely cold by the time Rick Beanblossom arrived at Swede Bjorenson's house. The temperature was hovering near zero. The street lamp was

out. A bright moon in a clear winter sky cast long dar
shadows over multiple layers of snow. The Marin
blew warm air into his leather gloves and then gav
the front door a good hard rap. There was no answe
No lights in the window. No sign of life anywher
Rick removed his gloves and knocked again. Loude
this time. Again, no answer. He bent over the rail an
peered into a window.

"They took her away."

Startled, Rick turned toward the sidewalk when sh
said that. He didn't like people sneaking up on him
He could make out the silhouette of a stout woma
standing below in the shadows. The man in the mas
couldn't see her face anymore than she could see his.

"They took her away," she said again.

"Who took her away?" Rick wanted to know. "A
ambulance . . . the FBI?"

"No, the coroner."

Rick froze. "She died?"

"Yes, Esther Kay died. This afternoon. I live acros
the street. The funeral and burial are tomorrow." Then
she added, "Oakland Cemetery," pointing up th
street.

Rick was crushed. "So soon?" he asked.

"That's the way Swede wants it. They were a ver
private couple. Besides, this wasn't unexpected. Ar
you family?"

Mrs. Bjorenson

y the time Rick Beanblossom passed through the ycamore Street gate at Oakland Cemetery the burial ervice was well underway. It was Sunday morning. he blizzards of March had been hard on everybody, ut this morning's snowfall was only a nuisance. Nee-les of ice danced in the frigid air before settling to the round, adding more snow to an already heavy base. Vinter seemed unbeatable.

In a city built on Indian graves, Oakland was the ldest Christian burial ground in St. Paul. Situated in e dilapidated neighborhood behind the State Capitol uilding, the medieval cemetery was a potpourri of eadstones jutting out of a landscape made heavenly hite by the weather. Everything from baroque mon-ments to Athenian temples appeared like candles in e snow. Here lay Minnesota's pioneers. The state's reat, near great, and not so great. Here too lay the umble. The man in the blue mask found the funeral arty on a small hill in the southwest corner. In newer raves were buried Minnesota's last wave of immi-

grants, the Hmong refugees of Southeast Asia. Ric
recognized family names. He had actually served wit
some of them in Vietnam. Had helped them come t
America.

It was a small gathering. The smallest flock Ric
Beanblossom had ever seen at a burial. Quite a con
trast to Saturday's funeral. A few family members,
few men from the *North Star Press*, and Mrs. Katherin
E. Howard. The owner and publisher of one of th
largest newspapers in the Midwest, the most influen
tial woman in the state, was attending a funeral for th
wife of a lifelong employee. A simple laborer. Only th
day before she had lead mourners at the funeral of
police officer. Was it any wonder why people love
her? Parked on the street outside the wrought-iro
fence were a couple of nondescript sedans, FBI agent
standing beside them.

Rick stood a respectful distance down the hill fron
Esther Kay Bjorenson's final resting place as the las
prayers were tolled, and the last tears rolled ove
cherry red faces, to be wiped away before they froze
Mrs. Howard walked over to Swede and kissed hi
cheek, embraced him as a mother would a child. The
she turned and walked away, alone, through th
snowy cemetery, tears still falling from beneath he
dark glasses. In some ways, it must be a curse to retai
a sharp mind well into old age. All of those memorie
and related emotions still intact, still lying in wait, t
be recalled in a split second.

The others paid their final condolences to Swed

jorenson, and then they too departed. Now the senior ressman stood alone in that god-awful moment that ll married couples know is one day coming, that noment when they are left standing alone at a ravesite. He was bundled in an overstuffed coat, a tie hoking his thick neck. His face was extra red from the old. With the tips of his ink-stained fingers, he rushed the casket of his dear wife, Esther Kay. Then e turned with a deep sigh and started down the hill. aught Rick's eyes and held his stare.

Rick Beanblossom hardly knew what kind of a reeting to expect. This was the man whose comatose vife he had accused of kidnapping his son. "I'm sorry, wede," he said, as the old man approached. "I am ruly sorry."

Swede Bjorenson stopped next to him. They were houlder to shoulder, two generations facing opposite irections. "She came down here from Little Falls to isit a friend. Married me. Moved into this crummy eighborhood . . . and never left. Fifty years. She eserved so much better. I tried . . . I swear to God, I ried."

"I'm sorry I don't know this, but did you have chil-ren?"

"No, my Esther Kay never wanted children. I did, but he insisted. Might have been a medical condition . . . I on't know. Women didn't talk to their husbands about hat sort of thing in those days. A gentleman didn't ask. ecrets and lies."

"How did you meet Esther Kay?" Rick asked him making awkward conversation.

The widower pulled a white handkerchief from his coat pocket. Blew his nose. "Mrs. Howard introduced us . . . she was her friend. They were both German immigrants, you know."

"No, I didn't know." Rick turned and watched Mrs Howard as she slowly walked along the shoveled path, dabbing at her eyes. The Swede seemed as if he wanted to talk. "So you've known the great lady that long?"

"Yes, great lady is right. She saved the paper, you know. If it weren't for her, the only newspaper we'd have to read in St. Paul would be that Minneapolis rag. Saved a lot of jobs too, including mine. Introduced me to my wife."

Yet the whole time the old man was extolling the great lady, Rick heard an off-key resentment in his voice. "Tell me more," Rick said.

"About Mrs. Howard?" Swede too turned and watched the old woman make her way past the graves. Her gray coat had the look of a dark cloud. "She was a big supporter of Democratic politics. Hubert Humphrey and his crowd. The paper was always endorsing Democrats in those days. She made a lot of enemies over the years. They spread some pretty nasty rumors about her . . . the death of her husband, and all."

"Walt Howard? What kind of rumors?"

"Oh, no autopsy. Quick funeral. That kind of thing."

"Suspicious circumstances?"

"Yes, suspicious circumstances. Men back then didn't like women in their politics. Things could get nasty."

Both men watched as Mrs. Howard stopped before a field of simple headstones. It was Soldier's Rest. Veterans of the Indian wars lay there; so did veterans of the Civil War, the Spanish-American War, and World War I. She seemed to be staring at one grave in particular.

"Is Walt Howard buried down there?" Rick asked.

"No," Swede told him. "We buried Mr. Howard at the Catholic cemetery . . . Calvary." He wiped his face and cleared his throat. "There are papers and such things at the house, Rick. A woman's life in boxes and drawers. If you think they might help find your little boy . . . you're welcome to go through them."

Rick turned back to Swede, his stomach churning. "They might clear up some questions. I know that many years ago Esther Kay was considered by some to be a suspect in the kidnapping of the Lindbergh baby . . . Grover Mudd seemed to think so. I simply don't know."

Swede Bjorenson placed his hand on the shoulder of Rick Beanblossom. "I pray for your son." He looked back one last time at the casket on the hill. "We prayed together for him. Every day." Then he shook his head, more in regret than sorrow. He shuffled away, leaving the Marine alone to watch Mrs. Howard standing before the graves down at Soldier's Rest.

"One more thing, Swede . . . if you would. The hunting accident that killed Walt Howard . . . who shot him?"

The big Swede stopped and glanced around, conspiratorially. Stared down at Soldier's Rest. Lowered his voice. "She did."

Stephanie

Rick Beanblossom spent the rest of the day grilling his colleagues at the *North Star Press*. Andrea Labore did the same at Sky High News. They had to be careful how they posed their questions, but the answers came back the same.

It was Sunday afternoon. Late afternoon. Rick Beanblossom and Andrea Labore were perched in front of a small fire in the nursery. They were like children hiding in their own house. The door was closed and locked. The light was off. A steady snowfall could be seen outside the window, the same window the monster had used to enter the house. The parents of the missing child were lying together on a thick rug that lay between the fireplace and the empty crib. Andrea was curled into Rick, her back to his chest. Rick's arm was draped over her shoulder; his fingers toyed with her hair. The baby's blankets were still in the crib. Paper sunshine hung on the wall. Fingerprint dust clung to the woodwork.

Spread before them were the writings of Grover Mudd, as well as the editorials of Walt Howard—two crusading journalists who may have unwittingly crossed the same woman. Now, decades later, two other journalists discussed their findings in whispers.

Andrea read from her notes. "Jasmine Allen, whose grandfather discovered the Lindbergh baby dead in the woods, gets a grant to study nursing in Minnesota. And that grant comes from . . . ?"

"The Howard Foundation," answered Rick.

"Jasmine Allen is placed in our home by . . . ?"

"By a recommendation from the Howard Foundation."

"How did you get your cushy job at the *North Star Press*?"

"Mrs. Howard offered it to me."

Andrea Labore flipped a page and continued. "Esther Kay comes down to St. Paul from Little Falls to visit her friend . . . ?"

"Mrs. Howard."

"Eligible bachelor and man in uniform Swede Bjorenson is introduced to Esther Kay by . . . ?"

"Mrs. Howard." Rick Beanblossom began to put the pieces together. "Katherine Howard may be the mysterious sister from Germany."

"And the handwriting?" Andrea asked.

"She got Esther Kay to write the ransom notes before she lapsed into a coma, or maybe she forged her sister's handwriting . . . I don't know . . . but she still has to be working with somebody." Rick was doing his detective work out loud. He glanced over his shoulder at the locked door. "It has to be somebody inside this house, or inside this investigation. Somebody young enough and strong enough to climb a ladder into this room."

Andrea closed her notebook and drew a deep breath, the sweet redolence of her child still in the nursery. "Did they kill him . . . like the Lindbergh baby?"

Rick pressed his hand over hers, gently but reassuringly. "Andrea, I know in my heart that Dylan is alive." He held her close, his mask brushing the side of her face. "What if, as some suspect, the Lindbergh baby died accidentally . . . in a fall, or maybe Hauptmann killed the baby against Esther's orders? What if, in some sick way, Katherine Howard is trying to get it right this time?"

Andrea breathed hard. "She successfully kidnapped our baby. She collected the ransom money. Why doesn't she give us back our son?"

"Maybe she doesn't know how . . . or maybe she's truly that evil," Rick answered in frustration. "We may have only a few hours before she learns we're on to her . . . if she doesn't suspect it already."

Andrea turned to face him. "*If* Mrs. Howard and her mysterious accomplice *don't* know that we're on to them . . . can't we somehow use that to our advantage?"

Rick's eyes lit up at the thought. "Talk to me, Grover. Talk to me." The Marine scrambled through the papers on the floor. "Here it is." He held up the unpublishe column and read, " *'How to catch this murderer? Lure h to a cemetery with false promises, as she did Lindbergh . . .'*

"How do we do that?" Andrea asked.

"My phone at the paper," he reminded her. "If it wa tapped . . . that means it's still tapped. Let's you and make a phone call."

"Do you mean a phony conversation?"

Rick spun around in front of her. "It's simpl Tonight we make a fake phone call about a new ran som demand . . . hopefully luring at least one of th kidnappers to Oakland Cemetery. Whoever is listen ing in is bound to show up . . . either to collect th money, or to try and stop someone else from collectin the money."

Andrea was dubious. "With all of the people wh may be listening to our phone conversations, it migh get pretty crowded in that cemetery."

"That's what I'm hoping."

Despite winter's firm grip, the days were gettin longer. The supernatural whiteness of the late after noon snowfall cast dark shadows through the win dows of the mansion. One of those shadows crept u the grand staircase and overlapped the balustrade o the second floor. Jasmine Allen stood within tha shadow, staring down at the fire in the grand hall. Th parents of Dylan Labore Beanblossom had been gon all day. When they finally returned to the house the locked themselves in the child's nursery, as if the were never coming out. Two hours later, Mr. Beanblossom grabbed his coat in a hurry and left the house alone. Andrea slipped back into the master bedroom.

Jasmine turned and peered down the hall at the bedroom door, which was slightly ajar. They were a strange couple, she thought, beauty and the beast. But which was which? Rick Beanblossom could say the most beautiful things, while it was Andrea Labore who could sometimes behave beastly. Who were these people, Jasmine asked herself? She'd worked for them for a year, cared for their baby, and didn't know them at all.

Rick Beanblossom had seen the dark side of life, but what of Andrea Labore? The kidnapping of her son may have been the first time in her life the queen of the evening news had faced real trouble.

Jasmine Allen approached the bedroom door, hoping to see if she could be of any comfort. She peeked inside. Andrea had her back to the room. The news anchor pulled a cellular telephone from her purse. A notebook was in her hand. Jasmine stepped back, just an inch. The FBI had tapped the house phones. Apparently, Andrea wanted this conversation kept private. Without knowing what possessed her to do it, the housekeeper put her ear to the open door and listened in.

"Beanblossom."

"It came."

"What came?"

"Another note. A cab driver just dropped it off at the house."

"What does it say?"

"Midnight in Oakland Cemetery. Soldier's Rest. Come alone, Masked Man."

"That's where Grover Mudd is buried. Did you show it to Koslowski?"

"No, I don't trust her. There's a dollar figure."

"How much?"

"Another hundred thousand."

"Christ, Andrea . . ."

"We can do that."

"We'll have to borrow. We haven't got much time."

"Please hurry."

How strange, thought Jasmine. No cab drivers had come to the house that she knew of. There had been no deliveries all day. Still, on this snowy afternoon, it wasn't the behavior of her strange employers Jasmine Allen was wondering about, as much as she was reflecting on the fire in that magical fireplace.

"The child is found in the church."

No, she hadn't imagined it. She heard it as clear as a cathedral bell. As clear as the night of the crying baby. The ghost that haunted the house spoke to her. The spirit of Stormy Day had been sending her messages for a week. The church of which she spoke had to be the Cathedral of St. Paul. If Stormy Day had lived in this neighborhood, if she had worked at this house in this city, that's the church she would have meant.

In the morning, she feared, the FBI lady would come for her. They would drive her over to Minneapolis and never again would she return to the house on Summit Avenue. The only way Jasmine could truly prove her innocence was to find the baby before morning. Rescue him. Tonight, she decided, in the hour after midnight, when Mr. Beanblossom was at the cemetery, and all was deathly quiet, she would slip out the back of the house and go to the church in search of the child.

Inspector Stephanie Koslowski moved to the third-floor window of the Summit Avenue mansion and watched the snow as it fell over the leaky dome of the great church. The light of day had disappeared from the early March sky. Another white night.

She had been among the first group of women admitted to the FBI training academy. Right out of the academy she was assigned to the field office in Seattle. On Thanksgiving Eve, her first year on the job, a passenger aboard Northwest Orient Flight 305, Portland to Seattle, handed the stewardess a note:

> Miss—I have a bomb here, and I would like you to sit by me.

Hijacked. A high-profile case. Highest in the country. Special Agent Stephanie Koslowski was added to the investigative team. She was young and eager, and determined to prove her mettle. The hijacker had purchased his ticket under the name D. B. Cooper. At ten thousand feet, to the amazement of all, he parachuted from the aft staircase of the Boeing 727 and disappeared into the cold night air of the Pacific Northwest.

Stephanie Koslowski stayed on the team and worked the case for two years. But the dream assignment turned into a nightmare. D. B. Cooper was never to be seen or heard from again.

On the rebound years later, Stephanie Koslowski became one of the first women at the FBI promoted to the rank of inspector. She was assigned to the Minneapolis office, with responsibilities from St. Paul, Minnesota, to Rapid City, South Dakota. Her grandfather had fought gangsters in St. Paul during the depression. But it wasn't gangsters she encountered upon her arrival. The first investigation she headed up was the disappearance of twelve-year-old Harlan Wakefield. Few things count for more in the FBI than solving a kidnapping case. Especially the kidnapping of a child. But as with the D. B. Cooper case, two years dragged by with no answers. Another nightmare, only this one had an ending. As it turned out, Harlan Wakefield wasn't kidnapped at all. He was shot to death by his twin brother and then dumped in the St. Croix River. And it wasn't FBI Inspector Stephanie Koslowski who solved the case. It was an arrogant reporter without a face who brought the Cain and Abel tragedy to light—a masked reporter with more secret sources than an undercover cop. The FBI is not kind to its women. It's even less kind to its failures. Stephanie Koslowski had failed twice.

But this case, this kidnapping, was going to be different. It was going to end with the baby rescued and the kidnappers in custody. The inspector would see to that even if it killed her.

She got along well with men. They respected her intelligence. Her dry wit. But she had never married. Had no children. Behind her back, colleagues speculated about her sex life. Retirement was in sight. At the bureau, that's age fifty-five. When that day arrived, Stephanie Koslowski would have all of the money she needed. Maybe she would go home to Chicago. Winter vacations in Florida. Maybe a second career teaching at a university. The kidnapping of Dylan Labore Beanblossom was a shot at redemption. Go out on top. She was sure if she could just keep that faceless son of a bitch out of her way, it would all come to a wonderfully happy ending.

He was so damn smug, hiding behind that blue mask of his, never mentioning the Wakefield case, but totally self-assured in the fact that it was always there, like a gun hidden in his back pocket. His newspaper, the *North Star Press*, was digging into her past. They went a lot further than just questioning her competency. The pressure was mounting. The inspector would have to work fast. Tonight, she would not let Jasmine Allen out of her sight. In the morning she would take the young housekeeper into custody. Bring her to the offices in Minneapolis. Sweat her. Break her. Schedule a press conference. Blow victory smoke.

The chimes began in the bell tower of the cathedral: 6 P.M. The snowfall seemed to intensify in the absence of light. Stephanie Koslowski was a lapsed Catholic of Polish descent. It had been years since she had made a confession. It wouldn't hurt to drop in, she thought, staring at the church. Maybe light a candle. Maybe whisper a prayer for a successful end to the kidnapping of Baby Dylan.

Taxi Driver

ṫ was now 11:55 P.M. Sunday, March 7. Six days since
he abduction of her son. The night sky over the
ıvenue was imperial white with snow. Andrea Labore
urned away from the bedroom window and walked
ɔver to her purse on the dresser. She lifted her service
'evolver and popped open the cylinder.

"Let's get our son back," Rick had said to her.

With those words Andrea remembered why it was
;he had married this man without a face. She had
watched with a loving wife's pride and awe as Rick
;lipped down the darkened stairs at the back of the
ıouse, and for the second time in a week set out into
he snow and the cold to pay a ransom for their son.
3ut this time the ransom was tissue paper stuffed into
ı hockey bag.

Rick would go alone. Andrea would follow, service
'evolver in hand. No FBI. The next move belonged to
he monsters who had stolen their child.

When the door had closed behind him, a blast of
rigid air swept up the stairs and hit Andrea in the

face. The girl from the Iron Range crept back to the bedroom and prepared to follow her husband. They'd agreed she would leave for the cemetery ten minutes after he did. Neither one of them liked the risks. But neither one of them felt they had a choice.

It was cold. Still, her gloves had to be light enough to get a good grip on the gun. She expected to use it. She chose the black leather gloves she used for driving. Then the bells in the cathedral tower struck twelve.

Andrea saw a movie once, years ago. A Western. Maybe Steve McQueen was in it. When the bad guy wouldn't talk, the good guys shot him in the arm. Then the other arm. Then the leg. The bad guy was running out of limbs when he finally spilled the beans. As a cop, she would never dare go that far. As a mother, she would go even further.

The former Minneapolis police officer had just holstered her gun beneath her coat when there was a rap at the bedroom door. Andrea jumped. She checked the clock. Five minutes past twelve. She had to get out of the house. Still, she didn't want to raise suspicions. She buttoned her coat. Opened the door.

It was Jasmine. "There's a man at the front door. A taxi driver."

He stood in the foyer at the foot of the staircase. A thin man. Ethiopian or Somalian. He looked frightened. The door behind him was open, letting the freezing air in, as well as the snowflakes. Jasmine moved down the stairs and stood a respectful distance to the side, but close enough to hear what the cab driver had to say. Which wasn't much. "I'm 'pose to give ya this." He handed Andrea a piece of paper.

I have what you are looking for
be at the church in the hour after midnight
in the stairs to the bell tower

The note hit her like an ice pick. It was the same beautifully ugly scrawl as the other notes. The same calligraphy as the good-bye note Esther Snow had written to Grover Mudd. It was the real thing.

Katherine

A heaven angry with snow provided a flat, sourceless light for the cemetery. Rick Beanblossom moved with caution past the graves, his sky-blue mask shielding his face from the weather. He had little trouble finding his way along the plowed path to Soldier's Rest. Tucked into the hillside, barely visible above a harsh winter of snowbanks, were the simple white headstones. They were fading to gray and stained with moss, but they maintained more dignity per square inch than all of the marble monuments and towering obelisks in the cemetery combined. The Marine placed the hockey bag on the frozen road and walked respectfully along the hallowed ground, dusting snow from the names until he found the stone he was searching for. He crouched down and wiped away the last white flakes from the inscription.

GROVER CLEVELAND MUDD
MINNESOTA
1 LIEUT. U.S. M.C.
2 DIV
OCTOBER 31, 1895
APRIL 3, 1936

After a minute, Rick got to his feet. He adjusted the collar on his flight jacket. He fidgeted with his gloves. Knocked snow from his hiking boots. Blew warm air into his fist. No, it wasn't the cold making him shake, nor the hopeful rendezvous with the kidnappers. It was a Marine's sense of pride and loss that was shooting at his heart. Threatening him with tears. For when the old soldiers die in the old soldiers' homes, it is not the sound of their beloved wife or their devoted children that they take to their graves, nor the playful barking of their favorite dog or their church choir singing their favorite hymn—rather it is the sound of combat they carry with them to their final resting place. The smell of powder and blood. The cries of victory, and the cries for help. The sight of young and fearless comrades lying soulless on the ground, never to go home, never to raise a family; denied a life of sharing and caring, and love, and aging gracefully with the seasons.

When the subzero winds kicked up, the chill cut through his mask and stung the scar tissue that was his face. This combination of emotion and weather made his eyes water. The Marine was smoothing away the moisture with the tips of his gloves when he spotted her coming down the hill. She walked like it was a stroll in the park. The breeze through the icy elms made crackling sounds that only added to her eerie arrival.

She wore a long black coat, with a high collar turned up to the falling snow. She moved toward him as if her boots were walking on top of the snow, not through it. Past the gravestones she floated, in and out of the shadows of the trees. As she came closer and closer, Rick was struck by the remarkable planes of her face. And for just an instant, for one brief shining moment with her countenance reflecting the snowflakes, she was young again. Her white hair was blond. Her skin was free of age. A woman stepping through time who was possessed of both grace and charm. The freezing cold seemed to throw a red glow into her face, and in that face Rick Beanblossom could see an incredible, haunting beauty. Then she stepped through the last shadows of the trees and paused at the grave of Grover Mudd. "Good evening, Richard."

For Rick Beanblossom, that was when it all came together—that moment of clarity he had been praying for since the night of the abduction. "Hello, Esther. *Sprechen sie Deutsch?*"

"Ja," she answered in her native German, *"ich spreche Deutsch sehr gut."* She had a musical voice, almost sexual and seductive for an elderly woman, as if she could have been singing an aria from a Wagnerian opera. "Where did I slip up?"

"Grover Mudd," he told her. "The more I read about you, the more I knew I was dealing with Esther Snow. The real Esther Snow."

When Jasmine Allen passed beneath the rose window of the Cathedral of St. Paul, she had complete faith in her belief that the kidnapping of Baby Dylan would soon be coming to an end. That the child could be found inside the church. She had watched Andrea Labore leave the house. Start for the church. Then she followed. Now with her gloved hand wrapped firmly around the iron door handle, Jasmine glanced over her shoulder at snow falling like a luminous shroud over Cathedral Hill. The snowfall threw shadows in odd directions, and despite her optimism she couldn't help feeling that she too was being followed.

The heavy door swung closed behind her. Suddenly it was hot, in stark contrast to the freezing air outside. She shed her wool coat, the heavy white flakes spilling onto the marble floor. Out of the corner of her eye, she saw a tall door swing closed near the baptistry. Not being Catholic, she felt like an intruder. She tiptoed through the narthex to the wide open doors of the nave, the heart of the cathedral. Peered inside. Not a soul in sight. But at the same time, despite its lordly dimensions, everything about the cathedral seemed warm and welcoming.

The young housekeeper had not been prepared for the enormous size of this church. Seven thousand square feet beneath the dome. She was awestruck by the ornateness of the gilded ceiling, and by the flood of colored light as it filtered through a hundred stained glass windows. The confessionals ran beneath the windows in the six transepts that flanked the aisles, north and south. Candlelight gave the interior a soft, radiant glow that could only be duplicated in heaven itself. The girl from New Jersey had never before seen such glory.

Jasmine Allen made her way down a long, lonely aisle to a red-oak pew near the sanctuary. A memorial plaque was attached to the side of the pew, commemorating a 1962 visit to the cathedral by President Kennedy. She took a seat. Laid her coat across her lap. Stared up at the altar.

Directly above her was the mosaic of an angel representing the cardinal virtue of prudence. In one hand this angel held a mirror, reminding the viewer that it is by looking back into the past that we find the wisdom needed to guide us into the future. In the angel's other hand was a snake recalling Matthew's scriptural injunction. *"You must be clever as a serpent . . ."* And above this heroic angel, at the base of the dome, were twenty-four windows of stained glass, depicting the angelic choirs of heaven.

Then Jasmine glanced heavenward into the gold-leaf dome, now marred by leaking snow melt. Where would one hide a baby in such a church? Or more likely, was the child being brought *to* the church?

No sooner had that thought crossed her mind when she heard the cry. She heard it as clearly as she had eard the apparition in the fireplace. The baby who ad one night come crying on the wind, was now crying in the great dome of the church, as if abandoned on is way to heaven. Then without warning, macabre rgan music reverberated through the marble walls, drowning out the weeping child. It was a heavy, harnonious, spiritualistic, breathtaking kind of music. And in the empty church, it was loud and frightening.

Minutes before Jasmine Allen passed beneath the rose vindow, Andrea Labore had entered the great church, ıer head covered with snow. It was warm inside, and Andrea hurriedly shook the snowflakes from her hair s she adjusted her eyes to the light. Candles lit the vay. She peered into the sanctuary at the lavishly adorned interior. Walls of golden stone accented the hiseled features of the statues of the apostles. The size of the church was breathtaking. Pews that could seat hree thousand sat empty, as if all those who had come o worship in the midnight hour had been ordered away.

The church had two towers, but only the south ower housed the bells. Andrea moved through the andlelight shadows, past the wrought-iron grille of he baptistry. Inside, the first baptism in Minnesota erritory was portrayed in a stained glass window. It vas performed on a dying Indian child by Father Louis Hennepin in 1680. Andrea paused just long enough to catch the inscription. *"That thou may have ife everlasting."*

The mother of the missing child glanced over h shoulder. Someone else was entering the church. A s of tall doors stood off to the left. Andrea pulled ope the doors. Stepped inside. Pulled them closed.

She found herself in the frost-coated stairwell th led up to the choir loft, and then up to the bell towe Andrea leaned back against the wall and tried to st the loud beating of her heart. The chill of the bric walls was penetrating, slipping like sin through h wet hair. From halfway up the steep stairs came th flickering glow of candles, presumably from the cho loft. And there was the silence, that cold, hollow kin of silence that is intensely magnified by being alone i a church where you don't feel you belong.

She listened for footsteps outside the door, but th footsteps never came. It occurred to Andrea th maybe she was in the wrong tower. Could the kidnap per of her baby be standing in the north tower, waitin for her? Andrea reached for the handle on the doc And that's when she heard it. She heard it as clearly she had heard it earlier in the week. It was the unmi takable sound of a crying baby. It wasn't coming fro the pews of the church, or the sanctuary, or even th baptistry. It was coming from above.

Not all crying babies sound alike. A mother instin tively knows when it's her child, and Andrea Labo believed in her heart that the crying baby was Dylan

The former cop reached for her gun. Then sh thought better of it. Left it holstered beneath her coa

She started up the stairs, hugging the walls. Movin

cautiously skyward through the shadows that snaked up the freezing stairwell. Then, halfway up, the music began. Organ music. Nightmarish music so loud and so intense it drowned out the screaming child. Passed clean through the soul of Andrea Labore.

The lighting was dim and got worse as she climbed. She climbed into darkness, and then through it. The frigid air of the stairwell was left below. Her heart was beating so fast, so loud, she thought it might fail. The gun remained hidden beneath her coat. Her only weapon in hand was her will, and it had turned to iron.

Andrea stayed in the shadows as she moved stealthily into the choir loft. Only a freestanding candelabra lit the organ. And that organ, now performing the requiem of the dead, was of biblical proportions. There were over four thousand pipes—and in the shadows of these giant pipes, these shrieking pipes, seated as if disembodied at the keyboard, was the equally giant silhouette of a monster.

There wasn't a lot of wind associated with it. It just kept snowing. The rolling hills of the cemetery appeared as heaven might appear on earth, calm and white.

"Ah, yes, *Herr* Grover," she said. Mrs. Katherine E. Howard kept her hands in her coat pockets. Maybe she had a gun. Maybe not. "Please go on," she said, in a voice cold as ice.

Rick Beanblossom put the puzzle together as he

spoke. "You masterminded the whole thing . . . used your money and your foundation to make it happen. You paid for the restoration of Fort Snelling . . . you saw the plans."

"That's what you came up with . . . that I saved a crumbling fort?"

"In your restoration work, did you come across an escape hole?"

"You are such a clever man . . . you tell me."

"You offered me a job, a ridiculous amount of money. You gave me an office, a free hand, and then you tapped my telephone."

"You and Andrea have had a productive day, Richard."

"That's how you found out about Les Angelbeck," he said, staring into her face. "Then you set the two of us up with the payoff at the fort."

Katherine Howard tossed off a laugh so contemptuous that Rick shuddered. "Do you think you were the only person in town that man fed news tips to? Les Angelbeck was feeding me the dirty details of crime stories before you were born. In return, I used my newspaper to build his legend."

"You were the reason he had a fascination with the Lindbergh kidnapping. He was on to you, wasn't he?"

"Yes, but he didn't know it. He suspected Esther Snow was still out there somewhere . . . maybe living right here in St. Paul. I'm afraid I couldn't afford to wait until he found her."

Her whole demeanor was melting before his eyes

sappearing in the snowfall. As she spoke of her
mes, the noble Katherine Howard Rick thought he
ew was gone. The great lady had been replaced by
s ice queen. "Do you know what really did you in,
ther?" Rick pointed to the grave of Grover Mudd.
ne lousy letter."

She stared down at the gravestone. "How's that,
chard?"

"Like a good reporter, Grover Mudd included your
ddle initial in his first story. Esther K. Trinka, he
ote. The *K* was for Katherine. Esther 'Katherine'
inka. Also known as Esther Snow. When all of the
ngsters were gone, you resumed life in St. Paul as
therine Something-or-other. You married Walt
oward when his ailing wife died. Then you handed
f your real first name when you brought your sister
wn here from Little Falls. Introduced her to the
ung Swede. The late Esther Kay Bjorenson, I'm
essing, was your sister?"

"Yes, and no. She was my daughter . . . from my
ther."

Rick was stunned, but the incestuous witch seemed
touched. Unmoved. He tried to shake off the shock
her horrible secret. Regain his composure. "That
ould explain the mysterious Mrs. Bjorenson," he
id, in a halting voice. "And the handwriting."

Esther Snow kept her eyes cast down toward the
avestone, as if in a trance. "My father was one of
ose famed aviators so worshipped by the German
ople . . . much like your Charles Lindbergh. You see,

Richard, I was once pretty. Perhaps as beautiful
your Andrea. My own father was such that he co
not resist me." She paused for effect, rememberi
"Father came through the Great War unscathed.
national hero. Ironically, he died with a bullet in
head. I put it there." Again she stood silent, the sn
falling about her, her mind wandering somewh
near the second decade of the century. Then she turn
and gazed up at the hill where only yesterday they h
buried Mrs. Swede Bjorenson. Her only child. H
daughter. Her sister. She put a gloved hand to her ch
as if to quiet her troubled heart. "He raped me at th
teen and then found me a husband at fourteen . . . j
before my baby was born."

Rick spoke softly, careful not to break the sp
"And what became of that husband, Esther?"

She released a scornful sigh, her breath visible. "
came home from the war on leave. Got drunk. Seve
days later he was found floating in a river, his he
bashed in with the butt of his own rifle. I rememb
hitting him so hard I could see his brains through
cracks in his skull. I used to tell people he was kil
during the war."

It was all being stated so damn cold and bold, R
believed every word to be the truth. "And then y
came to America," he said, prodding her along. "
New York you met a fellow German named Bru
Hauptmann."

"He was married . . . Anna was her name.
became lovers. Despite his flaws, we made quite

am. Our minds were as one. He hated the name
runo. He was always called by his middle name . . .
ichard."

"As you call me?"

"Precisely. Only Richard Hauptmann was a weak
an. Not to mention, a clumsy one. He dropped the
aby coming down that stupid ladder he built. The
aby hit the window ledge, broke his little neck. My
nly mistake in a perfect kidnapping. He was still
reathing . . . struggling for life . . . so I smothered
im. An act of mercy, I swear. After we had buried the
aby and were driving back to New York, I told
ichard the only way that he could truly prove his
ve for me was to take our secret to his grave."

Rick motioned toward the headstone. "Except
rover Mudd wasn't going to let that happen."

Esther Snow glanced down at the inscription on the
one, the beauty of her youth peering through her
res. "In Grover Mudd, I'd finally met my match. I
uldn't control the man. Couldn't buy him. Couldn't
in his love. So I left town and waited for nature, and
erman mustard gas, to take its course. But he wouldn't
ie . . . wouldn't stop writing. Even unemployed, he
as sticking his nose where it didn't belong. Right up
ntil the end he was begging Walt Howard to launch a
arch for the mysterious woman with the gold notes
om the Lindbergh kidnapping."

"Of course Grover, being sick and out of work, didn't
now that Walt Howard was already dating that mys-
rious woman."

"Yes."

"So you killed him?"

"Yes."

"Shot him down like a dog, right in front of his lit girl?"

"Yes."

Her callous confession to Grover's murder stru him hard, but he pushed on. "That should bring us u to 1948 . . . the infamous hunting accident."

"My husband was a very noble man. He had fac down some of the most notorious gangsters, and son of the most crooked politicians this country ever pr duced. He couldn't live with the fact that somebo had murdered Grover Mudd and had gotten aw with it. I begged him to let it go. But he had made his mind to launch another one of his editorial car paigns. Breathe new life into a murder investigati that was as dead as his war hero columnist."

"So you murdered your second husband. Made look like an accident, and took over the paper."

"Somebody had to take some control over t Grover Mudds of the world." Esther Snow now turn her full attention toward Rick Beanblossom. "If y had seen firsthand how the newspapers behaved du ing the Lindbergh case, you would understand. Th executed my Richard before the trial even began. was people like me that cleaned up their act. Ma them responsible again. Respected." Here her voi became frigid, increased with intensity as she set h sights on her final prey. "And now comes Richa anblossom . . . with his Pulitzer Prize, and his war edals, and his sanctimonious writings on the differ-ce between a gangster and a saint. I suspect that if I re that mask from your head, I'd find the face of rover Mudd. You remind me so much of him, you ake me ill."

The Marine moved slowly to his right, forming a tri-gle among himself, Esther Snow, and the grave of rover Mudd. "Why our baby?" Rick asked. "Why ndrea?"

"Simple . . . in this day and age, I couldn't find a ro . . . so I chose the next best thing . . . a celebrity." ther moved to her right, lengthening the triangle, e snow falling hard between them. "When your by was born, everything fell into place. I just had to ait until Anne Lindbergh died."

"You planned this whole thing in less than a week?"

"No. I've been planning this for seventy years." ey both stood silent in the snow. "Aren't you going ask me why?"

The man without a face shrugged his shoulders, wildered. "Ask the cancer why it kills . . ."

"That's too simple, Richard. You're smarter than at." Esther Snow stepped toward the grave of rover Mudd. Stared Rick Beanblossom in the eyes. 'ou see, Richard, if you live long enough, it all comes ound again. Anna Hauptmann lived to be ninety-e. Never remarried. Spent her whole life trying to ear the name of a husband who was guilty as hell. nne Lindbergh, poor little rich girl, went on to literary fame. Lived to be ninety-three. I'm the last on The last of three women whose lives crossed one col March night, a lifetime ago."

"I'm still waiting for the why."

"I told you . . . I only made one mistake. The Lin bergh baby was supposed to live. It was Charles Lin bergh who was supposed to die."

"I see . . . you were going to kill your father all ov again."

"We were going to lure the 'Lone Eagle' to a cem tery, then offer the baby's life in exchange for his life. desperately wanted to see what kind of principles th American hero really possessed. But after the bab was dead, I didn't really give a damn what Richar did with Lindbergh."

"So are you going to get it right this time?"

"Yes, Richard, your son is alive and well . . ." Sh pulled a small handgun from her coat pocket an stepped directly onto the grave of Grover Mud "... But I'm afraid you're not going to make it. won't insult you by making you choose betwee your own life and the life of your son." Esther Sno looked at the hockey bag lying on the path. "Wh do you have in the bag?"

Rick Beanblossom was searching the shadows of th trees for his wife. She should have arrived by now with a gun of her own. "Toilet paper," he answered.

"How clever. I'm sure you're proud of your litt ruse here, luring me to a cemetery, but aren't you fo getting something?"

"You're still holding my son."

"Yes, that . . . and the fact that all of my life I've ayed one step ahead of those who sought to destroy e. Andrea won't be joining us this evening, as you pected. She's decided to attend church. She should in the bell tower about now."

"What have you done?"

"It took me two whole seconds to figure out your one call about another ransom note was phony. Still, thought how appropriate it would be to meet you re, at Grover's grave. So I diverted your lovely wife the cathedral, where she too will meet her end."

sther Snow raised the gun, pointing it squarely tween the eyes of the mask that had sheltered him r years. "Good-bye, Richard. Some day may we meet gain."

Though the snow was falling heavily, the illumi-ated dome of the cathedral could still be seen—but st barely, almost a shadow. For a second the dome rew Rick's eyes away from Esther Snow as he ought of his wife roaming the cavernous church in arch of their child. But then with an odd flick of her rist, the old lady again arrested his attention.

At first Rick believed it was the cold, or her age, or en a pang of morality. The gun in her hand began to ake. Subtly at first, then violently. But even more amatic than her trembling hands was the look that d crept into her ancient eyes—something he had ly glimpsed once before, that day in her office, the

morning after his son's abduction. It was fear. Esth
Snow was scared.

The gun dropped from her hand to the foot of th
headstone and almost disappeared beneath the snov
She grabbed her left arm and squeezed. Squeezed as
her life depended on it. Then she fell to her knee
saliva spilling out the corner of her mouth.

"Richard, my heart pills . . ."

She had been standing in the falling snow lon
enough that her black coat was frosted white. He
head was crowned with flakes. And as the snowfa
increased, Esther could once again be seen returning t
the beauty of her youth.

Rick Beanblossom stood frozen in place, silen
watching, waiting.

She was on her knees now, clutching at her ches
Her tortured breath rolled out before her in painfu
spasms. "Richard, there's a phone in my car. Get me a
ambulance, then I'll tell you where to find the baby."

"Tell me now," said Rick.

"Do as I say, damn you."

"Who's your partner this time around? Wh
climbed the ladder for you? Judging from the way yo
smeared Koslowski's name all over your newspape
I'm guessing it's not her. That leaves Jasmine Allen .
am I right?"

"My pocket . . . the pills are in my pocket."

Rick Beanblossom moved not a muscle to help he
"Where's my son?" Esther Snow remained silent, arro
gant, even as she stared at death—determined to tak

her secrets to her grave. "Grover was right. You'll never tell. You don't have it in you."

She found her second wind. Esther reached into her coat pocket for her bottle of pills. She held on to the bottle for dear life, actually found the strength needed to open it. But the pills were white, and with thick gloves over trembling hands she fumbled the pills into the snow. She was dying, and she seemed to know it. Her enchanting blue eyes were being covered with the film of death. "I was born a hundred years ago," she cried, defiantly. "I am the twentieth century."

His blue mask was turning white with snow. Rick watched in awe as the years and the life paradoxically drained from her face at the same time. She had killed two husbands and her own father, the Lindbergh baby, and Grover Mudd. Maybe others. With delusions of grandeur she had gone from gangster moll to newspaper mogul, from the Nazi Party to the Democratic Party. Esther Snow was one for the books all right.

She pawed at the grave. "My pills . . . I only need one."

Rick Beanblossom stepped through the snow, but instead of picking up her pills, he reached down and picked up the gun. "You're yesterday's news, Esther." He pocketed the weapon. Glanced down at the headstone. "She's all yours, Grover." He turned and started after his wife. Left the old woman behind, on her knees in the snow.

"I will not die like a dog on this man's grave," she screamed.

* * *

The man in the mask topped the hill before the Sycamore Street gate. The Cathedral of St. Paul was now clearly visible, even through the arctic weather. Behind him could still be heard the dying but defiant voice of Esther Snow.

"You're too late," she was screaming. "You're too late."

He turned when she said that. Looked down the hill at her frail figure bathed in white. She was disappearing into the snow.

Then Rick Beanblossom turned back to the church, his eyes wide with horror. The first hellish flames burst through the windows of the angelic choirs at the base of the cathedral dome. And fire shot into the snowy night sky.

The Monster

Andrea Labore started up the heavily carpeted tiers of the choir loft, her hands at her sides, her fists clenched. She was on automatic pilot, couldn't stop now if she wanted to. She moved surreptitiously through the shadows, one silent step at a time. The requiem being played at the organ sang through the empty cathedral at ear-splitting decibels. The monster at the controls was huge. There were burlap sacks wrapped around the boots that worked the foot pedals. Black pants. Thick black arms, and black gloves with holes cut out of the fingers—long lissome fingers that skillfully manipulated the intricate keyboards. A black down vest hung over a black jacket. In the flickering flames of the candles, Andrea could see a gunnysack pulled over its head. The sack was tied at the neck with a rope. A pair of dark glasses stuck in the middle of the mask served as eyes. A floppy hat held everything together. A scarecrow ballooned out of all proportion. Andrea lived day in and day out with a man in a mask, but this was the mask of evil. Death come calling. And *it* had the baby.

Dylan Labore Beanblossom was wrapped in a blanket. He was lying on the right arm of the organ—on the far side of the monster, away from Andrea. This faceless creature didn't seem to notice the presence of the child's mother. Just kept on pounding at the organ in the spirit of the possessed. It was Mozart's *Requiem*—being played so loud, so ghoulishly, it made Andrea's skin crawl. But after a week of anguish, she was literally within reach of her missing baby. Only that brazen monster stood between them.

Then, as suddenly as it had begun, the music of the dead stopped. The monster turned in its chair and stared at the steely figure of Andrea Labore. Then it stood. With its boots it rose to a height of nearly seven feet, and all the time its dark glasses were fixed on the child's mother. Then the monster gently lifted the baby from the organ and held it in its arms, as if it were its own.

"Give me the baby," Andrea said, in a voice steady and firm. "The FBI is right across the street. If you give me the baby, I won't call for help. You can just walk away."

At first the silent monster stood unmoved, as if it had no pulse, no heart. But suddenly its attention was drawn to the doorway. Stepping out of the shadows was Jasmine Allen, a visitor neither Andrea nor the monster had seemed to be expecting.

"Give me the baby," Andrea repeated.

Jasmine blocked the doorway, the only escape. "I

was told you would be here," Jasmine said to the monster, as if they'd met before. Her voice was stern. Resolute. "You give the baby to his mother, and you do it right now."

The monster in the mask shifted the child into its other arm and squeezed him like a loaf of bread. With its free arm, it grabbed the candelabra. Lifted it high into the air. Now Dylan was screaming at the top of his lungs.

"Give me the baby," Andrea said, moving forward.

The monster raised the baby high into the air, along with the burning candles, as if it were going to smash them together. Andrea Labore felt her heart stop. Then, to her surprise, the monster tossed the child into the outstretched arms of Jasmine Allen. With its other arm, it violently flung the candelabra at Andrea.

She turned a shoulder to the flames. The candles hit Andrea on the back and burst around her. They toppled to the floor and lit the carpet on fire.

Jasmine squeezed the precious baby in her arms. "I've got the baby," she screamed until her throat hurt. "Thank you, dear God," she prayed aloud. She planted kisses on Dylan's cheeks, ran her fingers through his hair. Her cries of joy echoed through the deserted cathedral a thousand times.

Andrea Labore was shedding her own tears of joy, ignoring the fire at her feet. Now the monster seemed more interested in the baby's mother than it did in the baby. "Take him out of here, Jasmine," Andrea told her. "Take Dylan home and send some help."

Jasmine, holding Dylan to her breast, slowly backed through the door of the loft, into the stairwell, leaving Andrea Labore face to face with the monster who had stolen her child. The fire was spreading fast.

"I know you, don't I?" said Andrea. "What I don't know is, why?"

The monster was breathing hard, fighting off the smoke. It took one step forward, and Andrea reached for her gun.

The monster backed off, fast, kicked a path to the door. Then it was through the smoke and into the dark.

Andrea followed, gun in hand. Jasmine was standing on the top stair, the baby in her arms. Frenzied footsteps could be heard scuttling down a long, dark passageway that led around the dome. Smoke was pouring out of the choir loft. "Get Dylan out of here," Andrea ordered.

"You come too," pleaded Jasmine.

Andrea Labore shot a long, loving look at her baby boy, then turned and started down the passageway.

"No, Andrea, don't . . ." screamed Jasmine. ". . . We'll call the police."

Jasmine Allen watched as Andrea Labore, the former Minneapolis police officer, disappeared into the smoke. Fire alarms were screeching throughout the cathedral. With another kiss and hug for the baby, Jasmine started down the stairs, into the cold. But she hadn't gone two steps when she was confronted with Stephanie Koslowski pointing a gun up at her.

"FBI," Koslowski yelled. "Don't move."

"Don't shoot! The baby . . ."

"Put the baby down, Jasmine. Lay him right down at your feet and step back." Stephanie Koslowski kept her gun pointed at Jasmine's face.

"We found him here," said Jasmine, defensively, distrust thick in her voice. She was stepping away. "The kidnapper had him. Andrea is chasing him."

Koslowski kept inching forward, a controlled anger in her voice. Flames were climbing out the choir loft. "We can straighten all of that out later," she said, the smoke making her eyes tear. "Put him down on the stair and stand aside."

"I can't do that," Jasmine said firmly. "I got to take him home."

Andrea Labore followed the monster's footsteps down the dark passageway and up the narrowest steps she'd ever seen. The only light was the soft light that seeped in from the interior of the church. The crackle of fire could be heard behind her. Already smoke was clouding the darkness. Soon she lost even the faint shadow of the monster. Blindly, she felt her way along the dark shadows of the church rafters, following the choir of angels from the arch of one stained glass window to the arch of another. Steel trusses joined the copper roofing of the cathedral and the ceiling of the domed interior. The dramatic curving walls were studded with short, narrow steps and arching ladders. Snowmelt was leaking through from above; a dank odor permeated everything. This is where Andrea found herself, on a wooden catwalk between the domed roof and the domed ceiling. A circular maze. And it was filling with smoke.

Then Dylan was crying again. The church's crazy echoes made it difficult to tell exactly where the baby's cries were coming from. Andrea prayed Jasmine was carrying her weeping son out of the church. She heard the sound of footsteps coming up behind her. Candlelight from the sanctuary slipped through the cracked plaster of the ceiling and fell across a large shadow moving toward her through the smoke. She'd been outmaneuvered. The monster, she believed, had circled around.

The catwalk flattened into a platform. A ladder ran up and over the ceiling of the interior dome. Andrea swiftly holstered her gun and bolted up the ladder, into the dark. Her back was killing her. Holding on to the ladder was difficult. Painful. Then through the smoke below stepped Stephanie Koslowski, her own gun held out before her. Andrea stared down in breathless silence as the FBI inspector passed beneath her. What was she doing here? Whose side was Koslowski on?

Andrea got her answer, fast and furious. From above, she watched in horror as a black arm instantly wrapped itself around the inspector's neck. The black hand of the other arm covered Koslowski's gun hand

and squeezed until the bones in her fingers began to snap. She was hoisted into the air, her feet flailing wildly, frantically. And then Andrea heard the loud crack of her neck. She watched as the monster lifted the inspector's body above the rail, then tossed her to the stone below the catwalk as if she were trash. Perhaps in the end, Stephanie Koslowski had figured out what had brought her back to the church. It was more than just following Jasmine Allen. It was the last night of her life.

The masked figure reached down and fumbled for the gun on the floor. But the gun slipped over the side.

Flames now appeared over the shoulder of the monster. The fire was spreading over the insulation. Wailing sirens could be heard on the streets below. It wasn't as if Andrea could turn and run. The catwalk was narrow and pocked with steps and ladders. The dome was dark and smoky. The best light now was the light being offered by the flames.

The monster with the gunnysack over its head leaned back and focused its attention on Andrea, as if the whole time it had been aware of her presence above. It stepped toward the ladder. Fire or no fire, it wanted to do to Andrea what it had done to the FBI woman. Break her in two. Andrea reached for her gun.

But from her precarious perch, Andrea's police revolver spun through her fingers like a pinwheel, then it too fell to the catwalk below. Now the monster stepped away from the ladder at this sudden gift. Bent down for its second chance at a gun.

With catlike speed, Andrea leaped from the ladde
and landed atop the monster. They both tumbled t
the floor of the platform, amid the sound of splinterin
wood and crackling flames. But the heft of the beas
was too much for her. The monster shoved Andre
hard, sending her sprawling. The monster regained it
footing and stared down upon her. Only now it had
gun in its huge gloved hand.

Andrea back-pedaled fast and rested her shoulder
against the dome. Back spasms shot up her torture
spine. To her left was fire. To her right, hiding behin
a burlap mask, was the monster who'd kidnapped he
son. She closed her eyes and listened to the fadin
echoes of her crying baby for what she believed to b
the last time. Andrea Labore whispered a prayer. Bu
there was no gunfire. No attack. When she opened he
eyes, the monster stood paralyzed, staring into th
raging fire.

If an avenging angel were to storm the gates of hell, h
would surely appear before the devil the way Ric
Beanblossom appeared in the dome of the cathedra
that night, stepping through a wall of flames to do bat
tle with the kidnapper of his son. He stood like a rock
his silhouette blotting out the fire behind him. His wif
was on the floor in front of him. Beneath the burnin
rails he saw the twisted body of Stephanie Koslowski
her wide-open eyes staring up at the cross that toppe
the dome. The so-called monster before him, gun i

hand, he recognized in a heartbeat. The last piece of the whole tortuous week clicked into place.

Andrea Labore seized the moment, extended her leg, and kicked the police revolver from the monster's hand. The gun flew over the railing. But the move wrenched her back, and she doubled over in pain.

The skeleton of the dome was built of wood from the turn of the century. Dry and brittle. Rick Beanblossom stuck his foot through the burning posts of the railing. He picked up two limbs, wooden swords, both of them in flames. He tossed one of the burning sticks to the monster. "You're going to die, Freddie," Rick told her.

The muffled voice of Dr. Freda Wilhelm spoke through the mask. "I'm not the one you should be after."

"Mrs. Howard is dead, Freddie. Her real name was Esther Snow, but then, you already knew that, didn't you?" Rick stepped forward, placing a hand across Andrea's head, allowing his finger to run through her hair. He reached into his pocket and drew the small pistol he'd taken from Esther Snow. "Take this," he whispered to his wife.

"How did she die?" Freddie demanded.

"She died on the grave of Grover Mudd." He raised the flaming sword. "You might want to take off that silly costume now. It looks highly flammable."

"You were the first man that ever gave a damn about me."

"So you kidnapped my son?"

"I wanted a baby. Katherine Howard needed a partner to commit the perfect crime. She told me she knew
of a crime so perfect it was guaranteed to get me a
baby, along with the money needed to raise him. She
said the crime would put you and Les Angelbeck to
shame. When it came to solving crimes, I was smarter
than the both of you . . . and all the press did was make
me the butt of your jokes."

"So over the years you too were feeding news stories to Katherine Howard?"

"I loved that woman. And I fed plenty of stories to
you . . . don't forget."

Rick Beanblossom moved against her, his flaming
sword held with both hands, blade forward, the point
skyward. "She said she was going to let you keep the
ransom, didn't she? Said she could get you a job in
Florida. Of course the truth is when the old lady was
done with you . . . she was going to kill you. The baby
would have been killed. The kidnapping and murder
would go unsolved . . . leaving me and Andrea
scratching our heads, and our conscience, for the rest
of our lives . . . like the Lindberghs . . . wondering
what we did wrong."

"No, Rick, we were never going to hurt the baby. I
care for you too much."

The Marine's anger had been building with immea-
surable steam for a week. "Do you care enough to kill
me?"

Freddie raised her torch and charged him, screaming for her life, but quickly she discovered that despite

er size, she was no match for his skill with a weapon. ick swung his flaming sword like a man possessed. Ie backed her into the ladder above the catwalk. Fred-ie started up the ladder, kicking and flailing at the Iarine in pursuit.

Rick Beanblossom climbed after her. He jammed his orch up her back until her jacket and vest caught fire. he was stomping at him with her boots when the first ames reached her skin. Then she let out a scream that choed in circles around the dome of the church.

The man without a face was just about to finish off ne oversize coroner, when the smoke caught up with im and the coughing began. The Marine started chok-ng. This was something new, yet strangely familiar. moke was different than fire. It was slow and insidi-us, killed from the inside out. Rick Beanblossom was anging on to the mad doctor's fiery jacket with one and while the flaming sword was burning the fingers f his other hand. Over his head, the monster in the nask was baking in flames. Stomping madly. Then uddenly, his throat cleared. With one final, deadly hrust, Rick Beanblossom pulled down on the burning nonster with one arm, and with his other arm he mmed the burning stick through the ropes around er burlap neck. Then he let the burning witch climb ree.

She went screaming for air. She went climbing away rom the hell and into the cold night sky. By the time Dr. Freda Wilhelm reached the top of the ladder, her unnysack face was on fire.

As Freddie pushed through the trapdoor and int the spire atop the dome, the freezing air caught win of her and fully engulfed her in flames. Fire and snov Rick Beanblossom watched from below. She circled th lantern several times, her arms flailing wildly at th flames atop her head. Then, with a scream not of thi world, the Ramsey County chief medical examine flew off the dome. She rolled down the copper roo through the snow, bounced off the chapel of th Blessed Virgin, and landed in her own funeral pyr three hundred feet below.

Rick Beanblossom dropped down the ladder fo Andrea. They were surrounded by fire. Fighting he pain, Andrea got to her feet and started up the ladde Rick right behind her. They crawled into the lighte spire. The falling snow washed the smoke from thei eyes.

Rick spit the phlegm from his lungs. His ches soaked in the oxygen and his head began to clea almost as if he were being born again. His visio returned to normal. Down below, where Selby Avenu rolled onto Summit Avenue, the charred remains of D Freda Wilhelm were emitting a burning stench th masked Marine had hoped he would never smel again.

Snow blanketed the earth in the winter with no end They remained outside among this incantation o whiteness as the fire department battled its wa through the interior of the church, dousing the flames ndrea wrapped her arm in Rick's for support and aned her head against his mask. At the foot of the thedral steps, they could see Jasmine Allen holding eir son Dylan in her arms. A fire department blanket as draped over her shoulders. Jasmine looked up at e lantern with tears that were immune to the freez- g temperatures.

No divorce between history and place is possible. ıst before firefighters reached them, Rick Beanblos- om let his eyes wander out over the city of St. Paul. A onderfully banal little city that in the days of Grover Iudd had been the poison spot of the nation, a haven r criminals, a citadel of crime. It was the capital of a ıowy white land where the weather continually tried seduce them. Then kill them. But he loved it. Min- esota. *L'Etoile du Nord.* The Star of the North. The ıly state in America born of snow and ice. Rick ouldn't imagine living anywhere else. Any more than e could imagine living without Andrea, or without ylan. Standing atop the great church the feeling fell ver him that after years of suffering, years of struggle, e had reached the pinnacle of his life. The view was riceless. Our masked hero wanted to linger on and n. And he probably would have, had it not been so amn cold.

Perhaps we will all still be here together in the spring sometime—and happy.

—Anne Morrow Lindbergh
May 7, 1932
Hour of Gold, Hour of Lead

Epilogue

Above their heads, suspended from the ceiling, was a replica of *The Spirit of St. Louis*. Most people passed it by without paying it the least bit of attention. "Did he really fly all the way to Paris in that little thing?"

"Yes, he did."

Rick Beanblossom and Jasmine Allen were standing in the overcrowded and ever expanding Charles A. Lindbergh Terminal at the St. Paul–Minneapolis International Airport. They were waiting for Jasmine's flight to Newark.

"Wow," exclaimed Jasmine, as she gaped at the single-engine monoplane with no front window. "I wouldn't fly to Minneapolis in that little thing."

"He was a remarkable man," Rick told her. "And he was married to an even more remarkable woman." He pulled a book from a bag and handed it to Jasmine. "Here," he said, "Andrea wanted you to have this."

Jasmine took the book with the sky-blue dust jacket and held it in her hands. A poignant smile crossed her face. She read the title aloud. *"Hour of Gold, Hour of*

Lead. Anne Morrow Lindbergh. *Diaries and Letters 1929–1932.*" She ran her fingers over the black-and-white photograph. "She was so pretty."

"You remind me of her," Rick said. "A courageous and beautiful young woman . . . with a missing child."

Jasmine choked back the tears. "I'm going to find my baby."

"I know you are. If there's anything we can do . . ."

"You're proud of Minnesota, aren't you, Mr. Beanblossom?"

"Most of the time . . . yes."

"I know it might sound funny . . . but that's the way I feel about New Jersey. I'm going back to Camden. I'm a nurse now. That's where I'm needed."

Rick Beanblossom smiled, a rueful smile, but a smile nonetheless. "I was in love with a nurse once . . . a long time ago."

It was Memorial Day. The end of May. The man in the mask left the airport in the rearview mirror and drove through the tall gates of Fort Snelling National Cemetery. The afternoon temperature was nearing 80 degrees. A warm spring sun dominated a warm blue sky. The barometer was on the rise, and so was the grass. Winter seemed but a memory. The breeze from the southeast was light, but it carried with it the fragrance of the season. Ten thousand flowers on ten thousand graves. His father was buried here, as was his mother. And as a Navy Cross winner, a plot was reserved for Rick Beanblossom along Mallon Road, an avenue of Minnesota's most decorated soldiers that dated back to the Civil War. So the Marine knew in his heart that one day this hallowed ground would also be his final resting place.

Rick Beanblossom wandered through the perfect rows of white stones to a hill that overlooked the airport. These were the newer graves of the older veterans. Men who were born with the century. He read the dates as he walked. The twentieth century carved in stone. He found the stone he was searching for.

LESLIE H. ANGELBECK
U.S. ARMY
WORLD WAR II
1924 1999

Some men go through life with no father at all. Rick Beanblossom was lucky. He'd had two fathers. His real father, who taught his little boy how to face life like a man, and Les Angelbeck, who taught a young man crippled in body and spirit how to face the world with no face. Now Rick Beanblossom was the father. A new father who had lost his son, then got him back again.

Dylan Labore Beanblossom was in excellent health. He'd been in the care of a doctor the whole time. A mad doctor, but still a doctor. The hockey bag with the seven-hundred-thousand-dollar ransom was found in the home of Dr. Freda Wilhelm—tossed in a closet on top of her shoes. Perhaps a lifetime of autopsies drove Freddie to attempt the perfect crime. Or perhaps a lifetime of homeliness and loneliness, and the bewitching spell of another mad woman, drove her attempt to steal herself a child.

Andrea Labore had returned to the other side of the camera, but viewers saw a different woman. She anchored the news at five and six, but gave up the job at ten o'clock. News was no longer the most important thing in her life. She could live very well without it, thank you, which only made her more appealing to her viewers.

Inspector Stephanie Koslowski was returned home to Chicago with full honors. In a long line of Polish cops from the Windy City, she was the first Koslowski to die in the line of duty. She was buried alongside her great-great grandfather, an immigrant who once walked a beat on the lakefront.

The damage to the cathedral dome was extensive, but would be restored. In light of the fire, fundraising efforts went through the roof. The church was reopened for worship only thirty-six hours after the last flames were doused.

The world of Esther Snow was still unraveling. She had changed names and faces so many times that her life before she married Walt Howard was almost impossible to trace. And when the *North Star Press* got in trouble, around 1939, and Walt Howard's group wanted to buy the paper—his lovely new wife had put up thirty thousand dollars. The missing ransom money? Her death, and the meaning of her evil life, was now best left to the journalists and the dramatists.

Let them sort out the truths of her life, as they had been wrestling for decades to sort out the death of the Lindbergh baby.

Before she left for home, Jasmine Allen had told Rick about her vision of Stormy Day appearing in the fireplace and telling her where to find the missing child. And on the night they brought the baby home, Jasmine believed in her heart that the troubled soul of Stormy Day left the Beanblossom house for good and took her rightful place among the angels in heaven.

The man without a face stared out over the endless rows of white headstones, the antithesis of snowflakes—all were alike. The grave markers seemed to melt like clouds, right into the sky. Too many veterans. Too many wars. He thought of Lieutenant Grover Mudd and World War I. In many ways, Rick Beanblossom felt he knew Grover better than any newsman he'd ever worked with. Knew him better than any Marine he'd ever served with. Knew him like a brother. Perhaps in another life . . . but then you already knew that, didn't you?

Acknowledgments

Viking editor Al Silverman retired last year. *Silen*
Snow was one of the last books he edited. Al took m
from a self-published author to the national bestselle
lists. I am grateful for his guidance and his friendshi
And although I know he won't be slowing down an
I wish Al and his wife Rosa a well-deserved and
happy retirement.

My editor at Signet also moved on last year. Elain
Koster, past president and publisher of Dutton NAL
has formed her own literary agency. I wish Elaine an
her husband, Bill, the best of luck.

Special thanks are owed to my friends Celeste Ger
vais and Al Eisele for their support, and for their cri
tiques along the way.

To Larry Millett and Roger Stolley for their tour o
and information on the *St. Paul Pioneer Press*.

And to Mark Falzini at the Lindbergh Case Archive
at the New Jersey State Police Headquarters in Wes
Trenton, New Jersey.

As often happens in historical research, much of th

groundwork was done by those who went before me. I owe a special debt of gratitude to Jim Fisher, author of *The Lindbergh Case*: Rutgers University Press, 1987. To Anne Morrow Lindbergh, author of *Hour of Gold, Hour of Lead: Diaries and Letters 1929–1932*, Harcourt Brace Jovanovich, 1973. To Dr. Dudley D. Shoenfeld, author of *The Crime and the Criminal: A Psychiatric Study of the Lindbergh Case*, Covici-Friede, 1936. To Marda Liggett Woodbury, author of *Stopping the Presses: The Murder of Walter W. Liggett*, University of Minnesota Press, 1998. And to my friend Paul Maccabee, author of *John Dillinger Slept Here*, Minnesota Historical Society Press, 1995.

After several false starts, I began writing *Silent Snow* in August of 1996. It was completed in September of 1998. A special thank-you to Viking publisher Barbara Grossman, executive editor Pamela Dorman, and Washington, D.C., attorney Robert B. Barnett, who made publication possible.

S.T.

EOIN COLFER'S
Legend of . . .
SPUD MURPHY

by EOIN COLFER

Illustrated by GLENN McCOY

miramax books
Hyperion Paperbacks for Children/*New York*

 For information address Hyperion Books for Children, 114 Fifth Avenue, New York, New York 10011-5690.
First U.S. Paperback Edition, 2005
3 5 7 9 10 8 6 4
Printed in the United States of America
ISBN 0-7868-5501-0 (trade)—ISBN 0-7868-4911-8 (special market)
Library of Congress Cataloging-in-Publication data on file.
Visit www.hyperionbooksforchildren.com

To Seán:
welcome to Number 1

Contents

The Legend of

SPUD MURPHY

2

UGLY FRANK

I've got four brothers. Imagine that. Five boys under eleven all living in the same house.

On wet summer days, our house gets very crowded. If we each bring two friends home, then there could be fifteen of us crammed into the house. At least eight will be roaring like lunatics, and the rest will be dying to go to the toilet. The flusher on our toilet snaps off about once every three months.

When my dad came home one day and found three sons and four strangers covered with war paint, swinging on the bedroom curtains, he decided that something had to be done. It didn't help that the war paint was stolen from Mom's makeup box.

"No more bringing friends home!" Dad declared after the warriors' parents had collected them.

"That's not fair," said Marty, the biggest brother, mascara streaking his cheeks.

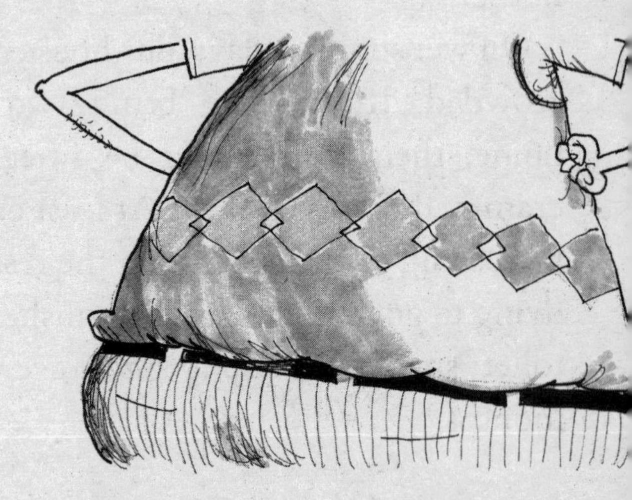

"That punishment really affects me because I'm popular, but Will's best friend is his Action Man."

Will. That's me. I love that Action Man.

Donnie, Bert, and HP started complaining, too. But only because they're little brothers, and that's what little brothers do for a living. I know that technically I'm a little brother, too, but I'm in the big-brother half of the family.

Having one little brother is bad enough,

but having three is too much punishment for one person. That's enough punishment for an entire housing development. The trouble with little brothers is that they are never blamed for anything. All Donnie, Bert, and HP have to do is bat their blue eyes and let their bottom lips wobble a bit, and they are forgiven for everything. Donnie, Bert, and HP could stick an ax in my head and they'd still get off with ten minutes' no TV and a stern look. The only things that Marty and I ever agree on is that our three younger brothers are spoiled rotten.

"This house is a madhouse," said Dad.

"And he's the chief lunatic," I said, pointing to Marty.

"I'm not the one talking to dolls," retorted Marty.

That hurt. "Action Man is not a doll."

"Quiet!" said Dad through gritted teeth. "There must be something we can find for

you to do during the summer. Something to get you out of the house."

"Not my babies," said Mom, hugging the younger-brother squad tightly. They gave her the full baby treatment—big baby eyes, gap-tooth smiles—and HP even sucked his thumb. That kid has no shame.

"Maybe not those three. But Will and Marty are nine and ten now. We can find something for them. Something educational."

Marty and I groaned. Educational hobbies are the worst kind. They're like school during the summer.

Marty tried to save us. "Remember the last educational hobby? The art classes. I was sick for days."

"That was your own fault," said Mom.

"I only had a drink of water."

"You are not supposed to drink the water that people use to wash their brushes."

Dad was thinking. “What about the library?” he said, finally.

“What about it?” I said, trying to sound casual, but my stomach was churning.

“You both could join. Reading. It’s perfect. How can you cause trouble reading a book?”

"Yes, of course, it's educational too," Mom agreed.

"How is it educational?" I asked, terrified by the idea. "I'd much rather be outside riding a horse than inside reading about one."

My mother tousled my hair. "Because, Will, sometimes the only horse you can ride is the one in your head."

I had no idea what that meant.

"Don't make us join the library," Marty begged. "It's too dangerous."

"Dangerous? How could a library be dangerous?" Dad asked.

"It's not the library," Marty whispered. "It's the librarian."

"Mrs. Murphy?" said Mom. "She's a lovely old lady."

The problem with grown-ups is that they only see what's on the outside. But kids

know the real truth. People forget to be on their best behavior around kids, because nobody believes a word we say. Every kid in our town knew about Mrs. Murphy. She was one of those people that kids steer clear of. Like Miss White, the teacher with the

evil eye, or old Ned Sawyer, the tramp with the drooling dog.

"She's not a lovely old lady," I said. "She's a total nut."

"Will! That's a terrible thing to say."

"But she is, Mom. She hates kids and she

used to be a spy in the army. Tracking kids from enemy countries."

"Now you're being ridiculous."

"She has a spud gun under her desk," added Marty. "A gas-powered one that takes an entire potato in the barrel. She shoots kids with it if they make a noise in the library. That's why we call her Spud Murphy."

My mother thought this was all very funny. "A spud gun! You'll say anything to avoid reading a book."

"It's true!" Marty shouted. "Do you know Ugly Frank, from number forty-seven?"

My mother tried to look stern. "You shouldn't call poor Frank ugly."

"Well, how do you think he got that way? Spud Murphy spudded him."

Mom waved her hands as if two annoying birds were flapping around her ears.

"I've heard enough. You two are going to

the library for the afternoon and that's it. We'll make some sandwiches."

We stood in the kitchen glumly. Sandwiches wouldn't be much use against Spud Murphy and her gas-powered spud gun.

STAY ON THE CARPET

Of course, the little brothers thought this was hilarious.

"Nice knowing you," said Donnie, shaking my hand.

"Yeth," said HP, the word whistling through the gap where his front teeth used to be. "Nithe knowing you."

Five years old and already a smart aleck.

"Can I have your Walkman?" asked Bert, who was already wearing it.

I swatted them with my Action Man. "Do you hear them, Mom? They're teasing us already."

"Oh, they don't mean it," said Mom. "Do you, my little men?"

"No, Mommy."

Mom gave them a gummi bear each. I thought my head would pop with the unfairness of it all.

"Now, Marty and Will, go upstairs and wash off the rest of my lipstick. We leave in ten minutes."

There was no escape. We pleaded and whined for ten minutes solid, but Mom was not giving an inch.

"The library will be good for you," she said, belting us tightly into the backseat of the car. "You might even learn something."

As we drove away, we looked back toward the house. Donnie was at the bedroom window, enacting a little play for our benefit. He had scrawled the name *Spud* across the front of his white T-shirt and was scolding a small figure standing on the window ledge. My heart jumped. It was Action Man. Donnie's scolding grew more and more furious, until eventually he picked up my unfortunate toy by the heels and began whacking him against the ledge.

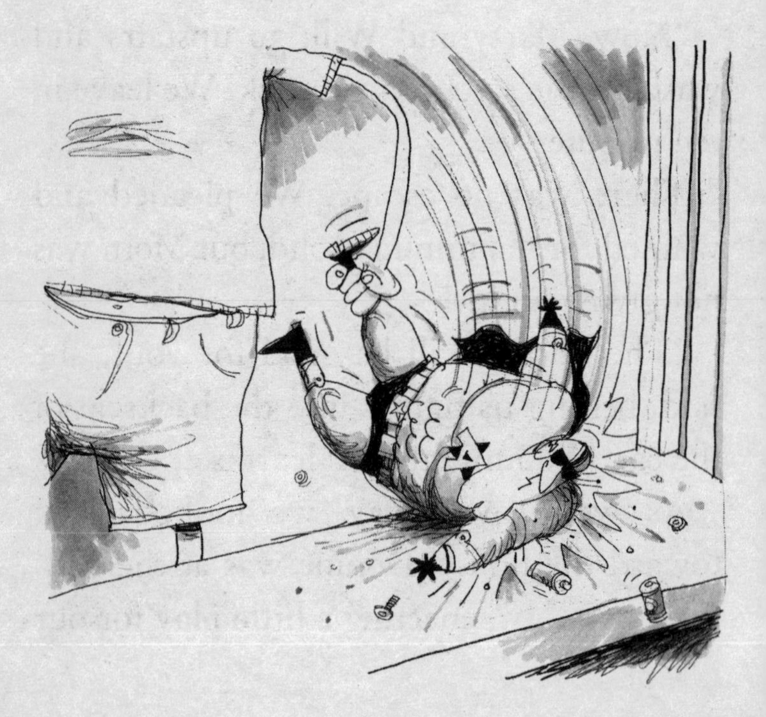

"No," I squealed. "Stop the car. Donnie is killing Action Man."

Mom laughed. "Really, Will. Killing Action Man. You'll have to come up with something better than that."

Through the window I could see Bert and HP clapping wildly as Donnie took a bow.

Mom dropped us at the library on her way downtown.

"I'll pick you up on my way home, after I collect your dad from work."

We nodded, both too scared to talk.

Mom pointed her fingers at us like two imaginary guns.

"Try not to get spudded, okay?"

She was joking, but we couldn't laugh. We couldn't even manage a smile. Mom would be sorry when she came back, and our faces had been blasted by soggy potatoes.

"Okay, off you go, up the steps. I'll just stay here to make sure you go inside."

I growled quietly. Our plan had been to hide around the back for a few hours. Mom was smarter than we thought.

We climbed the concrete steps to the library doors. I decided to go first because Marty told me to. You're probably wondering what we were so scared about. I bet you're thinking that we were a pair of gutless chickens who would have been better off at home sewing our names onto handkerchiefs. But that's because you think libraries are happy colorful places, where the librarians actually like children. That may be what most of them are like, but this one was different. It was a place where serious men read serious books, and nobody was allowed to show even a glimmer of a smile. A smile could get you thrown out; a titter could get you spudded. And if you

PUBL
LIBRA

laughed aloud, you were never seen again.

A little boy rushed out of the library, straight into Marty. The boy had tears coming out of his eyes, and someone had obviously been dragging him along by the collar.

He grabbed Marty's shirt. "Don't go in there," he cried. "For the love of God, don't do it. I was one day late with *Five Go to Smuggler's Top*. Just one day. And look what she did to me."

And just like that, the boy was gone, with only a puddle of tears to prove that he had ever been there.

"Wait," we cried after the fleeing figure. "Tell us what Spud did to you."

But it was no use. The boy had disappeared into the back of a dark car, which sped off to safety.

There was a porch outside the entrance to the library. The porch's walls were covered with posters about things like book groups and art competitions. All very educational. We looked at the pictures on the posters anyway. Anything to put off going into the library itself and facing Spud Murphy. We stayed there until Mom came up the steps and knocked on the window.

We had no choice but to go inside. It was just as I feared. There was nothing in there but books. Books just waiting to jump off the shelves and bore me silly. They seemed to watch me from their perches. I imagined them elbowing each other.

"Look," they said. "Two more kids having too much fun. We'll soon put a stop to that."

The library seemed to go on forever. Row after row of wooden bookshelves, bolted to the floor at the bottom and the ceiling at the top. Each row had a ladder with wheels on the upper end. Those ladders would have made great rides, but there was zero chance of children ever being allowed to actually have fun in here.

"What do you want?" said a voice from the other side of the library.

My heart speeded up at the very sound of that voice. It sounded like two pieces of rusted metal being rubbed together. I held my breath and looked across the huge room. An elderly woman was leaning on a huge wooden desk, her knuckles bigger

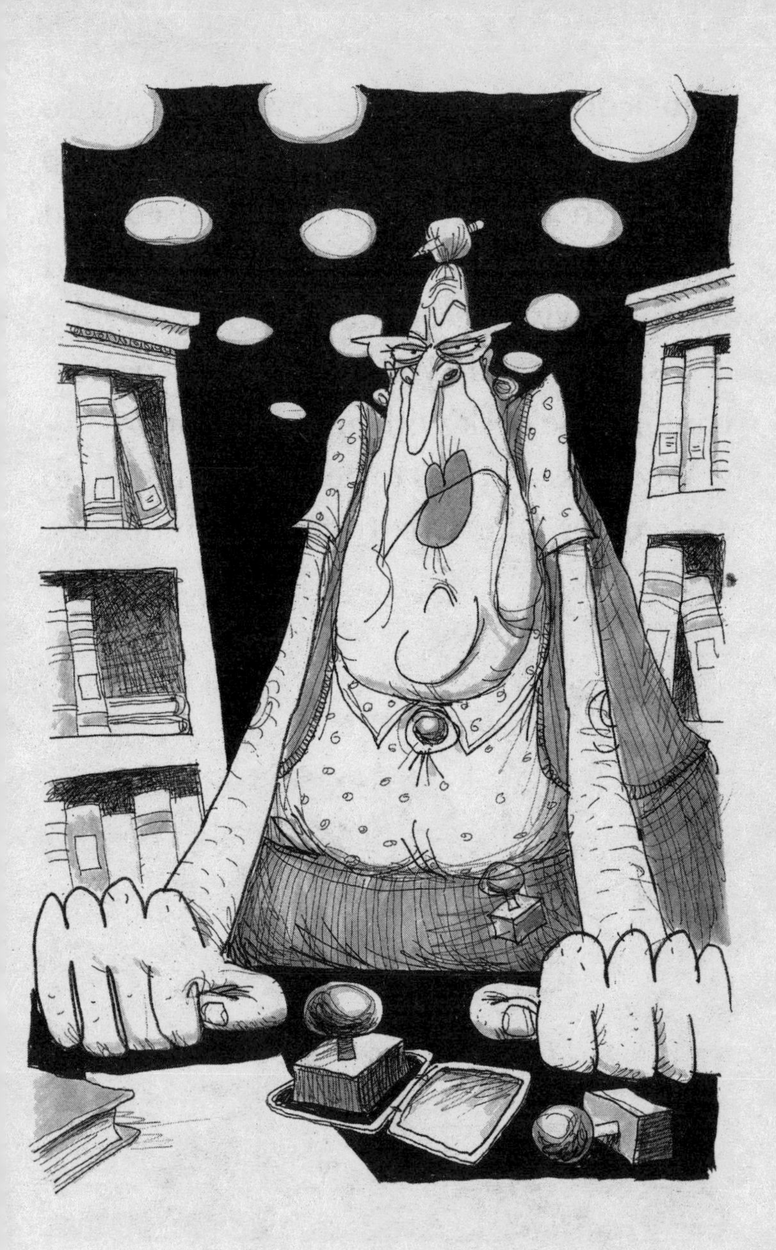

than acorns. Her gray hair was tied back so tightly that her eyebrows were halfway up her forehead. She looked surprised and angry at the same time. It was Spud Murphy, without a doubt.

"I said, what do you want?" she repeated, banging the desk with an ink stamp.

We walked across to her desk, clinging to each other like two frightened monkeys.

There was a whole box full of ink stamps on the desk, and two more hooked into her belt like six-shooters.

Spud Murphy glared down from a great height. She was big. Taller than my dad, and wider than Mom and my two aunties strapped together. Her arms were skinny like a robot's, and her eyes were like two black beetles behind her glasses.

"Mom says we have to join the library," I said. A full sentence. Not bad under the circumstances.

"That's all I need," grumbled Spud. "Two more urchins messing up my shelves." She took a pen and two cards from her drawer.

"Name?"

"M-M-Mrs. Murphy," I stammered.

Spud sighed. "Not my name, dummy. Your names."

"William and Martin Woodman!" I shouted, like an army cadet.

We had surrendered our names, and our address was next. I was a bit worried about that. Now Spud knew where we lived, and could track us down if we ever forgot to return a book.

The librarian filled in the cards, stamping them with the library crest.

"Pink cards," she said, handing them to

us. "Pink means junior. Pink means you stay in the junior section of the library."

Marty noticed that the toilets were in the grown-up section.

"What if we have to . . . go?"

Spud threw the stamp back in the box, slamming the lid.

"Think ahead," she said. "Go before you get here."

Spud led us down long aisles of wooden flooring to the junior section. She wore woolly slippers on her feet that polished the planks as she glided.

"That," she said, pointing a knobbly finger, "is the junior section."

The section was actually a single bookshelf with four rows of books. On the ground before it was a small patch of worn carpet.

"Do not set foot off that carpet until you leave," she warned. "Whatever boyish idea enters your head, ignore it. Stay on the carpet, or there will be trouble." She bent over almost double until her beetle eyes were level with my own. "Is that understood?"

I nodded. It was understood. No doubt about it.

THE TEST

On that first day on the carpet, Marty decided that we should test Spud. When Spud said there would be trouble if we stepped off the carpet, what exactly did she mean? Did trouble mean a strict talking-to? Or did trouble mean being suspended by your fingernails over a pit of alligators?

"I need to know how much I can get away with," said Marty, tying his sweater around his neck like a bib.

"I don't need to know," I said, remembering the boy who had run past us in hysterics. "I'll just sit here and pretend to read."

"You are such a chicken," said Marty. "No wonder Action Man is your only friend. I, on the other hand, am an actual hero type. I am prepared to take risks."

"Why did you tie your sweater to your chest?"

"Wait and see, chicken boy," said Marty.

My big brother walked around the edge of the carpet, checking to see if Spud would spot him.

"She can't even see us," he said. "We can do whatever we want."

I was starting to get worried. Whenever a boy did something wrong, grown-ups tended to blame the entire family. "What are you going to do?" I asked.

Marty smiled. "The best way to mess with a librarian is to put things back in the wrong place." He rubbed his hands gleefully. "They hate that. It drives them nuts." Marty was an expert on messing with librarians. There had been several notes home from the school library. "So I'm just going to switch a few books for Mrs. Spud Murphy. By the time she finds out, we'll be home watching cartoons."

Marty lay on his stomach and wiggled out

onto the wooden floor. He glided across the polished planks on a double layer of wool. I had to admit it. Marty was a master.

Like a crocodile swimming down the Nile, Marty slid to the nearest bookshelf with barely a sound. He climbed onto the bottom shelf, and perched there motionless. There was only one other person at this end of the library—a short man with gray hair and bushy eyebrows. Marty waited until he moved away before he began causing mischief.

One book at a time, he switched almost every single book in the section. He put mysteries with romance, adventure with bird-watching, and gardening with model airplanes. Spud would be furious. To make matters worse, Marty started to swap the reference sheets at the end of each shelf. These pages told the reader what kind of book was on that particular shelf. Marty

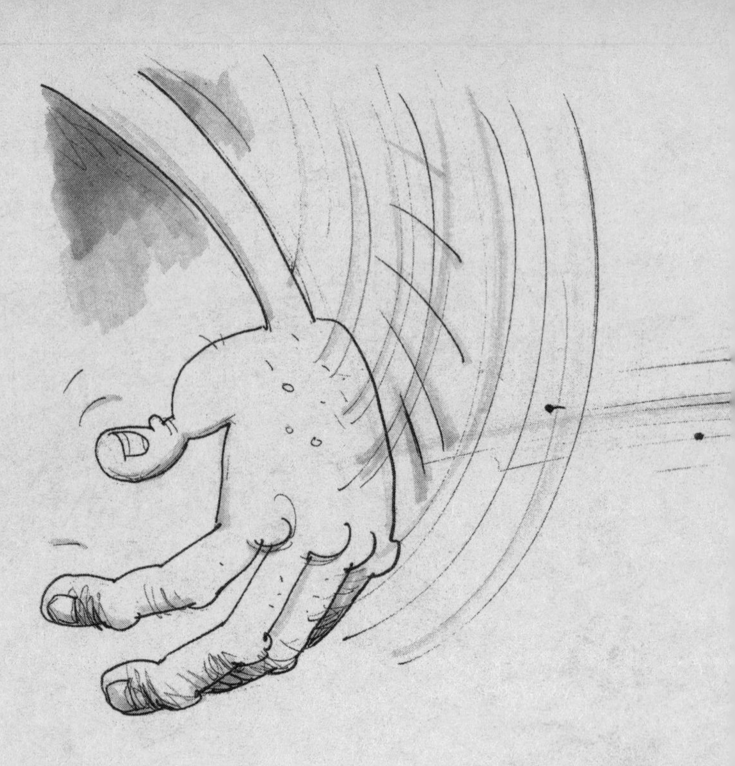

reached up slowly and tore the sheet from the clip that held it.

Suddenly, a shadow fell across my brother. It was a big sharp shadow, and it belonged to a big sharp person. I turned to look. It was Spud. She had appeared without a sound, like a ninja librarian.

Spud stood, slippered feet apart, with her hands hovering over the book stamps on

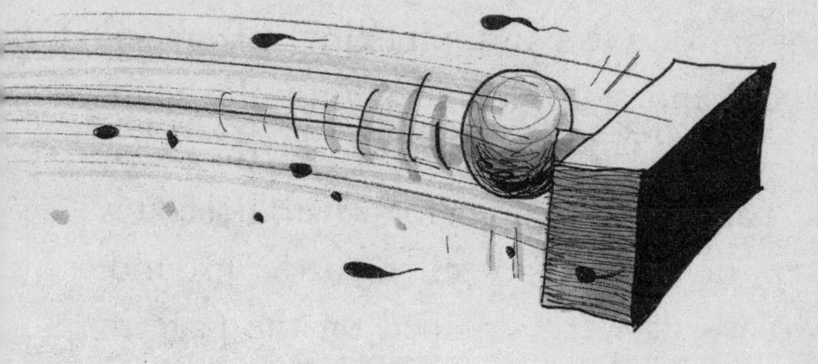

her belt. Marty hadn't seen her, and was still holding the reference page. It was too late to warn him. There was nothing I could do.

Spud's left hand moved with lightning speed, grabbing a book stamp and throwing it in one smooth precise motion. It tumbled through the air so fast that it hissed. Marty turned just in time to see the block of wood and rubber heading in his direction.

It was too late to move out of the way. All Marty could do was close his eyes and squeal like a kitten.

The rubber stamp snagged the reference page in Marty's hand, plucking it from his fingers and stamping it against the shelf. The force of the throw was so strong that the page stayed there for several seconds after the stamp had fallen to the ground. Two words were stamped on the page in purple ink: DAMAGED GOODS.

"I knew it," said Spud slowly. "I can always tell a troublemaker. I took one look at you, Master Martin Woodman, and I knew you'd be off that carpet before I was back at my desk."

"You set me up," said Marty, surprised.

"That's right. I was waiting behind the shelf. The sweater trick was good, but I've tracked a lot sneakier than you in my day."

Marty stood slowly, no sudden moves.

"I'm sorry, Spu—Mrs. Murphy. I'll never leave the carpet again."

Spud slid across the floor on her slippers. "Too late for that. Since you're already off the carpet, you can fix the damage you've done."

"But there are hundreds of books. I can't remember them all."

Spud ran a finger along the shelf. "Each book has a number. This section starts at number five hundred and sixty." She plucked a book from the shelf. "Here it is. I've started you off. You get these in order by the time your mother comes to pick you up, and maybe I won't have to tell her how you set off the fire alarms."

Marty's mouth flapped. "But . . . I didn't."

Spud put her hands on her hips. "I know you didn't, and I'm sure your mother will believe that. Unless, of course, you've been in trouble before."

Marty thought about it for a moment, then began rearranging books as fast as he could. He knew when he'd met his match.

Two hours and fourteen paper cuts later, Marty was finished. He sat on the carpet sucking his fingers.

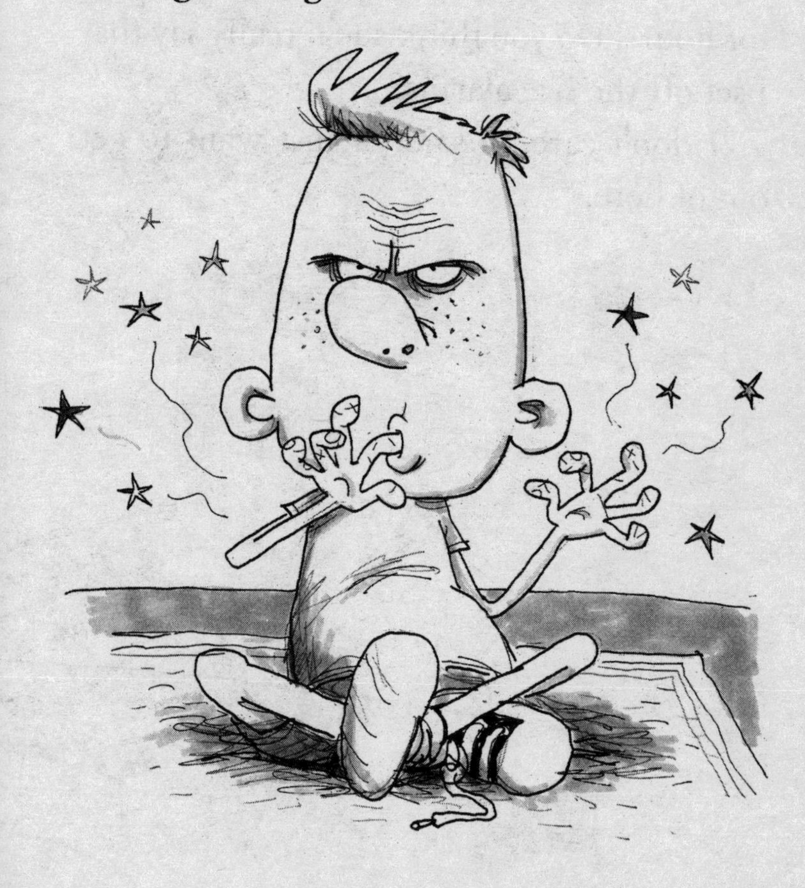

"That wasn't so bad," he said on the way to the exit. "I've had teachers meaner than her."

Marty was actually getting cocky again.

"Marty! Don't you remember the rubber stamp? She nearly took your head off."

"Yes. That was cool. She must practice for hours. Do you think she'll really say that I set off the fire alarms?"

"I don't care," I said. "I just want to get out of here."

Marty had started to wander over toward Spud. I couldn't believe it. Mom was outside, waiting in the car. I could see her through the swinging doors. We were almost safe, and Marty was going over to the librarian's desk.

"Excuse me, Mrs. Murphy."

Spud's head swiveled slowly, like a tank gun. Her eyes landed on Marty.

"Martin Woodman. Back for more. I

would have thought you'd keep well away from me."

"Just one question, Mrs. Murphy. You wouldn't really say I set off the alarms, would you?"

Spud smiled back at Marty. Her teeth looked like a row of icicles.

"Oh, wouldn't I?"

"I don't think so. Throwing a stamp is one thing. That was cool, by the way."

"You liked that, did you, Martin?"

"Sure did."

Spud opened the box on her desk. "I have a collection of stamps here. One came in last week you might like. It's in the shape of a pirate flag. A lot of the boys like me to stamp it onto their forearms, like a temporary tattoo." She began to close the box. "But maybe you're too young."

Marty was already rolling up his sleeve. "No. I'd love that. On my arm. Wait until

the guys at the swimming pool see this."

Spud selected a stamp, inking it on a blue pad.

"Are you sure, Martin? This won't wash off for a couple of weeks."

"I'm sure. Stamp away."

"Well, if you're sure."

Spud's smile widened. "Okay then. Keep still." The librarian rolled the rubber stamp across Marty's forearm. Across and back, three times. When she removed the stamp, we leaned in to examine the pirate flag. Only it wasn't a pirate flag. It was a short sentence of three words. The words were: I LOVE BARBIE.

"Oops," said Spud. "Wrong stamp. Sorry about that."

Marty couldn't speak. If anyone saw those words on his forearm, he'd be teased for all eternity.

"You boys had better hurry up," said

Spud, placing the stamp back in the box. "One more thing. Any more of your little games and I get nasty. There are worse things in this desk than rubber stamps."

We walked to the door. Marty held his arm in front of him as though it belonged to someone else.

Spud called to him as he opened the door. "Oh, Martin," she said, "enjoy swimming."

For the next few visits, I sat on the carpet pretending to read. I sat there until I felt sure the pattern from that faded old carpet had transferred itself onto my bottom. Marty spent most of the time licking his forearm, but it was no use. The stamp didn't fade, and now he had a blue tongue, too. Sometimes Mom arrived early to take us home and would catch me pretending to read.

"Now, there's a sight to make any mother smile," she said. "I knew you would love reading if only you would give it a try."

That was it. We were doomed. Three afternoons a week, Mom decided, we would spend two hours in the library.

So three times a week we pretended to read quietly. Sometimes we forgot to be quiet, and then Spud would pay the children's section a visit. I remember the first time it happened. We were arguing over who owned the air in our bedroom. I said

that Marty owned the air on his side of the room, but he said that he owned the air at ground level. This meant that I would have to climb onto the top bunk just to breathe.

Suddenly, a familiar shadow fell across the carpet, making me shiver. Spud stood there, feet apart, belt weighed down with rubber stamps. Without saying a thing, she pulled out a large flash card from her pocket. On the flash card was written the word *Shhh*. We got the message.

We couldn't fight, we couldn't shout, we couldn't make loud bodily noises. All the things young boys live for. Oh, the boredom! My head felt like it would fall off and spin across the wooden floor. I tried everything to entertain myself. Watching movies in my head, following the pattern in my carpet prison, eating strips of paper from the books. But most of all, I just dreamed of freedom.

Then one day, something strange happened. I was pretending to read a book called *Finn McCool the Giant of Ireland*, when something caught my eye. It was the first sentence of the story.

Finn McCool, it said, *was the biggest giant in Ireland*.

There was something about that sentence. It was . . . interesting. I decided to read a bit more. I wouldn't read the whole book, no way. But maybe just another couple of sentences.

Finn had a problem, said the book. *Angus MacTavish, the biggest giant in Scotland, wanted to fight him*.

Well, I couldn't stop now. Two giants fighting! Maybe I'd just see how that turned out. And so I read to the end of the page, and then I kept right on reading. Before I knew it, I was lost in the tale of Finn McCool and

Angus MacTavish. There was adventure and magic and battles and clever plans. Mountains exploded and wizards slew goblins. Magic goats talked and princesses turned into swans. It was another world.

"Ready to go?" said a voice.

I looked up. It was Mom.

"What are you doing here?" I asked.

There were shopping bags in Mom's hands. "What do you think I'm doing here? It's time to go."

I hugged the book to my chest. "But we just got here. It's only . . ."

I stopped talking, because I had spotted

the wall clock. It was five o'clock. I had been reading a book for almost two hours. I looked across at Marty. He was still reading! A book with a picture of a dragon on the cover. What was going on here?

"Come on now, your dad will be waiting."

To my complete amazement, I realized that I didn't want to leave my book behind. And neither did Marty.

"But, Mom . . ."

"Yes, Marty?"

"I haven't finished my book."

"Neither have I."

Mom put down the shopping bags, and gave us both a big hug. Right out in public. It's a good thing our friends didn't hang out in libraries.

"Do you think Spu—eh . . . Mrs. Murphy would let us bring them home?"

Mom picked up the bags. "Of course. You have your cards, don't you?"

For weeks, everything was wonderful. We had the time of our lives. Every new book opened the door to a new world. We floated down the great Mississippi River with Huckleberry Finn. Robin Hood taught us how to shoot a bow and arrow. We caught burglars with the Famous Five, and Stig of the Dump gave us fort-building tips.

Spud Murphy generally left us alone, so long as we returned our books on time and didn't make any noise on the carpet. A few times she had to show us the *Shhh* flash card, but we never got up to any real mischief. Until . . .

One Monday, we ran out of books to read. We had read everything twice, even the Nancy Drew mysteries. We sat on the carpet dreading the boredom that would soon set in. It wasn't fair.

Marty was so bored he was licking his forearm again, even though the Barbie stamp was long gone.

He stopped licking to complain. "What are we going to do?" he moaned. "I can't sit here for six hours a week with no books."

"Me neither."

"It's such a tragedy. The adventure section is right over there."

"The *adult* adventure section. We only have pink cards, remember?"

"I know, but if one of us just had the guts

to go over there. . . One book is all we need to get us through the afternoon."

I covered my head with a book. "No way. Don't even ask. I'm not listening."

Marty crawled over to me. "Oh, come on. I can't go. Spud has her eye on me."

"But what about the spud gun?"

Marty pinched my cheek. "You're the cute one. If Spud catches you, she'll probably give you a lollipop."

"No, Marty," I whispered in case Spud heard.

"I'll let you breathe my air in the bedroom."

"No."

"I'll let you hang around with me and the boys."

"I don't want to hang around with you."

"I'll tell you where Action Man is buried."

I gasped. "Action Man is buried?" I had been so distracted with my books that I hadn't even noticed he was missing!

Marty knew he had me. "Yes. Somewhere in the garden. The big garden. I'd say the worms are starting to nibble on him around now."

What choice did I have? Action Man

needed me, and I did really want something to read.

"Okay, Marty," I hissed. "I'll go. But only today. If you want a book on Wednesday, you'll have to go yourself."

Marty patted me on the shoulder. "That's fair," he said. ""Now, off you go. I want something really exciting."

I put one foot off the carpet, onto the wooden floor. It creaked like a bat squealing. Seconds later, Spud skated around the corner, her slippers gliding over the polished planks.

Shhh, said her card.

"Sorry," I whispered.

Spud's beetle eyes squinted at us suspiciously, but she continued on to the romance section.

"I knew you couldn't do it, chicken boy," said Marty. "Not even when Action Man is counting on you."

I stuck my tongue out at Marty. I wasn't beaten yet, not with Action Man buried in the garden. I would show Marty that I was no chicken boy. I stripped off my shoes and socks and tried again. With utmost care I lowered my big toe onto the boards, like a mouse testing a trap. No creak. Just beautiful silence. This could work. There were no adults at this end of the library, so I only had Spud to worry about. I took one little step. Then one more.

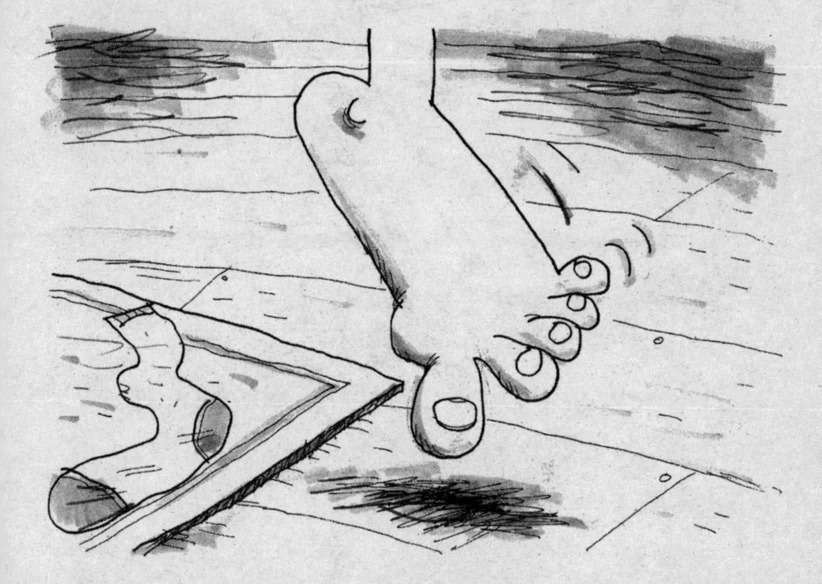

Every boy knows that if you want to cross a floor silently, then stick close to the wall. I stuck so close that I could almost feel my shadow tickling my back. Inch by inch, I made my way toward the adventure section. Every patch of skin on my body was sweating. It felt as though my teeth were sweating. What would Spud Murphy do if she caught me? Would I get the stamp, or the spud gun? Spud gun, I guessed. After all, Marty had already received the family warning.

A ladder blocked my way. A library ladder with wheels on the top. I needed this ladder to reach the adventure books. Gently I wheeled it along the shelves toward the adventure section. It didn't squeak once. Spud kept her ladders well oiled.

I could see the books now, just out of reach. I climbed the ladder slowly, waiting for the creak that would bring Spud running. One step, then two, then three. High enough to reach for a book. I made myself as tall as I could, stretching from the tip of my big toe to the point of my index finger. I took a book from the shelf and stuffed it down the back of my trousers. Success. All that remained was the return journey to the carpet.

The trip back was just as scary. I was sweating so much that I began to feel thirsty. The distance between me and the carpet seemed ten times longer than it had on the way over, and every tiny sound I made echoed around the high walls. But I couldn't stop now. If I did, Spud would surely catch me on her next round. Then I would be spudded for sure. So I took step after sweaty step until the ladder was back in its place, and I was safe on the carpet.

Marty pulled the book out of my trousers. "Well done, Will. I didn't think you had it in you."

"Now, tell me," I demanded, "where is Action Man buried?"

Marty grinned. "In the toy box, sucker, where he always is."

My big brother had tricked me again, but I was too relieved to be angry.

We took a look at the book's cover. *Spies in Siberia*, it said across the top in gold letters. Underneath there was a picture of a man skiing down a snowy mountain. Spud could tell from a hundred yards that this was no kid's book. So Marty borrowed a cover from one of the children's books and folded it over *Spies in Siberia*.

I put my shoes and socks back on, and

then we read happily for the rest of the afternoon. Those spies had a fine time with their fast cars and parachutes and kissing every girl they met. I could have done without the kissing, but the rest was great. It was the first time I had ever been this close to Marty for any length of time without an argument breaking out.

At four-thirty, Marty hid *Spies in Siberia*

behind a row of Enid Blytons, and we settled back to wait for Mom. I have to admit that I was feeling very pleased with myself. I had outwitted the famous Spud Murphy. Her tracking skills had been no match for my brain. I was the King of the Library.

Or was I?

Suddenly Spud glided round the corner

on her woolly slippers. She skidded to a stop before us, sniffing the air like one of those mean pit bull dogs. Her eyebrows seemed even higher than usual.

"Something's not right," she said in her rusted metal voice.

We smiled innocently. Like most boys, we did a great innocent smile.

Spud glared at us. "Innocent smiles don't

work on me, little men. Unless you really are innocent. Which I doubt."

I could feel my smile shrinking, like a banana being gobbled up from both ends. Stay calm, I told myself. Thirty minutes, and Mom will be here to save us.

Spud skated around the library floor in large circles, looking for something out of place. Her eyes flitted across the polished wood, like an eagle's searching for a mouse. Finally, she came to the spot where I had started my journey. She skated past it.

Whew.

Then, stopped and turned back.

Oh no.

Something had caught Spud's eye. Something in the exact spot where I had stood. She bent low to the ground, and followed my path to the ladder.

"Coincidence," whispered Marty, from the corner of his mouth. "Don't worry."

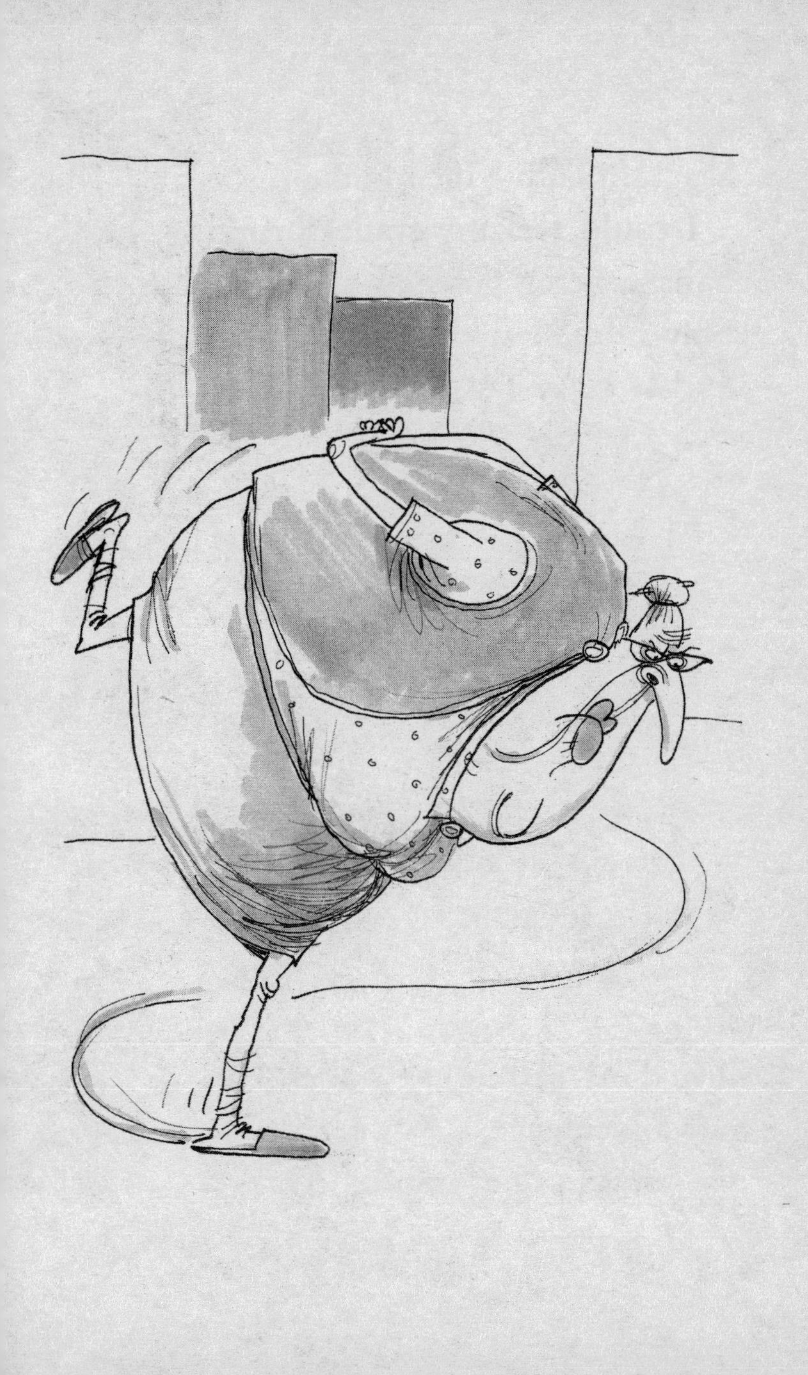

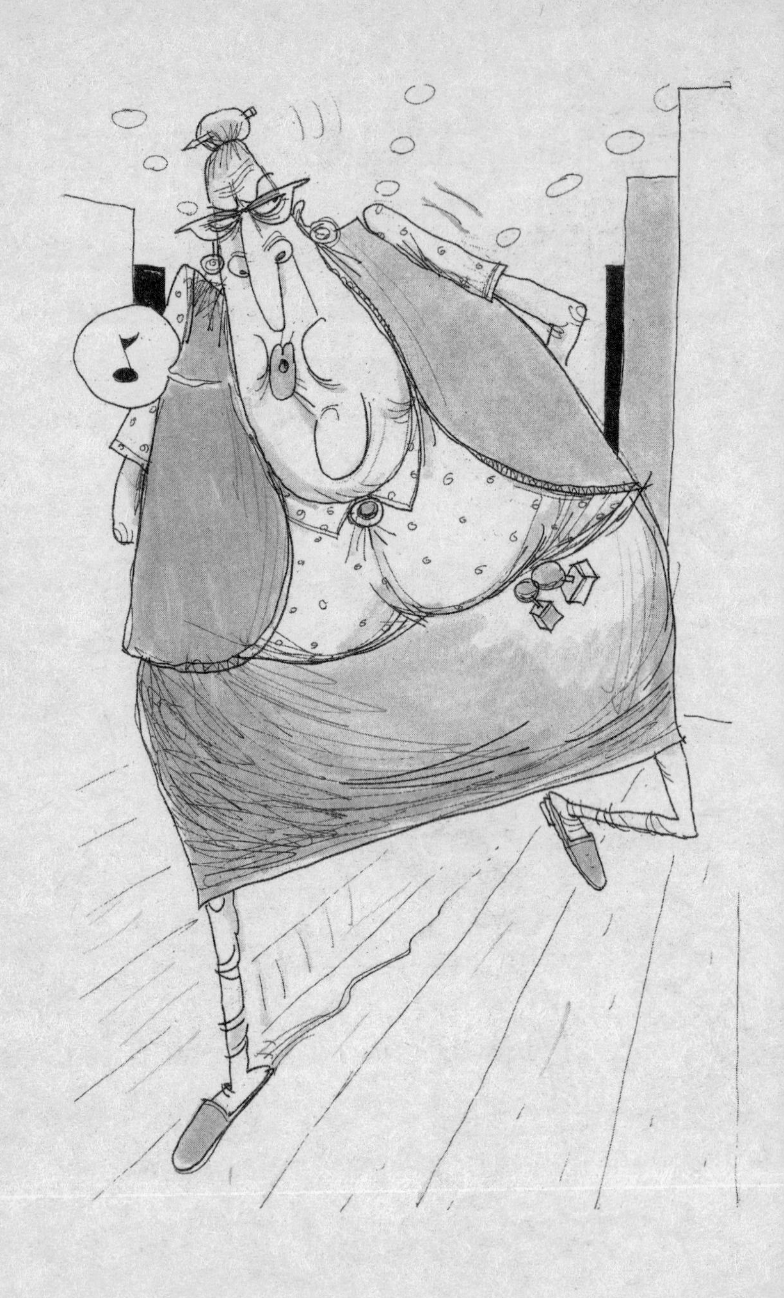

Spud placed one hand on the ladder, pushing it along the shelves. She stopped at the adventure section.

This couldn't be happening.

The librarian climbed to the third step, and reached out one knobbly finger. The finger pointed to a space on the shelf.

"Aha," she said.

I couldn't believe it. She must have some magical powers. I was in deep trouble. The deepest.

Spud climbed down and skated over to the carpet. She stopped before us and said three words.

"*Spies in Siberia*?"

I tried my innocent smile again. "Pardon?"

"*Spies in Siberia*. One of you took it from the adventure section. Hand it over."

By now I was too scared to speak actual words. I did manage to shake my head. *No*, the shake said, *it wasn't me*.

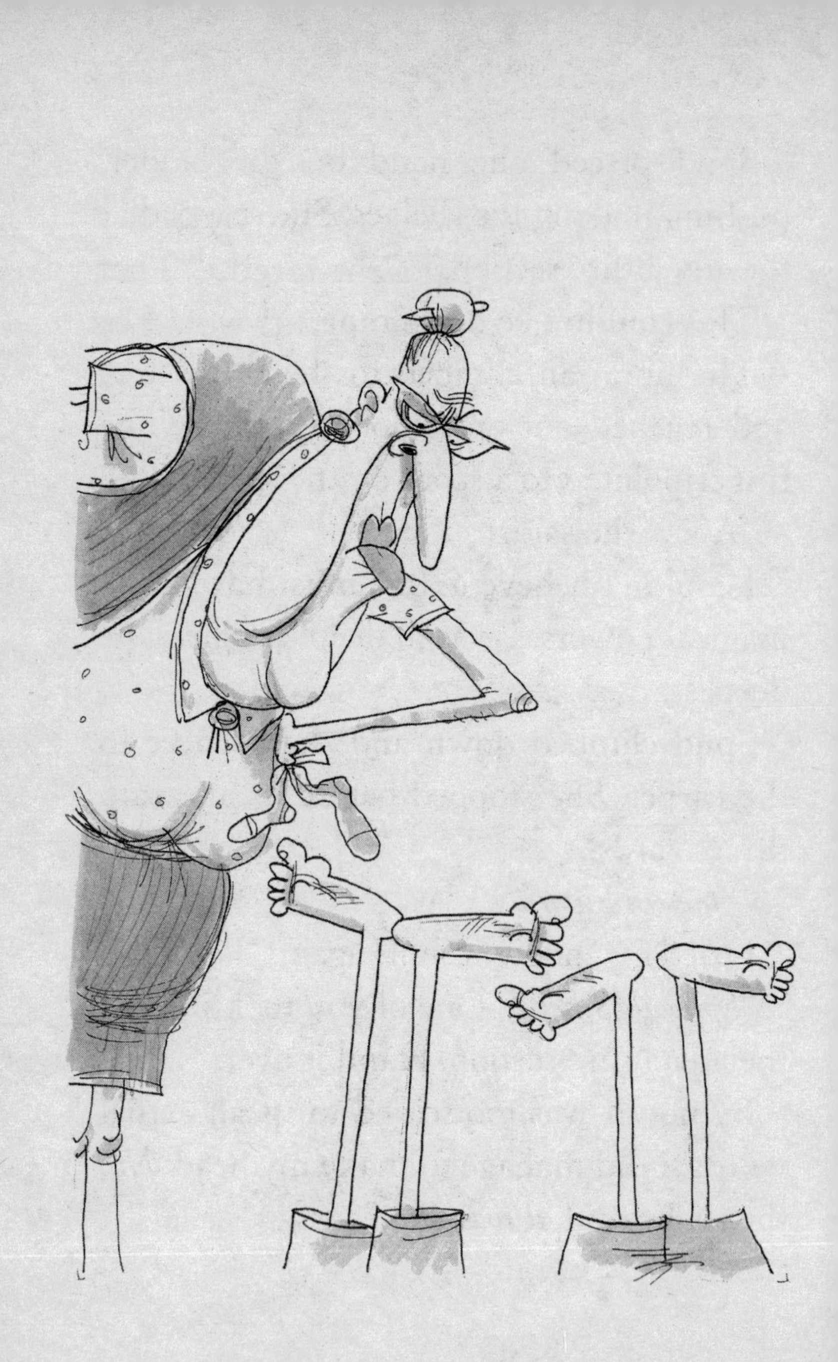

Marty did a bit better. "I would never ignore library rules and leave the children's section," he said, straight-faced. "That would be wrong and my parents would be so disappointed."

Spud squinted at us through beetle eyes. "So, that's the way it is," she said. "Okay, then, I want both of you to lie down."

We obeyed, and with deft movements, she whipped off our shoes and socks. She studied our bare feet, and eventually settled on me.

"Stand up," she ordered.

I did as I was told. Wouldn't you if Spud Murphy was looming over you?

Spud tucked her hands under my arms, lifting me fifteen inches straight up in the air.

"I think it was you, William," she said. "Because you left a trail."

What trail? I couldn't have left a trail.

Spud glided over to the wall where I had begun my journey, and set me down right on my own sweaty footprints. I had left a trail all right. A trail of drying footprints.

"Now," she said sternly, "hand over *Spies in Siberia*."

I was caught. Fair and square. The evi-

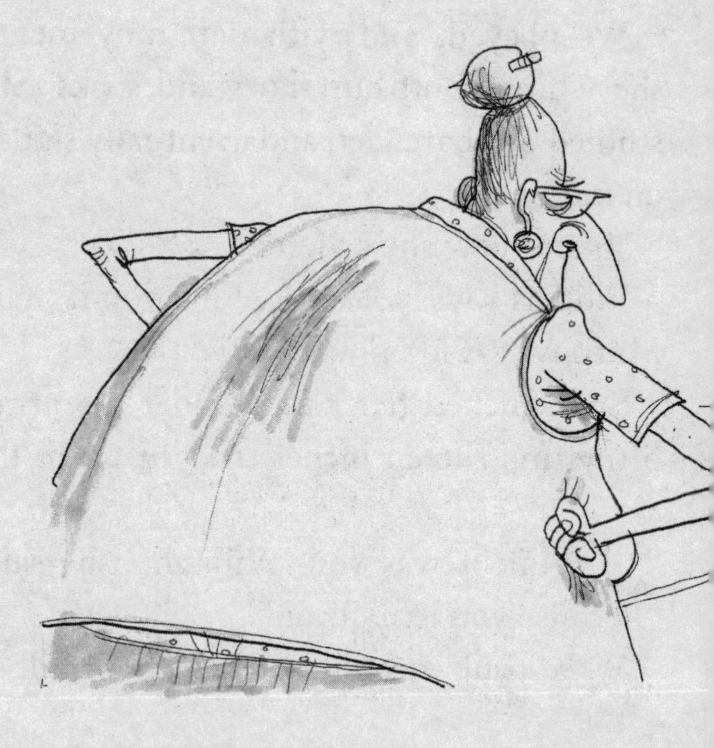

dence was against me. What could I do but return the book and beg for mercy? I trudged back to the children's section and took my borrowed book from the shelves.

Marty shook his head in disgust. "Shame on you," he said. "How could you break library rules?"

I ignored him, too busy wondering what terrible punishment Spud would inflict on me.

"Here," I said, handing her *Spies in Siberia*.

Spud shook her head in wonder.

"Why did you do it? Aren't you terrified of me? All the other children are."

At that moment, I made the best decision of the afternoon. I told the truth, or at least some of it.

"I wanted a book," I said in a shaky voice. "I had read all the others, most of them twice. I had to get a book."

"Even though you knew I might catch you?"

My bottom lip was trembling like Jell-O. "It was worth the risk."

"Right!" said Spud. "Stand in front of my desk. I have something for you. And it's not a rubber stamp."

Oh no! The gas-powered spud gun. I was going to get spudded. Time to beg.

"But . . ."

Spud raised her hand. "No buts. You're going to get what you deserve. Go on, in front of my desk."

I walked to the desk, more frightened than I had ever been in my life. This was it, the end of my time as a cute kid. From today on I would be known as Weird Will, the Spud-faced Kid. It was too much. I closed my eyes so I wouldn't see it coming.

My ears kept right on working, supplying noises for my imagination to add pictures to. Behind me, Marty was still making *tsk tsk* sounds of disgust, as though I had let him down. In front of me I heard Spud rooting around in her desk drawer. She was probably loading the spud gun, picking a really hard potato.

"Open your eyes!" she ordered.

"No," I moaned. "I can't."

"Come on, William Woodman. Look at what I've got for you!"

I took a deep breath and opened my eyes. Instead of the barrel of a spud gun, there was a blue card in front of my eyes. Behind the card was Spud's face. She was smiling and her teeth didn't remind me of icicles anymore. They looked friendly.

"A blue library card," she said. "Blue means adult. Blue means you can go anywhere you want in the library. All I ask is that you show me any adult books you pick, so I can check if they're suitable for you."

I was amazed. Could Spud be rewarding me for breaking the rules?

"W-w-why?" I stammered.

Spud smiled again. It quite suited her face.

"Because you left the carpet for a book. Not to cause mischief. Books are what this library is for. Sometimes even I forget that."

Wow. I had done something good, by accident. Wait till Mom heard about this.

Spud winked at me. “Maybe it’s time I expanded the children’s section, and got rid of that carpet.”

I thought about it. “Maybe you could leave the carpet where it is. But just as somewhere to sit.”

Spud put out her hand. "It's a deal."

I shook her bony hand. Winking and hand-shaking? Maybe aliens had abducted the librarian and left this Spud-shaped robot in her place.

"Mrs. Murphy, seeing as we're so friendly now, would it be okay if I called you Spud?"

The librarian put her free hand under the desk. She twisted something, and whatever she had under there began to hiss gently.

"Just try it once, Woodman, and see what happens."

I backed away slowly.

"Maybe I'll just wait for Mom on the carpet."

"Good idea."

Now, I know what you're thinking. Surely after Marty's terrible behavior I would stay well out of his reach. Well, you're nearly right. I did stay out of his reach, about fifteen inches out of his reach. I stood a yard off the carpet and waved the blue adult card at him.

"Get me a book," he begged.

"After that Action Man trick you pulled? Forget it."

"Come on. You can breathe the bedroom air."

"Well, okay," I said, and brought him *Roses in Autumn* from the romance section.

"Not this one," he cried, reading the back cover. "I don't want a book about someone called Penelope."

I was already halfway up the adventure section. I cupped one hand around my ear as though I couldn't hear him, and he didn't dare shout. When I glanced Marty's way, a few minutes later, he was twenty pages into the romance novel.

At ten past four, a horn beeped three times outside. One long beep, two short beeps. Our signal. Mom was waiting. We quickly chose books to take home. Marty was borrowing *Roses in Autumn*.

"There's a lot of sword fighting," he said as Spud stamped the book.

Spud stamped my book, too, and slipped my blue library card into a little envelope.

"You know, Will, now that we're so friendly, maybe you could call me Angela."

I tucked my book under one arm.

"See you Wednesday, Angela," I said.

Spud smiled. "See you Wednesday, Will."

And she did.

After surviving a summer with ninja librarian Spud Murphy, not much can scare Will and Marty Woodman. Until, that is, they travel with their family to a small seaside town famous for its resident ghost. Legend has it that when the rocks beneath the sea glow at night, pirate Captain Augustine Crow haunts the shore searching for a new cabin boy.

Of course, nine-year-old Will knows this can't be true. But one night, he is out late, and the sea is lit with an eerie glow . . . and, is that a ghostly voice calling his name?

Eoin Colfer is a former elementary school teacher who made a splash in the book world with the internationally best-selling Artemis Fowl series. His other popular books include *The Supernaturalist* and *The Wish List*.

To learn more about Eoin Colfer, visit his Web site at www.eoincolfer.com

Glenn McCoy is an award-winning cartoonist and animator. He has twice been named the Magazine Cartoonist of the Year by the National Cartoonists Society. He is also the creator of the book *Penny Lee and Her TV*. Glenn lives in Illinois with his family.